THE

CURSES

Public Library

First published in Great Britain in 2010 by Simon and Schuster UK Ltd
A CBS COMPANY

Text and chapterhead illustrations copyright © Michelle Harrison 2010

Simon & Schuster UK Ltd
1st Floor, 222 Gray's Inn Road, London WC1X 8HB

This book is a work of fiction. Names, characters, places and incidents
are either the product of the author's imagination or are used fictitiously.
Any resemblance to actual people living or dead, events
or locales is entirely coincidental.

A CIP catalogue record for this book
is available from the British Library.

ISBN 978-1-84738-450-8

5 7 9 10 8 6 4

Printed in the UK by CPI Cox & Wyman, Reading, Berkshire RG1 8EX

www.simonandschuster.co.uk

THE 13 CURSES

MICHELLE HARRISON

SIMON AND SCHUSTER

For Theresa and Janet

Prologue

As midnight approached in Hangman's Wood two girls fled through the forest, desperately searching for a way out. Every pounding step through the suffocating darkness brought the witching hour closer, and with it, a moment's fusion as the human world and the fairy realm intersected.

The smaller, dark-haired of the two girls ran the hardest. Through trickery and deceit, the moment when the two worlds connected would propel her into the fairy realm unless she made it out of the woods in time.

The second girl, lanky and boyish, led the way, her green eyes darting for any opening that signalled the end to the forest. Her hands throbbed as she ran; dripping blood from the stinging cuts on her palms. She had gained them from severing the bonds that had held her companion captive only moments before.

On and on they ran, threading through the trees and over the carpet of leaves and roots that was the forest floor. In the air above, fey creatures glided and swooped; waiting for the moment when the girl would be surrendered to them. Within the gnarly barks of the trees they passed, faces stirred and called out to them. Time was running out and the edge of the woods was nowhere in sight.

Breathing raggedly now, both girls had no choice but to persevere. But then came the moment when the inevitable could no longer be stayed.

'Stop,' the smaller girl muttered, slowing down.

'We can't stop!' the other hissed. 'Move. I said MOVE!'

Her dark-haired companion had stopped altogether, and sank to the ground, closing her eyes and clamping her hands over her ears to block out some noise that only she could hear.

'Get up!' the taller girl urged. 'Tanya, you can't stop now – get *up*!'

But Tanya was too far gone; slumping to rest against the woodland floor. Midnight had arrived and the transition was taking place. There was nothing either of the girls could do to stop it. Vines were crawling and snaking towards the fallen girl, snaring her, ready to pull her away into the dark recesses of the fairy realm. Whipping out her knife, the other girl slashed and sliced them away. There were too many. They had only moments before Tanya would be imprisoned in the fairy realm. Unless . . .

The solution was so blindingly obvious that the taller girl could not believe she had only just thought of it. Her bloody hands trembling, she reached into her pocket and removed a small pair of silver scissors. Kneeling at Tanya's side she pressed the point to the unconscious girl's thumb until a dark bead of blood formed there. Pressing her own wet, red thumb against the wound she held on tightly as Tanya stirred at the pricking sensation.

'How did I . . .?' she began.

'Take me,' the other girl whispered, pressing her hand tighter against Tanya's. Their blood mingled, and with it, so did Tanya's legacy. 'Take me instead,' she repeated. 'She has a life to go back to. I don't . . . take me instead.'

The vines crawling over Tanya slowed . . . then shifted their direction, edging towards the other girl. She felt the cool damp of the dark leaves against her skin as the branches crept over her. Ignoring her impulse to flee, she remained perfectly still, allowing the woodland to submerge her. The scissors fell from her hand, swallowed with the rest of her by the foliage. Humming began in her ears, a low swarm that eventually gave way into murmuring voices.

She felt herself being tugged at by the vines that covered her, pulling her this way and that, like a cat toying with a spider. The voices became clearer; the curious comments of fey creatures as they awaited the new arrival into their world. Then the foliage drew back as swiftly as it had advanced, leaving her huddled on the ground central to a crowd of fairy onlookers. They watched with glittering eyes; some merely curious and others with more intent; young and ancient, beautiful and hideous. As she watched them watching her, the girl leaped to her feet and launched into a run with a ferocious yell. At the sound of her cry more than half the fairies scattered back to their hiding places leaving several gaps in the mass that had gathered. Choosing the nearest, she ran.

Her lungs still burned, not yet recovered from her earlier running with Tanya. But now Tanya was gone, safely back on the other side in the human world. The girl heard scurrying behind her, and wings in the air. Branches moved, trying to trip her as she fled. Each jump to dodge them became harder as her limbs tired and grew heavier.

Then she saw it: a hollow in a huge old tree, a space big enough to hide. Drawing closer, she saw green berries among sprays of leaves and recognised them. No fairies would dwell here. Throwing her bag inside the hollow, she clambered in after it, arranging the foliage of berries to better conceal the hollow. Her body tensed as the scurrying passed her hiding place, then moved on. All became silent. She had done it. She had escaped.

Exhausted, the girl fell into sleep. When the sun rose hours later, she did not wake. Nor did she stir as night fell once more. All around her the forest grew, cradling the old tree and its hollow in leafy arms.

The girl in the hollow slept on.

1

VER SINCE FAIRIES HAD STOLEN
away her little brother, Rowan Fox – or
Red, as she now called herself – had
thought of nothing except how to get him
back. It consumed her and became her sole purpose, her
reason for being. His disappearance had occurred less than
two months after their parents' death eighteen months
ago. At the first opportunity, Red had run away to search
for him. During the months that followed she had lived
by her wits and refused to doubt – even fleetingly – that she
would find him. Her determination had been rewarded.
She'd made a breakthrough. *The* breakthrough.

She had finally gained access to the fairy realm.

It was dawn when she woke from a sleep that had been
like a black void. She was curled into the hollow trunk of an
ancient tree. Shivering, she reached out a stiff, cold hand to
push aside the tangle of branches and brambles concealing
her from the forest. As the mottled morning light filtered
through the undergrowth she saw the scars.

Both palms were caked with a dark substance. Dried blood.

Her skin was lacerated with thin slashes, crossing this way and that. There were too many to count, yet despite the blood, the injuries had healed to silvery scars. Her mind raced back, remembering how she had got them, freeing Tanya.

Her empty stomach growled. In addition, her full bladder was aching.

Grimacing, Red pulled herself from the hollow and stumbled away from the tree. She had pins and needles in her feet from sitting cramped for so long. Warily, she took a quick look around. Unable to hold on any longer, she lowered her trousers and squatted.

The woods were unnaturally quiet. When she was finished she stood up and collected her belongings from the hollow. From her bag she withdrew the knife that she always carried with her and strapped it into its holster on her belt. Then she took a few steps back and looked up at the tree. It was an old and sturdy oak, but thanks to the birds – or whatever else lived in the tree – seeds from another plant had found their way into some nook of the bark and taken hold, for it grew all over the tallest part of the tree. A spray of red berries caught her eye. They were rowan: her namesake, although she hadn't been called by her real name for a long time. Another lifetime. It was the reason she had chosen this particular tree. Legend had it that rowan offered protection against enchantment; the malevolent magic of witches . . . and fairies.

Uneasiness settled heavily upon her. The berries had been hard and green when she had entered the hollow shortly after midnight. Now they were red and soft, having ripened – overnight. Added to the healed scars on her hands, this unsettled her. It seemed that time had passed.

Quickly she tried to recall what she knew of the plant. The berries usually became red in autumn. But when she had entered the hollow just after midnight it had been July, the height of summer. Something was wrong. She had heard of time slips in the fairy realm, but if her guess was correct it would mean that more than two months had passed somehow.

Red glanced around the forest. Nothing stirred, but she knew that this scene of peaceful isolation was an illusion. She wasn't alone. Something would reveal its true nature eventually; a face in the bark of a tree perhaps, or a haunting song inviting her to dance. She had heard of the dangers of the fairy realm.

Now she was in it she had to be ready for them.

There was one last thing to do before setting off. Using the knots in the bark of the oak tree as footholds, she hoisted herself up to reach a rowan branch that was marginally thinner than her wrist. The branch snapped immediately beneath her weight and fell to the ground.

The length of rowan wood was about a foot shorter than she was tall. Resting it in the crook of her arm, she removed the knife from her belt and began hacking at the smaller twigs and branches that were growing from it, snapping them off to leave a staff of sorts. Now, with this added protection, she was ready.

She moved off. The woods were silent and cool, the early morning air swirling like wraiths in a low mist on the forest floor. Dew dripped from above. Red could smell the damp leaf mould on her clothes from being inside the hollow. It was mixed with the scent of her own sweat and blood. She reeked – and she knew it.

She walked relentlessly, following the sun as it moved higher in the sky. The air warmed a little but retained an autumnal chill. Still she walked, her staff poised and her eyes and ears alert for any sound that she was being pursued. As the forest awoke, leaves rustled with movement above her head. A few times she looked up to catch sight of fey eyes peeping down at her. Sometimes they vanished as their eyes met hers. Others, less wary, more curious, emerged further from their nooks for a closer look, their wings and markings blending with the newly golden, ruby and rich brown of the trees.

Presently, she heard the welcome sound of running water. Her heart lightened. She headed towards it until she found herself before the tiny brook that cut through the forest.

It trickled past, carrying the odd leaf here and there. Red knelt at its edge thankfully, placing the wooden staff carefully in front of her knees so that it remained close, should she need it. She pulled her backpack off and unzipped one of the compartments to withdraw her water flask. She shook it; it was almost empty, containing less than a mouthful of liquid. She unscrewed the lid and emptied the stale water onto the grass next to her, before taking the flask and plunging it into the water. It ran over her hand, icy and fresh.

Once the flask was full, she took several long gulps before returning it to her bag. Afterwards she turned back to the water and began to gently wash the blood from her hands, watching as it disappeared into the flowing stream like swirls of dark red paint. She scooped up handfuls of water and sloshed it over her face and neck. Refreshed, she sat back on her haunches and watched her reflection in the stream. It swayed with the movement of the water, and with another jolt Red saw that her hair had grown. Leaning forward, she lifted a hand to her head and touched her short, mousy tresses. She had cut it herself only days before, into a short, boyish style. But sure enough it was longer. Half an inch of her natural auburn showed at the roots. Time had definitely passed.

Suddenly a figure appeared in the water beside her reflection. Quick as a cat, Red grabbed the rowan staff and turned as the figure loomed towards her, just inches away. Red slid back in shock, losing her balance. She fell backwards into the brook, losing hold of her wooden staff. At the same time a swarm of birds and fairies scattered from the trees above, shrieking warning calls as they deserted the area.

As Red emerged spluttering from the chilly water, she glimpsed the rowan stick drifting downstream, out of reach.

A rough hand stretched towards her, accompanied by a low voice.

'Come, child . . .'

The face of the woman to whom the voice belonged was partially hidden in the shadow of the hooded green cape she wore. Beneath the hood long, grizzled hair spewed out, spilling over the woman's shoulders. There were things tied and knotted into the tendrils; pieces of rag and little rolls of parchment. Red could see little of her face. A crooked nose – thin at the bridge and broad at the tip – was the dominant feature. Her nostrils were large and pink-rimmed. Her mouth was thin and curved, her lips colourless like the rest of her skin, but when she spoke the inside of the mouth was unusually red. There were dried flecks of spittle at its corners. It was impossible to tell whether she was even fey or human.

'Come,' she said again, with difficulty, as though the words felt strange in her mouth. She hunched suddenly, giving a horrible, hacking cough.

Red stood her ground, not moving an inch. Her heart was still hammering from the woman's sudden appearance. How had she arrived so soundlessly? Water ran from Red in rivulets, and her hand gripped the hilt of her knife, ready to pull it. She saw the woman's head incline and knew she had noticed it, still sheathed firmly in Red's belt, at precisely that moment. Red moved her hand very slightly, as though she were about to draw it. Though she was unsure whether the woman meant her harm or not, something in her gut made her uneasy. She wanted the woman gone, and if it meant scaring her then so be it.

The woman backed away as silently as she had come, edging between the trees. Red watched, still motionless, as she slowly vanished from sight. There was something strange about the way the woman had moved; something she was unable to pin down. Red shook herself as goose pimples appeared on her arms. She was cold now, as well as hungry. She needed to find food – and soon.

She gathered her bag and made to move off, habitually checking her knife with a quick pat of the hand. The familiar feel of the cold hilt reassured her. Lifting her bag onto her shoulder, she set off, determined to set a quick pace in order to keep warm and dry off. Her wet clothes clung to her, and her hair dripped icy water down the nape of her neck. She shivered, and walked faster, cursing the fact that she had nothing else to change into. All she owned were the clothes on her back.

She had not walked very far when she saw another fairy. In the stillness of the wood, a subtle movement in the branches overhead caught her attention. A grey-skinned creature the size of a small child was hunched in the trees above. It was squat and rotund, its skin leathery like elephant hide. Either side of its dome-shaped head were large, bat-like ears. It looked like an ugly stone gargoyle. She paused momentarily before proceeding, never taking her eyes off it. The creature returned her gaze with an unflinching, amber-eyed stare, and crouched lower on the branch, holding on with ragged-looking claws. Its appearance made her realise that the other rustlings and whisperings had stopped. Either the fairies were being very quiet or this part of the wood was strangely lacking in their numbers.

Cautious now, she kept up her stride as she passed beneath the branches, the creature overhead. On the pathway before her lay a fallen tree, its thick trunk's width reaching the height of her knee. In front of it lay heavy bracken and other forest debris. She needed to watch her footing. Momentarily she took her eyes off the gargoyle-like thing above to step over the tree trunk. As she did so, two things happened at once. The first was a strange sound coming from overhead: the chink and clinking of metal on metal. The second was that as she lowered her foot to the earth beyond the fallen tree, the ground gave way beneath her.

As she plummeted forward, arms flailing, her left leg, still behind the tree, was forced into its bark; carried by her own weight. She felt fabric and flesh tear as it caught the rough surface, extending down the length of her shin as gravity propelled her over. She was falling, through branches and foliage into darkness. As the ground swallowed her, the last thing she was aware of was a high-pitched cackling before everything went black.

2

Eighteen Months Ago

THE FIRST DROPS OF RAIN FELL shortly after the thunder started. They met the windscreen of the car with fat, untidy splats, before being spread across the glass with a squeak as the wipers clicked on. Outside, the January afternoon was sepia-coloured, finally giving in to the storm it had been spoiling for.

It matched the mood in the car perfectly.

In the back seat, Rowan's head was lowered, her long, auburn hair falling forwards over her shoulders. Through the gaps in her fringe she could see her father's face in the rear-view mirror. Though his eyes were on the road, she could tell from the way his dark brows were knotted together that his concentration was not. He was angry. Angry with her. So far, the journey had been one of silence, but Rowan knew that it would not last. She did not have to wait long.

'You're grounded.' Her father's voice was level, but there was an edge to it. He was struggling to keep his temper in check.

She gave a small nod. It was no less than she'd expected.

'For a month,' he added.

At this, Rowan's head snapped up. 'A month? But . . . the school trip, next week . . . I've just got all the camping stuff!'

'It's all going back,' her mother said, from the front passenger seat. 'We've still got the receipts. You're not going.'

'But that's not fair! It's all planned – you have to let me go!'

'What's not fair, young lady, is your behaviour,' her father snapped. 'We were worried sick about you today.'

Rowan brushed her hair back. 'I was fine,' she muttered. She stared at the back of her father's head and resisted the urge to flick the bald spot that had taken nest in his once thick, dark hair.

'Fine? Fine?' her mother said. 'Anything could have happened to you! You can't do that – just bunk off school for the day and swan off to London on a whim! What were you thinking?'

'It wasn't on a whim,' Rowan said quietly. I planned it, she thought. She looked down at the small paper bag that was clenched in her hand. On the front of it were the words: The National Gallery. She turned the bag over in her hands distractedly.

'You're twelve years old, Rowan,' her father continued. 'You may think you're grown up, but you're not old enough to go off in London by yourself—'

'Let alone on the underground!' her mother interrupted. 'It makes me feel sick just thinking about it!' She raised a hand to her temple and massaged it. It was a gesture Rowan knew well.

'I've said I'm sorry,' Rowan muttered. She caught her father's eye in the mirror then, for the briefest of moments, before he turned back to the road.

'"Sorry" is only a word. And there's a difference between saying it and meaning it.'

'I do mean it.'

At this her mother turned round to watch her closely.

'You're not sorry you did it. You're sorry that you were found out.'

Rowan said nothing. It was partly true.

'Suspended, again!' her mum continued. 'Three schools in two years. And now you're on your last warning at this one—'

Her voice began to crack and she broke off.

Rowan lowered her head again. She'd heard it all before.

'This obsession of yours has to stop, Rowan,' her father said. 'I mean it. No more talk of seeing things, these creatures . . . these . . . these fairies.' He spat the last word out quickly, as if he couldn't bear the taste of it in his mouth. 'Or whatever you're calling them these days. Perhaps we humoured you for too long. The time for these stories and fantasies is over. Finished.'

'For you, maybe,' Rowan whispered. Her eyes downcast, she slowly reached into the paper bag and withdrew several postcards. She had bought them at the gallery. She stared at the first: the black and white photographic image of a girl whose chin rested in her hand as she gazed serenely at the camera. In the foreground, several tiny figures danced before her. The image was a famous one in a sequence of five photographs taken in the early nineteen hundreds. On the reverse of the postcard, a small caption stated: The Cottingley Fairies. She sifted through the rest, absorbing the images. A sepia watercolour painting of winged creatures flying over London's Kensington Gardens; a woman wearing a mask of green leaves. Each was beautiful, intriguing. And on the back of each card, beneath the title of the image, was the name of the exhibition: Fairies: A History in Art and Photography.

Carefully, she eased the postcards back into the paper bag. It crumpled and rustled beneath her fingers. In the passenger seat, her mother's fair hair bobbed as she turned at the noise.

'What have you got there?'

'Nothing,' Rowan said defensively, trying to stuff the bag in her backpack – but it was too late.

'Hand it over. Now.'

Reluctantly, Rowan passed the bag to her mother. As the postcards were slid out once more there, was a quiet moment in which all that could be heard was the thrum of the car's engine as it continued its journey along the packed M25. In that moment a small sigh caught Rowan's attention and, for the first time since she'd got in the car that afternoon, she glanced over at her baby brother, asleep in his car seat. His thumb was lodged firmly in a rosebud mouth; his wrist sticky with a line of dribble. He'd inherited his golden looks from their mother; blond curls and thick-lashed, wide blue eyes. Subconsciously, Rowan lifted her hand to her own unruly mane of red hair, cursing it again. Even in looks, she was the one who was different. Even in looks, she didn't fit in.

The sound of tearing paper brought her back to reality.

'What are you doing?' she demanded, lunging forward.

Her mother had torn the postcards into two, and was preparing to tear again.

'Don't!' Rowan yelled.

'Quiet!' her father hissed. 'You'll wake James!'

But all Rowan could see was her mother's hand wrenching at the pictures, and suddenly she didn't care about waking her brother. She was too angry.

'Stop!' she shouted. 'Stop it!'

Her voice collided with James's sudden howls as he woke up. Chaos erupted in the car. Rowan and her parents were shouting. The baby was shrieking. Rowan was straining against her seat belt, leaning forward between the two front seats as far as she could go, reaching for her mother's hands. Her mother was yelling at her to sit back. Outside, the rain lashed against the windscreen as the wipers worked furiously to keep it at bay. And then, realising the hopelessness of the situation, Rowan gave up, throwing herself back into her seat with tears blurring her vision. She blinked them away. Next to her, James continued to wail, and she reached over and placed her hand on his cheek, stroking gently. Beneath her fingers was a fish-shaped birthmark the colour of a tea stain.

As her tears dispersed, she became aware of a movement in the foot well. Looking down, she watched as a small opening appeared in her rucksack, and then two tiny, pale paws appeared through the gap, closely followed by a rodent-like head. The creature looked up at her disapprovingly before crawling out of the bag and scurrying up her leg. She winced as it bit her, twice. It was displeased with her for having the fairy images on the postcards, she knew. But not half as displeased as her parents would be if they knew she hadn't paid for them all. She had not been brave enough to steal the book accompanying the exhibition, but the postcards had been small and easy. In fact, the entire thing had been easy – except the part where she'd been found out.

Rowan had got up, eaten breakfast and brushed her teeth, then showered and dressed into her school uniform. She'd taken her lunch box from the kitchen worktop, then kissed James's fair head as he sat in his high chair, his face grubby with mashed up baby food. After calling goodbye to her mother she'd walked out of the front door, and out of her ordinary little street.

Only, today, instead of turning left to go to school she'd turned right at the end of the road, heading for the train station. Before buying her ticket she'd changed quickly in the toilets there, stuffing her school uniform into her bag and pulling on the jeans and top she'd stashed away the night before. A quick once-over in the mirror confirmed that out of uniform she looked older than twelve: fourteen at least.

It took just over half an hour to get to Fenchurch Street, then a further twenty or so minutes on the tube to get to central London. She hadn't enjoyed the tube journey at all. It was rush hour and she'd been crammed into the packed carriage with her nose wedged into a stranger's armpit. After leaving the train she hurried through the station, ducking her head and avoiding the gaze of all around her; the commuters, the underground staff, and the beggars reaching towards everyone who passed.

Once out in the air, walking across Trafalgar Square, Rowan had started to feel better. Dodging the pigeons she walked past the great stone lions and up the steps to the National Gallery. Inside, the gallery was bustling with visitors. Amongst hordes of tourists and schools on day trips it was easy to mingle anonymously. She picked up an exhibition guide and set off, ignoring the more famous attractions – the Botticellis and the van Goghs – instead making her way to the furthest galleries, the ones that held the exhibition of interest. There the rooms were quieter, with fewer visitors.

Rowan cast her eyes hungrily over the walls, questioning and absorbing what each image had to offer. The majority of paintings she disregarded; these were the saccharine notions of beautiful creatures nesting in flowers or perched benignly on toadstools. One quick glance was all it took for her to dismiss them for the fanciful dreams that they were. It was the others she was interested in. The darker images of masked beings camouflaged in woodland; the images of humans being made unwilling dancers to a bewitched tune; a child being coaxed towards a stream with one hand, while the other held another child beneath the icy water. These were the images Rowan was seeking. The images that held truth, as seen by those like her. Those with the second sight.

Rowan broke from her thoughts and came back to the present. The car was silent now except for a small whimper from James every now and then, but she knew that once they arrived home and James was out of earshot she was in big trouble. Her only consolation was that she'd at least done what she'd set out to do without getting caught. That part had come later, just after she'd left the gallery and was walking across the Square. When the hand clamped down on her shoulder, the last face she'd expected to see when she turned around was her father's, his expression of relief quickly becoming one of anger. Into her face he thrust a National Gallery leaflet detailing the exhibition – and which had train times printed on it in Rowan's writing. In dismay she realised that he must have fished it out of the bin after receiving the phone call from the school about her absence.

She still couldn't believe he had found her.

The creature that only she could see had made its way over to James, and was now nestling with him in his car seat, crooning a strange little sound; something like a lullaby. Rowan wondered if he could hear it. He couldn't see it, of that she was sure, but he did seem to be settling back into his slumber. She watched as the creature reached out with its paw and brushed a lock of golden hair away from her baby brother's eyes. As it did so, its whiskers skimmed his cheek, and for a moment his mouth curved into the faintest of smiles. And that was the moment Rowan's life changed forever. The moment the lorry came crashing through the central barrier with a deafening screech of metal upon metal and ploughed into the car.

Afterwards, Rowan would always remember those few seconds in horrifying detail. The shattering of glass that was followed by icy wind and rain. The scraping and creaking of the car as it buckled against the crushing weight of the lorry. James's helpless, confused cries mingling with her own as the car flipped onto its roof, spinning like a sycamore seed. Torn postcards fluttered around her head like broken fairy wings.

She would remember her wish to protect her little brother from this terrible harm . . . and how the ugly, nameless little fey creature had suddenly ballooned in size and thrown itself upon him, wrapping him in a furry, protective cocoon.

She would remember the flashing lights, and the side of the car being cut away; how she'd screamed when they pulled her out, snapping her arm in order to do so. But the thing that Rowan would never forget, and which haunted her most, was the complete silence from the mangled front of the car.

3

WHEN RED PULLED BACK INTO consciousness, the first thing she knew was that she had soil in her mouth. She spat in disgust and then clamped her hands to her aching head. Already she could feel a bruise forming at her temple. Thin rays from above lit her dim surroundings. She looked around with gritty eyes.

She had fallen into a hole of some kind, that much was clear. Underneath her, broken branches and roots sprawled like dismembered limbs. She ached as though she'd been kicked by them. Reaching out, she felt the walls of earth around her and gave a dry swallow. The damp earth clung to her fingers. She could feel roots protruding from it, some tiny, some large. Bracing herself, she stood up and raised her eyes, prepared to face her growing fear that she had been swallowed by one of the Hangman's Catacombs: one of the seven infamous deneholes in this area of forestland. Did the deneholes exist in the fairy realm as they did in the mortal world? The question hung in her mind, only to vanish when she saw that the branches loosely covering the hole were no more than about six feet above her.

Daylight poured in through the gap where she had fallen through. No, this wasn't a denehole, she realised. This was something worse. As her head was starting to clear her mind worked logically. Running her hands around the earthy walls again, she registered what she had missed the first time: the walls were not a natural formation. Apart from the roots they were smooth. The hole had been dug for a purpose.

The hole was a trap.

Calmly she sat down, ignoring the rush of adrenalin to her limbs. She had been in worse situations and she had learned that the most damaging thing she could do was panic. Quickly, she worked out the dimensions of the trap. Its diameter was about one and a half metres; its height about three. With practical thinking and the right tools, she might be able to climb out. She drew out her knife and, with a hard thrust, plunged it into the side of the hole. It slid in easily and sat there. Red tested its resistance by leaning a little on the handle. The blade held firmly, promising to take her weight. She withdrew the blade with some effort, then stood up and set about hunting for her first foothold.

On the other side, something shifted in the darkness. Red stopped moving immediately. Stupidly, she had not even considered that she might not be alone in the trap. Warily, she took another step, straining to hear. There it was again: shuffling in the dry matter beneath her feet, accompanied by a small sound. Whimpering. Slowly, she knelt and took a long, thin branch that had fallen from above. With it she began to turn over the leaves, lifting and sifting. Upon the third sweep of the stick Red found herself staring at the pitifully thin form of a young fox, its ribs protruding from its coat.

It stared back at her with the dull, hopeless eyes of something that has given up and is waiting for death. It did not look like it would have to wait long. Briefly, she thought of the water in her flask. Then, steeling her heart, she looked away, turning back to the task in hand. She had to think of her own survival. If the fox was dying of thirst then it must have been in the trap for a few days. There was every chance she could be resigned to the same fate.

Soon she found what she was looking for, a chunky root growing out from the side of the hole a couple of feet from the bottom. She tested it with her weight, and it held firm. Stepping up on it she felt around above, searching for something, anything else to grab on to. Her grasping fingers came into contact with something cold and rough: a piece of rock held tightly by the earth. Encouraged, she stepped back down. Now she needed something to place in-between the root and the rock, which could then serve as another foothold. She dropped to her hands and knees and began hunting. A piece of wood would be ideal – a strong branch which she could carve into a point with her knife and then drive into the walls of the hole.

It was then she made a second discovery. Her hand came

into contact with it as she rooted around beneath a pile of dead leaves. Somehow, even before she saw it she knew what it was. Her skin crawling, she held the object under the shaft of light. It was a little yellow shoe. A *child's* shoe . . . with tiny flowers stitched into it. It must have belonged to a little girl, she realised. A little girl . . . no more than three or four years old, trapped down this hole, alone in the dark. What had happened to her? Suddenly Red was afraid. Using her fingers, she shook out the dirt that was caked inside and for a moment just sat there, simply holding the shoe and staring at it. It looked like it had been down there for a long time. In places the leather had rotted away but the label inside confirmed it was from the human world. She shuddered and dropped it. It had belonged to somebody – a child, with a name and a family. Somebody's daughter. Somebody's sister, maybe. A child just like James.

She tried to tell herself that whoever – or whatever – had dug the pit, would surely only use it for the purposes of food; for catching wild animals. The child must have fallen into the hole by accident – but then, if she had been rescued, why had her shoe been left behind?

Unnerved, she glanced at the fox. It watched her with its empty amber eyes. Whoever had left the trap wouldn't have any use for the pathetic creature; it was nothing but skin and bone. It would barely make a meal for the crows. Despite her resolve not to get involved, she knew then that she could not just let it die. Slowly, she edged over and knelt at its side. It looked up at her and tried to shuffle away. Her ears caught the merest hint of a weak growl in its throat. This was promising, at least. It still had some spark of fighting spirit left. She reached into her bag, withdrawing her flask and a small tin camping dish she used for food – when she had food, that was. She poured a little water into it, careful not to overfill it in case the poor creature gulped it down too quickly. Then she dipped her fingers into the water and let a couple of cool drops fall onto the fox's hot, dry nose, before placing the bowl as close as she could to its mouth and then backing away into the corner. She had done what she could. Now it was up to the fox.

Rooting around, she found a sturdy wooden branch. She snapped it using the heel of her boot, then began to sharpen one end with her knife. Out of the corner of her eye she stole a glance at the fox. Its tongue had curled out of its mouth as it sought the droplets on its nose.

'Poor thing,' Red murmured. The fox's ears twitched slightly at her voice. To her amazement it then raised its head and leaned forward to the bowl of water.

'Go on,' she whispered, willing the animal to drink.

The fox lowered its muzzle to the water and began to lap at it slowly. It eyed her warily as it drank – and it drank for only a few seconds before lowering its head to rest, but Red was encouraged.

In the minutes that followed she continued to work steadily, sharpening her branch into a point, then beginning another. After a few minutes the fox lifted its head to drink a little more before resting again. Already there seemed to be a spark of life in its eyes. She carried on with her task. And, at intervals, the fox continued to drink. When the bowl was empty she filled it once again, listening as the fox lapped noisily. She wondered if the water would be enough to save it – for surely the maker of the trap would take pity on the skinny creature and release it – or whether, by helping keep it alive, she was simply prolonging its suffering. She pushed the latter thought from her mind. She was ready to put her plan into action.

She took off one of her boots and, using the heel, began to knock one of the sticks into the wall of the earth at about waist-height – halfway between the roots and the rock she had discovered earlier. With each whack of her boot she felt her underarms prickling with perspiration. By the time she'd finished, the branch was a sturdy peg in the wall of the hole, with a good few inches left for a foothold. Still holding her boot in her hand, she stepped up on to the root nearest the bottom of the pit then, with her free hand holding the thicker root above her head, moved up again onto the foothold she had just made. Then came the tricky part: while balancing on the foothold, she now had to repeat the process of knocking another branch into the earth. Only this time, she was balancing precariously on her foothold and pressed against the side of the hole while trying to drive the wood in with her boot heel. And this was where her plan began to fail.

As she attempted to hammer in the wooden peg, the earth above her crumbled and disintegrated, showering her in dirt as it broke and fell down on her. Some of it fell in clumps; other parts crumbled to a dust that flew into her eyes. She held her breath, determined not to inhale it, and persevered with the wooden peg for a further few moments, but to no avail. The earth nearer the entrance was brittle and dry, and would not allow her to knock the peg in. Dismally, she clambered down, shaking dirt from her hair and clothes. Her idea was not going to work.

She wiped the sweat from her brow and took a sip of water. It would need to be rationed now – for there was no way of telling how long she would be in the hole. She looked over at the fox, and saw that it seemed to have perked up a little, although it was still weak.

'Looks like you and I have more than just a name in common,' she told it. 'We're stuck down here together.'

She had not long finished the sentence when she heard a sound from above. Something was moving through the woods. Immediately she was alert, pressing herself against the side of the earthy wall beneath the shade of the branches above. The hole was plunged into darkness as the light was momentarily cut off; something was obscuring the gap in the branches through which she'd fallen. Then, one by one, the branches that had been placed across the entrance to the trap were being lifted off. She knew then that this was no animal, nor a passer-by. This was the setter of the trap. As the light filled the trap once more, Red knew there was no point in trying to stay hidden. In seconds there would be nowhere for her to hide.

Boldly, she stepped forward out of the shadows and turned her face up to the light. 'Hello?' she called. Sunshine dazzled her eyes. Silhouetted against it was a ragged, hooded figure with long, grizzled hair.

Red recognised her immediately. *The old woman!*

An odd mixture of feelings went through her then. A small glimmer of relief at being found was tainted by uncertainty. If the old woman had set the trap, how had she managed to dig the hole? She looked too frail for such a task. But then another thought occurred: perhaps the trap was old, dug by another, and the old woman had just found it and claimed it as her own.

Wordlessly, the old woman threw something into the hole. Red's concerns melted away as she saw it to be a strong-looking knotted rope. The woman was helping her to get out. Gratefully, she held it and tested it with a firm tug. The rope held true. Quickly, she grabbed her tin camping bowl from in front of the fox and shoved it in her bag. The fox was sitting up now, peering into the light above with fear in its eyes. Red shot it one last look, hoping that she would be able to persuade the old woman to let it go – for surely it would be worthless to her. Then she began to climb.

At first, she was able to use the footholds she had found earlier, but halfway up, when her sore hands were taking the brunt of her weight, the pain brought tears to her eyes. By the time she reached the opening her body was juddering with exhaustion. Soon, one arm was flung over the side of the hole, closely followed by the other. The old woman was standing before her silently, her face obscured by her heavy hood as it had been before. She reached forward and offered her hand to Red. This time, Red had no other option than to accept it.

As the gnarled fingers took her own, the old woman released a small breath that could have been from the burden of Red's weight. But as Red was tugged closer to her she was overcome by the awful, cloying scent of that one small exhalation, and as she played the sound back in her mind it became more like a sigh. It smelled like things that were rotten and decaying. She collapsed on her knees at the woman's feet, managing a single glimpse of the face that was concealed beneath the hood. The thin red mouth was twisted into a hideous grin.

Then, with one hand still clasped around Red's, tightening like a noose, the other was drawn back. Helpless, Red could only watch as it came rushing towards her . . . and dealt her a vicious blow to the head.

Although the blow to Red's head did not render her unconscious, it stunned her badly. Crumpling to the ground, she heard the low sound of something moaning – a creature in pain – and knew it to be herself. Mingling with it was another sound: the cackling of the gargoyle-like fairy in the trees above. She tried and failed to sit up, forced instead to lie helplessly on her side. Her vision clouded for a moment. She did not have the strength to put up a fight as her wrists and ankles were bound behind her.

Before her she saw the woman hunched over at the mouth of the hole, hauling something out of it. The fox was trapped within a woven net, and it was struggling feebly and whimpering. The woman turned towards Red, and then she felt something thrown over her also; something rough and scratchy. It was secured tightly above her head, and then she was being dragged over the ground. Stones scraped spitefully at her thin back and there was a peculiar pricking sensation at one of her ankles.

'Who are you?' Red managed. 'Why are you doing this? Let me go!'

The woman did not reply. Twisting her hands in their bonds, Red fumbled for her knife, already knowing that it would be gone. The woman must have removed it after striking her. Through the weave of the cloth Red could make out the sunlight, flickering through the branches above. Her head throbbed. Still, the creature in the trees screeched, its cries thinning as she was dragged further into the woods.

Soon she had recovered enough from the blow to start struggling. The fug in her head had cleared, but the woman paid no mind. Red yelled then, though it rewarded her with nothing but a sore throat. She quickly gave up calling out after noticing that the woman seemed curiously unconcerned. It meant that there was no one to hear her.

When the woman stopped, Red twisted around within the confinement of the sack. It smelled terrible and was stained with something dark. She pressed her face into the itchy fabric, squinting through the weave. A small wooden cart lay ahead. The woman unlatched the back of it, then Rowan felt herself being hoisted up. She heard the woman grunt with effort as she lifted her, and then she landed heavily into the flat wooden bottom of the cart. There was a smaller thud as the fox was tossed in on top of her. She felt its thin body roll off and land beside her. There was a bang as the hatch was slammed back into place and latched once more, preventing her from rolling – or jumping – out. Then came a creak and a clatter from above, and when she tried to sit up she found that some kind of mesh had been closed over the top of the cart too, forcing her to lie down.

'Where are you taking me?' she yelled. 'Please – let me go! You *have* to let me go!'

Her pleas fell on deaf ears. If the woman heard she did not show it. Instead Red heard her moving to the front of the cart, and then it began to rumble over the uneven ground.

Next to her she felt the fox, trembling with terror, its breathing shallow. When the cart stopped a short while later, the fox had stopped moving altogether. She heard the mesh thrown back and the hatch pulled down, and then something creaked: a door. The top of the sack was seized and once more she felt herself being dragged, out of the cart and over a threshold onto a hard floor. From the coldness of it seeping through the sack, Red guessed it was stone. Seconds later, when the sack was cut open, she saw that she was right.

She was in a small, ramshackle cottage. It was crudely built of stone, with a wooden door and small, uneven windows. In the furthest corner, a huge black pot bubbled over a fire, billowing thick steam. Stories of wicked old witches in the woods filled her mind. There was an awful smell about the cottage. As she looked up at the low thatched roof, the source of the smell was revealed as her eyes met with a gruesome sight.

Animal skins of every description hung from the rafters: some large, some small, older ones that were dry and newer, fresher ones still dripping grotesquely. There were pelts of badgers, rabbits, foxes, deer and squirrels, plus many more that she was unable to identify. The stench that filled her nostrils was death. In cages of wood dotted around the edges of the cottage, more animals were crammed in. These were still living, but Red could tell from their eyes that they knew the fate that awaited them. They had seen and they understood.

She squirmed, trying desperately to loosen her bonds. The woman had left the cottage and was outside, unloading the cart. A moment later she returned, throwing a smaller sack onto the cottage floor before disappearing again. It landed against Red, and she knew it to be the fox. She manoeuvred herself into a position to be able to rest her hands upon the sack. Through the cloth she could feel its pitiful body, still warm, but utterly motionless. It was dead, as she knew it would be, and Red was glad, for at least now it would be spared knowing what was to come – unlike the poor creatures trapped around her. She lay still as the woman's form filled the doorway once more, watching through narrowed eyes as a basket of herbs and plants was placed just inside the door. When the woman left for a third time, Red scanned the cottage for something, anything she might use as a weapon. Her sharp eyes caught sight of the hilt of a small knife on the hearth, next to a mound of vegetables. She wriggled like a caterpillar over the stone floor towards it, cursing that the fireplace had to be in furthest corner from her. She had made it only halfway across the floor when a wheezy laugh sounded from behind her. The woman had come back.

Red tensed, swallowing hard. She forced herself to roll over. The woman watched her, bemusement on her crooked face. Summoning the remainder of her strength, Red wriggled with all her might to close the gap between herself and the knife. But she was too slow, too awkward, and the woman had crossed the floor and was upon her before she'd got anywhere close. Grabbing her by the ankles, the woman pulled her into the middle of the cottage before releasing her. Then, slowly and deliberately, she threw back her hood and reached into the tangled mass of her hair. From it she untied a thick lock of grizzled grey hair and let it drop to the floor. It landed next to her, and Red could see small pieces of fabric knotted into it and, looped into a tiny plait, a tarnished locket. It was open, and inside were two portraits: one of a man, and another of a woman.

Confused, Red stared up at the old crone – and gasped. Before her eyes, the woman was changing. Her hair became lighter and smoother until it was the colour of honey. Her eyes were amber, and her limbs longer and slender. In a matter of moments the wizened crone she had first encountered was gone; replaced by a much younger woman. Her face was hard and thin; her mouth cruel.

It was like she was a completely different person.

Moving far more quickly now she had shed her disguise, the woman knelt and seized Red by the hair with one hand, forcing her head back. Red winced, but managed to refrain from yelling out. With her other hand, the woman tilted Red's chin slowly, as though admiring her.

'You're a feisty one,' she said softly. 'I came as soon as I heard about you. In my best . . . *garment*, no less . . . though you were not fooled, even by the appearance of a helpless old lady.' She paused and gave a soft little sigh, and once again Red was subjected to that terrible scent which was her breath; of things dead and rotting. 'I haven't had a young one for some time now,' she whispered. 'But I'm ready for a change. You're going to be very . . . *useful*.'

'What are you talking about?' Red said, horrified. 'What do you mean?'

The woman did not answer. Instead she stood and moved over to a thick animal pelt resting on the floor, serving as a rug, then kicked it back to reveal a trapdoor. She heaved it open, then pulled Red up. A dark little wooden staircase led down into a cellar. Cold, damp air drifted up from it.

Red swayed on her feet, the bones on the insides of her ankles digging into each other from being bound so tightly. Standing, she was able to see much more of the cottage – though none of what she saw was a comfort.

A large work surface stood at the back, smeared with dark stains. On it were several dead birds, some of which had been plucked. Their feathers filled a wicker basket nearby. Assorted animal skulls were heaped in another basket, next to a mortar and pestle containing a fine white power. Bottles and jars littered the other surfaces, their contents dark and slimy-looking. An unfinished iridescent garment glittered from where it lay folded over the back of a wooden chair, a needle hooked into it, waiting to finish the job. As she looked more closely Red saw that the material the garment was made up of was hundreds upon hundreds of tiny wings: butterfly wings, all stitched together. She turned to face the woman who by now she had guessed could only be a witch.

'I can't feel my legs,' she pleaded, swaying again.

The witch smiled back at her, and from the folds of her long dress produced something sharp and glinting: Red's own knife. Stooping, she brought the knife down in a sharp slash, slicing through the bonds that held Red's ankles. Then, with no time for Red to feel surprise or relief, a hard shove sent her flying into the depths of the pitch-black cellar, before the trapdoor was slammed shut and bolted from the other side.

With her hands still tied behind her back Red had no

means of saving herself, and though she tried to regain her balance on the steps, she failed. Luckily she did not have far to fall, and she broke it by landing heavily on her left side into a thin pile of damp, stinking straw. She lay there, too frightened and stunned to move.

Seconds later she received her next shock when a gloomy voice spoke out of the darkness.

'So . . . she got you too, did she?'

4

TANYA AWOKE WITH A START as the train she was travelling on juddered to a halt. She had been dreaming of fairies again. Not the cosy, friendly type portrayed in picture books, but the other type. Ones that did more than pilfer and pinch, and trick and lie. She had been dreaming of fairies that stole away human children, never to be seen again. *Real fairies*.

Tanya shook herself and wiped a thin layer of perspiration from her upper lip. She knew better than most that few people believed in fairies these days. Of those who did, even fewer had the ability to see them.

Tanya knew this because she was one of them.

Outside the window the sign on the shabby little platform read *Tickey End*. At her feet, her brown Doberman, Oberon, yawned and scratched, then stood up, sensing that their journey was at an end. Tanya got up and grabbed her luggage from the rack, then hauled it to the carriage door. As the train emptied of its last few passengers, she squinted through the sunshine, feeling the cool October air hit her warm cheeks, and stepped onto the platform. Oberon followed, eagerly sniffing the air.

'I'll take that for you, love.'

Tanya allowed the portly attendant to heave her bag from the train, correctly guessing that it wasn't often he saw thirteen-year-old girls travelling alone from London to Essex. Indeed, this was the first time Tanya had ever travelled alone. Normally, her mother would have driven her, but as their car was in the garage being fixed, Tanya had persisted in being allowed to take the train.

'Back for the holidays?' the attendant asked.

Tanya shook her head. 'Just visiting,' she said. 'I'm staying with my grandmother for half-term.'

'Where's that then, nearby?'

'Elvesden Manor,' Tanya replied.

The man's smile froze on his lips. 'Take care, now.' He gave a polite nod, and moved away to help someone else.

Tanya watched him go wordlessly. His reaction was not unexpected. Everyone who lived in Tickey End had heard the stories surrounding Elvesden Manor. Stories of how the wife of the original owner had died in a lunatic asylum, followed by the disappearance of a local girl just over fifty years ago – whom many believed to have been killed by the manor's groundskeeper at the time.

The house was shrouded in mystery, a never-ending source of tittle-tattle. But gossip was damaging. The accusations regarding the missing girl had tarnished the former groundskeeper's life, and now the old man was a recluse, never venturing from the second floor of the house.

However, the problem with the true version of events – which Tanya had had a hand in unravelling in the summer – was that the majority of people would not believe them. For the truth was that the missing girl had been trapped in the fairy realm for half a century, unable to leave unless somebody else took her place. Her attempt to return to the mortal world had almost resulted in Tanya exchanging places with her and becoming trapped instead. But Tanya had been lucky. Someone had saved her . . . by taking her place in the exchange. Her stomach formed a tight knot as she remembered that dreadful night.

She sat down on a nearby bench and waited, the autumn breeze blowing her long, dark hair around her face. Through the diminishing throng of the last passengers a lone figure was striding towards her. As the man approached, Tanya could see the lines in his weather-worn face. As always his dark hair, greying at the temples, was fastened back into a careless ponytail. His name was Warwick, and he was the groundskeeper of Elvesden Manor. He looked older than she remembered. He stopped before her and gave a slight nod.

'Good journey?'

Tanya shrugged and smiled. 'It was all right.'

Warwick gave Oberon a heavy pat on the head before hoisting Tanya's bag up onto his shoulder easily. Together they walked towards the car park. As they passed the ticket office Tanya saw unfriendly eyes aimed at her companion.

She stole a tentative glance at Warwick. His eyes were fixed straight ahead, giving no indication that he had noticed. Tanya glared back at the station staff, but if they saw they never reacted.

Warwick was well known in Tickey End for being the current groundskeeper of the notorious Elvesden Manor. But he was also the son of Amos, the old groundskeeper suspected of foul play in the missing girl's disappearance. Like Tanya, Warwick was one of the few people who knew of the fairies' existence – and of his father's innocence. Yet the knowledge was bittersweet, for it was something that would not, and could not, be accepted by the people of Tickey End.

They clambered into Warwick's battered Land Rover and exited the car park, onwards and out of Tickey End through the narrow, winding lanes of the Essex countryside. In the summer the trees had been lush and leafy, forming a thick canopy over the road. Now the branches stretched overhead were shedding their leaves like unwanted gloves. They lay across the road in a carpet of russet, scattering like birds or fairies as the Land Rover rumbled through them.

'Fabian's looking forward to seeing you,' said Warwick. 'I think he wants you to go trick-or-treating with him.'

During the summer, Tanya and Fabian, Warwick's twelve-year-old son, had become good friends. Fabian also knew of Tanya's ability to see fairies, though he did not share it.

'And your grandmother's just hired a new housekeeper,' Warwick added.

After the usual small talk silence settled. Warwick was not much of a talker at the best of times, Tanya knew, but today he seemed preoccupied. She wondered if he was thinking about the hostile stares he had received in Tickey End. Even though he had appeared not to notice, she knew he must have.

Warwick fiddled with the radio, flicking between stations. Strains of music were replaced by static, then he settled on a news channel and relaxed back into his seat. Tanya leaned back and stared out of the window, wishing that Warwick had chosen a music channel and not the news. A few minutes later, however, her head snapped up.

'A missing toddler who vanished last October has been found,' said the radio newsreader.

Tanya fumbled for the volume and turned it up.

'What is it?' Warwick asked, but Tanya barely heard him.

'Lauren Marsh went missing from a sweet shop in Suffolk. Today she was found unharmed near to where she originally vanished. Detectives are searching for fourteen-year-old runaway Rowan Fox in connection with this abduction and two others. Today it was confirmed that Fox's own young brother went missing last February while the two of them were in care. Fox has not been seen since July, and there are mounting concerns for her safety.'

A telephone helpline number was given for anyone with information on the abduction, and then the newsreader moved on to another story.

Tanya sat back in her seat, biting her lip. Out of the

corner of her eye she saw Warwick glance at her before turning back to the road. Then, the Land Rover slowed and he swung into a lay-by, cutting the engine.

'That was her, wasn't it?' he said, quietly. 'Rowan Fox. The girl who saved you. The girl who took your place.' He paused. 'The girl who calls herself Red.'

Tanya looked at him and nodded. His icy blue eyes were fixed on the road, and his mouth was set in a thin line.

'How can she have returned the child if she's still in the fairy realm?' he asked. 'It doesn't make sense.'

'It can't have been Red who returned the real Lauren Marsh,' said Tanya. 'Now she's in the fairy realm she'll only be searching for her brother – I'm sure of it. But I remember her saying there were other people involved. She had contacts – others doing the same thing. Someone else must have brought Lauren back.'

'So she hasn't . . . contacted you?'

'No,' said Tanya. 'She doesn't have any way of contacting me unless it's through the manor.'

Warwick exhaled slowly, shaking his head.

'What are you thinking?' Tanya asked.

Warwick started the engine, his face unreadable. 'I think she's still there, in the fairy realm. And I think she's got herself into a lot of trouble, that girl. On both sides.'

'On both sides? You mean . . . here, and . . . the fairy realm?'

'Aye. That's exactly what I mean.'

'Do you think she'll find her brother?'

Warwick looked as if he was considering his answer carefully.

'Finding him is one thing. Getting him back may be quite another.'

The last ten minutes of the journey were in silence. Finally the Land Rover lumbered through a set of open iron gates, either side of which, mounted on a pillar, a stone gargoyle glared down. Then, looming before them was the magnificent, ivy-wreathed building known as Elvesden Manor.

Warwick parked the Land Rover at the side of the house, next to his little den. Then he, Tanya and Oberon got out and made their way to the front of the house, their feet crunching through the gravel. As he pulled his keys out, Tanya stared up at the many windows, ivy trailing over them. The house was huge, with nearly twenty bedrooms, and was far too big for its few inhabitants. Even so, her grandmother stoutly refused to move to somewhere smaller, and had expressed her intention that the house would, one day, belong to Tanya. Given the manor's past, Tanya still wasn't sure how she felt about this prospect.

The sturdy old front door creaked as Warwick pushed it open, and then they stepped into the dark hallway. Tanya sniffed a few times and wrinkled her nose. She was used to the house smelling musty but today there was another, unfamiliar smell, something sickly and synthetic, like furniture polish or air freshener. They moved further into the house, passing the staircase leading up to the first and second floors. On a small landing halfway up to the first floor stood a grandfather clock, silent except for a light scuffling from inside. As they approached it Tanya could make out the voices of the fairies that lived there.

'Not *her* again!'

'The tricketty one? *Already?*'

Warwick gave her a sideways glance, but neither of them mentioned what they'd heard. 'I'll take your bag up to your room,' he said, moving onto the stairs.

'Thanks,' said Tanya, heading for the kitchen with Oberon at her heels. 'I'll unpack later.'

Voices could be heard from the kitchen. Tanya bounced through the door eagerly. As she entered, her grandmother, a woman in her mid-sixties named Florence, turned to face her, her thin face breaking into a smile.

'There you are!' she exclaimed. 'We were wondering where you'd got to.'

She stepped forward, kissing Tanya's cheek.

'This is Nell, our new housekeeper.'

Tanya turned and looked behind her. Two other people were sitting at the kitchen table. One was Warwick's son Fabian, a tall, spindly boy with unruly fair hair and thick glasses. He was grinning at her, his blue eyes dancing with mischief. On the table in front of him was a fat pumpkin. He was still in his school uniform, his tie loose around his neck. He leaned down to make a fuss of Oberon, who had positioned himself under the table, contentedly crunching on a bone Florence had produced from a brown paper bag for him.

The other person at the table was one of the oddest-looking women Tanya had ever seen. She was middle-aged, probably in her early fifties. Her hair was like coarse brown straw, resting on plump shoulders in a messy heap. The next thing Tanya noticed was her shape: the top half of the woman seemed strangely out of proportion to the rest of her. From her double chin to her fleshy bottom, she was large and plump, with a rounded tummy; but her legs were thin, and did not look strong enough to support the weight of the rest of her. Her clothes, a baggy, cheap-looking blouse and tight leggings meant for much younger women, only accentuated the strangeness of her shape. But it was the smaller details that really held Tanya's interest – details such as the chipped nail polish on the woman's stubby nails, and the equally stubby toes that reached over the ends of shabby pink flip-flops.

'Hello,' said Tanya, politely.

Nell beamed as Florence set a steaming cup of tea in front of Tanya. She took a sip, and then her eyes settled on Fabian, who was sketching a pumpkin design on a scrap of paper, the tip of his tongue protruding from the corner of his mouth in concentration. Tanya went and sat next to him, peering at the drawing.

'Do you want to help me carve it?' he asked.

Before Tanya could respond, Nell spoke.

'It's a bit early, isn't it?' Her voice was high-pitched and slightly too loud. 'It'll be rotten by Hallowe'en if you carve it now.'

'I'm not carving it yet,' said Fabian. 'I'm just working out the design.'

'Hmm,' said Nell, wrinkling her nose. She squinted at Fabian's drawing as if she couldn't quite work out what it was of.

Just then the phone rang in the hallway. Florence rose from the table and left the kitchen. She returned a moment later.

'It wasn't the phone after all,' she said. 'It was that bird of yours, Nell. He's learned to mimic it rather well.'

'You've got a bird?' Tanya asked. 'What kind of bird?'

'He's an African Grey parrot,' said Nell.

'Why don't we bring him in?' Florence suggested. 'He's been cooped up in the sitting room all day.'

'What's his name?' Tanya asked.

'General Carver,' said Nell, her chest swelling with pride. 'Yes, all right, but that dog better not get too near him.' She trotted off into the hallway, in the direction of the sitting room. They heard the door being opened, then came the squeak of wheels. Nell appeared a moment later, pulling a silver cage that was even taller than she was, and twice as wide.

'There we are, dearest,' she crooned, positioning the cage in front of the fire. 'That's better, isn't it?' She beckoned for Tanya to come nearer.

'Isn't he handsome?' said Nell.

Tanya edged closer and looked into the cage dubiously. Handsome was not a word she would have used. Vicious seemed more appropriate. The General was sitting as still as a statue on a wooden perch. He was grey all over, except for a curved black beak and a few red feathers in his tail. He stared back with cold yellow eyes, narrowed to a pinpoint.

'Talk to him,' said Nell, nudging Tanya's arm enthusiastically. 'He likes you, I can tell.'

'I don't think he looks like he likes *anyone*,' said Fabian. 'Not even you. In fact, he looks as if he'd like to peck someone's eyes out.'

Tanya privately agreed. 'Why's he called General Carver?' she asked.

'Well,' said Nell, her cheeks reddening. 'I named him after an old flame, see? General Reginald Carver. It was love at first sight. I was a bit of a looker in my day, you know.'

At this Fabian gave a loud cough, but Nell continued, oblivious.

'It all ended suddenly,' she said.

'Did he die?' asked Tanya.

'No,' said Nell. 'He went back to his wife.'

Florence gave a disapproving tut.

'So you never married then?' Fabian asked.

'Oh, yes, eventually,' said Nell. 'He was a good old boy, my Sidney. Dependable, he was. Passed away last year.'

Tanya was saved from thinking of something to say by the General giving an ear-shattering screech. At this, Oberon, who had just plucked up the courage to raise his nose to the cage for a better look at the strange creature inside, fled and hid under the table.

Nell chuckled. The General chuckled too.

'How rude,' he said, in a perfect imitation of Nell's voice. 'How *rude*. Young whippersnapper.'

'My clever boy,' trilled Nell.

The General blew a raspberry and puffed his feathers out so he appeared twice his normal size.

'Look,' said Nell. 'He's got his suit of armour on.'

'Pop goes the weasel! HOW RUDE!' the parrot screeched, puffing himself out even more. 'Skulduggery, that's what it is!'

A small movement caught Tanya's eye. On the worktop, the lid to the tea caddy had lifted, and the shrivelled little face of the old brownie that lived there peered out. He blinked grumpily and brandished his walking stick at the General, before slamming the lid back down and burrowing under the teabags again. Tanya caught her grandmother's eye. Like her, Florence had the second sight, but no one else in the kitchen had seen – or was able to. The only other fairy that lived in the kitchen was a shy little hearthfay whom Tanya had seen dart behind the coalscuttle a few minutes before.

'I bet I could teach him some new words,' said Fabian.

'I'd rather you didn't,' Nell answered. 'If he starts to swear I'll know exactly who to blame and I'll wash your mouth out for you with a bar of soap.'

'As if I'd do *that*!' said Fabian, pretending to be shocked.

'I'm sure Fabian will respect your wishes,' said Florence, giving Fabian a hard look. 'Won't you, Fabian?'

Fabian's only response was a vague 'Hmm.'

'Bleedin' pest! Bleedin' nuisance!' said the General.

From the look on Nell's face it was clear she agreed.

Later that evening, after Tanya had packed away her things and let Oberon out for a run in the back garden, everyone except Warwick had eaten dinner and was now gathered in the kitchen in front of a roaring fire. The General had, thankfully, had a dark cloth draped over his cage and been wheeled away for the night. Oberon was stretched out with his paws on the hearth, snoring softly. Florence was knitting for a charity jumble sale, her needles clicking and clacking away, and occasionally answering Nell's questions about the house. Tanya stared into the flames of the fire, half listening to them, and half thinking about Red and the news bulletin she'd heard on the radio. She wanted to talk to Fabian about it, and had hinted several times for them to leave the room. Fabian, however, was sprawled out on the rug next to Oberon, finishing homework that he insisted he wanted out of the way so it didn't ruin his half-term. Every so often he complained about Oberon's breath and wriggled away in disgust.

'Where does that staircase lead to?' Nell asked, her eyelids heavy with the heat of the room.

Tanya looked at the old staircase next to the fireplace. It

curved up and around, disappearing behind another wall partition.

'It used to lead up to the first and second floors,' said Florence. 'It was used by the servants years ago. It's blocked off now, though.'

Tanya and Fabian shared a secret glance. It was true that the kitchen's entrance to the staircase was blocked off, but what Florence had declined to say was that access could still be gained to the old staircase from a hidden door on the second floor. Unbeknown to Florence and Warwick, Tanya and Fabian had found the door and explored the servants' staircase during the summer.

Just then, Warwick came into the kitchen through the back door, followed by a gust of cold air and a few stray leaves. He had been out all afternoon, and now looked cold, tired and hungry.

He hung his coat on the back of the door and moved to the oven, where he knew his dinner would be waiting for him, but Florence rose from her chair.

'Let me,' she said. 'I'll make a nice cup of tea and get your dinner while you check on Amos.'

Warwick's tired face brightened. He licked his lips and disappeared to check on his old father upstairs. Minutes later he returned and took a seat at the table.

'It's stew,' said Florence, cutting two slices from a crusty loaf.

'With dumplings?' Warwick asked happily.

'With dumplings,' Florence replied, opening the oven. 'Oh!'

'What's the matter?'

'It's not here,' said Florence, in obvious confusion. 'I left it in the oven to keep it warm, and it's gone!'

Nell sat up, suddenly looking nervous. She heaved herself out of the chair and lumbered towards Florence.

'Well . . . you see, er . . .' she began. 'I thought . . . well, I mean, I assumed that . . . oh *dear* . . .'

'Yes?' Florence enquired, eyes beginning to narrow.

'I thought it was for the old man,' said Nell. 'Amos – I thought it was meant for him . . . that he hadn't wanted it . . . and well, I was doing the washing up anyway, so—'

'Where is it?' snapped Florence.

All eyes were on the housekeeper as she very slowly turned towards Oberon.

Over the crackling of the fire, a loud gurgling could be heard from the dog's stomach.

'Oh!' said Florence.

'It was drying out!' Nell squeaked.

'You gave my dinner to the dog?' Warwick said thunderously.

'I didn't bleedin' well know it was yours, did I?'

'But I told you, Nell!' said Florence. 'I thought I'd made it quite clear what the eating arrangements are – Amos has his meal very early on in the afternoon, Warwick takes care of that!'

Nell looked as though she were about to cry.

Warwick stared disbelievingly at the two pieces of bread before him.

'It's my favourite too,' he said, glaring at the housekeeper.

'Well, it's done now,' said Florence. 'And Nell, please don't do that again – it's a terrible waste. Plus that stew was full of onion and will probably upset Oberon's tummy.'

'And he's fat enough already,' Fabian pointed out, yelping as Tanya elbowed him in the ribs.

Nell gave a miserable little nod. 'I'll just go to bed now then, shall I?' she said in a small voice.

'Goodnight,' said Florence abruptly.

Nell's footsteps faded as she sloped off down the hallway. Warwick stalked over to the toaster and pushed the two pieces of bread into it before opening a tin of beans.

'She's a strange one and no mistake,' he said. 'Whatever were you thinking of, hiring her?'

'Oh, I don't know,' Florence answered, irritably. 'I just met her at the market one day, and we got talking. She said she'd just been made redundant and I felt sorry for her. She needed work and a roof over her head, and we needed a housekeeper. It seemed ideal.'

'She'll be more trouble than she's worth,' said Warwick darkly. 'You mark my words.'

5

THE PLACE ROWAN AND JAMES *were taken to was grey and cold, a Victorian building that smelled of disinfectant and beds that had been wet. It had once been a school. Now, it was a children's home.*

Rowan was numb by the time they arrived. James clung to her, his head heavy on her shoulder. Rowan's good arm ached from carrying him. Over the past twenty-four hours he had cried for his mother, and screamed when anyone tried to take him from Rowan. And so he had remained with her the entire time; during the questions and examinations at the hospital following the crash, and the introduction to their social worker, a young woman named Ellie.

Ellie put her hand gently on Rowan's free shoulder.

'Want me to take him?'

Rowan shook her head. Her red hair hung in greasy tendrils and her swollen eyes were sticky with tears.

'He'll wake up.'

Ellie led the way towards the back of the building, and finally they stopped outside a door on the right. Its paintwork was chipped, and from underneath it, light could be seen in the dim hallway. Ellie put down the suitcase containing Rowan and James's belongings and knocked. The door opened almost immediately and a grey-haired man beckoned them inside and offered them seats in front of his desk. Rowan sat, glad to rest herself from James's weight. She readjusted him in her arms, the movement wafting the smell of a full nappy to her nostrils. The grey-haired man sitting opposite regarded her kindly, and though she thought she saw his nose twitch too, he did not mention it. Ellie sat down beside Rowan.

'I know this is a terrible time for you both,' the man began. 'And it's late, so I'll keep this brief.'

Rowan glanced up at the clock on the wall behind the man. It was nearly ten o'clock in the evening.

'My name is John Temple, and it's my job to oversee that everything runs smoothly, and that everyone here is happy.'

His words entered Rowan's brain but had no real meaning. He meant well, she knew, but his talk of happiness was pointless, because she would never be happy there. She didn't think she'd ever be happy again.

'You'll be introduced to the rest of the staff over the next few days. In the meantime, Ellie will continue to see you, and we will of course be looking into finding somewhere more permanent for you and James.'

'You mean a foster home,' said Rowan.

John Temple nodded.

'Yes. Foster care looks likely, though we're still checking every possible avenue for any extended family members.'

'Have you managed to contact my Aunt Rose?'

'Ah. No, we haven't yet made contact with Miss Weaver, your aunt, but rest assured, we'll keep trying.'

'It's like a zoo, her house,' said Rowan. 'It smells funny. Six cats, three dogs and even two geese. She'll end up being evicted, my dad says . . . said.' The word stuck in her throat like sawdust, and she rushed on quickly, tears stinging her eyelids. 'And that's without the ducks and the g-goat in the garden . . .'

She was crying now.

'All right, love,' said Ellie.

'We want to go to bed now,' Rowan whispered, pulling James closer. 'Please.'

'Yes, of course,' said John, rising from his chair and ushering them to the door. 'Let's take you upstairs.'

Upstairs was little better than downstairs. It was clean but shabby, the carpets worn and the walls in need of a lick of paint. As John led them through the darkened hallways, Ellie pulled the suitcase of Rowan's belongings behind them. It rumbled softly over the carpet until John paused outside a door that had been left ajar.

'A bed has been made up for you,' said John in a low voice. 'There's a cot for James for tonight, but tomorrow he'll be moved to the nursery with the other babies and toddlers. The bathroom is two doors down on the left. You'll be woken at seven-thirty for breakfast at eight.' He gave a sympathetic smile. 'Try to get some rest. This is a good place. One of the best.'

With that, John said goodnight and left, leaving Rowan, Ellie and James outside the bedroom door. Rowan pushed the door open. A chink of light from the hallway spilled in, highlighting a single bed and a cot. A slim wardrobe stood to the side, and a desk with a chair and a few drawers was beside it. Everything was empty and bare.

As Ellie quietly lifted Rowan's case onto the bed and unzipped it for her, Rowan gathered some of her belongings from her suitcase. Everything she needed for now had been packed at the top, as Ellie had instructed. She pulled her wash bag and nightdress from it, then collected a towel and face flannel that had been left folded on the bed.

The bathroom was spacious and cold, and when Rowan filled the sink with hot water, steam clouded the air and fogged the glass of the mirror above the basin. Together Rowan and Ellie changed James's nappy and washed his face and hands. Then while Ellie left to get James into his pyjamas, despite his protests, Rowan washed her own hands and face, taking longer to do everything now that her left arm was in a sling from the crash.

Shivering, she looked over at the shower cubicle. As long as her arm was in plaster she was limited to sink washes or shallow baths.

A gurgle came from the plughole in the bathtub, drawing her attention. Gleaming yellow eyes stared up at her from the darkness. Something was down there, and from the way it watched her she knew it was fey. She moved closer. Frog-like fingers slid through the plughole, gathering soap-scummed hair that had collected in the drain. The slurping, squelching noises that followed told her that the hair was being eaten. She let out a small sound of disgust. The slurping continued, oblivious.

She turned away, stepping out of her clothes and into her nightwear, and snapped the bathroom light off as she left. Ellie had already put James into the cot and was ready to leave. She whispered her goodbye in the hallway and told Rowan she'd be back the following day. Then she was gone. Rowan stepped into the darkened bedroom, pushing the door to but not fully closing it. She could hear more whispering downstairs between Ellie and John, and then the front door opened and closed before the building was left in silence.

She edged between the cold sheets of the bed, shivering. James was breathing rhythmically from the cot at the foot of the bed, already in an exhausted slumber. She stared around the room. Her suitcase stood in the corner. It contained only essentials, nothing personal save one thing: an old book of fairy tales that had belonged to her mother. She had insisted on bringing it. Everything else, the rest of her beloved books and James's toys were at home.

Only, it wasn't home, not any more. Now it was just a house, where a family had once lived. Choking on her sadness, it took her several moments to notice that the bedroom door was opening, slowly and soundlessly. She held her breath, wondering if this was the strange creature from the bathroom, but as the gap widened a small hand curled around the edge of the door, and then a face appeared; a face surrounded by an elfin crop of hair. In the next heartbeat, a second, identical face with short, cropped hair appeared just above the first. Twins, Rowan thought, aged about eight or nine. Quickly she half closed her eyes, watching them through her lashes.

'See?' one said in a whisper. 'Told you there was a new girl.'

'Your chin's digging into my head!' the other complained.

'Shush!'

'You shush. You'll wake her up!'

'Thought you wanted to wake her up?'

The twin on the bottom shrugged. 'New girl? Are you awake?'

Rowan didn't answer. She just wanted to be left alone. But the twins were not about to give up so easily.

'New girl? What's your name?'

'Leave her alone, she's asleep,' the other whispered.

Then Rowan heard one of them take a step into the room. 'Look. There's a baby – they said she had a brother.'

'Who said?'

'John. I heard him telling Sally. They were in a car crash. Their mum and dad died.'

There was a beat of silence.

'Poor things.'

'Come on. Let's go back to bed.'

'Wait a minute,' whispered the other.

'What are you doing?'

'I'm giving her Mr Bones.'

Rowan squeezed her eyes shut tighter as the twin came closer to her. Her heart thudded. What was Mr Bones, she wondered, some horrible children's home trick that was played on the first night?

'What for?' the first twin hissed. 'She won't want that stinky old thing!'

'Yes she will,' the approaching twin whispered defiantly. 'He'll make her feel better. Don't you remember our first night? The first night is always the worst.'

Rowan tried to breathe deeply and convincingly, as though she were in a deep sleep. Then something was placed on the pillow beside her face, something warm and soft, and faintly smelly. She lay there, breathing the scent of it as the twins left. Only when she was sure they were gone did she open her eyes.

On her pillow was a stuffed toy dog. Its ears looked pulled about and one was longer than the other. It was patchy and bobbled, and only had one eye and no tail. It had the look of a toy that has always been loved the best.

Picking it up, Rowan pulled it closer, hugging it under her chin. Hot tears ran down her face and were absorbed by Mr Bones. She turned her face into the pillow.

The twins were right. The first night really was the worst.

6

HOCK STOLE OVER RED LIKE A CLOAK as she sat unmoving in the dark cellar. She strained her ears, wondering if she'd imagined it – but no. The voice came again in a low, exhausted drawl.

'You'll have to forgive us for not preparing for your arrival. We've been a little . . . tied up.'

Red squinted in the pitch darkness. She could see nothing. The voice had sounded from directly in front of her.

'How many of you are there?' she asked, listening for any other sounds of life but hearing none.

'Oh, there are a few of us down here,' the voice said slowly, betraying something that sounded like a hint of amusement. 'But I'm the only one you'll get any conversation out of.'

Red felt her scalp tingle as her hair stood on end. The voice was male, and sounded older than herself. There was something sly about it, something that made her immediately on her guard.

'Who are you?' she asked, shifting on the damp straw beneath her. The movement sent an acrid smell through the air. It caught in her nose and throat, sending her into a fit of coughing.

The voice waited for her spluttering to subside.

'Call me Eldritch.'

There it was again; that same, sly inflection of the words. In that sentence Red understood two things: firstly, that whoever – or whatever – sat across from her was not to be trusted. The name she had been given was not genuine, and on no account should she reveal her own name. Secondly, the manner in which a true name had been withheld strongly suggested that the being sitting opposite was a fairy. The last point was cemented in her mind with the voice's next words.

'And what might *your* name be?'

Never give them your name, not if you can avoid it, for they'll be sure never to give you theirs. Names are powerful.

'Call me Red.'

'Wise,' the voice remarked, and Red noted how it was less amused now, and more wary. Withholding her name belied the fact that she had knowledge of the fairy realm – that she was not someone who had blundered blindly into it.

Her eyes had now adjusted. A chink of light from the trapdoor was making its way into the cellar – it was not in utter darkness as she had first thought. She could just make out a shadowy form ahead of her. The features were indistinguishable but she could see that one arm was pinned to the wall, held in place by a manacle.

She twisted her body away from the stinking straw.

'Another good move,' Eldritch said dryly. 'Out of all the places you could have landed, that was the least ... fortunate.'

Red shuddered in disgust. The wet stench that now clung to her suggested that the patch of straw was a makeshift latrine. She fought the urge to retch.

'How long have you been down here?' she asked. 'When did she capture you ... and who *is* she? What does she *want*—'

'Patience,' Eldritch whispered. 'Please, I'm weary and weak.' He coughed suddenly. 'One question at a time.'

'I don't *have* time,' Red hissed. 'We need to get out of here and escape from that ... that *thing* upstairs before we find out what she's got in store for us! And judging by the state of the poor creatures – or what's left of them – up there, I don't think she has anything pleasant in mind!'

'We can't escape,' Eldritch said flatly. 'No one ever escapes.'

Lying on her side, Red tried to clear her head. Fear was clouding her thoughts. She forced herself to remain still, and drew in several calming breaths as she fought with her mind to work logically. Once she'd calmed herself a little, she rolled onto her back. Then she rocked backwards, easing her hands down towards the base of her spine.

'All right,' she said, still wriggling her bound wrists. 'Let's start at the beginning. Who, or what, is she? The woman upstairs?'

Eldritch's eyes glinted.

'She's known as the Hedgewitch,' he said quietly. 'No one knows her real name, or where she came from. But most have heard of her. She's the reason this part of the woods is desolate. They call it the "Dead Wood" now, because of her. Nothing in it lives for long. Few are safe from her.'

Red grunted and continued writhing her hands behind her back. Slowly, she was managing to manoeuvre her bound wrists over her thin hips. If she succeeded in getting them underneath her and over her legs so that her hands were in front, she had a better chance of freeing herself. But it was a difficult task.

Eldritch paused and was watching her curiously.

'Go on,' Red said, resting to relieve the aching in her wrists.

'She's a glamour-maker – a trader of dark magic. The animal skins above aren't just clothing, not after what she does to them. Put on one of those cat- or fox-skins and it's what you'll become. Her magic extracts the essence of the animal – its soul, if you like – and traps it within the skin. And these are no flimsy surface glamours, designed to fool only ordinary humans. They're infallible – even fey eyes would be deceived by them. She's a master of disguise.'

'She had her own disguise,' Red interrupted. 'When she found me she was an old woman . . . she looked harmless.

And then, upstairs . . . in the cottage, it all melted away somehow. She became . . . younger.'

Eldritch nodded. 'It's what she does . . . how she fools people.'

Red rocked back again, pushing her bound wrists further down her back.

'How long ago did she catch you?'

'Three, maybe four moons ago. I've lost track of time. My companion and I fell into one of her traps.'

'You had a companion?' Red asked. 'What happened to them?'

'He's over there.' Eldritch inclined his head slightly.

Red looked at a dark, silent shape a short distance away. Like Eldritch, a hand was manacled to the wall. The head was slumped forward, the face not visible.

'He's not moving,' she whispered.

'He stopped moving two weeks ago.'

Red's head snapped back. '*Weeks* ago? I thought you'd only been here for three or four days? Unless . . . oh, no . . .' Her voice shook. 'When you said "moons" I thought you meant nights. But you didn't. You meant months, didn't you?'

Eldritch's slow nod sent a tremor through her.

'Why?' she croaked. 'What does she want with us? Why does she keep us down here?'

'Mainly she captures for trade. She'll work to discover your . . . qualities. Then she'll wait until she has a buyer.'

'I don't understand.'

'Someone comes to her, someone who has lost their sight perhaps, and who wants to regain it. The Hedgewitch can give them their sight back – or, more specifically, she can give them *your* sight. For what could be better than a young, healthy pair of eyes?'

Red gasped in horror, but Eldritch was only just beginning.

'Or perhaps someone comes to her who can see perfectly well . . . someone who has red or yellow eyes, and wants to be able to pass for a human . . . or simply someone who is bored and feels like a change—'

'Stop!' Red cried. 'That's not true, it *can't* be true!'

'But it is,' Eldritch said, warming to his theme. 'Want a cure for baldness? The Hedgewitch can provide you with whatever locks you wish for! It's only a matter of waiting for a suitable source to come along. Or how about a singing voice that would sweeten even a toad's croak? Simply slice out the tongue of a young choirboy, and it's yours!'

'Stop it!'

'Or to wish an enemy ill, buy a high-quality curse; a heart full of hatred to bury in some discreet corner of your foe's land! Or a plague of warts, supplied by my own good self . . .' Eldritch finally paused for breath and emitted a manic cackle. 'She was welcome to them . . . just not the thumb they were attached to.' He gave a sudden four-fingered wave and then fell silent, his sudden burst of energy spent.

Red shook with fear and rage.

'She's not having me,' she vowed. 'Using me in her spells and curses – I won't let it happen.'

'You don't have a choice,' said Eldritch. 'I told you, you can't escape. No one has – not unscathed. And in any case, it looks as if she has other plans for you.'

'There's a first time for everything,' Red began, and then stopped. 'What do you mean "other plans"? What other plans, and how do you know?'

'Because I heard what she said before she threw you in. You're going to be her new disguise.'

7

WARWICK'S HUNCH ABOUT Nell soon proved to be correct. The next day, something she did culminated in a great deal of trouble.

The day began ordinarily enough, but with one notable difference. When Tanya awoke in her bed it was to silence. For the first time there were none of the usual shouts or tantrums from Amos, above on the second floor. The house was peaceful. Casting her mind back to summer, Tanya recalled learning that the herb rosemary had the power to extract memories from a human's mind if used correctly. Knowing that many of Amos's troubles stemmed from his past, Tanya had suggested extracting the memories that disturbed his mind. The quietness of the manor confirmed that the old man's past tormented him no longer.

When Tanya entered the kitchen Oberon jumped up at her in an enthusiastic morning greeting. She groaned as his enormous paws landed heavily on her shoulders. His hot dog breath tickled her nose and she pushed him away, laughing.

'He did that to me, too,' said Fabian, grouchily, from over near the fireplace. 'Only, when he jumped up at me he'd just come in from the garden.' He stood up next to the mantel-piece. Two dirty paw prints were smudged on his thin jumper.

'What are you doing skulking around over there?' Tanya asked.

'Nothing,' said Fabian. 'I'm not skulking.'

'You are. You're looking for the hearthfay, aren't you?' she guessed.

Fabian shrugged. 'Might be.'

'I told you before, she's shy,' said Tanya. 'If you want to see a fairy, your best bet is the brownie in the tea caddy. It's always there – but just watch out for its teeth.'

'I've already looked,' said Fabian, his voice taking on a mournful note. 'I can't see it – I think it's because I've just used the last of the eye drops Mad Morag gave me, and there wasn't quite enough left for both eyes.'

'You've used it all?' Tanya asked.

'I get curious,' said Fabian. 'There are so many of them in this house.'

'What a waste,' said Tanya.

In the summer, the old gypsy woman who lived in the nearby Hangman's Wood had foreseen the dangers that awaited Tanya and Fabian, and had given them a number of gifts to help. One was a tiny glass bottle of murky green liquid, a drop of which into each eye had allowed Fabian a temporary second sight. The other items were a pair of silver scissors that would cut through almost anything and a compass that would always lead the person who possessed it home. On the night Tanya had almost vanished into the fairy realm both had aided her and Fabian in their escape – but Tanya had not seen the scissors since. They had vanished with Red. Now Fabian's eye drops were gone, only the compass remained.

'I've been thinking about the compass,' she said, chewing her lip.

'What about it?' said Fabian. He pushed his thick glasses up his nose, leaving a smear of coal dust on the bridge.

'We should check to see if it's still working. Morag said she'd like it returned once it stops because that means it's no longer any use to us, and she'll pass it on to someone else who might need it.'

'Does this mean you're going to see her in her caravan in the woods if it's not working?' Fabian asked. 'If you are, I'll come.'

Tanya nodded. 'I'll check it after breakfast.'

She gave Oberon a dog biscuit and then took the lid off the tea caddy. Using a teaspoon, she carefully lifted a heap of teabags, and jumped as a gnarled little hand shot out and rapped her over the knuckles with a tiny walking stick. Wincing, she replaced the lid and rubbed her sore hand.

'He's still there all right,' she muttered, turning at the sound of footsteps.

Florence came into the kitchen, beaming at them, and then set about preparing breakfast. Shortly after, Warwick joined them and swept out the remnants of yesterday's fire from the grate and laid a new one. Nell was the last to come downstairs, a duster tucked in her waistband and her flip-flops slapping the quarry stone floor.

'There's a funny smell up on the first floor,' she announced, wrinkling her nose in Fabian's direction. 'It's coming from your room.'

'It's probably yesterday's socks,' Fabian replied.

'Well, I'm doing a spring clean, so if there's anything important lying around put it away.'

'Funny time for a spring clean,' Fabian muttered. 'It's autumn.'

Nell pursed her lips and tossed the duster into the washing machine.

'You know what I mean.'

After breakfast she collected the General from the sitting room, wheeling his cage into prime position in front of the fireplace. Oberon backed away, his tail between his legs. The General paid no attention. Instead he preened and then settled back, regarding everyone superiorly from over his hooked beak. Tanya watched as Nell opened the top of the cage and repositioned the wooden pole to allow the parrot to sit in the open.

'Won't he fly off?' she asked.

'Oh, no,' said Nell. 'Not unless something frightens him. He'll just sit there like a good boy.'

Tanya could not imagine that anything would frighten the General.

'All the same, don't leave him unattended,' said Warwick, piling plates in the sink. 'There's Spitfire to think of. He may be old but he's still got that killer instinct.' As he made his way past the General he gave a sharp exclamation.

'What is it?' asked Florence.

'He *pecked* me!' said Warwick, holding his arm and looking outraged. The General cackled, as if to insult further.

'Oh, dear,' said Nell. 'You must've frightened him by walking too close.'

'He looks petrified,' Warwick answered sarcastically. He glared at the bird and left the kitchen.

'How rude,' said the General. 'Off with his head!'

It had been three months since Tanya had last prised up the loose floorboard in her room. From the space beneath she pulled out a shoebox that was wrapped in a red scarf. This was not for decoration – she used the scarf because the colour red acted as a camouflage to fairies. With the scarf covering the box, it was safe from tampering. Removing the lid, she cast her eyes over the contents. Amongst them was an old diary of Tanya's, a handful of photographs, a heavy silver charm bracelet, and a tarnished brass compass. At first glance, the compass seemed quite ordinary, but on closer inspection there was something odd about it: there were no directions marked on it except for a single letter 'H' where the letter 'N' for 'north' would normally be. This 'H', Tanya had discovered, stood for 'home'.

'Well?' said Fabian. 'Is it still working?'

Tanya lifted the compass from the box.

'No. The needle is just spinning, as if it's broken. If it was working the needle would be steady on the "H".'

'Oh, well,' said Fabian, grudgingly. He reached past her for the bracelet. 'Do you still wear this?'

'No.' She regarded it solemnly. 'Not since . . . the drain-dweller.' There had been thirteen charms on the bracelet to begin with, but one, a tiny silver cauldron, had been taken by a fairy that had then attempted to steal the rest of the bracelet. This had resulted in a chase that had ended in the fairy's death when it had crossed Spitfire's path.

'Where's the cauldron charm now?' Fabian asked.

Tanya shrugged. 'Probably still in the sink pipe with the rest of the things the drain-dweller stole.' She put the lid on the box and then pushed it back under the floorboards, keeping the bracelet to one side. 'I don't even want it any more. I can't bear to look at it – I'm going to give it back to my grandmother.' Glancing up at the window, she got to her feet.

'Come on,' she said. 'Let's go and return the compass to Morag while the weather's good.' She picked the bracelet up. 'I'll give this back to my grandmother on the way out.'

But when they arrived downstairs there was nobody around; just a note from Florence to say she had gone to buy groceries in Tickey End, and a rhythmic snoring from the brownie in the tea caddy. There was no sign of Warwick or Nell either; just a mop and bucket in the kitchen.

Tanya collected Oberon's leash from where it hung on the

back of the kitchen door. 'Let's go out. If anyone asks we can just say we're walking Oberon.' As an afterthought, she left the bracelet on top of Florence's note before they left the house. She would explain her feelings to her grandmother later.

The vast back garden was as overgrown as ever, only now it looked as if an artist had taken to it with an autumnal palette. Tanya tilted her head back and sniffed the scent of leaf mulch.

In the summer, three goblins had often been found on the rockery. Now, though, there were none to be seen. Tanya had befriended one of them, a gentle-natured creature named Brunswick who had been bullied by his two vicious companions. She wondered what had become of him.

Soon Tanya, Fabian and Oberon were through the gate and heading towards the forest. They paused before the little brook that dissected the land between the manor and the woods, then used the stepping stones to cross. Fabian made to dash into the fringes of the forest but Tanya called him back.

'Wait! Don't forget that the woods are full of fairies – you need to protect yourself.'

Quickly, she took her jacket off, turned it inside out and then put it back on again. Fabian watched, and then did the same.

'Ready?' he asked.

Tanya nodded. 'Let's go.'

And with that, they stepped into Hangman's Wood.

The old gypsy woman's caravan was difficult to find.

Tanya had found it once before with the help of the goblin, Brunswick, but now she and Fabian were wondering how to go about finding it again. Fabian, ever logical, had a theory.

'Mad Morag likes her privacy, obviously. Why else would she live out in the woods? She'll be tucked away somewhere, but not too far out.'

'What makes you so sure?' Tanya interrupted. 'And for goodness' sake, stop calling her *Mad* Morag. She's not mad, she's eccentric—'

'Eccentric? She's a witch,' Fabian said rudely. 'As I was saying, she's old, so she won't want to walk further than she has to. She goes to Tickey End for her groceries so she'll probably live over on this side of the forest . . .' he paused and pointed off to the left, 'and she'd want to be near to the stream for her water supply as well. So we should follow the stream in this direction.'

Tanya didn't argue. Fabian's idea seemed sensible.

'Let's go,' she said.

They set off, kicking through the woodland undergrowth. As they drew deeper into the wood Tanya saw patches of fairy rings; red, pale brown and flesh-coloured toadstools growing in wide circles between the trees, and, in some cases, around them.

'Careful,' she said. 'Don't step into any of these fairy rings. I've read that they can be dangerous.'

'Dangerous how?' asked Fabian.

'You can get pulled into a fairy dance that goes on all night, or sometimes even years. So avoid them.'

'Easier said than done,' Fabian replied. 'I can hardly take a step without being right on top of one.'

It was true. The fairy rings were everywhere. They walked on carefully, and as they went further still into the woods Tanya could make out familiar chattering noises in the trees. She kept her eyes trained ahead, but remained wary. Often, the fairies kept to themselves unless they were meddled with, and today Tanya was more comfortable in the knowledge that their business was not with them.

Soon the fairy rings became fewer, before disappearing altogether, but then they happened upon something else. Silver-grey railings went round in a circular shape, guarding a massive, cave-like hole in the ground. Oberon trotted ahead, sniffing the foliage at the foot of the railings, then cocking his leg against them.

'How big do you think this one is?' Tanya asked.

'About three metres,' said Fabian. 'It's similar in size to the large one we saw in the summer.'

The cavernous holes were known as the Hangman's Catacombs, due to the numerous people that had gone missing in the woods over the years before the railings had been constructed. The real name for such a hole was a 'denehole', and it was known that they tunnelled for miles below the earth into a twisting labyrinth of caves. This was the third Tanya had seen, but it had no less impact on her than the first. They were truly sinister, and no real explanation had ever been found for their existence.

'Come on,' said Fabian. 'Look. There's a path.'

Oberon waited ahead for them and was wagging his tail. As they approached, he lowered his nose to the ground and snuffled along as though picking up a scent. After a short distance he paused again and waited, his tongue falling out of the side of his mouth.

'Looks like he's picked up on something,' said Fabian.

'He has,' Tanya replied. She glimpsed a flash of yellow through the greenery. 'He's been here before. He's found her.'

The caravan was just as she remembered; vibrantly painted, old and ornate. They crept up to the sky blue front door. Tanya was a split second from knocking when voices from the open window stopped her. Shocked, she whipped round to face Fabian.

They had both immediately recognised one of the low voices as Warwick's.

'What's he doing here?' Tanya mouthed.

'I don't know!' Fabian whispered. 'But he'll skin us alive if he sees us, you know we're not supposed to come into the woods!' He darted closer to the caravan and pressed himself to its side beneath the open window, beckoning for Tanya to join him.

'What are you doing?' she whispered.

'Let's listen,' he said quietly. 'I want to know what he's doing here. We can hide under the caravan if we need to.'

Tanya scurried to Fabian's side, her pulse racing. Warwick's voice was a murmur, drifting through the open window.

'So you can't tell me anything then?'

Morag spoke, her aged voice a croak. 'No, I cannot – she is not known to me, not at this time.'

'But if you see anything, you'll send for me?' Warwick continued. 'It's important.'

'If she appears to me I will let you know,' the old woman promised.

Moments passed wordlessly inside the caravan.

'What's going on?' Fabian hissed, clearly bewildered. 'Who are they talking about?'

'I don't know who,' Tanya answered. 'But she's talking about her visions. Your father is asking her for information, things she might have . . . *seen.*'

They both looked up at the open window.

'I'm getting something else,' Morag could be heard saying at last. 'It's hazy, but it's something to do with a new arrival . . . at the manor. Something in the past . . . a child. A child that was lost. It's never been forgotten. And ahead there lies trouble, this I can see clearly.'

'What kind of trouble?' Warwick asked sharply.

'The kind you are already familiar with,' Morag replied.

There was a shuffling from inside the caravan, and the sound of heavy footsteps approaching the door. The secretive meeting was over.

Tanya and Fabian looked at each other in panic, then scrambled beneath the caravan, each rolling to the opposite edges in order to conceal themselves behind one of the four huge wheels. The caravan door opened above them, and Warwick's mud-encrusted boots descended the tiny set of steps. Midway, he turned back to face the direction he had come from. To Tanya's alarm, Oberon's tail began to thump at the familiar scent of Warwick. She placed a warning hand on his collar, praying that he would not reveal their presence.

'When will the tonic be ready?' Warwick was saying. 'I'm almost out.'

'By the next full moon,' said Morag. 'In three days' time.'

'I'll return for it then,' said Warwick. He turned again and came down the remainder of the steps, and was heading away from the caravan when the door could be heard closing.

Tanya and Fabian watched as he strode back through the forest. Tanya became aware of Oberon's head cocking to the side, but the dog seemed to understand that he was to stay with Tanya, and made no attempt to follow Warwick. They waited, leaving several minutes until Warwick was out of sight before edging out from their hiding places.

Tanya looked at Fabian.

'We can't go to see Morag now,' she said in a low voice.

'I know,' said Fabian. 'If she's in contact with my father we shouldn't take the risk. She might tell him we've been to see her, and as far as he's concerned, we're still forbidden from coming into these woods.'

They set off, hurrying away from the caravan silently.

'Who do you think Warwick was trying to find out about?' Tanya asked.

Fabian narrowed his eyes behind his thick-lensed glasses.

'I don't know,' he said. 'But the person Morag did see in her vision had to be Nell. She's the only new person in the household.'

'I wonder what happened in her past,' said Tanya. 'Morag said she saw a lost child. Perhaps she had a child that . . . died.'

'She's never mentioned any family,' said Fabian. 'Apart from her dead husband.'

'What about the person Warwick was asking about, the first one? Who do you think that might be?'

Fabian shook his head. 'I can't think who else he would want to find out about.'

They pondered this for the remainder of their journey back to the manor, but even by the time they arrived, neither of them had come up with any answers.

As they moved through the house there were signs that Florence and Warwick had both returned before them. Warwick's muddy footprints marred Nell's mopped floor and Florence's keys were on the side. The charm bracelet, Tanya noticed, had gone from where she had left it, and she made a mental note to mention it to her grandmother when she saw her next.

However, when she went upstairs to put the compass back beneath the floorboards Tanya saw the needle as she took it out of her pocket.

The compass was working again. With that, all thoughts of the old charm bracelet slipped her mind entirely.

8

ANYA LEFT HER ROOM AND crossed the landing, eager to tell Fabian about the compass. She was almost at his door when it was flung open from the other side, making her jump. Fabian stomped out, his nostrils flaring.

'Look at this!' He brandished something beneath her nose. 'A mouse trap! It would have taken my toe off if I hadn't seen it in time.'

Tanya frowned. 'It's not like my grandmother or Warwick to use mouse traps.'

'That's because they don't,' Fabian said hotly. 'Florence doesn't like them, and we've never needed them with Spitfire in the house. It has to be Nell's doing!'

'Well, I daresay my grandmother will put a stop to it,' Tanya said impatiently. 'Listen, about the compass—'

A terrible, high-pitched squeal of agony prevented her from finishing the sentence.

'What was that?'

Fabian looked blank. 'What?'

'A scream, down on the landing.'

The compass forgotten, Tanya edged away from Fabian and towards the staircase. 'You didn't hear it?'

Fabian shook his head but followed her anyway. A whimpering noise drifted up to them. She descended the staircase. She knew in her gut where the sound was coming from, and the fact that Fabian could not hear it did not bode well. Each step brought her closer to the grandfather clock on the landing. The sound was coming from the other side of it. She approached, ignoring Fabian, who was prodding her and demanding an explanation. Already she had a horrible premonition about what she was going to find.

Fairies resided in the clock, and the space beside it was also one of Spitfire's favourite snoozing places. The combination made for a deadly possibility. Tanya's stomach lurched as she took another step. She had witnessed the death of one fairy at Spitfire's claws. She had no wish to see another.

This time, when she peered round the side of the clock, Spitfire was nowhere to be seen, though the sight that met her was no less gruesome.

'Oh, no . . .' Tanya murmured.

Three pairs of tiny fey eyes met hers; a mixture of anger and terror. They huddled together in such a way that, even as one of them bared its teeth, Tanya could see that they were afraid. Behind them a fourth fairy was the source of the whimpering. It looked up at her, its eyes huge with fear and pain. Just in front of it lay a pale cube of cheese.

'What is it?' Fabian asked.

Tanya swallowed. 'One of the fairies from the clock. Its wings are caught in another trap.'

She dropped to her knees, deaf to the cries of the trapped fairy's companions. She had never before seen the inhabitants of the grandfather clock, and had always imagined them to be ugly creatures with good reason to hide themselves away. But the lodgers, as she'd always thought of them, were actually rather beautiful; small, silvery beings with bluish skin and white hair, and they were dressed in tiny mouse-skins.

'Let me help,' she told them, but as she reached out they fled and hid behind the clock. The trapped fairy shrieked in distress.

'Stay away, tricketty girl!'

'I'm trying to help,' she muttered, wondering if she should just take the whole thing – trap and fairy – to her grandmother. But she simply could not bear for the fairy to suffer any longer. Gently, she released the trap, disabling the spring that held the snapping arm in place, and eased the fairy into her hand. It was moaning incoherently now, while its companions looked on from the foot of the clock.

'I'm taking you to my grandmother,' said Tanya. 'She'll know what to do.' She stood up. Fabian hovered helplessly at her side.

'Search the house for any more traps and dismantle them,' she told him, starting down the stairs. 'If more fairies become injured we could be punished.'

'How badly is it injured?' Fabian asked.

'Its wings are completely crushed,' she said in a low voice. 'I don't think it'll ever fly again.'

Fabian took off, back up the stairs. Doors opened and slammed as he searched the rooms. In the kitchen, Oberon bounded over and tried to jump up at her, but Tanya shooed him away, afraid he would further injure the fairy in her hand.

Through the back door she could see Florence pegging laundry out to dry. Tanya called to her and waited in the doorway, next to the General's cage. The bird tilted his head to one side, staring at the fairy quivering in her palm with interest. He gave a loud click suddenly, making both Tanya and the fairy jump. A moment later Florence came in and closed the door. She took one look at Tanya's hand and pressed her thin lips into an even thinner line.

'How did this happen?' she asked. 'Was it Spitfire?'

'No,' Tanya answered. 'A mouse trap.'

'A *what*? Who on earth would—'

'Nell,' Tanya finished.

Florence's eyes narrowed and she held out her hand urgently. Tanya placed the fairy into her grandmother's palm as gently as she could. The creature moaned.

'Where is Nell?' Tanya asked.

'She's gone to the post office in Tickey End,' said Florence. 'But I'll be having words with her when she gets back.' She marched out of the kitchen and started up the stairs. Tanya hesitated, then went after her.

Her grandmother's bedroom door was ajar as they approached, and Tanya wondered if she would notice. Fabian must have been into Florence's room in his search for the traps, but if Florence realised then she did not mention it.

As they entered Tanya heard a thump from a few doors away. Fabian was still engaged in his search. Florence motioned for Tanya to close the door, and then sat on the bed. If the situation had been different, Tanya would have enjoyed the opportunity to look around her grandmother's room, for she had not often been into it. But now was not the time to satisfy her curiosity.

Florence nodded to the oak chest of drawers under the window.

'In the second drawer, there's a needlework kit. Fetch it for me.'

Tanya did as she was asked. The sight of a framed photograph on top of the chest momentarily distracted her. It was of her and her grandmother, taken only a few weeks ago.

'Open the box,' her grandmother told her, snapping her back to the present. 'There's a red pouch at the bottom.'

Tanya fumbled through the contents, pricking her fingers on errant needles. Beneath a tangle of embroidery thread was a small, blood-red drawstring pouch. She pulled at it, velvet soft between her fingers, and slipped her forefinger inside.

Something soft and cool to the touch met it. She

withdrew a small skein of gossamer-like thread. It glittered as the sunlight coming in through the window hit it.

'You know what this is, don't you?' her grandmother said.

Tanya nodded. 'Spidertwine.' She looked up at her grand-mother, bewildered. 'Why do you have it?'

'It's not just used by the fairies,' Florence replied. 'It can be used by us too, if we know how to, and how to obtain it in the first place, of course.'

'You got it from Morag,' Tanya guessed.

'Yes. And I keep it here, hidden, for times like these,' said her grandmother. 'It has healing properties – it can bind a wound and restore health more effectively than any medi-cine we know of – if it's used quickly enough. I need you to cut some off, and thread a needle with it.'

'How do I cut it?' Tanya asked, confused. 'I thought it was unbreakable by anything other than magic.'

'It's unbreakable by mortal hands,' her grandmother con-tinued. 'But there are other ways, and not all of them involve magic.'

'How, then?'

'There's something else in the pouch.'

Tanya lifted the pouch and felt a small, hard object still inside. She shook it out into her hand. It was a tiny wooden pillbox. She opened it. Inside, there was an assortment of odd objects: animal teeth and fragments of bones, and sev-eral small half-moon shaped things – cats' claws.

'Are those . . .?' she began.

'Yes, Spitfire's,' said Florence. 'A few from when I've

trimmed his claws, and some from where he's shed them through sharpening them on the furniture.'

'What are they for?' Tanya asked.

'Cutting the Spidertwine,' her grandmother explained. 'As you probably know by now, Spidertwine can't be destroyed by humans as it was used to make the nets fairies use to capture human children in the changeling trade. But it can be broken by things that are naturally designed for cutting, such as teeth or animal claws. Whatever's used must be living, or must have come from a living being. If the object is detached from the living creature, like these are, then each can only be used once.'

Tanya nodded. She understood now how valuable the scissors Morag had given her – the scissors she had lost – really were. Unravelling a length of thread, she selected a grimy claw from the box. As she touched it to the Spidertwine's surface, it separated effortlessly from the remainder, which she returned to the velvet pouch.

'Now thread a needle,' said Florence.

Tanya reached for the lid of the needlework box, where a few needles were stuck in the underside of the lid.

'No, not those,' said Florence. 'They're steel. Steel consists of iron, which will dispel the Spidertwine's magic.'

'So what do I use?' Tanya asked. Her eyes rested on the small shards of bone in the wooden box. She carefully lifted one and inspected it, correctly guessing that there would be an eye at the blunter end through which to direct the thread.

Quickly and deftly, she threaded the Spidertwine through it and handed it to her grandmother.

The fairy was now limp and quiet in Florence's hand. It had finally passed out from the pain.

'Will it fly again?' Tanya asked, watching as her grandmother skilfully began to sew the torn shreds of wing back together again.

'I don't know,' said Florence, fretfully. 'It's possible we acted in time, but the damage is bad. I don't know what Nell was thinking of, using traps when there's a cat in the house. Most of the fairies know to stay away from Spitfire, but I've never used traps for fear something like this might happen.'

Tanya watched as her grandmother continued to sew. The next few minutes passed in silence, but it was shattered by a thundering of steps on the landing outside the room, and then raised voices from downstairs.

'Now what?' Florence snapped. 'If that's something to do with Nell I'm going to be very cross. Go and see what's the matter, will you?'

Tanya got up and left the room. She hurried down the stairs, but paused by the grandfather clock. Muffled sobs were audible from inside.

'It's going to be all right,' she whispered to the clock. 'My grandmother is helping.' The sobbing ceased, and Tanya ran on, towards the kitchen, where already, an argument had ignited.

'We don't use traps,' Fabian was saying coldly. 'There's a perfectly good cat to catch rats and mice!'

'Perfectly useless, more like,' Nell retorted. 'He can just about manage to chew his food with what's left of his gnashers!'

Tanya burst into the kitchen. Fabian and Nell were glaring at each other. Nell's coat was draped over one of the kitchen chairs, and she had just put the General on his perch outside the cage.

'I don't see why you're making such a fuss about it,' Nell said indignantly. 'There's vermin in this house – I can hear it in the bleedin' walls, scuffling and scrabbling. They're even in that old clock on the landing!' She shuddered, her plump shoulders wobbling. Her voice had taken on a shrill note, and in response, General Carver was bouncing up and down on his perch, clearly agitated. Oberon, too, appeared upset, his paws folded over his nose as he lay in his basket.

'All the same, Nell,' Tanya said, trying to mask her own irritation. 'We don't use them. My grandmother is quite cross.'

'Cross?' said Nell, disbelievingly. She picked up her coat and threw it on to a hook on the back door, startling the General. 'Cross? Anyone would think it's acceptable to have vermin in the house, the way you lot are carrying on!'

Cold air rushed into the kitchen as Warwick came through the back door. From the look on his face it was clear he was aware he had walked in on an argument.

'What's going on?'

This latest interruption proved too much for the General. With a squawk and a flap of his wings he took off from his perch and flew over Warwick's head, through the open door and out into the garden.

'Now look what you've done!' Nell cried. 'Come back, Carver!'

Warwick fell back against the doorframe as Nell pushed past him. Tanya and Fabian ran to the door, watching as the General led Nell a merry dance around the garden.

'Will someone tell me what's going on?' Warwick demanded.

Fabian pointed to the array of traps he had collected. He had set them on the table.

Warwick sighed, raking his long hair back from his face.

'Does Florence know about this?' he asked. 'Where is she?'

'Upstairs,' said Tanya. 'One of the fairies from the clock got caught in another one of the traps. It's badly injured – she's trying to help it.'

Warwick looked outraged. 'I said she would be trouble.' Turning back to the garden, his expression darkened further. 'Now where's she got to?'

The garden was quite empty.

'There,' said Fabian suddenly. 'Through the gate – look!'

A rotund figure was rapidly growing smaller in the distance beyond the garden walls. Above it, Tanya could just make out a speck in the sky before it vanished altogether.

'Oh, no,' she breathed. 'I think the General has just flown into the woods . . . and Nell's about to follow him!'

Warwick made a noise like a dog growling, then turned on his heel and strode out into the garden.

'Where are you going?' Fabian called.

'After her, of course!' came his father's indignant reply. 'She can't possibly go into those woods alone. It's not safe.'

Tanya and Fabian exchanged glances, and then the two of them pulled on their outdoor shoes and coats and raced after Warwick. Tanya whistled to Oberon, who was only too glad to come bounding after them. By the time they caught up with Warwick he was a short way beyond the garden gate, striding quickly across the sodden land.

It was only the afternoon but darkness had begun to draw in, bringing with it a damp autumnal chill that crept around Tanya's neck like the tentacles of a sea creature. She could see Warwick's breath coming out of his nose in short little puffs that gave him the appearance of an angry dragon.

'What are you two doing?' he asked them, his voice gruff. 'You're not to come into the forest. Go back.'

'We know how to protect ourselves,' said Fabian, pointing to his coat and Tanya's, which they had automatically put on inside out. 'And you might need our help.'

Warwick gave a low snort. 'Just stay close to me. If I tell you to do something – if I tell you to do *anything* – you obey. Immediately, got it?'

'Got it,' they answered in unison.

'And this doesn't mean you can go gallivanting off whenever you feel like it, either,' Warwick continued. 'This is a one-off.'

They had reached the brook. For the second time that day (unbeknown to Warwick) Tanya and Fabian crossed at the stepping stones, and followed Warwick across the border of trees that marked the edge of the woods. It was almost dark now, and Tanya's teeth had begun to chatter, though this was less to do with being chilly and more with the memory of the last time she had been in the forest after sundown. The night she had almost become imprisoned in the fairy realm . . .

'Now what?' she heard Fabian ask.

'We wait, and listen,' said Warwick. 'She'll probably be making enough racket to rouse half the forest. That way we can track her.'

Before he had even finished the sentence they heard a shrill voice, calling out from within the wood. 'General Carver! Where are you, dearest?'

Tanya felt an unexpected pang of sympathy as she heard Nell's quavering voice. She sounded afraid as well as worried for her pet.

'This way,' Warwick said quietly, leading them along a narrow trail. 'And be careful where you walk – there are fairy rings everywhere this time of year. Don't step into them.'

Tanya and Fabian said nothing, each remembering their conversation about the very same thing earlier that afternoon.

'Carver! I insist you return this instant!' Nell's voice was closer now. Ahead, they could hear the swish of low branches being pushed aside and the crackle of undergrowth under a heavy tread. They were close.

'Goodness knows how many traps are still lying about,' Fabian mumbled. 'She's probably killed off half the fairies in the manor—'

'Quiet,' Warwick hissed. 'Something's wrong – listen!'

They froze at his words and strained their ears. Nell was wailing; a piercing, high-pitched sound of surprise. Beneath it Tanya could hear music; a violin or a fiddle of some kind, a tin whistle, and an irregular beat, like a drum.

'What's she yowling like that for?' said Fabian.

'And what's that music?' Tanya wondered aloud. 'The tune sounds familiar somehow, but I can't place it . . .'

'Music?' Fabian looked at her, his blue eyes curious. 'I can't hear any music, just her squawking.'

They both looked up at Warwick. His expression was worrying.

'Neither can I,' he said. 'And that's not a good sign!'

He raced ahead, Tanya and Fabian close behind. Tanya jumped as a pair of eyes in a leafy nook of a tree blinked at her crossly. She sped on after Warwick, until Fabian drew level, then took over.

Suddenly, Nell's wailing was upon them and Warwick halted abruptly. Fabian skidded to a standstill just short of his father and stood, open-mouthed in astonishment. Tanya drew up behind them, her chest heaving with short, painful breaths.

At the centre of a large ring of bright red toadstools were four figures, dancing frantically to a strange little melody. Three of the figures were musicians, and fey. Nell was the fourth, jigging away to the tune with a bewildered look on her face. It was clear to Tanya that Nell had absolutely no control over her limbs, and that, much to her horror, now that she was inside the ring she could see her musical companions as well as Tanya could.

'Nell, what on earth are you doing?' said Fabian. 'Have you gone barking mad?'

'Help . . .' Nell panted. 'Make them stop!'

'Them?'

'She's not alone,' said Tanya, knowing that Fabian was oblivious to Nell's odd companions. 'She's under some kind of enchantment.'

'What do you see?' said Warwick. 'Describe them.'

Tanya glanced at him in surprise. She had assumed that Warwick would be able to see the fairy revellers, for although she knew he did not have the second sight, she was aware that he used the same eye tonic as Fabian had had in order to allow him to see fairies temporarily.

'I used some eye drops earlier,' he said, reading her thoughts. 'They've worn off now, and I've run out.'

Tanya nodded. Now she understood why Warwick had allowed her and Fabian to accompany him into the woods – he needed Tanya as a lookout.

'There are three of them in there with Nell,' she said in a low voice. 'They're playing instruments and dancing along with her. One has a fiddle. He's as tall as Fabian, and looks like he's half man, half goat. He has goat's legs and cloven feet, and two little horns growing out of his head.'

'What are you? What are you?' Nell was gasping.

'A faun,' said Warwick, his eyes narrowed. 'And the others?'

'A goblin,' Tanya said, with certainty. 'Knee height, grubby-looking. It's beating a dish with a spoon.' As she spoke, the goblin eyed her sneakily and grinned, showing the characteristic large, yellowing goblin teeth.

'The third is a little old man, wearing old-fashioned clothes. He looks a bit like the brownie in the tea caddy, but skinnier. He's playing a tin whistle.'

'Anything else?' said Warwick.

'They're dancing around an empty flask.'

'How can you tell it's empty?'

'The flask is on its side and the cork is beside it.'

'Drunk,' said Warwick, disgustedly, but there was a measure of relief in his voice. 'It's likely that they're just mischief-makers, but they could be on their way to the fairy realm. We need to get Nell out of there.'

'How do we do that?'

'I'm going to reach in and pull her out,' said Warwick.

'Will that work?' Fabian asked doubtfully.

'As long as I keep one foot out of the circle and grab hold of her firmly, it should do.'

'Do something!' Nell shrieked, now hopping madly on one foot.

Warwick planted one foot heavily in the soil of the forest floor, ready to leap at the right moment.

'Stand back,' he ordered Fabian and Tanya. Then to Nell, who was about to lap the circle again, he added, 'Get ready. On the count of three . . . one, two—'

As Nell came almost level with Warwick she reached out to take his hand. Warwick placed one foot inside the fairy ring and leaned towards her. Their fingers brushed briefly, but then Nell stumbled and tripped over Warwick's foot. Staggering forward, she almost went over completely but somehow managed to right herself at the last minute. The effect of this was disastrous. Hot on Nell's heels was the faun, who quickly reached out and took Warwick's hand in place of Nell's. His momentum caught Warwick off-guard completely . . . propelling him headlong into the fairy ring with Nell and the rest of the revellers. All he could do was dance helplessly to the enchanted fey music.

'Dad!' Fabian yelled, rushing forward. Tanya grabbed him and yanked him away.

'Stay back!'

'What do we do?' he cried. 'How do we get them out?'

'Don't try anything!' Warwick shouted. 'Go back to the manor at once!'

'But—'

'Just go! *Now!*'

'Come on,' said Tanya, pulling at Fabian's arm. 'We need to get help. We can't take any more risks – they could pull us both in as well.'

They backed away from the circle, taking care where they placed their feet. After they had taken a few steps, the tune being played by the fairy revellers shifted and went off-key. The dance changed, and before Tanya and Fabian's horrified eyes, the revellers leaped from the fairy ring into another that was alongside it, continuing their dance there for a minute or two. Then once again, a key shifted and they moved on, into another nearby fairy ring, gradually moving further into the woods and away.

'Where are they being taken?' said Fabian, his breath coming in short bursts.

'I don't know,' Tanya answered. 'But we need to go, and quickly.'

As she spoke, the revellers, Nell and Warwick vanished from sight, swallowed by the woods.

'Which is the way back?' Fabian asked, panicking. 'I can't think – I can't remember which direction we came in from!'

Tanya reached into her pocket and pulled out the compass. 'This way,' she said, reading the needle and pointing calmly.

Fabian stared at the compass in confusion. 'But this morning . . . we were going to return it to Mad Morag . . .'

Tanya shook her head. 'I know. That's what I was coming to tell you when you found the first trap. It's a good thing we didn't manage to return it – it's still working.' She glanced into the trees at the space where Warwick and Nell had last been visible. 'Which is just as well, because we're going to need it.'

9

ELDRITCH'S WORDS ECHOED IN Red's head.

'Her new . . . *disguise?*'

'Sounded that way to me,' came the sly reply. 'She's been the old beggar woman for some time now—'

They both flinched as the trapdoor above was flung open and, with a triumphant shriek, the Hedgewitch threw another body down into the cellar with them. It landed beside Red with a grunt. In the seconds before the trapdoor was snapped shut again, Red was able to glimpse the new captive.

It was a man. He looked to be no older than her father had been, which would make him around forty years old, and there was nothing about him that suggested he was fey. He was dressed scruffily in outdoor clothes; a long, dark overcoat and thick corduroy trousers. They were mud-spattered, like his black boots. His hair was dark, although grey in places, and was long, just past his shoulders, and unkempt. His face was contorted with pain – with good reason.

He had been bound; his arms were pinned to his sides and his ankles were positioned in a way that looked both uncomfortable and unnatural. In places she could make out a hint of something glistening; almost invisible to the eye, something that looked like spiders' web. As she stared she caught sight of the same glistening material around the man's mouth.

She recognised it now. Tiny precise stitches, sewn with Spidertwine. Red's own mouth formed an 'o' of revulsion: the man's lips had been stitched together.

The man began to moan, as if attempting to speak from behind his sewn up lips. All that was audible was a low humming sound, coming through his nose.

'You'll have to speak up,' Eldritch said. 'I didn't quite catch that.'

'You're despicable!' Red hissed, unable to tear her eyes away from the man's lips. The sight was truly gruesome. Something inside her ignited then – some primal instinct for survival. She began struggling again, fighting to manoeuvre her bound hands from behind her to in front. Using the last ounce of her strength, she fought to push her hands past her skinny hips, praying that her boyish figure would be her saviour. On the fourth attempt her wrists slid past her hips, and, with a low cry of joy, she slipped her numb hands from behind her heels to in front. It was a small triumph, but a triumph nevertheless. She lay back, shivering on the freezing stone floor, trying to regain some of her strength. Her respite did not last long; the prickling sensation at her ankle was back, and even worse than before.

Wriggling her fingers to encourage some semblance of life back into them, she probed along her lower leg, over the top of her trousers. It was not long before her fingers came into contact with something small and hard, the added pressure of her hand sending a twinge of discomfort into the skin below the fabric. Wincing, she used her crooked fingers to hook the hem of her trouser leg up. There had to be some bramble or thorn caught in her clothing from the woods, pricking her. But it was not a bramble or thorn caught beneath her clothes.

A tiny pair of ornate silver scissors was tangled up in a loose thread in her trousers. They were open, and one of the points was digging into her skin; a dark smear of blood where it had punctured the surface. Her heart soared with hope at the sight of them. These, she knew, were no ordinary scissors. They belonged to Tanya and would cut anything except metal, wood or stone. Edging her thumb and forefinger into them, she twisted them and snipped at the thread they were caught in.

'What's that you have there?' Eldritch said, suddenly alert. 'Show me what's in your hand!'

'Quiet,' said Red, concentrating. To her immense frustration she was unable to position the scissors in a way that would let her free her hands. She attempted for several minutes, eventually giving up as her fingers cramped and the scissors clattered to the floor for the third time. With a growl, she crawled over to the man with the stitched lips. He eyed her, and the scissors in her hand, warily. His eyes were pale, she saw, grey or blue – it was hard to tell which in the dim light.

'I'm going to cut the stitches in your mouth,' she whispered fiercely. 'And then you're going to talk. You're going to tell me how you got here. If I believe what I hear then I'll free you, on the condition that you return the favour by cutting the ropes on my wrists. Understand?'

The man nodded vigorously, his eyes wide and bloodshot.

'All right,' said Red. 'Now keep still.'

'What about me?' Eldritch whined. 'I've been here longest! See if you can help me!'

'Shut up,' Red snapped. 'I'll come to you in a minute.' *If you're lucky*, she added silently. She reached forward, straining in the dim light. The gossamer-like appearance of the Spidertwine was helpful in one respect: the stitches glistened, enabling her to see them. Leaning over the man, she edged the tip of the scissors beneath a stitch that looked to be the loosest. A dot of dark red appeared on his skin as the scissors nicked him, but the man did not make a sound. She snipped, and the Spidertwine separated. Removing the scissors, she repositioned them again, beneath a second stitch. This one was tighter. The man's eyes clamped shut as he tried not to jerk away instinctively. Beads of sweat were forming on his lined forehead. She cut again, and then again and again, until every stitch had been broken.

'It's done,' she said finally. 'You can open your mouth now.'

Tentatively, the man separated his lips.

'Thank you,' he whispered. 'Thank you, thank you . . .'

Red allowed him a moment to compose himself before moving on. There was no time to waste. The Hedgewitch could re-enter the dungeon at any moment.

'Who are you, lad?' the man asked.

The word 'lad' momentarily confused her, before she remembered her appearance. She looked like a boy now, with her short, spiky hair and men's clothing. With everything that had occurred since arriving in the fairy realm she had completely forgotten about her disguise. She lowered her voice before answering.

'You can call me Red.'

She thought she saw a spark of something behind the man's eyes then, a fleeting glimpse into whatever was going on in his mind. But before she could attempt to read it, it had vanished.

'I see,' he said, coughing suddenly. 'I forgot about the thing with names in this place. I'll have to think of one for myself, some kind of alias for you to call me.'

Red was instantly alert. 'What do you know of the fairy realm?'

'Enough to know not to give my real name away,' said the man. 'But clearly not enough to have escaped the clutches of whatever that thing is upstairs.' He eyed Eldritch, then turned his gaze back to Red. 'How long have you been here?'

'Less than a day,' she answered, keeping her voice low and boyish. 'Only hours, in fact.'

The man regarded her silently, but again she had the feeling that something was going on behind those pale eyes – that he knew something about her. It made her uncomfortable.

'Enough about me,' she said, narrowing her eyes. 'How did you end up here?'

From his corner of the dungeon, she sensed rather than saw Eldritch lean in closer to hear the man's answer.

'By accident,' the man said. 'Trying to help someone. Our housekeeper. She ran into the woods after her pet bird flew off. I ran after her, and found her dancing in a fairy ring. I tried to pull her out, and instead ended up getting pulled in with her. There were three other revellers, dancing, singing and playing instruments. We were carried away with the dance, the music was enchanted . . . impossible to resist.'

'Where is she? This housekeeper?'

'I don't know. We became separated when I got my foot caught in a trap.' He looked down. Red followed his gaze. In his left boot, puncture marks were visible in the leather, like a crocodile had snapped at the foot. Blood welled in the indents. 'They carried on dancing and moved off through the woods,' he continued. 'I don't think they realised I was no longer following. I don't know where she is now, but I need to find her and get us both out of here.'

'But you knew about the fairy realm?' Red asked. 'You knew the housekeeper was caught in the fairy ring? How do you know about fairies, do you have the second sight?'

The man's gaze shifted to Eldritch. He seemed reluctant to answer.

'No,' he said quietly. 'But other people I know do. And I've used something before – a solution to enable me to see them – but I wasn't using it today. It was all so fast and unexpected. I ran into the woods without fully preparing.'

Red nodded, relaxing slightly. 'I believe you,' she told him.

'Good,' said the man, weakly. 'Now cut me free, and let's get out of here.'

'You think it'll be that easy?' Eldritch sneered. 'Even if you're untied, getting out of the cottage will be a different matter. The trapdoor will be locked, and I guarantee the Hedgewitch will have used magic to prevent anyone from leaving against her will.'

'We'll deal with that when we come to it,' Red answered, glaring at him.

'Where did you get those?' the man asked her, eyeing the scissors in wonder.

Red faltered. 'They belonged to someone else. I ended up with them accidentally.'

'You thieved them!' Eldritch crowed.

'No, I didn't!' Red retorted. 'I didn't even realise I'd brought them with me. They were caught up in my clothing, that's why the Hedgewitch never found them—'

She broke off abruptly as a scraping sound came from above. The latch to the trapdoor was being pulled back.

'She's coming!' Eldritch hissed.

Red scrambled away from the man, hiding the scissors in the first place she could think of: beneath the damp straw. She retched as the stench was disturbed, forcing herself to push the scissors deep into the putrid pile. She had only seconds to throw herself back into place before the Hedgewitch pulled back the trapdoor and set foot on the first step leading down into the cellar.

Her heart was thudding as the witch drew closer. She was alone and Red knew that this meant she had come for one of her prisoners.

Her heart pounded like that of a rabbit sighted by a fox. It had never been in Red's nature to freeze with fright, instead her instinct was to run. But now she was forced to stay still, to fight the urge, for there was no point in running if there was nowhere to escape to. Even so she eyed the steps leading up to the cottage. Could she make it, if she ran hard and fast enough? Without her hands free to steady her it seemed futile. One stumble would see the end of the attempt if she had no hands to brace a fall. And she had no doubt that the Hedgewitch's wrath would be terrible and instantaneous. So she remained still, waiting.

The Hedgewitch approached, skirting around the filthy straw. Red's fears were confirmed as the woman knelt beside her, her smell of decay filling the air. She seized Red's hair in her fist, turning her head to face her. Light from the cottage above glinted against something . . . a shard of broken mirror that came slicing down towards her.

Red caught sight of her own eyes, wide in terror, in its reflection. There was a small cutting sound as it severed a strand of her hair, and then the witch released the rest of her hair, breathing heavily. Red's scalp tingled. She saw the witch shaking the hair carefully into something oval, pale and smooth: a hollowed-out eggshell. Then, raising the mirror shard once more, the witch grabbed Red's hand and pulled it towards her. Red felt a sharp sting in her thumb and knew the skin there had been pierced. Wordlessly, the witch lifted Red's thumb and squeezed it painfully, collecting three drops of blood in the eggshell along with the lock of hair. The shard of mirror joined them seconds later. Red gasped, instinctively pulling away. With a throaty laugh, the witch released her and crossed the cellar, climbing the steps to above once more. The slam of the trapdoor sounded like a tomb being sealed.

'What is she doing?' Red croaked, sucking her bleeding thumb. 'Why did she take hair and blood from me?'

'Haven't you figured it out yet?' Eldritch replied. 'Why do you think she's taken your hair, and blood? Why do you think she took them using a fragment of broken mirror? And why do you think she's brewing them in an eggshell?'

Red stared at him, rolling his words around in her mind. 'Hair . . . blood,' she whispered. 'A broken mirror . . . reflections. An egg . . . new life . . .'

'That's right,' Eldritch said ghoulishly. 'You're going to be her glamour. Her new disguise.' He tilted his head and looked towards the ceiling. 'Any minute now, you'll hear her. I've heard it twice before.'

Red lifted her head. Above, the Hedgewitch began to chant.

'Through my veins your blood shall flow,
Three drops this shell does brew.
Through my scalp your hair shall grow,
And old will become new.
Reflection of the garment past
Mixed with the garment fresh
A new glamour is being cast
This spell will change the flesh.
Warp and twist, fool and convince
The onlooker's perception
Mortal, fey, pauper or prince
Succumb to this deception.
Like a snake this skin is shed
A new one grown in place,
Chameleon tail, foot and head
Allow swift shift of face.'

The chant paused briefly, then took up again from the beginning.

'Through my veins your blood shall flow, three drops this shell does brew . . .'

Red turned to Eldritch. He was eyeing her craftily from the shadows.

'What's going to happen to me?' she asked urgently. 'How long do I have before she . . . before she turns into me? And what will happen once she does? Will I turn into her, or whoever she's pretending to be now?'

Eldritch stared back at her, a rakish smile on his lips.

'Answer me! What will happen?'

'You won't turn into her, no,' he said eventually. 'But when she's . . . you, you'll start to feel strange . . . displaced. You'll begin to have visions of things you haven't seen or done, and memories that aren't yours, but hers. The more she uses you, the less like you you'll feel.'

'But how can that be?' Red whispered, horrified.

'Because she'll be out there; seeing things, doing things and experiencing them as you. Whereas you'll be down here, with only these four walls, and misery and despair. It'll take time, months even, before you stop feeling like you altogether. And she will be more *you* than you are.'

'How long before her spell transforms her into me?' Red asked, trying to keep her voice from shaking. 'How long have I got?'

Eldritch shrugged. 'Difficult to say. It's been different for each of the others she's used before. One took only a matter of minutes. By the time she'd taken the hair and blood they were half out of their mind with terror, which seemed to accelerate the spell. The other took longer – it was dawn before it took effect. She was chanting all night, I thought I'd never get the words out of my head . . .' He trailed off.

'We need to get out of here,' the other man said, hoarsely.

'We can't,' said Eldritch. 'I've told you, she bolts the trap-door. And it's the only way out.'

'Then we'll wait until she comes down next,' said Red. 'And we'll have to make a run for it.'

'What about me?' Eldritch demanded. 'I can't run any-where – not with this holding me in place!' He jerked his wrist, trapped in the manacle, and then cursed under his breath. 'The only way I'm getting out is with the key. Someone needs to overpower her, take her by surprise.'

Red glanced at the human man, trying to read his expres-sion. He remained silent, looking thoughtful. His face was half hidden in the shadows.

'Yes,' he murmured at last. 'Overpowering her is the only way all three of us can escape. So that's what we have to do.'

'Very well,' said Red. Steeling herself, she plunged her hands into the fetid pile of straw and groped for the scissors. Eventually she found them and pulled them out, wiping them dry on one of the few unsoiled patches of straw. Moving over towards the man, she began to hack at the Spidertwine pinning his limbs into place. Within a couple of minutes he was free, shaking life back into his limbs. Red waited, trying to curb her impatience as he pulled himself into a sitting position. He held his hand out for the scissors, looking her in the eye.

'Give them to me and I'll cut your bonds.'

She hesitated.

'If you try anything, anything at all, I'll make you sorry,' she threatened.

The man looked at her, taken aback. 'Like what?'

'Like not giving the scissors back,' she said. To make her point, she stared pointedly at his injured foot. 'If you try to run you won't get far. I'll make that injury ten times worse.' She held his surprised gaze and hoped she sounded convincing, despite her heart fluttering like a caged bird.

Eldritch gave an amused chuckle.

'I won't try anything,' the man said calmly, meeting her glare.

Finally she handed him the scissors. In silence he cut the ropes binding her wrists, waiting patiently as she hurried to rub warmth and life back into her freezing hands. She had pins and needles, but even so she snatched the scissors from the man's palm and tucked them away into an inside pocket of her trousers.

'So now what?' she said to Eldritch. 'How long before she comes down here again?'

'Impossible to guess. Could be minutes or hours.'

Though it had stayed unspoken, Red knew that the talk of overpowering the Hedgewitch meant that it would have to be her that did it. The thought scared her more than anything had in a long time. But there was no other option: Eldritch couldn't move, and the human man's foot was injured too badly for him to be able to move quickly enough. It all depended on her. And all there was left to do now was wait.

'Let's talk,' she said eventually, desperate to think about something, *anything* except what was yet to come.

'What do you want to talk about?' said Eldritch.

'Why don't we begin with ourselves?' the man suggested. 'That seems as good a place to start as any.' He paused, shifting to loosen the laces of the boot on his injured foot. 'If we're going to be working together to get out of here then we should get to know one another.'

Red nodded. Above, the Hedgewitch's chant continued, low and steady.

'*Warp and twist, fool and convince the onlooker's perception . . .*'

She shuddered, eager to block out the terrible sound.

'Fine, I'll go first.' She closed her eyes, allowing herself to look into the past. 'I'm here because of my brother. He was taken from me last February. I've come to get him back.'

10

ON THE FIRST MORNING IN THE children's home, Mr Bones was gone when Rowan awoke. One of the twins must have come in quietly and collected him. She had slept fitfully and, as she sat up, snatches of bad dreams pricked at her like poisoned thorns.

She pushed back the covers and swung her legs over the side of the bed. On the dressing table there was an alarm clock. It was still early, just coming up to seven o'clock in the morning. She looked over to check on James. He was awake, lying quietly in the cot. As she leaned over and reached in to him, his face broke into a smile. He grabbed hold of her good arm and pulled himself up, then clung to the side of the cot, stamping his feet as he took in his surroundings.

'Want Mummy,' he said.

'I know,' Rowan whispered. 'So do I.' She patted his chubby little hand, then moved away to unpack her suitcase.

'Want Mummy,' James repeated, his little voice rising. 'Want Daddy.'

'Shush, now,' said Rowan, glancing back at him. His large blue eyes were following her in confusion as she started to put clothes into drawers.

By the time she had unpacked and got to the bathroom the water was tepid and once again the plughole was clogged with hair, soon slurped up by the disgusting fairy in the drain. After she'd washed and dressed, a staff member from the nursery came and took James, and after a short protest she had to be content with being told that she would see him later in the morning.

The first breakfast was the worst. Rowan had never enjoyed being the centre of attention, but now, being the new girl, the centre of attention was exactly what she was. Some of the girls whispered or pointed at her. Some offered tentative smiles, some offered words of comfort, and others simply stared with unabashed curiosity. None of it was returned. Rowan stared at her bowl, half-filled with some kind of sugary cereal. Her stomach growled, yet the thought of food made her nauseous. Instead she sipped at a chipped cup of lukewarm tea. Soon, she was joined either side by two slight figures.

'Hello,' the one on the left said, in a chirpy voice. 'What's your name?'

Rowan looked up into a friendly, freckled face that was surrounded by a shock of short, dark hair. She recognised it as one of the twins who had peeked around her door the night before. 'My name's Rowan,' she answered.

'I'm Penny,' said the twin. 'And this is my sister, Polly. We're nine, but Polly's twenty-four and a half minutes older than me. We've been here for two months now. We—'

'Stop rabbiting,' the other twin interrupted. 'Can't you see she wants to be left alone?'

Rowan turned to look at the second twin, Polly. She had the same, friendly face as her sister, but it was tinged with concern. Rowan tried to smile, but her mouth didn't want to.

'She talks too much,' said Polly. 'I keep telling her about it but she doesn't take any notice.' She reached up and scratched her mop of dark hair. 'If you need any help learning your way around, just ask us. We'll show you.' She turned to her twin. 'Come on, Penny.'

'Wait,' said Rowan, suddenly not wanting to be alone. 'Perhaps . . . perhaps you could show me around after breakfast.'

There were several other girls in the wing that Rowan shared, though as the day wore on, many of their names escaped her. She paid attention only to those that she thought she would have closest contact with.

'There's Sally, she's nine, the same as us,' said Polly. At the sound of her name, Sally looked up and gave a friendly smile. Rowan gave a weak smile in return, but then her attention was caught by a scared-looking girl who was alone and seemed to be hiding behind her hair.

'Who's that?' she asked.

'Oh, that's Lara,' the twins replied in unison.

It turned out that, like Rowan, Lara had a younger sibling, a sister aged three. Rowan often saw them in the nursery when she was there with James. Sometimes she made small talk with her, but for the most part Lara kept to herself. Rowan wondered what Lara's story was; how she had come to be there. Most of the children were there due to unfortunate family circumstances.

Some, like the twins, had been neglected. But no one seemed to know Lara's story. And no one seemed to care much, either. In fact, no one took much notice of her at all – until the day her little sister disappeared.

It was late afternoon when it happened, three weeks after Rowan and James had arrived. Rowan was sitting on the floor in the common room staring at her book of fairy tales with James on her lap. Across the room, the twins were embroiled in a noisy card game, while Sally and two other girls were playing a board game. They had given up trying to get Rowan to join in, instead leaving her to her book. On her lap, James gurgled contentedly. Already, he was crying less for their parents. In private, Rowan was crying more for them.

Her broken left arm was still in plaster but healing well. Unfortunately, she happened to be left-handed and so until the plaster was removed, the things she could do were limited. Getting dressed was difficult enough, however the thing Rowan really wanted to do was to write a letter. And this was the kind of letter that couldn't be written right-handed. It was an important letter which had to be perfect, and the more that time passed and the more she thought about it, the more monumental a task it became.

She was going to write a letter to her Aunt Rose, her mother's younger sister. Aunt Rose, with her shabby cottage full of animals, whose name always brought about a little worry line on her mother's forehead, and a crease on the bridge of her father's nose. It was true that Aunt Rose was an oddball. But she was also the only family Rowan and James had left. So Rowan had decided that her letter was going to ask Aunt Rose to take her and James away from there.

Rowan was staring at the pages of her book, only half seeing the beautiful colour plates that lay before her. The illustrations were of The Little Mermaid by Hans Christian Andersen. It was one of Rowan favourite tales, but today her mind was occupied with how to begin her letter. If she got it right, the letter could be her ticket out of this place.

The door to the common room flew open and Lara dashed in, her face ashen.

'Has anyone seen my sister?' she demanded, her voice uncharacteristically loud. 'Well?' She scanned the room. A sea of blank faces, Rowan's included, stared back. 'Has anyone seen her?'

'What do you mean?' asked Polly. 'She's in the nursery, isn't she?'

'I've just come from the nursery,' said Lara. She was breathing very quickly. 'I was there, with her, then I went to get a glass of water. Two minutes later I came back and she'd gone. We've been looking everywhere and no one can find her. I wondered if she'd managed to walk this far down.'

Just then two harassed-looking members of staff rushed into the room. One of them Rowan recognised as one of the nursery attendants, and the other was the cleaner, an odd-looking woman with a mop of untidy brown hair and a pair of flip-flops on her feet despite it being January. It was she who spoke first, addressing Lara.

'Is she here? Have you found her?'

Lara shook her head, and the worried expression on the two adults' faces deepened.

'Don't worry, pet,' said the cleaner, kindly. 'She can't have gone far, now, can she? She's probably just playing at hide-and-seek. We'll find her.'

Rowan got to her feet, snapping her book shut.

'I'll help you look for her.'

'So will we,' said the twins.

A flurry of activity ensued as the place was turned upside down in the search for the little girl. Every room and every cupboard, every little nook was explored, yet seemingly Lara's little sister was nowhere to be found. Minutes dragged by, and the staff were beginning to panic. People were calling out as they burst into rooms; to the little girl: 'Megan? Megan?' and to each other: 'What was she wearing?'

'A green dress, her sister says.'

Though an effort was being made to keep calm, the confusion and chaos was frightening. Then, just as Lara began to cry, there came a shout from the twins.

'Here! She's here – we've found her!'

Rowan followed Lara, who was now sobbing, along the corridor to Lara's room, where the twins' voices had come from.

There, fast asleep in Lara's bed, with her thumb in her mouth, was Megan. She was burrowed down into the covers like a little dormouse, stirring only when Lara pushed her way into the room and swept the little girl up into her arms, hugging her tightly.

'Where have you been?' Lara wept, but there was only relief in her voice, not anger. 'Don't ever wander off like that again!'

Megan yawned widely. 'I'm hungry,' she said.

'How on earth did we miss her?' Sally wondered aloud. 'We searched this room already.'

'Like a little creature hibernating, she was,' said the cleaner, who had been second to arrive on the scene.

As more people arrived, Rowan slunk away, not wanting to crowd poor Lara and Megan. Now the drama was over, she went back to the empty common room and picked up her book before quietly going to her own room with James. She lay down on her bed with James in her arms, reading to him in a low voice, and, without meaning to, she dozed off.

She woke with a start to find that the room was in darkness. Hours must have passed, for night had fallen. Her mouth was dry, and she was cold. She sat up, shivering, shifting James in her good arm. He was awake and smiling placidly. Only when she looked towards the doorway did she see that someone was standing there, silhouetted against the lit hallway.

She jumped, squeezing James a little too hard.

'Sorry,' said a quiet voice. 'I didn't mean to frighten you.'

'Lara,' said Rowan, recovering herself. 'Is everything all right?'

Lara hesitated. 'No,' she whispered finally. 'Everything isn't all right. I think . . . I think there's something quite wrong.'

Rowan got up and snapped on the light, making them both blink with the sudden flood of brightness. A quick glance at the clock showed that it was nearly eight. It would soon be bedtime.

'What's going on?' she asked.

'It's Megan,' said Lara. 'She's not herself. She's acting . . . strangely.'

'Perhaps she's not well,' Rowan answered. 'Ask someone to take her temperature.'

'No, that's not it,' said Lara. 'She's not ill, she's just . . . different. No one else has noticed, but she's . . . not her normal self. I'm the only one who'd notice – I know her. I spend time with her. Just like you and James. That why I came to you.'

'You're not making any sense,' said Rowan. A trace of annoyance had crept into her voice. She immediately regretted it as Lara's eyes filled with tears. 'Look,' she continued hastily. 'Sit down. Take a minute to think and try to tell me what's bothering you. Be specific.'

Lara walked to the bed and sat down on the rumpled covers. Rowan sat down beside her.

'She's talking less,' Lara began. 'She's normally a chatterbox, but this afternoon she's barely said a word.'

'Maybe she's tired,' Rowan said, but Lara shook her head.

'No. It's like . . . like she's taken a step backwards, or several. She's asking what things are, like a book, or a cup, things she should know. Things she does know. It's almost as if she's relearning things. And her voice is different, too. When she speaks it sounds odd, higher at first, but then sounds more normal as she carries on. And she hasn't stopped eating. She's been demanding food all afternoon, when normally she's picky about what she eats. Now she'll eat anything that's put in front of her.'

Rowan frowned.

119

'No offence, Lara,' she said carefully, 'but maybe you're tired, or upset from when Megan got lost earlier. Perhaps you're just imagining things—'

'Don't tell me I'm imagining it!' Lara smacked her hand down on Rowan's pillow in frustration. Fresh tears began to stream down her face. James's eyes widened at the outburst, and then he began to howl. But Lara took no notice. Instead she stood up and walked to the door.

'I came to you because I thought you might understand. Your baby brother means the world to you, just as Megan does to me. You'd know if something was wrong. And I'm telling you, something is definitely wrong with my little sister!' She sniffed suddenly, and wiped the cuff of her sleeve across her face. 'But what do you care? What does anyone care?'

'Wait, Lara,' Rowan began, startled at the usually gentle girl's outburst. 'I do care! I just . . .' She trailed off. She was talking to an empty corridor. Lara was already gone.

'Great,' she muttered. She sat there on the bed for a few minutes, trying to decide whether to go after Lara and try to make amends or just to leave her alone until her anger had burned itself out. Eventually guilt got the better of her. Sighing, she got up again, shushing James, who was still grizzling softly into her shoulder, and went out of the bedroom. On the way to the stairs Rowan passed the common room, where most of the older girls were sitting, making their bedtime drinks last as long as they possibly could to snatch a few extra minutes of television or games. She ignored the twins' calls to join them and carried on.

The nursery was situated on the ground floor, at the furthest end of the building. It was a large room, full of cots, toys and playpens, and several murals were painted on the walls. Towards the rear of the room was a set of French doors that looked out onto the garden.

Lara was sitting by Megan's bed, a few feet away. As soon as Rowan entered the room, it was clear that Megan was having a tantrum. Lara simply stared back at her, unmoving.

'Pick me up!' the little girl shouted, and even Rowan winced at the tinny, scratchy quality to her voice. James wailed even more loudly.

Lara shook her head, biting her lip.

'For goodness' sake, pick her up!' Rowan said fiercely, but froze as she drew level and saw Lara's face. It was a mask of fear. She stared up at Rowan with glassy, shocked eyes.

'Her hair,' she whispered. 'It's grown. In a day. I thought I was imagining it, but look! I'm not, am I? Tell me I'm not!'

Rowan stared at the little girl. With a jolt she realised it was true; the child's hair had grown at least two inches. Her fringe was now in her eyes.

'No, you're not.'

Suddenly the child stopped screaming, and looked Rowan directly in the eye.

'I'm hungry,' she said, licking her lips.

'But I fed her!' said Lara, in despair. 'I fed her only twenty minutes ago!'

Rowan did not answer. For, there, right before her eyes, something was happening. Something deeply unsettling. Megan's eyes were starting to change colour. As she watched, the pupils

121

dilated, larger and larger, until they completely filled the brown irises. But even then, they did not stop. They continued to grow, to spread like black ink that had been spilled, until the whites of the eyes were black too.

Rowan blinked, trying to make sense of it all. Her eyes must be deceiving her, surely. But then she gasped audibly as Megan's dark hair and skin began to pale drastically, then flooded with a pale, sickly green tinge.

'What?' Lara said. 'What is it?'

'Nothing,' Rowan managed, clasping James to her and holding his head tightly into her neck. Somehow she knew that it didn't matter; that if he looked at the little girl on the bed he wouldn't see what she was seeing. For it was evident that Lara could not see the horrifying spectacle either. She took a step back as the child's ears suddenly protruded from her hair either side of her face. They were now pointed. She took another step back as its limbs seemed to ripple and elongate; the hands and feet large and out of proportion to the rest. She knew what she was seeing, then, in the same moment that she knew she could never tell anyone. For she wouldn't be believed. She could barely believe it herself.

'When . . . when did you first realise something was wrong?' she whispered.

'Within a few minutes of finding her, after she got lost earlier. But I thought I was imagining it.'

That confirmed it then. Even as the child on the bed stared back at her, a scowl forming on its face, Rowan knew what had happened.

Someone or something had taken Megan, and left a creature that wasn't her in her place.

Whatever it was that sat on the bed was an impostor. It wasn't Lara's little sister. It was something else. It was fey.

'Rowan, what is it? Why are you looking at her like that?'

Rowan was unable to tear her eyes away. To her relief, the creature on the bed slipped back into its imitation; its imitation of Megan. The fairy features dissolved, and morphed into something human once more.

'Nothing,' she stammered. 'I don't know anything.'

She pushed her way past Lara and ran to the door, her good arm clamped tightly around James. Somehow, she was short of breath, as though she'd run a great distance, but she did not stop running until she reached her room, and had shut the door behind her.

She would never tell anyone. She couldn't, and wouldn't. There was nothing she could do, she told herself. The real Megan was gone. Now Rowan just needed to concentrate on getting herself and James out of this place.

She really believed she wouldn't tell.

11

ED'S TALE WAS INTERRUPTED by a chilling shriek from the cottage above. She stopped speaking and shrank back. Something shuffled over the trapdoor above, then silence.

'What happened next?' Eldritch prompted, unfazed.

'What's going on up there?' Red asked, her past momentarily forgotten. The terrible scream had chilled her through and through.

Eldritch leaned forward, as though listening intently. Then he shrugged.

'Perhaps someone's come to the cottage,' Red said, her voice lifting. 'Perhaps we're going to be rescued!'

Eldritch laughed darkly. 'I doubt it. If anyone's come here, then it's not to do any good. Don't waste your time hoping.'

'There's always room for hope,' the other man said. Red looked at him and saw him staring at Eldritch through narrowed eyes.

Eldritch ignored him and settled back against the wall, closing his dark eyes. A film of sweat clung to his skin.

Without warning the bolt on the trapdoor shot back, making all three of them jump. There was a long pause before the trapdoor began to lift; slowly, maddeningly. Then a foot appeared on the first step.

'Quickly!' Red hissed. 'She's coming down again!' She scrambled back to the foul-smelling straw and lay down, eyes squeezed tightly shut and breathing raggedly, positioning herself to look like she was still tied up. Opposite her, the man did the same.

A stomach-churning groan made them both turn towards the stone steps. What they saw instantly made them sit up, their pretences forgotten.

The Hedgewitch was staggering down into the cellar, one hand clutching at her throat, the other clawing at the wall for support. She was staring at Red.

'What . . . have you . . . done . . . to me . . .?' she rasped. '*Poison . . . you've p-poisoned . . . me! Should have skinned you . . . should have gutted you like a rabbit straight . . . away!*'

Red scrambled to her feet, tingling with adrenalin. What was happening to the Hedgewitch?

The woman took another step towards her, her hand outstretched. The skin on it bubbled, as though something was simmering under its surface.

'You'll pay . . . for this!' she hissed, her eyes burning with malice. Then she doubled over with a howl. 'Make it . . . stop . . . I beg . . . you . . . make it stop! *Please* . . .'

She thinks I did this, Red realised, confused and terrified. *She thinks I've poisoned her somehow!*

'What's happening to her?' Eldritch crowed, leaping to his feet. His face was animated with excitement. The chain attached to his manacled hand rattled manically.

'Poison . . . *poisoned me . . .*'

Red had no idea what was going on, but she knew that this could be their only chance of escape. She *had* to seize it.

'Release us,' she said. Her voice was firm, and cold. It was a voice she had rehearsed well.

The witch collapsed at her feet, writhing on the ground.

'Make it . . . stop!' she screamed.

'*Release us!*' Red repeated.

'Yes! Anything . . . just make . . . it . . . stop!'

'Give me your word,' Red said coldly. 'That you will let us go safely from here. And I'll make it stop.'

'I will . . .' The witch's body twitched with spasms. 'I'll release you . . . I promise!'

'The keys!' Eldritch yelped. 'Don't forget about me! *Get the keys from her!*'

'Give me the key,' said Red, unwavering. 'Where is it?'

'Up-upstairs . . .'

'Where upstairs?'

'Please . . .' the witch gasped. Her eyes were bulging now, with the effort of speaking. It was like seeing a fish out of water, the life draining away. 'I'm dying . . .'

'The key!' Red snarled, forcing herself to remember everything the Hedgewitch had done. All the lives she had stolen. Her evil threats. And in her heart she found no pity for her.

126

'In the . . . chimney . . . loose brick . . . now make it . . . stop. Save . . . me . . .'

The man was on his feet too now, next to Red. He leaned over the witch, his mouth open as she wheezed out another fragmented sentence.

'Help . . . me . . .'

I can't, Red thought. She almost said it then, out loud, but something stopped her.

'No,' Red said flatly.

The Hedgewitch's face contorted with fury and pain. Then, as Red, Eldritch and the man watched, it crumpled. Literally. And then it was replaced with another face; that of a young man with twinkling eyes.

'May I carry your basket for you?' he said, before his words melted on his lips. His hair fell out and his skin bubbled. Another face formed; this time a little girl with blonde ringlets. The ragged clothes of the witch rippled as the body beneath shrank and became smaller, to that of a child.

'I've lost my mother!' she cried. 'Will you help me to find her?'

The little girl became an old man.

'I'll show you the way, come with me!' he said.

The old man became a peddler woman . . . then a scruffy youth . . . then a woman in Victorian clothes . . .

Red turned away, unable to watch any more. These had been the victims of the Hedgewitch, that much she could guess. These poor people had never had a chance, falling into her hands, unaware that their fate was to end up as nothing better than a garment; a disguise of trickery.

She heard the witch gurgling incoherently, and battled the urge to clamp her hands over her ears. There were a few last thrashes from the witch's limbs, and then finally she fell still and quiet. Eldritch chortled.

'She's dead! I don't believe it, she's dead!'

Red felt a wave of disgust roll over her at his evident glee. Reluctantly, she turned to face what was left of the Hedgewitch . . . and almost screamed as she saw what was there, on the hay.

It was a distorted version of herself, visible in the light that streamed down from the open trapdoor: the pale, freckled skin, and green eyes that were glassy and staring. The face was twisted into a snarl. Oddly, the hair was not the mousy colour she had dyed it, but her natural auburn. It was as she looked at it that a thought occurred to her. The witch had taken a lock of her hair, not knowing that she had recently dyed it. Could the ingredients in the hair dye have been responsible for poisoning her?

The man stepped over the lifeless body and limped towards the steps.

'Come on,' he said to her. 'We'd better go and find that key.'

Red shook herself, and knelt to search the body, purposely avoiding the face. In the folds of the witch's clothes she found what she was looking for: her knife. She pushed it into her belt and then kicked straw over the prone body, before moving up the stairs into the cottage. Her skin prickled with goose pimples as she came into the warmth of the upstairs, and bizarrely, the sudden heat set her teeth chattering. She hadn't realised how cold and damp she had become down in the cellar.

The cottage was as the Hedgewitch had left it: candlelight flickered from wall sconces, a fire burned in the grate of the fireplace, and, over the hearth, two pots bubbled. Red approached, her stomach gnawing. It had been a long time since she'd eaten. She raised her hands to the heat from the flames and peered into the nearest pot. Something thick and brown with chunks of dark meat simmered there. Her mouth watered but she did not dare to touch it. The man appeared beside her, and as she watched him breathing in the scent of the food, she knew from his expression that he was thinking the same: they did not know what else might be in it. Whatever had killed the Hedgewitch could be in the contents of this pot. Wistfully, she leaned further forward and looked into the other one. She met with an unpleasant sight. A lock of brown hair that she recognised as her own was being tossed about in a dark, blood-red mixture. Fragments of an eggshell swam beside it, and as the foul mixture turned over, more of its contents were brought to the surface: a piece of snakeskin and something that looked like a claw.

'Destroy it,' the man said quietly, beside her. 'Throw it into the flames.'

Using a piece of rag that lay on the hearth, Red lifted the pot and threw its contents onto the fire. Instead of dousing the flames as she expected, they shot up briefly, before dying down to a merry dance once more.

The man took the rag from her and gripped the handle of the stew pot. 'We can't eat this,' he confirmed. 'I'll make something fresh. That way we'll know it's safe.'

'We shouldn't wait around,' said Red. 'We need to get out of this awful place.'

The man shook his head. 'No point in leaving now.' He motioned to the cottage window. 'It's going dark. We're best to stay here for the night, eat, and take whatever supplies we can. If we stay it'll give us the chance to prepare properly.'

'But surely it's dangerous,' Red argued.

'No more dangerous than being out there,' he replied. 'And now that thing in the cellar is dead, the main threat is out of the way.'

'You haven't forgotten about me, have you?' Eldritch called from below. 'Hurry, find that key!'

'You get the key,' said the man. 'I'll throw this away and make something else to eat.'

Red nodded and stood up. She waited for the man to walk outside with the pot, heard him scraping the contents out.

'I'm going to the stream,' he called through the open doorway. 'Back in a minute.'

As soon as he vanished she played her fingers over the brickwork of the chimney above the fireplace. For a moment she thought the witch had lied and that there was no loose brick, but then she found it, moving slightly in its

130

place. Deftly she began to nudge it with her fingers. It was wedged tightly in place and it took her several minutes to remove it. Sure enough, when she did, there was a hollow cavity behind it, containing several small objects. She cast her fingers over them, withdrawing and examining them one by one. Just then, the man came in from outside with the newly-cleaned pot.

'You found the brick,' he said. 'Is there a key there?'

'No,' Red answered. 'There are lots of other bits and pieces, but no key. The witch lied.'

The man's face fell. 'It must be somewhere. We'll have to keep looking.' His eyes scanned the caged animals in the cottage, and rested on a small hutch containing some rabbits. He strode over, and took one out. It was large and fat. Red suddenly felt sick as she realised he intended to kill it. He caught her eye and collected the small knife from the hearth.

'Sorry,' he said. 'But we need to eat something that's substantial. We don't know when we'll next be able to find food. It'll be quick, I promise.' He moved towards the door once more with the rabbit under his arm, then hesitated and turned back. 'Perhaps you should go and tell Eldritch about the key, and let him know we're still looking.'

Red nodded again, not trusting herself to speak. Steeling herself, she clambered back down the steps to the cellar, choking on the smell that she'd become so accustomed to only a short while before.

Eldritch glowered at her. She could smell him, rank with sweat and grime.

'What are you doing up there?' he hissed. 'Why haven't you unlocked me yet?'

'There's a problem,' said Red. 'The Hedgewitch lied about the key – it's not where she said it would be.'

Eldritch threw back his head and gave an anguished howl.

'You should have checked first!' he yelled. 'Now it's too late! What if we never find it?'

'We'll keep looking,' said Red. 'It has to be somewhere.' She eyed Eldritch's wrist, hanging in the manacle. It was horrific; a ring of red, raw flesh circled it like a gory bracelet. Evidently her thoughts showed in her face, for Eldritch spat on the ground suddenly.

'Iron,' he said. 'This is what iron does when it comes into contact with fey skin.' He looked at her, almost accusingly. 'It *burns*.'

'Like I said, we'll keep looking,' Red answered curtly. She turned and made for the stairs again, eager to escape the rancid smell of the cellar. 'There'll be some food soon. We'll bring some down to you when it's ready.' She scrambled back up the steps, and was tempted to slam the trapdoor shut. It would be easier to forget that way, that the cellar was now homing the dead Hedgewitch and the remains of the other poor creatures who had been her victims. But even though she did not like or trust Eldritch, it would have been unforgivable to shut him in the darkness. So instead, she turned her back on the trapdoor and began exploring the rest of the cottage.

Through the mesh of their cages, the animal captives watched her, their eyes distrustful. She walked over to the nearest cage, which held a fox. It growled as she knelt next to it, but shrank back, away from the door. Readying herself, she knocked the peg out of the latch, and quickly stepped back as the door swung open. The fox was out in a flash, bolting through the open door of the cottage and away, out into the night.

One by one she released the caged animals: rabbits, more foxes, stoats, and a box full of moths and butterflies that she took outside prior to opening, for fear they would fly towards the light of the candles or the fire in the hearth. Upon her return to the cottage one creature remained, a rabbit huddled in the corner of its cage. It was lame – its back leg crushed from a trap. Otherwise it was fat and healthy. Regretfully, Red bolted the cage. It would not survive in the wild. Now she knew it would be an ideal candidate for the pot.

The man returned to the cottage then. He set the pot over the fire, stoked it and then began to move around the cottage, poking into various sacks and corners. Red caught him glancing at the empty cages.

'I freed them,' she said, unnecessarily.

'So I see.' He made no other comment, just returned with a few potatoes and a couple of old-looking carrots, which he then peeled, chopped and threw into the pot. That done, he got up and began rooting around again.

'That key has to be here somewhere,' he muttered.

Red got up and followed him into the corner.

'Be careful what you touch,' he said, running his hands over a large wooden chest. It had no lock, and so he threw the lid back. Red gasped.

'My bag!'

She snatched it and checked her belongings. Everything was there, packed in just as she'd left it. Beneath her bag were countless other items: bags, shoes, watches, clothing. Each had belonged to someone. Most would never find their owner.

The man reached in and took something out as well. It was a knife twice the size of Red's and she eyed it warily.

'This is mine,' he said. 'It's made from iron.' He slipped it into the empty holder on his belt and continued digging around in the contents of the chest.

Red moved away, looking over a table at the back. A pile of books caught her eye. She picked up the one on the top and opened it. In the topmost corner there was a handwritten name: *Agnes Fogg*. Red wondered if it had belonged to one of the Hedgewitch's victims. As she began to flick through the book, some of the phrases and notes jumped out at her.

Remedy for warts: apply dandelion milk by light of waning moon. Repeat for three nights . . .

'What's that?'

The man's voice next to her ear made her jump, and she dropped the book onto the table. It hit the surface, bounced and then fell on to the floor. As it did, a strange thing happened. Tiny black insects scurried from the book and spread out over the floor, rushing into the dark recesses of the cottage. Red frowned and picked the book up.

'It looks like a book of remedies, or spells,' she began, opening the book. One of the insects ran up her arm. She made to brush it away, and then stopped and leaned in closer. For the insect was not an insect at all. It was a tiny letter 'A'.

'What on earth . . .?'

'Bewitched,' the man said. 'There must be a spell on it to destruct if the wrong hands touch it.'

Red flicked through the pages of the book. Every one of them was now blank; the words had run away, letter by letter.

'There was a name written inside,' she said. 'Agnes Fogg. Do you think she was another victim? Or maybe the Hedgewitch stole her book for the magic it contained?'

'No, I don't think that's it,' the man said slowly. 'I know of an Agnes Fogg. She lived around two hundred years ago in Tickey End. She was a wise woman – a healer and a midwife – and was befriended by Elizabeth Elvesden, the first lady of Elvesden Manor, who she began to teach about natural remedies. But after a child Agnes delivered died, and then a sickness spread throughout the town, the people of Tickey End accused both women of witchcraft. They drove Agnes out and banished her to the woods. Elizabeth Elvesden ended up dying in a lunatic asylum.'

'So you don't think the Hedgewitch got Agnes Fogg?' Red asked.

The man shook his head. 'I think the Hedgewitch *is* Agnes Fogg – or at least was once.'

Red placed the book back on the table.

'How do think she came to be known by that name?' she asked. '"Hedgewitch" sounds so sinister.'

'It doesn't have sinister origins,' the man said. 'The word "hedgewitch" simply means "solitary witch". It comes from olden times, when a witch often lived on the furthest outskirts of a village, close to a bordering hedge. The hedge would often be part of a garden of their herbs and plants used in their craft. Until now, I'd always thought of it as a gentle term.' He moved back to the fire, stirring the pot. The aroma of the food made Red's stomach cramp with longing.

'How do you think she ended up in the fairy realm? Doing such evil things?'

'Who knows?' he answered darkly. 'She wasn't evil to begin with, from what I've heard. Perhaps she was tricked into coming here. Or perhaps she grew bitter and resentful at the way she'd been treated, and found a way to escape and have her revenge.'

'She did that all right,' said Red. She began to move around again, feeling restless and twitchy after being held captive in the cellar. Ducking under a collection of drying animal pelts, she saw a fox-skin coat hanging from a stand in the corner. The sight of it disturbed her, but at the same time she needed a coat. She reached for it and threw it around her shoulders, fastening a small catch just below her chin.

She felt immediately odd. The room around her loomed suddenly huge, and the man towered over her. Every hair on her body stood on end for a split second, then her senses sharpened. She could smell the thick stew, and her hearing was impeccable, magnifying every bubble of the cooking liquid. Looking down at her hands she saw they were gone, instead replaced by two red-brown paws.

The man's face was etched with astonishment.

'It's amazing,' he breathed.

'I'm a fox!' she gasped.

The man's mouth dropped open. 'You can still talk!'

Then Red panicked.

'If I've got paws instead of hands how do I get it off? How do I unfasten the catch?' Her claws scrabbled uselessly at her chin.

'Calm down,' said the man. 'You still have hands, not paws. Remember, it's glamour. An illusion.'

Red forced herself to be calm. In her mind's eye she pictured her hands and held the image of them in her head. Then she lifted them to her chin to find the hook. Her fingers found it and with relief she slid the coat off.

'Eldritch told me the Hedgewitch's powers go beyond the ordinary,' she said, remembering. 'He said these were no surface glamours, that they'd fool even fairies. If that's true then I'm guessing humans with the second sight wouldn't be able to see through them either. Try it,' she said, offering the man the gruesome garment. He took it and, after a moment's hesitation, threw it around his shoulders and fastened the hook. Nothing happened – he stood there waiting while

Red watched expectantly. Still he remained just a man in a fox-skin coat, looking vaguely ridiculous peering out from beneath the fox's ears.

'It's not working,' she said, disappointed not to witness the coat's power. 'Why did it work for me and not you?'

The man took the coat off and handed it to her.

'I don't know. Maybe the coat can only work for one person – the person who wears it first of all. How did you feel when you tried it on?'

'Weird. All sort of . . . hairy. It felt as though the fur wasn't just on me, but that it was part of me, actually growing out of my skin.'

The man's eyes widened. 'That's it then. The coat has fused itself with you. It has to remain yours now, it's useless to anyone else.'

'Maybe we could find one for you,' said Red. 'A different disguise.'

But after they searched the rest of the cottage, none of the other garments wielded such power, though there were plenty of furs and skins which they gathered and piled up in front of the fire to sleep on.

'It can only mean one thing,' said the man. 'That coat has been made to order. Someone will be coming for it, and soon. We need to leave this place at first light.'

It was a sobering thought. They busied themselves eating the stew the man had cooked. It was thin and the meat was fatty, but Red was glad of it. It was nourishment and she did not dare to take it for granted.

She was spared entering the cellar when the man took down some of the stew to Eldritch, along with some furs to wrap around him. Red heard him whining from below, demanding to know why they hadn't yet found the key. She huddled into the thick furs; her knife at her side once more. With food in her belly and the flames of the fire warming her thin body, she dozed a little in front of the fire every so often, but every knock of the shutters and rattle of the door jerked her awake. Soon the man returned and settled a little way from her, and out of the corner of her eye she saw him staring into the flames of the fire, as if lost in thought.

She closed her eyes, determined to rest as best she could, but she was just too jittery.

Next to her the man's breathing slowed, and soon she felt certain he was asleep. She was surprised then, when she glanced over and saw his blue-eyed gaze fixed upon her.

'So,' he said softly. 'Tell me the next part of your story.'

And she did.

12

HEN TANYA AND FABIAN arrived back at Elvesden Manor, Fabian threw the kitchen door open with such force that it bounced off the wall. Oberon immediately bounded over to his bowls, checking for food first, as always, before greedily lapping from his water dish, sending droplets all over the floor.

Florence was sitting at the table, nursing the fairy from the clock. She looked up in surprise at their riotous entrance.

'For goodness' sake, Fabian,' she scolded. 'You'll have that door off its hinges one of these days.'

'Sorry,' he gasped, throwing himself down into one of the chairs. Tanya pulled out a chair between him and Florence, also fighting to get her breath back from running.

'What's going on?' Florence asked suspiciously. 'Tanya, why are there leaves and twigs in your hair?' She cast a cursory look at Fabian. 'And you look untidier than ever, not that I'd have thought it possible.'

'Something's happened,' Tanya managed. 'In the woods.'

She pulled a strand of hair from her mouth. It was sticky with sweat.

'You've been in those *woods?*' Florence's voice was suddenly shrill. 'What have I told you? Haven't you learned anything from what happened—'

'We were with Warwick,' Tanya interrupted.

Florence's frown deepened. 'I don't know what he was thinking of. Where is he? And where's Nell and that wretched bird of hers?'

'That's what we're trying to tell you,' said Fabian, and began to explain what had happened.

Tanya listened as he spoke and saw her grandmother's expression grow solemn. The sight of the old woman's obvious fear only served to heighten Tanya's further. How were they ever going to find Warwick and Nell now?

Florence's hand had frozen in mid-air and, for the first time since they had entered the kitchen, Tanya noticed something glistening on the tip of her forefinger. In her other hand sat the injured lodger from the clock. It was apparently much better, staring at the suspended finger in earnest. It was smacking its lips, and there was something golden and sticky around its mouth. Then Tanya saw the open jar of honey on the table in front of her grandmother; a treat for the traumatised fairy. She peered closer at the creature's wings but could see no obvious signs of repair. Her grandmother's work was immaculate.

'Warwick was right,' said Florence, her voice quivering,

after Fabian had finished their tale. 'Nell and her pest of a parrot really have got us all into a fix.'

'What are we going to do?' asked Tanya. 'How do we find them?'

'I don't know,' said Florence. 'All I can think of is to call upon Raven, Gredin and the Mizhog. Maybe they'll know what to do.'

'Call upon them?' said Tanya. 'You can do that? You can actually summon them?'

'Oh, yes,' said Florence. 'It can be done, though I don't do it if I can help it. They don't take kindly to it, you see. They much prefer coming when they choose to come.'

'I see,' said Tanya, her mind turning over this piece of news. It was some time since she had seen the fairies now. In the past they had visited far more frequently, although their visits had been by no means pleasant. The possibility that they could be summoned was one that had never occurred to her.

'How do you do it? How do you call them?'

'Come with me and I'll show you,' said Florence, reaching for the lid of the honey pot. 'Oh!' she exclaimed suddenly, looking down at the fairy in her hand.

'What?' Fabian asked, confused. Tanya reminded herself that Fabian was the only one present who was unable to see the fairy in her grandmother's hand.

'The little beast bit me!' Florence brushed the fairy onto the table and discarded the lid to the honey.

'It's a fairy, isn't it?' Fabian said mournfully. 'I wish I could see them.'

'Be careful what you wish for,' said Tanya.

'Ungrateful creature,' Florence muttered, rubbing her finger. She got up and motioned for Tanya and Fabian to follow her. Oberon trotted after them, rubbing his wet muzzle against Tanya's leg to dry off. Florence led them out of the kitchen, pausing to shut the door – presumably to keep Spitfire away from the fairy – and headed further into the darkened corridor before the stairs. As they went after her, Tanya saw her grandmother pull a bunch of keys from her pocket. They walked in silence through the musty hall until they reached a door that Tanya was familiar with: the library. Florence unlocked the door and swept into the room, heading straight for the bookshelves.

Tanya watched as her grandmother ran her fingers along the spines of the books, searching. It was then that she noticed something was amiss. She started to scan the shelves herself, her eyes narrowed. She had been into the library before, in the summer. The first time she had found two things of interest – a book containing valuable fairy lore which had later been destroyed by goblins, and a newspaper cutting about the missing Morwenna Bloom, her grand-mother's former best friend. The second time she had found the entrance to one of the manor's secret passages behind the bookcase – and the runaway Rowan Fox using it as a hideout. Shortly after her first visit however, Warwick had cleared the library of its books on the pretext of giving them to charity. Her hand came to rest over a small book wedged into the shelf: A Midsummer Night's Dream.

Tanya lifted it from the shelf and leafed through it while her grandmother's back was still turned. It was no surprise when the familiar newspaper cutting came loose in her hand.

Tanya snapped the book shut pointedly, and her grandmother looked round. Her face fell as she saw the book in Tanya's hand and realised her mistake.

'These are the same books,' Tanya said quietly. 'Warwick never got rid of them at all, did he? It was just for show. Just pretend.'

'I'm sorry we lied to you,' Florence said. Her voice and face were calm. 'But it was necessary that you believed the books were gone for your own protection. There was too much information at your disposal and too much at stake. I knew that once you knew about the library, simply locking the door wouldn't be enough.'

Fabian glanced at Tanya guiltily and she guessed what he was thinking. Together, after Fabian had stolen skeleton keys belonging to both Florence and Warwick, the two of them had managed to explore a number of locked doors that would otherwise have remained off-limits.

'So what's changed?' Tanya asked, gesturing to the books. 'How come you don't mind me knowing the books are here now?'

Her grandmother crossed the room and took Tanya's face gently in her hands.

'Everything's changed. You know now that I have the second sight. And I hope that, if or when you need help, you'll come to Warwick or me first. Just as you did today.'

Tanya said no more and both she and Florence went back to their searches. Her grandmother was right; not to have lied, but in wanting to protect her. It was true that Tanya's discovery of the newspaper cutting had been the beginning of the dangerous events in the summer.

'What's the name of the book you're looking for?' Fabian asked.

'It's called *One Hundred and One Perfect Puff Pastry Recipes*,' said Florence, flicking at a cobweb. It landed on Oberon's nose, making him sneeze.

'How is puff pastry going to call the fairies?' Fabian asked in puzzlement.

'You'll see,' said Florence, still scanning the shelves. 'Oh, bother, it really isn't where I left it – it must have been put back in a different place when Warwick replaced the books.'

Five minutes later, Fabian called out.

'It's here!' He pulled it from the shelves near to where the secret passage leading to the tunnels below the house was. He blew dust from the cover and handed it to Florence. Tanya joined them. Her grandmother leafed through it, mustiness coming off the old book's pages. Its deep red fabric cover was tatty and faded. *Red to keep the fairies away*, Tanya guessed suddenly, *and a title that would keep children away. The perfect hiding place.*

From the middle of the book, Florence removed three things: a tiny green leaf, a black feather and a long, thin whisker. Tanya recognised them all. They belonged to the fairies. Her grandmother snapped the book shut.

'What you're about to see you must promise never to reveal to anyone,' she said.

Tanya and Fabian murmured their solemn agreement. Florence returned the book and beckoned them out of the room. Tanya noticed that she did not lock the door behind them this time. They followed her back into the kitchen and waited while Florence disappeared into the pantry. A minute later she returned, clasping a tiny wooden box. She prised it open to reveal a pile of tiny, dried and pressed green leaves.

'Clovers,' said Fabian.

'*Four-leafed* clovers,' Florence corrected. 'If you ever find them you must keep them, for they hold a lot of power. They connect humans to fairies in more ways than one.' She knelt before the fireplace with her assortment of objects.

Tanya and Fabian followed suit, and as Tanya did she saw a flash of movement from behind the coalscuttle. The little hearthfay had skittered away from them. Tanya watched as her grandmother gazed into the flames. A wisp of her long, grey hair had worked its way loose from the tight bun at her nape, and floated to rest at her jaw.

Florence lifted her hand, and in it was Raven's black feather. To this she added one of the four-leafed clovers and a single hair plucked from her own head. With a flick of her wrist she threw all three things into the fire. A curl of smoke wreathed up the chimney, and as it did Florence called:

'By the powers that be, I call thee to me.'

She plucked another hair and added it to the Mizhog's whisker and another four-leafed clover, then threw them into the flames, uttering the same words a second time. As she reached for the third item, a leaf from Gredin's clothing, she hesitated, then stretched her hand towards Tanya.

'Here.'

'You want me to . . . to do that?'

'Gredin is your guardian,' said Florence. 'You, more than any other, have the right to call upon him.'

Nervously, Tanya took the leaf from her grandmother. She licked her finger and dipped it into the box of clovers. One of the leaves stuck to the tip, and she shook it into her palm. With her other hand she pulled a hair from her head. The flames sizzled once more as she threw the three items into them.

'By the powers that be, I call thee to me,' she said in a clear voice.

'Now what?' Fabian asked anxiously.

'We wait,' said Florence.

It was over an hour before the fairies arrived. Tanya, Fabian and Florence were sitting in a subdued silence in the kitchen, staring into the fire. It was beginning to go dark outside now, and the strain of worrying about what had become of Warwick and Nell had started to show. Florence kept making endless cups of tea that went cold because nobody felt like drinking them, while Fabian had been snappy and obnoxious, ensuring that conversation dried up before it ever began.

Other than the crackling of the flames, Tanya could hear several other sounds: a light rain outside tapping at the windows; the occasional hiccup from the clock fairy who had gorged itself silly on honey; and Oberon's snoring along with the odd leg twitch and a half-yelp as he chased rabbits in his dreams.

'Why aren't they here yet?' Fabian said, scowling at Florence. 'What's the use of calling them if they don't come straight away?'

'As I've already explained, they'll come as soon as they're able to,' Florence replied.

Fabian remained quiet for a moment, but Tanya could tell he was no calmer. His nostrils were starting to flare as he breathed, a signal of his increasing agitation.

'Will I be able to see them?'

'I don't know,' Florence said. 'If they know you're aware of them, then yes. They may choose to show themselves. But don't be surprised if you don't see a thing.'

Fortunately they did not have to wait much longer to find out, for just then, the back door flew open, and in with a fine spray of rain came two figures, their cloaked forms filling the doorway.

Immediately Fabian jumped up from his chair, his pale face lit with sudden hope. 'Dad?'

Tanya, however, had noticed the way the flames dimmed and the telltale twitching of her eyelids. A scent of woodland swept into the kitchen, tangy and fresh. These were no ordinary visitors.

The two guests threw off their cloaks to reveal an ivory-skinned woman, dressed in a gown of black feathers, and a dark-skinned young man in a suit of leaves. Like Fabian, Tanya's mouth had dropped open. She had never before seen the two fairies at life-size. They had only ever appeared to her as tiny, doll-like versions of what now stood before her.

'Raven, Gredin,' said Florence. 'Please, sit down.'

The fairies acknowledged the invitation with curt nods, pulling up seats beside Tanya and Fabian in front of the fire. Tanya avoided their eyes, feeling awkward. She had yet to become used to the fairies visiting without expecting a punishment of some kind, and neither of them looked pleased to be there. Before sitting, Raven reached into the folds of her dress and gathered a small brown snuffling creature about the size of a guinea pig into her arms. She set it down on the rug before the hearth, where it proceeded to sniff at Fabian's boots while folding its moth-eaten wings behind its back.

'Is that . . .?' Fabian began in wonderment.

'Yes,' Tanya finished. 'The Mizhog.'

As they watched, a small beetle scurrying across the hearth caught the Mizhog's eye. It moved surprisingly fast, and with a lick and a gobble, the beetle was gone.

Florence vanished into the pantry once more, returning with a container of something that she stirred into cups of hot water and then passed around. Tanya sniffed hers dubiously. It smelled of herbs and was strangely bitter. She blew on it before tasting, and it was just as unpleasant as she had expected.

Florence was the last to sit. The fairies eyed her expectantly.

Gredin spoke first.

'Why have you called upon us?' His lip curled slightly, as though he was baring his teeth.

Florence pushed her cup on to the mantelpiece.

'Something serious has happened. Warwick has gone missing in the woods, along with our housekeeper, Nell. They were taken by fairies.'

Gredin's yellow eyes narrowed.

'How do you know this?' Raven asked frostily.

'We saw,' said Tanya, hesitantly. 'I mean . . . I saw. Nell wandered into a fairy ring and was caught up in some kind of enchanted dance. Warwick tried to pull her out but got pulled in himself . . . and they ended up getting taken away with the revellers, from ring to ring through the woods.'

'How did this Nell end up in the fairy ring?' Gredin asked. 'Does she have the second sight?'

'No,' said Tanya. 'At least, I don't think so.' She looked at her grandmother questioningly.

Florence shook her head. 'I think she just stumbled into one of the rings accidentally.'

150

'How many revellers were there?' said Raven, her tone softening slightly. 'Can you describe them?'

Tanya closed her eyes and recalled them: the goblin, the faun and the little old winged man. When she had finished, Raven and Gredin talked in low voices amongst themselves for several minutes. Finally, they turned back.

'These three are known to us. They are mischief-makers. It sounds as though they are on their way to Avalon for the Samhain festivities, collecting unsuspecting human-folk on their way to be used in the entertainment.'

Tanya frowned. 'What's Avalon?'

'And Samhain?' Fabian added, finally finding the courage to address the fey visitors.

'Avalon is a name for one of the entrances to the fairy realm,' said Raven. 'The most famous of all the entrances, and also the most dangerous, for it is the location of the fairy courts. It is on an ancient hill that was once an isle.'

'And Samhain,' Gredin continued, 'is an old word that means "summer's end". It is the night humans call "Halloween", the night of the changing of the fairy courts from the Seelie rule to the Unseelie. It is a dangerous night.'

Tanya's heart sank.

'You think that's where Warwick and Nell have been taken? To the fairy courts, for their twisted games and celebrations?'

Raven nodded, the movement causing the tips of her

pointed ears to appear through her black hair. 'It seems likely.'

Fabian leaped up from his seat.

'We have to do something! We have to find them and bring them back!'

'Sit down,' Gredin said coldly. '*You* will do nothing except stay here and wait, in case they return of their own accord. Raven, the Mizhog and I will search for them.'

'Let me come with you,' Fabian begged. 'Please!'

But Raven and Gredin were already rising from their seats.

'It's too dangerous for any of us,' said Florence.

Raven turned to Gredin, who was draining the last of his bitter drink.

'We must leave at once. If we can intercept them before they reach the court, they might stand a chance.'

They stood and threw their dark cloaks around their shoulders once more, drawing their hoods up to conceal their faces. Florence walked with them to the door, wrapping her arms around herself as the damp breeze flew in from outside.

'We will return when we have news,' said Raven.

These were the only words of goodbye. Without further ado or even a second glance back, Raven and Gredin transformed suddenly, shrinking to the smaller size Tanya was familiar with, and, accompanied by the Mizhog, took flight. Tanya and Fabian joined Florence at the door, watching as they flew up and over the garden walls, towards the forest before vanishing from sight.

Florence closed the door and locked it.

'It's not fair!' Fabian burst out.

Tanya turned to face him and was shocked to see that his anger and frustration had manifested through tears. He was crying openly.

'They should have taken me,' he sobbed, throwing himself into a chair. 'I could have helped. I want to help!'

Tanya watched, stricken. She had no idea what to say to comfort him. She felt useless, but then Florence drew a chair up beside him and pulled him into her arms. Tanya could not help but notice the ease of the gesture – it had never existed between herself and her grandmother. Yet she was not resentful. Florence was the closest thing to a mother that Fabian had ever known.

'I know, Fabian,' said Florence. 'I know. But all we can do is wait.'

'What use is waiting?' Fabian said bitterly, his voice muffled from Florence's shoulder. 'We should be *doing* something!'

A loud knock at the back door interrupted them.

Fabian was up in an instant, skidding to the door.

'Maybe they've changed their minds!' he gasped. 'Maybe they've come back to take me with them!' He unlocked the door and threw it open.

Instead of the two dark fairy figures Fabian had been hoping for, there on the doorstep stood a very old woman in raggedy clothes, her patchwork shawl and long, braided grey hair both dripping with rain. Shivering next to her, a plump woman clutched a blanket around herself. Her flip-flopped feet were blue with cold.

'Mad Morag!' Fabian exclaimed. 'And Nell!'

'Just *Morag*, if you please,' the old gypsy woman snapped. 'May I come in?'

13

AFTER WITNESSING MEGAN'S switch, Rowan avoided
Lara whenever possible. Every time Lara entered a room Rowan
left, and if Lara lingered in the corridors Rowan chose a different route, even if it meant she had to go out of her way entirely.
When conversation was unavoidable, Rowan told Lara nothing,
insisting that any differences in her little sister's behaviour were
imagined. Eventually, Lara stopped asking altogether.

Rowan's own mind was in turmoil. As well as trying to cope
with the loss of her parents, she now feared that James or another
child would suffer a similar fate to Megan. The knowledge that
the child sitting only metres away from her baby brother in the
nursery was not human weighed on her mind like lead. The
differences in the child had been noticed by the staff – the hair that
grew too quickly and the insatiable appetite – but within days both
diminished and the appearance and behaviour of the little girl
became more fitting with that of the children she was surrounded
by. Soon it was forgotten.

Rowan was not fooled. She knew that it was an illusion, and
whenever possible removed James from the nursery and refused
to let him out of her sight. Her broken arm hindered all that she

did, and she longed for the approaching day when her plaster cast would be removed. Writing the letter to her Aunt Rose was at the forefront of her mind, and she was still figuring out what to say that would convince Rose to give her and James a home.

It was the first week of February; four weeks had passed since the car crash. During this time Rowan had spent many hours with a counsellor, talking through her feelings, hopes and fears. It was decided that once she was ready, a private tutor would be employed to school her. Until then, and between visits and days out with Ellie, Rowan lost herself in books. The home had a small library, but weekly trips to the town library also took place. One afternoon, as they walked in a group through the cobblestone streets of Tickey End, Rowan thought how pretty it was, with its crooked little buildings and lanes.

The town's library was small and not very well kept. Even so, the group descended upon the children's section gleefully. Rowan selected several books for James and settled down with him on some plump cushions in the corner, letting him look through them. No sooner had she got comfortable than the twins flopped down beside her, with a shriek and a giggle that earned them a scowl and a 'quiet, please' from the sour-faced librarian at the counter.

Penny pushed a chewed-looking book at her.

'Will you read it to us?'

Rowan sighed and took it from her. But when she looked at it properly, she shook her head and handed it back.

'I don't like this story,' she said stiffly. 'Choose something else.'

Penny pouted. 'But I want this one.'

'Well, I don't,' said Rowan. 'So if you want to hear it you'll have to read it yourself.' She ignored Penny's hurt expression and turned away. The truth was that the story was one she used to like. It was about the Pied Piper of Hamlyn, who led children away with his magical tunes. But now, following Megan's disappearance, the thought of reading anything to do with missing children frightened her.

'I can't,' Penny whined. 'That's why I asked you. I'm not a good reader. You're mean.'

'Just choose something else,' said Polly, flicking through another book that was in an even worse condition than the one her sister had picked up.

'What are you looking at?' Rowan asked, eyeing the tattered pages in disdain.

'It's about fairies,' said Polly, turning the pages carelessly. 'I'm just looking at the pictures – the ones that are left. Lots of pages have been torn out.'

Rowan's ears pricked up at once. She looked over casually, expecting a twee, sentimental storybook. But to her surprise it looked to be neither. Its dark green cover was missing its dust jacket.

'Are you sure that's a children's book?' she asked.

Polly shrugged. 'I found it in the children's section so it must be. It had fallen down the back of the shelves. I only found it because I dropped a different book down there.' She flicked through the pages disinterestedly. 'It's stupid, anyway. Everyone knows fairies don't look like that. They're meant to be pretty, not ugly. And it's been scribbled in.' She got up and wandered off, leaving the book in a stack on a trolley while she searched for something else. In the meantime, Penny returned with another book which she sulkily offered to Rowan.

Rowan began to read, but did not take in a word. Her mind was on the book that Polly had discarded, but she knew that she should not make a big deal of it. The last thing she wanted to do was draw attention to herself. Every few minutes her eyes flitted to the book, anxious to check that it was still there. She held her breath and forgot to read at one point when the librarian paused by the trolley. A poke from Penny forced her to continue, and when she looked up again, the librarian had gone and the book was still there.

Then a strange thing happened. The middle section of the book lifted and, as Rowan watched, a tiny woman stepped out of it, blinking as though she had been hibernating amongst the pages. The surprise on her pointed little face quickly turned to rage. She had been nesting in the old book, Rowan realised. That must have been the reason it had been found down the back of the bookshelves. Its location was no accident – the fairy had hidden it there purposely, and Polly had innocently fished it out.

The little woman's hair was long and matted, twisting around her body like fur. Beneath it Rowan could make out a raggedy dress of a material that looked very old, grey and crumpled – like the fairy herself. She was barefoot and her arms and legs were twig-thin. Looking around the library she caught Rowan's eye and shot a furious glance at her.

Penny poked her again.

'Why aren't you reading?' she complained.

'I've had enough,' Rowan snapped, closing the book. 'I want to read to James.'

Penny let out a huff of annoyance and got up to find someone else to pester. Rowan grabbed a book from James and pretended to read. James sat placidly in her lap, chewing on a strand of her long red hair.

She waited to see what the fairy would do. She didn't have to wait long.

With a screech that reached Rowan, the fairy woman kicked the book off the trolley. It hit another book jutting out on its descent, and landed in an untidy crumple on the carpet.

The creature leaped from the trolley and landed on the librarian's counter. At that moment the woman was reaching carefully for a steaming mug; as the only person authorised to eat or drink in the library. But as her fingers brushed the handle, the fairy gave the mug a vicious shove that knocked it over. Its contents slopped all over the desk, saturating a pile of books and a stash of paperwork.

At the librarian's gasp, several people looked over at the apparent accident and tut-tutted, and another member of staff rushed to help. The fairy gave a triumphant cackle as she admired her handiwork, then, unfolding a crusty set of wings, she took flight, landing on one of the nearby desks. There, she kicked a stack of books and papers to the floor, much to the confusion of the young man seated at the desk. Then she stomped on, flicking the pages of a book a teenage girl was diligently making notes from, losing her place.

159

Her rampage continued: books fell from shelves and were knocked out of hands; hair was pulled; shoelaces were knotted together; library cards were mixed up; pens leaked ink.

Rowan watched it all. And as the fairy drew nearer and nearer, she noticed something odd. A group of local school children was completely bypassed by the fairy, who appeared not to see them at all. Next she ignored a middle-aged man who was peering over his newspaper in bemusement at all that was going on around him, and went on to torment a little old lady, unpinning her hair from its neat bun before moving on to the next person. Everyone in its path was attacked, seemingly without reason, so Rowan wondered why the school children and the man had escaped the fairy's attention. She continued to watch as the fairy drew closer to where she sat. Then it happened again: the fairy bypassed the twins and went on to jab Sally in the arm with a stolen hairpin. Sally slapped her arm and looked about herself suspiciously, as if expecting to see a bug of some kind.

Rowan was openly staring now, her mind racing, trying to figure out what was going on. The fairy seemed unwilling to spare anyone from its tirade, so why had it ignored certain people? What was it about these people that was different from everyone else in the library?

They must have something in common, she thought to herself, something she was missing. But what? An idea struck her then. What if the people the fairy had spared were able to see it? Perhaps it only preyed on those who were oblivious to the existence of fairies. But even as she thought it, her mind was already dismissing it. She would have noticed if someone else had the second sight – especially the twins.

So what was it? She examined the people again, looking for some obvious similarity or shared characteristic. Finally, she saw it.

They were all wearing red.

The children's matching school blazers were a rich crimson. The man, in turn, was wearing a pair of bright red corduroy trousers, and the twins were wearing matching red dresses.

Rowan glanced around, looking for whoever was next in the fairy's path. It seemed to be heading back in the direction of the bookshelves, and she wondered if it was going back to its nesting place. Only two people stood in her way now: a father reading to his young child, a boy a little older than James. As it passed the child, the fairy slammed the book closed on the little boy's fingers, catching the father's thumbs, too. Luckily the book was thin, and so the action would not have caused an injury, but the shock of it was enough to make the little boy's face crumple, and he burst into tears.

Content now with the chaos it had caused, the fairy gathered its horribly matted hair around itself and leaped through the space in the bookshelves, vanishing from sight.

As the occupants of the library began to pick up their dropped books, clean the spilt drink and rub their sore fingers, Rowan heard more than one nervous laugh and a few embarrassed coughs.

'There must be something in the air today,' she heard some-one mutter.

The group gathered their belongings and chosen books, readying themselves to leave. Rowan grabbed the books she had selected for James, and asked Polly to hold her little brother's hand as she took the books to the counter. On the way, she added to her pile the tattered book that the fairy had crawled out of. Her heartbeat quickened as she picked it up, for although it was badly damaged, she could already see that it was no whimsical read, but something that contained folklore – something that could be of great use to her.

As she waited for the librarian she flicked through it, looking at the strange old pictures. Some were paintings, others were grainy woodcuts. It was one of the woodcuts that caught her eye. It depicted an ugly, shrivel-faced creature in a baby's crib, and a woman looking on anxiously. Beneath the picture were the words: 'A changeling left in place of a human baby may be a fairy child, an old fairy, or even a piece of carved wood enchanted to look like a real child.'

Changeling. The word was eerie. She turned the page, but then her pile of books was slid along the counter by the librarian.

'Wherever did you find this old thing?' the woman enquired. 'It's in a terrible state.'

'It was down the back of the shelves,' Rowan explained. 'It seems to have been there a long time, too.'

'I'll say,' said the librarian. 'Let me see if there's another copy. Now, what's it called?'

The book was so badly worn that neither Rowan nor the librarian could decipher the title on its cover or spine. In the end the librarian looked inside the book for a reference number before going off to another desk and checking records.

'I'm afraid it's for reference only,' she said when she returned. 'You can't take it out of the library.' She wrinkled her nose. 'It'll have to be thrown away anyway – it's not even fit for a jumble sale.' She picked the book up and put it behind the counter.

'You're going to get rid of it?' said Rowan. 'Why can't you just let me take it?'

The librarian sniffed, and suddenly Rowan had the feeling that she was being deliberately obstructive. 'I can't release sub-standard books. It reflects badly on the library.'

'So you'd rather throw it away than give it to someone who wants to read it?'

'I don't make the rules, young lady.'

'Will there be a replacement?'

'I shouldn't think so. It's probably out of print.'

Rowan narrowed her eyes. There was a self-satisfied air about the woman's words.

'Please,' she tried again. 'It's important. I . . . I need to read it.'

But the woman shook her head. The conversation was over.

Later, when James was asleep, Rowan rifled through her clothes, looking for something red. Eventually she found an old bobbled cardigan and pulled it on. Next, she searched for something red for James, but all she could find was a pair of pyjamas that would be impossible to get him into with only one functioning arm. Scouting the corridors, she found a red towel draped over the banister, and wrapped it around her little brother. Then she crept into the bathroom.

At first she did not think the fairy was there, but she waited, listening, and soon heard a telltale gurgle. A moment later it emerged from the drain warily and looked around. Immediately, Rowan knew that it had not seen her. She watched in silence, for several minutes, as the creature moved around the bathtub, slurping on stray bits of hair and even an old piece of soap. Then its bulbous eyes bulged as it spied something on the side of the bathtub: a thin necklace with a star pendant left by one of the girls. The creature grabbed the piece of jewellery with a delighted squeak.

'You slimy little thief,' Rowan murmured.

The creature looked up in obvious shock. It had seen her. As it slid down the drain, Rowan tried to make sense of what had happened. It hadn't seen her at first, she was sure of it. But when she had spoken . . . it had broken the spell somehow. The colour red acted as some kind of camouflage to the fairies, but it wasn't totally foolproof. But now she could be certain of two things. Firstly, she had a way to hide herself and James from the fairies.

Secondly, if there was one way, then there were bound to be others.

14

ED AWOKE AT DAWN, HER HEAD
aching from lack of sleep. The Hedge-
witch's cottage was still and silent, but
for the breathing of the man who was
slumbering a few feet away from her. Light and a freezing
draught forced their way in through the gaps in the window
shutters. Red fought the temptation to burrow back into the
thick furs that covered her. Every breath clouded in the air.

She studied the man's face. In sleep, he was less stern-
looking, and there was a trace of something that might
have been handsome about him once, in another lifetime.
She still didn't know his story; didn't even know his name
or what to call him, in fact – and she found she didn't want
to. She hadn't yet told him all of her story. Now she
doubted she ever would. In a split-second decision, she
knew that she was going to leave the Hedgewitch's cottage
alone.

Quietly she rolled the furs back into a bundle. They were
going with her. Next, she stood up and took the fox-skin
coat, which she'd used as a pillow, and pushed it into her

bag. She scanned the cottage a final time, making sure she had all her belongings and anything else that could be of use.

Soundlessly she lifted the latch on the cottage door.

'Leaving without saying goodbye?' a voice said.

She spun round. The man's blue eyes were open, watching her. 'I had a feeling you might do that.'

'Goodbye,' she said pointedly, turning back to the door.

'I know who you are.'

Red froze. Her instinct told her he was bluffing; yet she couldn't be sure.

'No, you don't.'

'Really? You mean that you're *not* the girl who steals the changeling babies, returning them to the fairies in the hopes of exchanging one of them for her missing brother? You're *not* the girl who hid in the tunnels below Elvesden Manor, until you were discovered by the granddaughter of the owner? And you're *not* the girl who intervened when that same girl was in danger of being drawn into the fairy realm, taking her place?'

The latch slipped from Red's fingers.

'Who are you?'

'I'm the caretaker of Elvesden Manor. And the girl I just spoke of told me about you – how you saved her.'

'I didn't save her,' Red answered. 'I did what I did for myself, to get me here for the sake of my brother. I didn't do it for Tan—' She stopped herself just in time, remembering not to reveal the name. From his place in the cellar Eldritch was likely to be within earshot, and though Tanya's absence meant she could not be connected with the name, Red still did not want to risk speaking it with a fairy nearby. 'I didn't do it for *her*,' she finished.

'I don't think that's completely true.' The man threw back the furs covering him, and blew into his hands.

'I don't care what you think. I'm leaving.'

'I know you are. But I'm coming with you.'

Red stared at him, infuriated. He was up now, sweeping out the remains of the fire and calmly laying another.

'I'm going alone,' she said coldly. 'You're injured. You'd only slow me down. And I don't want you with me. I don't know you, and I don't trust you.'

The man did not even turn around.

'Maybe it's time you started to. Because I know who you are. I know your name. Your *real* name.'

Red felt her mouth suddenly go as dry as sand.

'You can trust me because I haven't revealed it, and I won't,' he continued. 'Ever since I found out about you, you've played on my mind. Knowing you were here . . . alone. I felt responsible somehow. Even though it was an accident that I came to be here, now that I am, I'm glad.'

'Glad? *Why?*'

'Because now I can help you, and I don't have to feel guilty.'

Red shook her head, confused. 'Why should you feel guilty? Why should you feel *anything?*'

'Because I already have responsibilities.'

'A family,' Red guessed. 'Children?' The word stuck in her throat like a hot potato.

He nodded. 'A boy of twelve, nearly thirteen.' His voice was wistful when he next spoke. 'That's a lot of years to make up for.'

'What do you need to make up for?' Red asked, intrigued, despite herself.

A haunted look came into the man's eyes. 'Many things.' He tossed a log onto the fire. Longing to warm herself, Red stepped closer. 'Perhaps I'll tell you about them on the way.'

'On the way to where?'

'To the courts,' he replied. 'That's where you're heading, isn't it?'

He correctly took her silence as an agreement.

'So am I. Because it's our best chance out of this place.'

He motioned to the furs beside him.

'Why don't you sit awhile, and have something to eat while you think about it.'

Red slipped her bag off her shoulder and walked over to the hearth. In the few steps it took, she had already made her decision. It would be good to have a companion in this strange world, for a while at least. She had been alone for so long and the thought of company was surprisingly comforting. In addition, his connection to Tanya had softened her. She watched him. At the very least, he could cook. And if she decided it wasn't working, she could run, and set off alone. She lowered herself down and held her hands to the flames. Neither of them spoke for a few minutes.

'So,' she said finally. 'If we're going to be travelling together, what should I call you?'

The man looked up and smiled – then winced, bringing his hand up to his swollen mouth. He gestured to his lips. 'I think . . . Stitch. Call me Stitch.'

He left her by the fire, staring into the flames. She heard the door opening, then she was alone in the cottage as he went outside. Sometime later, she started to worry and got up to look out of the window. But before she could open it the latch lifted and Stitch returned with a basket of berries and fresh water from the stream.

'We have to get out of here,' he said, placing some berries before her. 'Eat quickly, and then gather your things. I need to have another look for that key.'

As if on cue, Eldritch hollered from below.

'Are you eating up there?'

Stitch grimaced. 'On second thoughts, you look for the key and I'll go and see to him. Check everywhere, twice. Make sure there's not another loose brick.'

Red wiped blackberry juice from her chin.

'Are you sure we should free him?'

Stitch raised a finger to his lips. 'If we don't he's as good as dead. I wouldn't wish that fate on anyone. Plus he could be of use to us.'

'And he could also be dangerous,' Red whispered.

'True. But if we free him, then he'll owe us. He knows this

realm – at the very least he might guide us to where we need to get to.'

Stitch vanished into the dungeon with a share of food and water for Eldritch. Red continued to eat, her fingers stained with berry juice. It was a paltry breakfast, and the berries were long past their best, but it was better than nothing. She washed it down with icy stream water, then got up and began looking around the cottage once more.

Stitch clambered back up into the cottage, looking peaky. The stench of the cellar clung to him, and he crossed the floor and threw a window open wide, gulping in the fresh, cold air.

When he turned back he looked a little better. He left the window ajar and limped to the tables at the back of the cottage. There, he began lifting glass jars and bottles and scanning the contents.

'What are you doing?' Red asked.

'Making use of what's available.' From one jar, he pulled a handful of dark leaves; from another, a piece of withered root. Placing them into a small stone bowl, he grabbed a nearby pestle and began grinding the contents together.

'You have healing skills?' Red asked.

'Not skills, exactly. I know a little, enough to get by on.' He continued to pound and mix. 'This should help with Eldritch's wounds – and mine. Any sign of the key?'

'Not yet,' Red answered. She knelt by the wooden chest that her bag had been found in, and opened it. After finding her bag before, she had abandoned the chest and left

Stitch to search through. Now she wanted to have another look at the many possessions the Hedgewitch had claimed.

She sifted through the contents. Her chest constricted as she found a small girl's shoe – the twin to the one that she had found at the bottom of the Hedgewitch's trap. She wondered what had become of the child, then pushed the unanswered question from her mind. Many of the items were of no use or interest to anyone but their owner: a pair of wired-rimmed spectacles, one lens missing; a set of false teeth; and even a staring glass eye. Then she found something interesting: a simple drawstring bag of the softest leather. It was knotted tightly, and did not appear to have been opened even by the Hedgewitch. Red lifted it from the chest and began to pick at the knots. Gradually they loosened and eventually she was able to pull the bag open and reach inside.

The first thing she found was a fine cylinder, seemingly carved from wood by hand. She inspected it for a short while before realising that one end was removable. She twisted it and it came free, revealing a hollow in its centre. Something had been rolled carefully and tucked inside. With her index and middle fingers, she eased it from the hollow. It was a piece of thick, yellowing parchment. She unfurled it, weighting the ends with a shoe and a pair of field glasses.

As she leaned over the parchment, a shadow fell onto it from behind her.

'What is it?' Stitch asked.

'A map,' Red answered, staring at the document.

Stitch dropped to his knees at once.

'That's not just any map.' His voice was trembling and he pointed to a word in the south region. 'You see that?'

'Avalon,' Red read.

He nodded. 'That's where the courts are located. That's where we need to get to.' He ran his finger over the surrounding areas and turned to face her. 'This is a map of the fairy realm. It'll lead us straight there.'

Red felt a shudder of excitement ripple through her. She looked back at him, smiling, but then her face fell.

'What is it?'

'How can we get there if we don't know where we are now?' she said. 'It's all very well knowing where we need to go, but not if we're lost before we even begin.'

'We're not lost,' said Stitch, thumbing the edge of the map. 'I know exactly where we are.'

'How?'

'Don't you recognize the shape of the map over all? Doesn't it look familiar to you?'

Red leaned back on her heels, studying the map as a whole, and then looked back at him amazement. She had been sitting so close to it that she hadn't noticed what was glaringly obvious.

'That's right,' he said quietly. 'It's the British Isles – only through the eyes of the fey. We're here, in Essex . . . where we entered the fairy realm in the first place.'

'I don't understand.'

'The earth is the same, but the two worlds are on a different plane to each other. They coexist.'

'So this is . . .' Red trailed her finger over to Avalon.

'Somerset. Glastonbury, to be precise.'

'So how long will it take us to travel there?'

'On foot? Around five days. But we're not going by foot.'

Red's eyebrows shot up. 'We aren't?'

'There are horses tethered behind the cottage, and a small tack room. They must have belonged to the Hedgewitch – or her victims. We'll take them – it'll halve the travelling time.'

She heard him retreating, still mixing the herb-scented paste, and then his footsteps faded as he took the mixture down to Eldritch.

Red rolled the map and fed it back into the cylindrical tube before placing it into her bag. As an afterthought, she emptied the leather bag that the map had come from, to check nothing else of value was concealed in its depths.

Two things fell out. One was an empty water skin, which she kept. The other was a finely-bound book with gilt-edged pages. Something inside her stirred at the sight of it; a distant memory. She reached for it and pulled it closer to her, reading the faded title on the cover.

Her hand flew to her mouth.

'*The Fairy Tales of Hans Christian Andersen*,' she whispered from behind her fingers. It was exactly like the one that had belonged to her mother . . . the one she had treasured. The one that had gone missing with her brother.

Her eyes were filling before she had a chance to stop them, and she pressed the heels of her hands into them, forcing the tears away. She hadn't cried in a long time. Not since she had been Rowan. She sniffed a couple of times, bringing herself back under control. *You're not Rowan any more*, she told herself. *You're Red, and Red doesn't cry.*

Composed now, she stroked the book's cover and opened it, wanting to see the familiar list of contents. Instead she saw something that made her fingers whiten as they gripped the edges of the book.

There was a bookplate on the first page; the kind where the owner of the book writes their name. Red had seen it a hundred times before, and would recognise it anywhere; the little pen and ink illustration of a witch on a broomstick, reading a book.

More importantly, she could never mistake the name written on the bookplate itself.

She sprang up clutching the book, her tears forgotten. All she felt now was a cold rage – and fear. She turned and flew down the steps to the cellar, oblivious to the putrid air. Stitch was kneeling before Eldritch, applying the paste to his raw red wrist. They both looked up, Eldritch eyeing her hopefully.

'You've found the key?'

'No.' She thrust the book at them. 'I found this.'

She was completely unprepared for what followed.

'That's mine.' Eldritch reached out with his free hand.

'You found my belongings? Bring them to me . . . there's a map—'

Red snatched the book back with a reflex quicker than a scalded cat's. 'What did you just say?'

Eldritch hesitated. 'There should be a map,' he said. 'A map showing—'

'*Before* that!'

'I said . . . it's mine,' Eldritch answered, wariness creeping into his voice. 'I mean . . . I think it is. Let me take a closer look . . .'

'What's going on?' Stitch asked, setting his bowl aside.

Holding the book out of reach, Red knelt, elbowing Stitch out of the way, and leaned forward until her face was only inches from Eldritch's. She could smell the filth of his hair, skin and clothing.

'Could be mistaken . . . of course.' He ran his tongue over dry lips. 'In fact, yes . . . I don't believe that's mine at all.'

'Oh, you're mistaken all right,' Red hissed. 'In fact, you've just made the biggest mistake of your life.'

'What's going on?' Stitch repeated.

Red did not take her eyes off Eldritch.

'He recognised this book – says it's his. Well, it's not.' She opened the book and turned to the bookplate, holding it up before Eldritch's face. 'Do you see this name? Do you recognise it?'

Eldritch shook his head.

'I do,' Red continued. 'It's my mother's maiden name. This book belonged to her when she was a little girl. She used to read from it to my brother and me. And when she died, the book was one of the last things I had left to remind me of her. Then it was stolen from me. Stolen on the same night as my brother.'

At this she caught Stitch's sharp intake of breath.

'I said I was mistaken—'

'Shut up. I found this book in a bag with a map. You knew about that map – and you knew about this book. Now you're going to tell me how you got it, and it had better be good. Because I'll be listening very, very carefully.'

'We don't have time for this,' said Stitch, glancing up at the trapdoor. 'We need to go.'

'I'm not going anywhere until I get some answers,' said Red, her voice dangerously low.

Eldritch remained silent, but then Stitch crouched beside Red.

'You'd better start talking,' he threatened. 'Before I make you talk.'

Eldritch was sweating heavily now. His skin looked waxy and his black hair hung in a greasy curtain around his face. 'I didn't take it,' he said at last. 'It wasn't me.'

'Not good enough.' Stitch reached out and tugged the chain attached to Eldritch's wrist. Eldritch screamed as the iron cut into his skin, and fell against the dungeon wall, writhing.

'I didn't take it,' he repeated at last, through gritted teeth.

Red reached for the chain again and Eldritch flinched.

'It's the truth!' he whined. 'Someone gave it to me.'

Red regarded him coldly. 'Who?'

He stared into his lap. 'Knowing won't do you any good.'

'I'll decide that. Who was it?'

'He was my travelling companion.' Eldritch jerked his head into the darkened corner of the dungeon – as he had done only yesterday. 'He's over there, like I told you.'

Red and Stitch scanned the dark recesses of the cellar. Several shapes littered it – the Hedgewitch included. All were in varying states of decay.

'He's one of the dead?' said Stitch.

'Correct,' said Eldritch, leaning his head back against the wall. 'And even if he was still alive it would have been too late to question him – what with the Hedgewitch removing his tongue.'

'Was he the one who took my brother?'

Eldritch shook his head. 'I don't know. I don't know anything!'

'Yes, you do,' said Red. 'Otherwise you wouldn't have tried to lie about the book. You know something, all right.' She stood up and slowly walked over to the figure that was slumped forward, manacled to the wall just as Eldritch was. Clenching her jaw, Red grabbed a handful of the long hair covering the face, tilting the head back. To her horror and revulsion, the hair came away in her hand and, as the head shifted, she saw that it was no longer recognisable. She released it, letting the hair drop to the ground, and roughly wiped her hand on her trousers. Bending down, she began to go through the clothing.

'What are you looking for?' asked Stitch.

'I don't know,' she said. 'Anything . . . some kind of clue.'

'You won't find anything,' said Eldritch. 'The Hedgewitch would have taken anything of value from him.'

Suddenly Red spied something, glinting in the faint glow from above. She reached out for it.

'What is it?' Stitch asked. 'Have you found something?'

'A ring,' said Red. She turned the body's skeletal hand over and the ring rattled free from the bone and fell into her hand; no flesh to hold it in place. 'Why didn't the Hedgewitch take this from him?'

'It was stuck on his finger,' Eldritch answered. 'It . . . it became welded to his skin one night in an . . . accident.'

Red felt herself growing cold as she turned the ring over in her hand. It was silver and chunky, with a smooth black stone at its centre. Carved into the stone was a pair of wings. She recognised it immediately . . . the image was seared into her mind. Forcing away her revulsion she ran her hand over the shoulder blades of the body. Through the clothing she felt two bumps – stumps of where wings had once been. She stood up and strode back to where Eldritch and Stitch were.

'I've seen this ring before,' she said quietly. 'Only once, but I'll never forget it. It was worn by the fairy who took my brother. And I had a feeling about you, Eldritch. I knew you weren't to be trusted.' She knelt before him once more. 'We've met before.'

Eldritch looked as though Red were the Hedgewitch herself. He looked terrified.

'I haven't seen you before!' he protested, but the lie was wasted upon her.

'Yes you have. Only I had red hair back then. Long, red hair. Now do you remember?'

'I don't!' Eldritch snivelled, starting to weep now. 'I don't remember you!'

'Then perhaps you'll remember this!'

She swivelled around, and with her left hand reached up to pull the neck of her top down.

'Does this look familiar?' she snarled.

But Eldritch refused to look, cowering into his knees with his face hidden. She could sense Stitch, however, staring at the back of her neck in horror.

'If you won't look, then let me describe it to you,' she said, turning back around. 'It's a burn, branded into the back of my neck, and it's in the shape of fairy wings – the same fairy wings that appear on this ring. The ring became stuck to his hand when he was burning me – and his own wings caught fire. It was the only reason he stopped!'

Eldritch looked up then. 'He burned lots of people. Anyone who crossed him – it was his signature. You were the only one who burned him back somehow. He lost the power after that. You did something to him . . . just like you did something to the Hedgewitch!'

Stitch's eyes bored into Eldritch.

'What are you doing here?' he asked suddenly. 'You didn't just fall foul of the Hedgewitch by chance, did you? You and your companion knew too much for that, and you were too powerful. You were here for a reason. There's no evidence upstairs to suggest she caught fairies for her glamours – only humans.'

Eldritch hesitated, then nodded. 'We did business with her sometimes. Nothing too serious,' he put in hastily. 'Just plants from afar, and things from the human world. Animals, if we could get them. She was always after fresh stock. Snatcher – my companion – traded with her for curses to repay those who crossed him after he lost his burning ability. It all worked well enough until she gave him a curse on condition that he would repay her later – he didn't have anything valuable enough to trade at the time.

'The price was one hundred four-leafed clovers or primroses – both valuable to fairy magic, and rare. It took us many moons to find enough on our travels. Eventually we did. But Snatcher was greedy. On our way here to deliver the goods he had the idea to pretend we'd been robbed and lost most of them, in order to keep half for ourselves and sell them at a later date. He thought he could fool the Hedgewitch and that her pity would allay the rest of the bargain. He was wrong. She pretended to go along with it at first, even offering us wine after our ordeal. The next thing I knew we were both here, in iron manacles – powerless. She'd drugged the wine. She told us that if we hadn't the goods to pay for the curse Snatcher took, then we'd pay with ourselves. She started with Snatcher's tongue: the tongue of a liar. Apparently she got a good price for it. And I've been here ever since.'

'Forgive me if I can't feel sorry for you,' Red interrupted sarcastically. 'Now, where's my brother?'

'I don't know where he is. I never got involved with all that.'

'All what?'

'The changeling trade. I've never been part of it, I swear to you.'

'Knowing about it makes you involved,' said Stitch, his voice full of disgust.

'Yes, I knew about it,' Eldritch hissed. 'But I never stole any children, even though . . .'

'Even though what?' Red shouted. Her fingers twitched at her sides. It was all she could do not to strike the despicable creature before her.

'Even though I was tempted,' he finished. 'The money's good. And the connections are . . . better. But I never did. I kept out of it. I saw things, though, and heard things. The one with the book sticks in my mind. Snatcher had been watching the child for days, a little golden-headed boy he was.'

'That's right,' Red whispered.

'He bragged about it – it was an easy target, he said. A children's home . . . no parents around to notice the differences between the children that were taken and their replacements. And the first few he got away with easily. But the golden-headed child was proving a challenge. He had an older sister who clearly had the second sight and could see what was going on. She wouldn't let him out of her sight, and even found ways to ward off the fey. So Snatcher waited, knowing that one day there would be a mistake that would allow him to take the child. And it was only a matter of time before he was right.'

'I didn't make a mistake that night,' Red murmured. 'Something went wrong . . .'

'The book he only took as an afterthought,' Eldritch continued. 'He saw the word "fairy" in the title. It amused him, so he took it. Later, when he realised that there were no fairies in the book at all, he no longer wanted it. I liked it though, so he traded it to me.'

'Where's the child now?' Stitch asked.

Eldritch shook his head. 'That I can't tell you.' His eyes widened in terror as Stitch reached for the chain once more. 'Please!' he cried. 'I'm telling the truth! I don't know – he never told me what he did with them, and I never asked. He mentioned a meeting with a fey woman – I don't know who! But I'll help you – I'll help you look for him. Just . . . just get me out of here . . . out of these chains . . .'

'I believe you,' said Stitch, shortly. 'The problem is, we can't find the key, and Red and I can't wait around. So I'll give you a choice. You can either stay here and take your chances, or I can get you out . . . but it won't be pretty.'

'What do you mean?' Eldritch croaked.

By way of reply, Stitch drew back his long overcoat, revealing the hilt of his dagger.

Eldritch pushed himself back against the wall.

'Oh, no . . . oh, no, no . . .'

'Forget it,' said Red. 'He's not coming with us. He's not going anywhere. He's a worthless coward.'

'What?' Eldritch's voice rose in terror. 'I'll help you find your brother, I swear—'

'You were there the night I was burned. You hid your face in your hood while those wings were branded into my skin, and you did nothing.'

'But I wasn't the one who branded you!' he cried. 'It wasn't me!'

'No,' Red roared. 'But you could have stopped it. And you did *nothing*! You knew about the children being stolen. And what did you do? NOTHING! So now I'm going to repay the favour.' She leaped to her feet and plunged her hand into her pocket until her fingers met with something small and cool to the touch, which she held aloft.

'The key!' Eldritch gasped. 'You had it all along!'

'It was exactly where the Hedgewitch said it would be. And now it's coming with me, and you're staying here. Because now you're going to know what it feels like, to need help and the only person who can help you does . . . *nothing*.' She turned her eyes on Stitch, shoving the key back into her pocket. 'Let's go.'

'No!' Eldritch yelled. 'No, wait! Please! Don't leave me here!'

But Red was already on the steps leading up to the cottage, with Stitch close on her heels. When they reached the top, Red turned back to stare into the dungeon for the last time. Eldritch's face twisted into a snarl like a rabid dog – his pretences gone at last.

'You'll regret this, girl!' he growled. 'I'm going to get out of here, and when I do, I'll track you down and make you pay for this!'

Red stared back at him, her emerald eyes clouded with hatred.

'I don't think so.'

With that she slammed the trapdoor shut, and then she and Stitch collected their belongings and exited the cottage with Eldritch's cries ringing in their ears.

15

LORENCE HURRIED MORAG
and Nell into the kitchen and fetched
warm, dry blankets for them both. As
Morag hobbled across the threshold into
the house, Fabian made a face and tried to catch Tanya's
eye, but she refused to get caught up in his superstitious fear
of the old gypsy woman.

'Nell, where on earth have you been?' Florence cried.
'We've been worried sick!'

'And where's my dad?' Fabian asked. 'What's happened to
him?'

Nell looked at them, eyes wide with shock.

'They took him,' she said.

'Who did?' Tanya asked carefully.

Nell refused to meet her eyes, and in that instant, Tanya
knew that she was too afraid to relate her experience.

'It's all right, Nell,' she said. 'You can tell us.'

Nell wrung her hands together and shook her head. 'I
can't. You won't believe me. You'll think I'm crackers.'

'I think we should all sit down,' said Florence.

Everyone sat, except for Florence, who set about brewing a fresh pot of tea. Tanya got up and started to help, but nerves made her jittery, and after she'd broken a saucer Florence told her to sit down. The tea was poured in silence.

Morag sipped at her tea, nodding appreciatively. Tanya wondered when the last time was that the old gypsy woman had had a cup of tea made for her. She lived a lonely life, out in the woods where no one would bother her.

'I . . . oh, hello again,' said Morag, her birdlike eyes noticing Tanya properly for the first time. 'I didn't know you lived here.'

'Tanya is my granddaughter,' said Florence in surprise. 'I was unaware that you knew each other.'

'We've met,' said Morag, with a twinkle in her eye.

'In Tickey End,' Tanya added, keen to shield her grandmother from the true extent of her disobedience in the summer. Her visit to the gypsy woman's caravan was something she had only shared with Fabian.

Morag nodded her agreement, much to Tanya's relief. Her secret was safe.

'Where did you find Nell?' she asked.

Morag drained the rest of her tea in a single gulp and glanced surreptitiously at the teapot. Florence dutifully leaned over and refilled her cup. The old woman beamed.

'She was in the woods. Came knocking on my door, in a dreadful muddle.' She paused to give Oberon a pat; he had rested his large brown head on her knee and was sniffing at her many layers of clothing with interest. 'I could see she was disoriented and exhausted. She could barely walk.'

A deep line had appeared in Florence's forehead.

'Nell, you have to tell us what happened,' she insisted.

'They made me dance,' Nell said in a small squeak, then pressed her lips tightly together as if she had revealed too much.

Tanya looked down at Nell's feet, protruding from beneath the blanket. They were dirty and grass-stained, and there were cuts and blisters all over them. Her flip-flops were barely in one piece.

Morag helped herself to a custard cream from a small dish Florence had placed on the table. At once, Oberon started to drool over her knees.

'That's about all I could get out of her, too,' Morag said through a crumbly mouthful.

'Was my father with her?' Fabian asked urgently. 'Did she say anything at all about where she had been?'

'No, nothing,' said Morag. 'She was alone, like I said.'

'She got lost in the woods earlier this afternoon with Warwick,' Florence explained.

'We were looking for General Carver,' Nell mumbled, staring into the fire. She was still shivering hard.

'Her parrot,' Tanya explained, seeing Morag's baffled expression. 'He flew off. That's why Nell and Warwick were in the woods in the first place. I saw what happened. They were pulled into one of the fairy rings by some ... well, some fairies—'

'Naturally,' said Morag, as though such occurrences were commonplace. 'I thought as much. That would explain the dancing.' She dunked another biscuit in her tea. 'Dangerous time of year for it.'

'This is just a bad dream,' Nell murmured, starting to rock. Her eyes were fixed and staring on the fire. 'There's no such thing as fairies. I'm going to wake up any minute, and when I do, the General will be here and everything will be all right and— Oh! What did you do that for, you little tyke?'

Fabian had leaned forward and pinched her.

'Because that's what you do when you think you're dreaming,' said Fabian. 'You pinch yourself to check if you're awake or not. But obviously you weren't going to do it, so I thought I'd help.'

Nell's eyes filled with tears.

'I don't want to stay here,' she sniffed. 'I want to find General Carver, and I want to leave. He'll be terrified out there, alone and in the dark.'

'I'm rather more concerned about Warwick,' Florence said stiffly. 'I know you've had a terrible shock, Nell, but we need you to cooperate. The things you saw in the woods are real, and now Warwick is in danger. We need you to tell us what happened so we can find him . . . just tell us what you can.'

'There were three of them,' said Nell through her tears, looking at Tanya as if to back her up.

Tanya nodded encouragingly.

'They were playing this tune . . . it was like nothing I'd ever heard. My body was moving of its own accord – I couldn't control it. All I could do was dance, round and round. They kept changing the notes, shifting, moving to other circles to dance in. We were moving through the woods. I was tired, so tired. I begged them to let me stop but they just carried on, getting faster and faster—'

'And my father,' Fabian interrupted. 'What was he doing?'

'The same,' Nell continued. 'Just dancing, he couldn't stop either . . . but he wasn't as tired as I was. We kept on and on; I thought it would never stop. And all the while they kept laughing and singing, and they were so strange . . .' She shuddered. 'I only got away because my flip-flop got caught on the root of a little tree, laden with red berries – it hooked me back, and broke the dance somehow.'

'Red berries,' said Morag, thoughtfully. 'Sounds like it was rowan – protection against dark magic.'

'They didn't even realise I'd fallen behind,' Nell continued, in a quavering voice. 'They just carried on until I lost sight of them. Warwick was still with them.'

There was a long, brooding silence.

'But there's still a chance,' said Fabian, desperately. 'Perhaps my father isn't far away . . . perhaps he managed to break the spell as well, somehow. He could be in the woods right now!'

'It's possible,' Florence said quietly. 'But unlikely. If Warwick had managed to get away he would have found his way back by now. I'm sure of it.'

'But he might be injured,' Fabian protested. 'He might not be able to make it back! We should go and look for him . . . If Nell got away then he might have, too!'

Florence shook her head. 'Much as I want to believe that I think the chances are slim. We'll wait here until Raven and Gredin bring news.' She gave Tanya and Fabian a warning look. 'And that's final.'

Morag got up, folding her blanket. She reached for her shawl, still damp, and threw it around her shoulders before walking to the back door.

'I must go now,' she said. 'But I will see . . . what I can see. An answer may present itself.'

'She means her visions, doesn't she?' Fabian whispered to Tanya.

'Thank you, Morag,' said Florence. 'But I'd hate to think of you walking through the woods in the dark on a night like this. Stay with us – we have plenty of rooms we could put you in.'

'Oh, don't worry about me,' said Morag, with a sudden cackle. 'I can take care of myself.'

'I'll bet,' Fabian muttered under his breath, and Tanya dug him in the ribs.

Florence opened the back door and peered doubtfully into the night.

'I really don't like the idea of you going back into the woods this late alone. In fact, I have an idea . . .' She stepped out into the darkness and gave a tuneful little whistle. Only the wind replied, throwing leaves back at her. She stepped out further, and whistled again, more loudly.

Nearby, a bush parted and a man of only knee-height stepped out. He was wearing funny little trousers made from tea towels and a jacket of thick material that had evidently once been a curtain: it fastened down his middle with hooks and eyes.

'Brunswick!' Tanya exclaimed.

'Where?' Fabian demanded, craning his neck and squinting through his thick spectacles.

Florence put a finger to her lips and motioned to Nell, who remained in a shocked silence by the fire. To the goblin she said:

'It's all right, Brunswick. You can show yourself.'

The goblin smiled shyly and stepped forward. Unlike the last time Tanya had seen him, he looked happy and healthy, his face free of the usual bruises that were the result of beatings from two other goblins. Then, though Tanya saw no visible change, she heard Fabian catch his breath as the goblin revealed himself.

'Brunswick lives here now, in the garden,' Florence explained. 'The other goblins don't trouble him any more – Warwick banished them from the grounds when we saw how they were treating him.'

'How did he manage that?' Tanya asked. Somehow she could not imagine the two hateful goblins taking orders from anyone.

'He told them that if he ever saw them again he'd lock

them in iron cages and throw them into the catacombs,' her grandmother said, matter-of-factly.

Fabian gave a low whistle. 'That ought to do it.'

'Brunswick, would you mind taking our friend safely home through the woods?' Florence asked the goblin, gesturing to the old gypsy woman.

Brunswick beamed and offered his hand to Morag.

'Safe you'll be if you accompany me.'

'He still speaks in rhyme sometimes,' Florence explained. 'Just out of habit. He spent so long in the company of the other two goblins that he slips back into his old ways from time to time.'

Tanya remembered how Brunswick's old companions had only spoken in (and responded to) rhyming speech. Later she had found out that this was a common punishment for fairies that had been banished from their own realm for wrongdoings.

Morag accepted Brunswick's hand, and the strange pair set off through the garden, over the rockery and through the gate towards the forest.

Back in the kitchen, Florence locked the door for the second time that night, and smoothed her silvery hair back into its bun. The events of the day had crept up on her. Her face was drawn, and the colour of white laundry when a dark sock is accidentally thrown in.

'I'm going to check on Amos,' she said. 'And after that I'm going to make some supper. We need to keep our strength up.' She left the room, and they heard the tread of her footsteps going up to the second floor where Amos's room was.

Tanya and Fabian stayed with Nell, who was rocking again in her chair in front of the fire. Her face was white, her eyes glassy. When Oberon nosed her hands in her lap she did not respond.

'Do you think Florence will tell Amos that Warwick is missing?' said Fabian.

'No,' said Tanya. 'It would only upset him, and that's the last thing we need.' She was starting to get a tight ball of worry in her chest. She glanced Nell, then at the window. Through the grimy glass she could see the trees against the moon being whipped back and forth like reeds in the wind. If Warwick was out there, alone, would he be afraid?

16

IVE HORSES WERE TETHERED behind the Hedgewitch's cottage. Between them, Red and Stitch chose the three that appeared the healthiest, saddling up one each to ride, and a third to carry their belongings. Red chose a palomino mare, while Stitch quickly bonded with a sturdy stallion. The third horse was an energetic, creamy-coloured colt.

'It's best we take three,' Stitch said, fastening the buckle on his saddle. 'It gives us a chance to rest the horses and covers us if one should go lame.'

They freed the other two horses, knowing that there was now no one to care for them, and watched as they meandered off into the woods. Then they set off, keen to leave the awful events of the Hedgewitch's cottage behind them. They rode in silence, walking at first. Not only was this to gauge the horses' temperaments, but Red had forewarned Stitch about the trap she had fallen into. Neither of them wanted to run the risk of overlooking another one.

Soon they heard the trickling of the stream and headed towards it, dismounting to fill their flasks. Stitch took out the map and spread it on the grass, chewing his lower lip as he studied it. By the time Red had bundled the water on the horses and led them to the stream to drink, he had rolled it back up and put it away, and was watching her when she mounted the palomino once more.

'Why are you looking at me like that?' she asked, unsettled.

'Are you really willing to leave Eldritch chained up in that dungeon?'

Red stared at him coldly. Raising herself in the stirrups, she removed the Hedgewitch's key from her pocket and hurled it into the running water.

'Does that answer your question?'

Stitch stared at the bubbles on the water's surface.

'Perfectly.'

She clicked the horse on, moving through the dappled shade of the trees. Stitch followed, drawing up alongside her.

'How did you become like this?' he asked. 'You're just a child.'

Red laughed mirthlessly. 'I think my childhood ended the night my brother was taken.'

'Are you going to tell me what happened that night? With Eldritch, and that burn of yours?'

'I'm tired of talking about myself,' Red answered shortly. 'I want to hear about you.'

'What do you want to know?'

'I want to hear what you know about fairies, and how you know about them. You said back in the dungeon that you know people . . . people with the second sight. How did you become involved with them?'

Stitch pushed an overhead branch away from his face.

'I work for one of them, the owner of Elvesden Manor . . .' he lowered his voice and glanced about, checking their deserted surroundings, '. . . Florence. She has the second sight, but it wasn't until Tanya was born that I knew anything of fairies, even though I'd been surrounded by them all my life.' He paused, as though still not quite believing this fact. 'I grew up at the manor. My father was the groundskeeper before I was – he'd worked there since he was sixteen. But Morwenna Bloom's disappearance shaped the rest of his life.'

He faltered, looking up through the trees.

'Until thirteen years ago, I never knew for certain whether my father had something to do with her disappearance. I had to trust that he didn't, despite the rumours and sly comments as I was growing up. Sometimes I felt angry, and other times, ashamed. There were few people in Tickey End who didn't judge or ignore me, and I'd decided to leave as soon as I could. But then I met someone.' His frown eased suddenly. 'Someone wonderful. A girl named Evelyn, who ended up becoming the mother to our son. So I stayed. Everything seemed bearable suddenly – it didn't matter what strangers thought. But then thirteen years ago everything changed.

'Florence knocked on my bedroom door one night in a panic. She'd just returned from visiting her newborn granddaughter, so I couldn't understand why she was so distressed. She should have been happy, or so I thought. She said she had a story to tell me, an unbelievable story that involved my father, and that I was to listen without interruption. I promised her I would – then immediately broke it by laughing in her face when she said that the missing girl's disappearance was to do with fairies.

'I nearly walked out then and there, but something in her voice made me stop. I started to wonder if she was mad – she seemed to genuinely believe in what she was saying, and I had noticed fairy books in her library before. Then she offered to show me, and thinking no such thing was possible, I agreed.

'Into the fire she threw a black feather, and muttered an incantation. We waited, and she told me of how the girl, Morwenna Bloom, had vanished into the fairy realm leaving no trace of her whereabouts. How she eventually craved to be released, and turned her hatred against Florence. I was still unconvinced, but then a large, black bird landed on the window ledge outside. It was let in, and within seconds morphed into a woman who wore a black, feathered gown. I stumbled backwards in shock . . . almost fell into the fire. But finally, I believed her.'

'But the story didn't finish there. It continued with Tanya. Florence had seen that Tanya had inherited her ability – the fairies were all around her. And she knew then that she had to distance herself from Tanya, in order to prevent her becoming a target for Morwenna's revenge.

'I listened to all she was saying, but I still didn't understand what she was asking of me. Then her reasoning became clear. My job as groundskeeper was now secondary. My primary task was to protect the house and patrol the woods to guard against whatever might come out, searching for Tanya.'

'You mean, protect the house against fairies?' Red interrupted.

He nodded.

'How would that work if you can't see them?'

'That was what I argued to Florence. But I soon discovered other ways to see them. Following Florence's instructions, I visited the old gypsy woman who lives in Hangman's Wood. She gave me a small phial of tonic, with which to anoint my eyes. It was a temporary solution, but an effective one. I used it that very moment, before journeying back to the manor. The things I saw in the woods astonished me – and terrified me. Suddenly knowing that these creatures, these *things* were all around. Unseen. Watching and listening. I hurried back to the manor as fast as my legs would carry me, and locked the potion away. I told Florence that I couldn't do it.

'I expected her to be angry, yet all I saw on her face was sadness and disappointment, which somehow made things worse. I couldn't sleep that night. Instead I turned things over in my mind. The injustice of how my father had been treated, and the thought that Tanya could be in danger. I knew I couldn't turn my back on them. I also knew my life had changed. There was no going back.

'The next day I took the phial out. The potion had worn off by then, so before I could change my mind I used some more. Even in the house, there were fairies. On that first day, Florence showed me the ones that resided there with her permission. Any others, she told me, were to be removed – taken back to the woods and forbidden to return.'

'She allowed fairies to live in the house?' Red asked, deeply entrenched in Stitch's tale now. 'What were they like? Are they still there?'

'Most of them,' Stitch answered. 'One or two have died since, of old age and in . . . accidents.'

'What kind of accidents?'

'Cat-related accidents,' he said. 'But most are still alive and well, making nuisances of themselves.' He frowned a little. 'I don't know why Florence allows it, really. I've always told her she's too soft with them.'

'Tell me about them,' Red persisted. She was curious to know how the strange old house functioned, with its inhabitants both fey and human.

'Well,' said Stitch. 'There's a hearthfay in the kitchen. She helps keep pots warm, and keeps an eye on them to make sure they don't boil over. Then there's the brownie in the tea caddy – waste of space, if you ask me. Used to be helpful for a few drops of cream. Now he's more likely to sour it if he's disturbed – he's always asleep, you see.'

Red smiled. 'Go on.'

'There was a drain-dweller, like a thieving magpie, it was. Anything shiny or glittery and it'd take it—'

'I've seen one of those!' Red exclaimed. 'It used to come into the bathroom in the children's home I was in! It ate the hair and soapsuds that collected in the drain.'

'In Tickey End?' Stitch asked. 'It could have been the same creature that came to the manor – it used the network of drains to move around.'

'Is it still there?' she asked.

Stitch's eyes clouded with regret.

'No. The cat got it. By the time I heard the commotion it was too late.' He pulled a silver bracelet from his pocket. 'Funnily enough, one of the things it stole was a charm from this bracelet. I found it in the sink of Tanya's room when I was doing my repairs before she came to stay. I found it yesterday morning . . . I was going to fix it for her, as a surprise.'

Red glanced at the bracelet. She remembered seeing it on Tanya's wrist, and had thought it an odd choice for a young girl. She told him so.

'It was Florence's to begin with,' Stitch said. 'Passed down through the family, from the first owner of the manor.' He eased the bracelet back into his pocket.

The trees became knitted more closely together now. Stitch led the way, with the colt following and Red close behind. The forest was eerily silent; only the sounds of the horses' breath and tread found her ears.

'It's too quiet,' she murmured. 'Eldritch said this part of

the forest is called "the Dead Wood". How long before we're out of the woods?'

'Hard to say. A couple of hours, maybe. Once we find the border we'll rest awhile.'

A rattling sound above broke the silence, causing them both to halt. Red's head snapped up. She knew that noise. It set the hair on the back of her neck on end like the hackles of a dog.

'Did you hear that?' Stitch whispered.

She saw it hunched on a branch overhead, watching them. The gargoyle. Stitch saw it a moment later.

'What is that?'

'I don't know,' said Red. 'But I saw it before falling into the Hedgewitch's trap. It was screeching . . .' Her mind reeled with a sudden realisation. 'It was looking out for her – telling her when something had gone into the trap.'

As though it had understood, the gargoyle bared its teeth and hissed. It lifted its wings and launched itself at them, swooping with a snarl.

'Go!' Stitch yelled, but before either of them could spur their horses on, the gargoyle was jolted backwards, only inches from Stitch's horse. It screamed and flew at them again, only to be jerked back once more.

'It's chained up,' Red breathed. 'Look, there on its leg.'

The gargoyle's ankle was in an iron shackle, tethering it to a long chain secured to the tree. The chain rattled as the creature moved, and finally Red understood the source of the noise.

'It was a spy for her,' Stitch said grimly.

The gargoyle made a chattering sound, rather like a jack-daw, as they began to move away.

'Be careful,' called Red. 'The trap must be close – it was just beyond a fallen tree trunk.'

'I see it,' Stitch answered. He diverted his horse around the trunk, avoiding the trap, and Red followed.

They continued onwards with little conversation. Soon they found a path, and once on it they could talk again, for there was room enough for them to ride side by side.

'So, you told me about the fairies that are allowed in the house,' said Red. 'What about the ones that weren't?'

'There weren't so many at first,' Stitch said. 'Just the odd one or two, coming in out of curiosity, or to scavenge scraps of food. Most of the time they were seen off by the cat, if not the other fairies – territorial, they are. We started to believe we were safe, Florence and I. Then, one weekend when she was about six months old, Tanya was brought to stay.

'We knew it was dangerous for her to be in the house, and Florence had tried to discourage it – but it was unavoidable. We took precautions, always dressing her with her clothes inside out, and, whenever possible, in red. Florence refused to let Tanya out of her sight, even moving her cot into her own room. On the second night I was awoken by a shout from Florence's room. I rushed to investigate, unsure whether it was something fey, or perhaps a burglar. I could hear Spitfire hissing and spitting from inside. As I entered the room, I saw Florence standing by the cot with Tanya in her arms. She was plainly scared out of her wits. Something was sitting on the side of the cot, watching Tanya – but because her nightclothes were inside out it couldn't touch her. When I came in the creature was startled. It tried to escape up the chimney, but it knocked against the poker, which fell and trapped it. All at once, it screamed and the room filled with the smell of burning. As I ran over I realised that it was the flesh of the fairy, searing beneath the iron poker. When I lifted the poker it escaped.

'The next day I ordered a knife crafted from iron. It's barely left my side since. After that, Florence was terrified to have Tanya in the house at all. She even hid all the photographs of her. But the damage was done – the secret was out that Florence had a grandchild with the second sight – and the fairies kept on coming. I began to build iron cages to hold them in. A few days of imprisonment persuaded most not to return. Others needed further convincing.'

Red's skin prickled as she wondered what level of 'convincing' Stitch might be capable of.

'So they continued to come,' Stitch said. 'And I continued to hold them at bay.'

'And your family?' Red asked. 'Did you tell them what was going on?'

Stitch's hands clenched the reins of his horse tightly.

'No,' he said. 'They never knew a thing until recently. I hid it all. Then my son discovered everything.'

'What about your wife? Surely he couldn't manage to keep it a secret from his own mother?'

A look of anguish crossed Stitch's face. 'No. Evelyn never knew. I'm sure Fabian would have told her, if he'd had the chance. But by the time he found out about the fairies, his mother had been dead for seven years.'

He looked at her with damp, bloodshot eyes. 'If she'd known she might still be alive. It was the not knowing that got her killed.'

17

TITCH'S WORDS HUNG BETWEEN them like cobwebs. He lowered his head, his expression haunted, and sank his fingers into the mane of his horse, combing through the coarse strands of hair. Red waited for him to continue. Already, she sensed that this was a matter he had not spoken of in some time – if at all.

'Actually,' he said hoarsely, 'that's not completely true. The fact that she knew nothing of fairies . . . it was a factor in her death. But the truth is that she wouldn't have needed to know about them if I hadn't been involved. The fairies would never have come near her if it hadn't been for me.' He disentangled his fingers from the horse's mane and took hold of the rein once more. 'So the real truth is that I'm to blame. She died because of me.'

'I'm sure that's not true,' Red said softly.

Stitch smiled grimly. 'I've had seven years to think about it. It *is* true, no matter which way I look at it. I've always known. I've just never said it . . . out loud before. I thought I could protect her. I was wrong.'

'What happened?' Red asked.

Stitch paused to swig some water from his flask.

'It was made to look like an accident,' he said. 'Evelyn loved music. She was a talented musician. She played piano every day – Fabian loved to listen to her.

'I'd been hunting fairies for about six years by then. I knew a lot more about them by that time, and leading a double life had become second nature. Even so, Evelyn sometimes asked questions that I couldn't answer: why I spent so much time in the woods. How I ended up with so many cuts and bruises that I couldn't explain. Why I had to keep my knife so perfectly sharp when I never seemed to use it. I soon learned how to cover my tracks, occasionally bringing home a dead rabbit to keep up the pretence that I was hunting. In reality I've never hunted for sport – never will. I knew it was something Evelyn disapproved of. But I needed her to believe it, even though it killed me to know she thought less of me.

'One day, I found a rabbit in the woods. One of its legs had been taken off by a poacher's air rifle. It was bleeding to death. As I approached, two other rabbits that had been nearby ran off. I wrung the creature's neck to put it out of its misery, then took it back to the manor.

'Evelyn was in the garden with Fabian when I got back. Fabian saw the rabbit and burst into tears. Evelyn said nothing. She just looked at me with her mouth pinched and took Fabian inside.

'That evening Florence was out, so Evelyn and I ate alone

with Fabian. It was a meal of few words. She was still angry with me. To try and make amends I was playing some silly game with Fabian to try to make him laugh. It wasn't working. When someone knocked on the back door, he'd just tipped his food everywhere, so I asked Evelyn to answer it while I cleaned up.

'On the doorstep stood a woman and a child of about Fabian's age. They were peddlers; the woman carried a basket containing what I thought at first were bundles of firewood. But then Evelyn exclaimed that they were in fact little flutes, hand-carved from wood. She went out of the room to fetch her purse, leaving Fabian and me alone.

'"Take good care of your son," the woman at the door said suddenly. I looked up to find that she was staring at me with the utmost hatred. Her eyes were red-rimmed, and the child at her side was also crying, burying her face into her mother's skirt.

'"Take *very* good care of him," she repeated. "For today my son was lost to me."

'For the first time I noticed what she and her daughter were wearing: long coats of thick brown fur. Rabbit fur. Only then did I realise what I'd done . . . that the rabbit I'd killed earlier that day wasn't really a rabbit.

'Just then, Evelyn called to ask if I'd seen her purse anywhere. I snapped back at her that I hadn't, and in my panic I used her name. The fairy woman heard it, and she smiled.

'"You have taken something dear to me," she said. "Now I shall take something that is dear to you."

'I held on to Fabian tightly, terrified she was going to steal him away. He must have picked up on my fear because he started to cry. Evelyn came back at that moment. She'd found her purse and was rummaging for some coins. I wanted to slam the door on the fairy woman then and there, but the shock of what I'd done had left me frozen. All I could do was mumble to Evelyn not to buy anything from the woman – but she just frowned at me, assuming I was being rude to the woman because she was a peddler. She handed over the money and accepted a thin, wooden flute in return. The fairy woman smiled, and then turned and made her way back through the garden towards the woods.

'I was shaking when I bolted the door, but if Evelyn noticed, she never commented. I watched her put the flute down on the mantelpiece, then she took Fabian upstairs, trying to placate him. As soon as she'd left the room I threw the flute into the fire, and stood watching as it burned away to nothing. Afterwards I collected the dead "rabbit" from the compost and looked it over. At first there seemed to be nothing out of the ordinary. Then I found it: a tiny button, almost like a waistcoat button, on the underside of the dead creature. I didn't dare to unfasten it. I couldn't bear to see what was really underneath the glamour. I went out to my den, and stayed there for the rest of the evening, waiting for Florence to arrive so I could warn her about what had happened in case the fairy came back. When I heard the car pull in later that evening, I went back into the house.

'I heard it the moment I stepped through the door – the flute was playing in the kitchen. I ran to the room. Evelyn was playing and laughing, showing the flute to Florence – the same flute I'd thrown into the fire earlier that evening. She stopped smiling when she saw my face. I asked her where she'd found it. She looked puzzled, and told me it was on the mantelpiece where she'd left it.

'I knew then that the flute was enchanted, and that it could not be destroyed by normal means. I waited until Evelyn had gone to bed, and then I hid it in my den, wondering if perhaps it could remain hidden as long as I didn't try to destroy it. I told Florence what had happened, and she told me to go and ask the old gypsy woman's advice in the morning.

'That night I lay awake for hours, too afraid to sleep. Eventually though, I must have dozed off, because I awoke with a start. The room was still dark, and beside me the bed was empty. Evelyn was gone. I reached over and touched the space where she'd lain – it was still warm, so I knew she hadn't been gone long. I lay back, thinking that maybe she had gone to check on Fabian. Then I heard the faintest strains of a flute playing.

'I was up and dressed in seconds, out of the room and shouting to Florence to check on Fabian. I ran through the house, calling Evelyn's name and running into every room. It started a complete commotion – Fabian was crying, and upstairs my father was upset too. I had no time to comfort either of them. I raced downstairs. The kitchen door was open slightly. That's when I knew she'd gone outside. I ran round to the front of the house, unlocked my den and went in. The flute was where I'd left it, yet still I could hear faint notes being played from an eerie melody behind the house. I ran back through and into the garden, calling her name. Through the gate I saw a figure in the distance, walking towards the woods, as though in a trance. It was Evelyn, still in her white nightgown, lit by the moon.

'I chased after her, calling her name, but she never turned back. It was as though she couldn't hear me. Then she vanished – one minute she was there, and the next she was gone. I ran towards where I'd seen her last, just about to cross the brook on the stepping stones. I arrived no more than two minutes after she'd stood there, yet there was no sign of her. I didn't know what to do. I yelled until I was hoarse. I crossed the water and ran into the woods, and out again, twice. And all the while that flute was playing its awful, cursed melody.

'By then the sun had started to come up. I forced myself to think, then I remembered something about running water breaking enchantments. I suddenly had a strong feeling that she wouldn't have crossed the brook. Taking a chance, I started to jog to the right, following the brook. For the next few minutes I saw nothing. I was about to give up and go back to the manor to call for more help. Then I saw her.'

Stitch's voice broke then. Red said nothing, knowing that he had come to the most painful part of his past.

'She was face down in the water, tangled in the weeds. I jumped in and pulled her out. She wasn't breathing. Her eyes were open, but unseeing. Her skin was blue and icy cold from the water. I tried to resuscitate her – but it was too late. She was gone. Only then did I realise that the wretched music had stopped . . . with her heart, so it would seem.

'I carried her back to the manor and called for help. Soon after, an ambulance arrived, along with the police. I told Florence to stay out of the room and to keep Fabian away. When they took her away, I knew they thought I was responsible. Why was she out in the night like that? Why was she in her nightgown? Why hadn't I called for help as soon as I knew she was missing? They just kept firing questions at me.

'To make matters worse, there was a wound on the back of her head. And then later . . . as the brook was searched for clues, traces of her blood were found on one of the stepping stones. She'd tried to cross, slipped and hit her head. She was unconscious when she drowned.'

'How did they find out you weren't responsible?' Red whispered.

Stitch wiped his face across his face and sighed.

'From Evelyn's medical history. Records proved she was prone to sleepwalking, something she'd been doing since she was a teenager. I remembered her talking about it but had never known her to do it in the time we'd been married – apparently it was something that was triggered by stress. But I knew she hadn't been sleepwalking, and I knew what I'd heard. That ghostly tune, echoing out over the fields. It lured her to her death. When I went back to my den the following day, the flute was gone. I never saw it again.

'After that I asked Florence to lock the music room. I never went into it again, and I didn't want Fabian in there either. Soon he gave up asking. I promised myself that I'd explain it all to him one day . . . that I'd tell him the truth about how his mother had died. That it wasn't the accident he'd grow up believing. I told myself that once he was old enough to handle it, I'd tell him about the fairies. In the end he found out on his own.'

'About how his mother died?' Red asked.

Stitch shook his head slowly.

'About the fairies. I'm still searching for the right words to tell him the rest. Somehow I never seem to be able to find them.'

'You should just tell him. I've heard your story and I don't think it was your fault.'

'I don't know if he'd see it that way. And I don't think I could bear it if he wouldn't forgive me. Still, it's only what I deserve.'

'You think you deserve to be unhappy?' said Red.

Stitch shrugged and rubbed his nose.

'Maybe. Who knows. I don't think I'll ever be happy again, not truly. Not without her.'

He pulled his horse up short and pointed to the ground suddenly. 'Look.'

There was a dirt path, overgrown but still just visible beneath the horses' hooves.

'It's a good sign,' said Stitch. 'We must be nearing the edge of the woods. We need to keep our wits about us now – no more talking. This must be where the Dead Wood ends.'

He was right. Presently, Red noticed a significant change in their surroundings. Birds sang and chirruped, undergrowth twitched and rustled, and once or twice she caught sight of small tree fey, peeping out from their nests. She jumped as something caught in her hair, and reached up to try and extract herself after halting her horse. There she found a thick, twiggy branch of a knobbly old tree. As she twisted around, she could swear the tree moved – swaying a little – and the twigs curved further into her hair.

'Stitch! I'm caught up.'

He turned and trotted back, waiting momentarily as the colt trailing behind paused to rip up a mouthful of grass.

'Keep still,' he said, studying the tree. 'It's just curious. It probably hasn't seen many humans in its time.'

Red slowly lowered her hand, staying very still, not daring to look up at the living tree. Her scalp itched with each brush of its gnarled fingers, and a couple of times she felt strands of hair get caught and plucked out. Then it withdrew, and gave a long, creaking sigh.

'Come on,' said Stitch. 'Keep moving.'

The next hour passed without incident, although fairy life was far more prominent now they were out of the Hedgewitch's domain. Soon Red smelled a familiar scent in the air; one that somehow reminded her of Sunday lunch. It was masked by another smell; something unpleasant that was earthy and musky. She looked at Stitch and saw him staring through the trees at the stream. Only then did she realise there was something odd about it.

'It's flowing uphill!' she exclaimed.

Stitch nodded. 'I've heard of this place. That smell – the herby one – is rosemary. But not just any rosemary. It's piskie-tainted.'

'Piskie-tainted?'

'Look down.'

Beneath the horses' hooves, clumps of dark, stinking matter were being trampled; some dried and cracked, some fresh and oozing.

'Piskie dung,' said Stitch. 'This is their domain. The rosemary that grows here is very magical – it can tamper with memories. We should pass as quickly and quietly as possible. Piskies can be volatile if they're disturbed.'

Sure enough a jabbering sound had begun around them. The next thing Red knew, a pine cone hit her in the temple. She winced, turning to a giggle and a doughy-looking, spiteful little face ducking out of view.

Stitch was hit next by a pebble, lifting his arm a fraction too late to defend himself as another small figure bobbed out of sight.

'Hurry,' he muttered, clicking his horse on. Soon the jabbering faded as they left the piskies behind.

Red wondered how long they had been on the move now.

She was hungry; her stomach gurgling. She placated it several times with huge gulps of water but its protestations gradually grew louder. She was about to ask Stitch if they could stop for a break to eat, when they came upon the edge of the woods. Her heart leaped at the promise of finally being free of the gloom, out beneath the sky instead of the branches.

'Let's stop over there,' said Stitch, motioning to a dip in the grass beyond the woods. 'It's sheltered from sight, and we can tether the horses over there – it's right by the stream. It should be safe for us to stop a while and eat.'

Red followed him gratefully, urging her horse on a little faster to be free of the trees. They were almost on the border when Stitch's horse suddenly reared up in terror. She saw him sliding from the saddle and gasped, but then he managed to grasp hold and right himself, bringing the frightened animal back under his control.

She stiffened as she saw what had made the horse rear up. Two figures stood silhouetted in the opening of the trees, blocking their exit from the woods.

18

NSTINCTIVELY, RED TUGGED HER horse's reins to the left, preparing to head back into the woods at speed.

'Hold it!' Stitch yelled, before she could dig her heels in. He dismounted his horse and went to stand next to the two figures, waiting expectantly for her to join them. Slowly, Red brought the horse back around but stayed in the saddle.

'It's all right,' said Stitch. 'They're not going to harm us.'

Red eyed the two strangers properly for the first time. The first was a young, dark-skinned fey man with gleaming golden eyes. Beneath a black hooded cloak, he wore an impeccably stitched suit of leaves.

The woman next to him was older, her colouring a stark contrast to the fairy man's. Her ivory skin was almost translucent, and her black hair carried the same oily blue-green sheen as her gown of ebony feathers. Red recalled Stitch's account of the large black bird that had transformed into a woman before his eyes.

'You're the raven, aren't you?' she said.

216

The woman stared back at her, her black eyes glistening.

'It's one of the names I go by, yes.' She motioned to her yellow-eyed companion. 'And this is Gredin.'

Red stayed in the saddle. Stitch gestured to the grassy knoll they had been heading for before Raven and Gredin had found them.

'We've been travelling since daybreak,' he told them. 'We were just about to rest awhile and eat.'

'Good,' said Gredin, curtly. 'We will join you. And then we can start thinking about how to get you out of this mess.'

They tethered the horses by the water and ate after Stitch and Gredin made a kill.

Raven had removed from her cloak a small, hedgehog-like creature, which was now snuffling for insect life near to where Red was sitting. Red was unable to take her eyes off it.

'I can't tell you its real name,' Gredin said, watching her. 'But Tanya calls it "the Mizhog".'

Red looked up into Gredin's intense golden stare. Evidently Stitch had told Gredin about her connections with Tanya whilst they had hunted in the woods.

'I've seen one before,' she muttered, turning back to the Mizhog. 'It used to follow me everywhere before . . . the accident.'

Gredin nodded. 'Your guardian.'

'My *what*?'

'Your fairy guardian,' he repeated, bemused. 'All children born with the ability to see fairies have one.'

The Mizhog settled by her foot to chew on a worm.

'I didn't know,' Red said. 'It was just . . . there. I never questioned it. I don't even know if it had a name. I never gave it a name of my own.' She gazed at Gredin. 'If Florence was able to call upon Raven then that must mean that Raven is . . .'

'Florence's guardian,' Stitch interrupted.

'So, I'm guessing you're Tanya's guardian, then?' Red asked Gredin.

'Yes.' Gredin was watching her intently. 'If it's any consolation, she didn't know about guardians until recently, either.'

'So what does a guardian actually *do*?' Red asked.

'We protect our elected human's best interests,' said Raven. 'Those of relevance to the fairy world, that is. If we think a human will benefit from knowing more – or less – about the fairy world, then we endeavour to make it so.'

'How would we benefit from knowing less, though?' Red persisted. 'Surely it's better to know *more*?'

'Not if it leads to trouble,' Raven said, her birdlike eyes fixed on Red in a penetrating stare. 'We tried to shield Tanya from too much knowledge, yet she still managed to find certain things out.' The fairy woman's tone was suddenly icy, and Red knew that her relation of fairy information to Tanya had not gone unnoticed, or forgotten.

'And look where it led her,' Gredin said softly. 'Into a situation she thought she could handle, when really she had no idea of what she was getting herself into.'

'But Red's fairy, this rodent-like thing,' Stitch interrupted hastily. 'What happened to it?'

'It died,' said Red, shooting him a grateful look. 'Protecting James from harm in the accident.'

'Protecting your best interests,' Gredin reiterated, then turned away dismissively.

Stitch recounted the events that had brought him and Red together. Much of it had already been told to Gredin on their trip into the woods, and so it appeared to be more for Raven's benefit.

Red found herself distracted by the Mizhog. It had dribbled pieces of chewed worm on her trouser leg and was now licking at it frenziedly. Red dragged her soggy leg away, but the greedy little Mizhog trotted after it determinedly. She gritted her teeth and moved again, but the Mizhog looked up at her with such a mournful expression that she found herself moving her leg back and allowing it to continue its disgusting feast.

'We can get you out easily,' Gredin was saying to Stitch. 'We know of an entrance we could use with little chance of complication.' He cast a glance at Red. 'With you, it's not so simple. We could get you out, but you'd only get brought back again. When you traded places with Tanya, you effectively gave yourself to the fairy realm. To get out you must trade places with someone else with the second sight or arrange some other kind of bargain.'

'I'll worry about that after I've found my brother,' said Red.

Gredin's eyes gave away nothing, but when he spoke next, there was a measure of respect in his voice.

'Very well. Raven will take Stitch back to the manor. I will accompany you to the courts. But be warned that I can have no sway over what happens there – I hold no power in the court. Once you're there, you're on your own.'

'No,' said Stitch. 'I don't think you understand. I've pledged to help Red now. I'm not going back without her.'

Red shook her head. 'You've already helped me. You should go back.'

'I'm staying,' he repeated. 'Whatever happens.'

Raven and Gredin exchanged a look.

'Then Gredin will guide you both,' said Raven. 'I'll return to the manor with the news that we've found you.'

Stitch nodded, a worry line appearing in his forehead. 'Tell them that Nell is still missing, too.'

Stitch and Gredin went over the map, discussing the quickest route to their destination. Gredin, already familiar with the realm, had little use for the map except to demonstrate to Stitch the best path for them.

Too soon, Stitch was looking up at the sky as he made ready the horses.

'We should get going. There's still a long way ahead of us.'

They said their goodbyes to Raven before her bird form took over once more. Then she was in the air, soaring above the forest, and gone.

They mounted their horses, Gredin leaping lithely onto

the third. His golden eyes narrowed as he surveyed the landscape, and then they moved off onto the open land, the fey man slightly in the lead and Stitch and Red on either side of him.

Miles of nothingness stretched before them, but for green hills and a ribbon of road threading through it. They headed for the road, heads down against a rising wind. There was little conversation; Gredin was not a companionable guide. Soon the sun was gone, enveloped by murky rain clouds. Red threw the fox-skin coat around her shoulders but did not fasten it, instead holding it closed with her hand. When the rain started the coarse fur kept her dry and warm, and beneath the pointed ears she dipped her head to keep her face out of the wind.

Through the wind hissing past her ears, she heard Gredin shouting for them to move faster.

Her thighs burned with the effort of staying on the horse. Dirt and grit flew up from the horses' hooves and, though she stayed quite dry, soon she began to tire. Onwards they rode in what felt like the longest journey of Red's life.

The first sign of shelter was another traveller on the road, coming in the opposite direction. It was a carriage, drawn by two horses that were foaming at the mouth.

'Whoa!' Gredin cried, slowing his horse and moving to one side to allow the carriage by. As it passed, Red glimpsed the coachman. At first sight he looked almost human, yet as her gaze travelled down she saw that one leg ended in a wet-looking frog's foot which was splashing happily in the water sliding across the coach's wooden surface.

'Over there,' called Stitch, pointing further along the road once the way was clear once more. Red looked through the sheets of rain. Beyond, there was the faint outline of a town.

They drew nearer. With darkness descending, it was plain that they would be resting here for the night.

'Stay behind me,' Gredin warned. 'Do not accept anything to eat or drink without my say-so, and let me do the talking.'

Shabby cottages of wood and stone fringed the town. In one or two places a wooden door in a rocky face or a hole in the ground belied the dwelling of some fey creature. The gravel road gave way to cobblestone, and further in the buildings knotted together to form streets and alleys; much to Red's surprise there were even little shops nestled in-between.

Gredin halted outside an inn.

'Wait here,' he told them, sliding neatly off his horse and vanishing through a wooden door that was at least a head smaller than he was.

While she and Stitch waited for him to return, Red peered up at the building. Hanging from the wall was a faded sign displaying the name of the inn: *The Pauper's Platter*.

When Gredin reappeared he was accompanied by a goblin less than half his height with an enormous nose.

Taking his horse's reins from Stitch, Gredin beckoned as the goblin innkeeper hurried around the side of the building.

'Leave your horses here,' the innkeeper grunted, pushing open a high, wide door that led into a stable. 'They'll be looked after.' He summoned a stable-hand with green-tinged skin as they dismounted and then made their way back out to the inn door.

'The rooms are small, but they're warm and dry,' their goblin host continued, ushering them through. Once inside, he left them.

The inn was dimly lit and the air was thick with a herby smoke. Red kept her head down but took in her surroundings from out of the corner of her eye, careful not to meet anyone's gaze. At the centre was an ancient tree, its trunk so stout that Red suspected that even if she and Stitch and Gredin were to join hands they wouldn't be able to meet around it. Its branches curved and dipped overhead, and from some of the branches lanterns glowed.

On the floor there were places where the roots had pushed up through the ground; the stonework floor had been laid to accommodate them, and in one or two curves of the exposed roots fairies sat whilst they supped at their ale.

'Take a seat,' Gredin said, gesturing to a darkened nook. 'I'll collect our key, and something to eat and drink.'

Red and Stitch slipped into the space to sit either side of a small wooden table. It was enclosed due to a partition of branches that hung low. They sat in silence until Gredin returned. Red could tell that they had attracted a few curi-ous glances already – but whether it was because she and Stitch were human, or merely strangers, it was impossible to say. When Gredin came back he placed a key on the table and took a seat.

Without warning, one of the tree's branches suddenly swooped towards them. Impulsively, Red ducked, but Gredin gave a low chuckle.

'It's all right.'

She sat up again, feeling foolish. She realised now that the branch hadn't come to attack, but to set a platter on the table before retreating. Looking around the inn, she waited for a few moments, and then another branch swooped out carrying another platter to a different table.

The platter held bread and some hard-looking cheese, meat, some fruit, a bowl of eggs still in their shells, a full pitcher containing a dark liquid, and three stoneware mugs. Gredin poured himself a little of the liquid, drinking cau-tiously and warning Red and Stitch with his eyes to wait until he gave the go-ahead. After a sip, he nodded and filled their mugs, then took a slow bite of the bread. He did not nod this time, but simply divided the portion into three and pushed it towards them.

Red sipped her drink dubiously. It tasted sweet and vaguely familiar, yet there was a slightly bitter aftertaste.

'What is it?' she asked.

'Beesmead,' Gredin answered. 'It's made from honey and a small amount of hops.'

'It's nice,' she said, taking a gulp that almost emptied her mug. She held it in her mouth to savour the taste. Gredin noticed.

'Eat and drink as much as you like,' he said. 'You'll never go hungry here.' He took her mug and placed it back on the platter. There was a light gurgle and the mug refilled.

'How did you do that?'

Gredin reached into his cloak and removed a small drawstring pouch. He cupped it in his hands and drew the drawstrings through his fingers repeatedly.

'Ever heard of the Thirteen Treasures?' he asked, looking at first Red, then Stitch.

Red nodded and glanced at Stitch. He was brushing crumbs from his increasingly bristly chin.

'I know a little of them,' he said. 'An old legend, isn't it? To do with the fairy courts? In fact, that reminds me . . .' He wiped grease from his fingers and pulled the old charm bracelet out of his pocket. 'I'm pretty sure this is based on them. It belonged to the first lady of Elvesden Manor, who was a changeling.' He passed the piece of jewellery to Gredin.

'I remember this,' said Gredin, his dark brow furrowing as his long, thin fingers moved over the charms like spiders' legs. 'It was the cause of the drain-dweller's unfortunate demise.'

'Let me see.' Red held out her hand for the bracelet, and examined each of the charms in turn. She knew them by heart, having committed them to memory with the rest of the information she'd hoarded in her mind. 'The Sword, the Book, the Goblet, the Cauldron . . . they're all here,' she muttered. 'I never paid attention to it when I saw it before.' She set it on the table, then looked at Gredin expectantly.

'So, what do the Thirteen Treasures have to do with this place?'

Gredin twisted the cord of the drawstring bag around his fingers once more.

'One of the treasures – the Platter – was enchanted so that it would never let its owner go hungry. There's a story that once, before the division of the great court, a human man – a farmer – and his family showed hospitality to a fairy in disguise, even though the family was poor and had little for themselves. As repayment the fairy took the man before the court and requested that he be rewarded. The court bestowed the power of the Platter upon the farmer and his family for all their days – and for their descendants. Their farm prospered from that day forth. As well as every meal that was prepared replenishing itself until each member had eaten their fill, their crops grew well, and their livestock was healthy and plentiful. Many years later, when the farmer was old and had passed the care of the farm over to his son, the fairy who had visited all those years ago paid the farm another visit. This time his daughter accompanied him, and at first sight she fell in love with the farmer's son. The farmer agreed for his son and the fairy girl to marry, and so the farmer's son returned to the fairy realm with his new wife and set up a little inn to trade from and to live in. Bestowed with his father's good fortune, the inn flourished with its portions of food and ale that would never fail to satisfy any appetite, and . . .' Gredin spread his hands wide, and glanced around them, '. . . it continues to do so today.'

'This is the inn?' Red asked, with another happy sip of the beesmead.

Gredin shrugged. 'So it's said.'

She leaned back. The story was comforting, almost like one of the fairy tales from her book. She yawned, full and suddenly drowsy.

'We should rest,' said Stitch. 'We've still got a long way ahead of us, and we should start out early again.'

Gredin nodded, finally opening the drawstring bag in his hand and shaking out several silver coins. Red reached for one of them.

'I've never seen fey money before,' she said curiously. On one side, a tree in full blossom was etched into the coin's surface. She flipped it over to see what was on the other side. 'It's a tree again,' she said aloud. 'Only this time it's like a skeleton, without any leaves.' She replaced it and reached for another. This one was larger, and showed six familiar symbols on one side.

'What do you see?' asked Gredin.

'A platter, a heart, a candelabrum, a dagger, a staff, and a key.'

'And on the other side?'

Red turned it over.

'A book,' she said slowly. 'A ring. A sword, a cup . . . a goblet, a mask . . . and a cauldron.'

'The Thirteen Treasures,' said Stitch.

Gredin nodded. 'Every fairy coin represents the two faces of the courts: the Seelie and the Unseelie.' He pointed to the coin with the tree. 'The side that's in bloom represents spring and summer – the Seelie Court. The other side, where the tree is barren, is autumn and winter – the Unseelie.' He arranged the coins carefully on the table.

'You're leaving them all Seelie side up,' Red noticed.

'It's the custom,' said Gredin. 'Coins used in payment must be offered with the side up that represents the court that is currently ruling. To do otherwise is believed to be bad luck. If witnessed by a member of the courts it could be seen as treachery or disrespect, resulting in a penalty. So we always give them the right way.' His face clouded then. 'And in two days, it changes once again.'

Red suddenly went cold.

'What do you mean, "two days"?' she asked.

'The changeover of the courts,' Gredin replied. 'From the Seelie to the Unseelie. We call it Samhain, but I believe you humans know it as "Hallowe'en".'

'*What?*' Red jumped up, knocking her stool over and upsetting her beesmead. Across from them, a fey woman with a scarred face looked over.

'SIT,' Gredin hissed, his golden eyes ablaze.

Red obeyed, but fear rose within her.

'I don't understand,' she said hoarsely. 'How can it be in

two days? I knew some time had passed but I had no idea how much! How can it be almost Hallowe'en now?'

Stitch placed his hand on her arm.

'Red,' he said gently. 'Nearly three months have passed since the night you came into the fairy realm. I don't know how long the Hedgewitch kept you in that cellar . . . it may have only felt like a day, but you've been here a lot longer than that.'

'It wasn't the Hedgewitch,' Red said slowly. 'When I first got in I was being chased. I needed a place to hide, so I climbed into the hollow of a tree with rowan berries grow-ing around it . . . they were green when I went in. And when I awoke the next morning they were red . . . ripe.'

'Anything else?'

'Yes – my hair had grown . . . and before I got in I cut my hands on Spidertwine. But the next day the cuts had healed.'

'A time slip, then,' Gredin muttered. 'It's not uncommon when a human enters the fairy realm. The clash of one thing from one world entering the other can often result in a slip. Sometimes it can be years . . . decades, even.'

Red stared at her scarred hands. 'You make it sound like I should be grateful.'

'You should,' said Gredin, unflinching.

'Why didn't it happen to Stitch?' she asked, turning to him. 'How could you come into the realm and meet up with me? Wouldn't there have been another time slip?'

'No,' said Stitch. 'Because I didn't come in alone, or of my own accord. I was brought in by fairies – in which case there would be no time slip.'

Red began to tremble. 'We need to get to the courts before they change over! It has to be the Seelie court that gives me an audience – it can't be the Unseelie! It *can't*! We have to leave, right now! We have to keep going!'

'We are making good time,' Gredin said stiffly. 'The Seelie court will see you and hear the case for your brother – I am confident of that. Tonight we rest, and tomorrow we ride hard. But before that, I want to hear about the night your brother vanished.'

Without hesitation, Red began.

19

SLEEPING WAS PROVING *difficult for Rowan, especially since she now feared for James's safety whenever he was out of her sight. Since the trip to the library, she'd hunted out every red item of clothing in the home that might be suitable for James to wear. She stole some red flannelette trousers and a pair of red socks from other children's wardrobes and the laundry.*

She dressed him in them only when she knew he was going to be out of her sight, but the thought that he would only remain safe for as long as he stayed silent worried her a great deal. He was prone to waking and calling out for her. As a result, her own sleep was fitful; she awoke three or four times every night to check on him.

Making the items last was also a challenge. Twice she dug the little red trousers out of the laundry basket to use again, once the backs of the watchful staff were turned.

Although she hoped that what had happened to Megan was a one-off, she took no chances. Her fears were soon realised. One day, three weeks after the trip to the library, Rowan went into the nursery to check on James. Straight away she could tell something was wrong. Two worried-looking carers were hovering around one of the cots, speaking in low voices. She stepped closer to catch what they were saying.

'. . . doesn't look good. How long has he been like this?'

'Since first thing this morning.'

'I think we need to call the doctor.'

Rowan stepped aside as one of the women turned to leave the room quickly, brushing past her.

'Is something wrong?' she called to the one that remained.

'Nothing to worry about,' came the forced cheerful reply. 'Why don't you take James out for some fresh air?'

Rowan eyed James, who was sitting up in his cot, gurgling to himself. Something – perhaps curiosity, perhaps intuition – made her draw closer to the crib with the sick child.

As soon as she laid eyes on it she could see the child had been switched – like Megan. Only this time, the thing that lay there instead of the human was plainly very ill. There were dark shadows beneath its eyes and its breathing was shallow. It looked up at her, and whatever mask it wore slipped beneath her gaze; it was a fairy, no question. And the reason it had been switched was its illness, she felt sure of it. It had been switched with a healthy child.

'Best keep James away,' said the carer. She flitted over to the other cots, checking on the children one by one. 'Oh, no . . .' She paused beside another of the children.

Rowan's heart lurched. Already she knew what was coming.

'It's another one, isn't it?' she asked. 'Another one is . . . ill.'

'Yes. I think you'd better take James out, now.'

Rowan did as she was told. She hugged James to her

tightly. How many more children would be taken? And was there anything she could do to make it stop? Before she could change her mind she hurried towards John's door and knocked loudly.

'Come in,' he called mildly.

Once inside, she closed the door behind her.

John looked up from mounds of paperwork on his desk.

'What is it, Rowan?'

'There's something wrong in the nursery,' she said, her words coming out in a rush. 'Something's happening to the children.'

John leaned back in his chair and gestured for her to take a seat opposite him.

'Yes, I've just heard there's an illness going around,' he said. 'But you needn't worry, the doctor has been called for. Just keep an eye on James and let us know if anything develops—'

'You don't understand,' she said. 'The children . . . they aren't . . . themselves.'

'Well, of course not,' said John, his frown deepening. 'People – children – often behave strangely when they're unwell, particularly if there's a fever—'

'No!' Rowan shouted, making James jump. 'They aren't themselves! They've been switched!'

James began to cry, and John simply stared at her, saying nothing.

'You've got to listen to me,' she said urgently. 'The children are being replaced with . . . things that aren't human.'

John continued to watch her in a way that made it plain she was being assessed.

233

'Rowan,' he said gravely. 'What exactly are you proposing the children are being switched with?'

'Fairies.' She said it firmly but quickly, and her eyes did not waver from John's. There was, she noticed, a curious lack of reaction.

Wordlessly, John got up and walked over to an ugly grey filing cabinet. He rifled through the drawer labelled 'F' and selected a file. He carried it back to his desk and opened it.

'Changelings?' he said gently. 'I'm familiar with the concept. Rather fond of Victorian fairy art. It's a common theme.'

She gritted her teeth. 'Yes.'

'I looked at your file before you arrived.' He flicked to a page that had been bookmarked with a yellow Post-it note. 'It says here that, in your statement to the police following the car accident, you admitted that you wouldn't normally have been in the car with your parents at that time or on that route. It was unusual, wasn't it?'

She nodded.

'Can you tell me why it was unusual?'

'Because . . .' She cleared her throat. 'Because I should have been at school. But instead I went to London that day. We were only in the car because my parents found out where I was and came to find me. If . . . if I'd gone to school then I would have walked home as I normally did . . . the accident would never have happened.'

'The accident would still have happened,' John said. 'It would just have happened to someone else. I've set up a meeting for you with a counsellor who is going to explain this to you in more

234

detail, as it's important that you understand that it wasn't your fault. For now, though, I want to discuss what you were doing that day, instead of being at school.'

'There was an exhibition,' Rowan said. 'Of fairies in art and photographs. I went to go and see it.'

'Why did you go alone?' John asked. 'Why didn't your parents take you at the weekend, or in the holidays?'

'They didn't like me talking about fairies,' Rowan said.

'Why not?'

'Because they refused to believe what I'm telling you now – that fairies are real. But if someone doesn't start believing me, the children here are going to be switched, one by one.'

John leaned over and scrawled a note on a piece of paper.

'What makes you think that the children here are at risk? To be snatched by fairies, I mean?'

Rowan opened her mouth to answer, then paused to consider the question carefully.

'Perhaps it's because the children here are more vulnerable,' she said tentatively. 'If they have someone to love them already, and care for them, then they'd be missed. Maybe that's it – they take the ones that they think won't be missed.'

'I can see why you might think that,' John said gently. 'And why this interest of yours has escalated since your parents' death. It's normal to want to believe in something. It's your mind's way of coping.' He closed her file. 'I think that's enough for now.'

Rowan got up. The conversation was over, and she felt foolish to have even attempted to convince another adult of the truth. By the time she reached her room, her embarrassment had been replaced by anger. She had to get herself and James out of this place. The letter to her Aunt Rose was her only hope. Following a hospital appointment that afternoon, she was gladdened to hear that her plaster cast would be taken off in two weeks. When she arrived back, she began drafting out her letter to Aunt Rose with her right hand. Her writing looked dreadful, but each version was improved in content.

The next morning, Rowan awoke to pandemonium. Footsteps thundered along the corridors accompanied by low voices.

Rowan jumped out of bed and pulled her cardigan on over her pyjamas, then crept out into the corridor. Ahead of her, the cleaner was hurrying downstairs after John and two other staff members. Rowan followed, her bare feet allowing her to be stealthy as a snake. Her pace quickened as she realised they were heading for the nursery. Some of the other children were up, milling around, and being barked at to go back to their rooms.

Outside the nursery door, Rowan paused and listened. Through a crack by the hinges she could see that James was in his cot, and at once her pounding heart began to slow. He was safe. But something else was going on. She pressed her ears against the crack.

'They can't have just disappeared!' John snapped. 'Don't keep telling me that!'

'But they have,' a female voice insisted.

'It's bleedin' odd,' said the cleaner. 'But they must be some-where. Someone's playing a trick, I'll say. Too coincidental, what with the other little girl wandering off the other week. Still, we found her, so the other two can't have gone far.'

Two, Rowan thought. Two children have vanished.

'I think you're right,' John said, his voice suddenly hard. 'Someone's playing tricks. And I think I know who.' His footsteps thudded towards the door. Rowan looked around and saw that there was nowhere she could get to quickly enough to hide, so she simply stood there, waiting.

The door was flung open and John regarded her. He didn't seem at all surprised to see her there.

'I want a word with you,' he said.

'Pardon?' said Rowan.

'Into my office. Now.'

Numbly, Rowan followed, with one last glimpse over her shoulder to ascertain that James was safe.

'All right,' said John, before the door was even closed. 'Two of the babies weren't in their beds this morning. Do you have any idea of where they are?'

'What?' Rowan said, feeling sick. 'You can't think . . . that I had something to do with this?'

'Bit of a coincidence, isn't it?' John said grimly. 'The day after you insist children are being stolen by fairies, two children mysteriously vanish?'

'It's nothing to do with me,' said Rowan, angrily. 'I'd never play a trick like that! I'll help you look for them.'

'People are already looking. They've been looking for an hour. And what's interesting is that one of the children can only crawl, and the other has only just learned to sit up! Common sense says they couldn't have gone far. And my common sense is telling me that they were moved by somebody.'

'It wasn't me,' Rowan repeated.

'Is that the truth? Because to put the safety of others at risk is more than a simple prank, Rowan. It's serious.'

'I swear to you, I don't know where they are,' she whispered. 'How can you think that?'

John's expression relented suddenly.

'Very well. Collect James from the nursery, and then go back to your room.'

Hours passed, and there was no sign of the missing children. A horrid nagging feeling ate away at Rowan like a rat. If the fairies were to blame, then why hadn't they left replacements for the children? Surely they wouldn't just steal two babies . . . snatch them away into thin air? But as the morning went on, and the children were not found, it seemed the likeliest explanation.

It was noon before the children were called down from their rooms for something to eat. Extra staff had been called in to deal with the crisis, and the police had been called and were asking everybody questions. When Rowan's turn came, she told the absolute truth about what she had seen and heard – which was nothing. On the subject of fairies she maintained a sensible silence.

'Have you heard what's happening?' Polly said breathlessly, rushing over to her after she rejoined the common room. 'We're being moved. They're transferring us to other homes!'

'They are? When?'

Polly gestured to her twin. 'We've been told to pack up our

things this afternoon! We're going to Kent.' She scanned the room. 'Sally's been given a place in a foster home,' she said enviously. 'She's leaving tomorrow. I suppose it's only fair. She's been here longest.'

'What about me?' Rowan asked, but Polly was already shaking her head.

'You'll have to wait and see what John says.'

Just then, the cleaner came bustling over.

'All right, pet?' she said to Polly, patting her on the head. She turned to Rowan. 'Mr Temple has asked for you.'

Rowan leaped up and ran to John's office, bursting in without knocking.

'Are you moving me and James?' she demanded.

'Yes,' John said. Through his worry, he managed a smile. 'I've some good news. We finally managed to contact your Aunt Primrose.'

'It's Rose,' Rowan said nervously. 'She doesn't like to be called Primrose, my mother says . . . said.'

John nodded. 'Rose has agreed to care for you and James on a permanent basis. There are a few matters that need ironing out, such as the living conditions,' he wrinkled his nose, 'and you'll be visited by a social worker during the settling-in period, but it's wonderful news.'

Rowan's eyes filled with tears of relief. Now there was no need for her to write the wretched letter!

'Thank you,' she said with a sniff. 'When is she coming?'

'She doesn't have a car,' John answered. 'And she needs a home check, which normally takes a few days. However, she's been abroad, which is why we had problems contacting her, and she's become rather ill on her return, so it's likely to be a couple of weeks until she's well enough to come for you. You have one more night here, and then you'll be off to London for a couple of weeks. She'll collect you from there, and she'll be coming by train.'

He crossed the room and patted her arm awkwardly.

'You're going to be fine. You're a good girl. Now, why don't you make a start on that packing?'

It was during the manic packing process that a staff member with an inventory spotted the 'mix-up' with the babies' clothes and returned the two items Rowan had stolen to their rightful owners. Rowan could have cried with frustration. It was close to bedtime, and she had nothing to protect James. Luckily, it had been agreed that James could sleep in her room in his cot for that final night.

Then, as Rowan helped with the bedtime drinks, she spied a bright red tea towel in the kitchen. It was grubby but she didn't care. She snatched it and stuffed it under her dressing gown.

Later, when everything was packed, she folded down the lid of her suitcase, keeping it unzipped for the last few bits in the morning. Fresh clothes were laid out on top of it for them both.

James was curled up like a hamster, his thumb wedged in his mouth. Pulling the tea towel out, she gently laid it over his bedclothes and then clambered into bed, reading from her book of fairy tales until she was drowsy. When her eyelids eventually began to droop, she laid the book on the bedside table and turned out the light.

*

She did not know what it was that woke her, although at times later on she wondered if it had been the smell. It was the first thing she had noticed; that earthy, damp scent that filled her nostrils. The second thing she saw, through her sleep-narrowed eyes, was the outline of a figure standing over her. Muzzily she lay there, assuming one of the staff was going to extra lengths to check on the children that night. However, something about the way the figure was standing alerted her to the fact that it had been there for some time, silent and watchful. And it was for this reason that, although she had started to tremble, she kept her eyes narrowed and pretended to be asleep.

The figure reached out and ran a finger along something on the bedside table. On the finger was a silver ring with something inscribed into its stone. A familiar shape jumped out at her: a set of wings. There was a low noise then: a barely disguised masculine guffaw. Then the item, which Rowan now realised was her beloved book, was lifted and slipped into the folds of the figure's coat. This action was enough to make Rowan react, her fear overridden by anger. As her eyes snapped open with her mouth, ready to shout, the figure turned away from her.

As it did, Rowan's words died on her lips. A waft of air fanned from two great wings protruding from the intruder's back. The fairy moved towards the door, pausing by James's cot and gazing in. Its reason for being there could not have been clearer.

Not James, Rowan thought. Not James. He's protected. Even though she was terrified, she was comforted by the thought that the protection of the red tea towel would shield her brother from fey eyes. So when the fairy, after one last glance her way, reached inside the cot, Rowan was paralysed with shock as her sleeping brother was effortlessly lifted into its arms. Then, through the door it went, as soundlessly as it had arrived.

Suddenly, Rowan snapped out of it. She threw back the bedclothes and flew out into the empty hallway. Her hair whipped into her eyes as she turned her head this way and that, searching. At the end of the corridor was the fire exit: a sturdy wooden door with a set of stone steps leading to safety in the back gardens. Now the door was open, and through it she saw the fey creature cradling her brother at the top of the steps. From the fairy's size and features, now she was able to see more clearly, it was male with a hard-faced, flat-nosed profile. A lumpy scar bisected his upper lip.

To shout and raise the alarm when no one but herself would see the intruder would have been pointless. Her only weapon was the element of surprise. As the fairy's wings lifted and flexed in the air, Rowan broke into a stealthy run. He had lowered into a crouch, ready to take flight, when, hearing her approaching footsteps, he turned suddenly. By then, Rowan had launched herself into the air. He grunted as her attack made contact – and then, knocked off balance, they toppled over the handrail and plummeted four metres to the grass below.

Rowan had the advantage of being the lighter. The intruder landed on his back, bearing the brunt of both their weight. In the seconds following their landing she realised he was winded and struggling for breath. She heaved herself backwards, and reached out to snatch James from the fairy's grip. He was crying plaintively now, and as the sound echoed into the night Rowan felt sure someone would wake and come out. But as she looked back up at the fire exit she saw that the heavy door had quietly closed behind them – shutting her, and most of the sound, out.

Strong fingers snared her wrist. Gasping, she turned back. The intruder had recovered sufficiently to grab her and was now twisting her hand cruelly behind her back, forcing her down on her knees into the grass. The intruder stood up, still twisting.

'Why doesn't she call for help?' His low voice, evidently addressing someone other than her, came as a shock.

'Probably because she knows it won't do much good,' said another voice, a little way away.

Rowan forced her head to the side, searching the moonlit gardens. There, beneath the apple tree was a second figure. A lookout. The voice was male also, but his face remained hidden in the shadows.

'Take the child,' the first fairy instructed his accomplice.

'What? Wait, now . . . Snatcher, all you said was that I would have to keep watch. That's it. I don't want any other part of this.'

'I said, take the child,' Snatcher hissed. 'And keep it quiet.'

'Please, don't take him!' Rowan begged. A jerk to her arm shut her up.

Reluctantly, the second figure slid out from under the tree. His face was obscured by a hood.

'Please,' she tried again. 'Don't take my brother. Don't hurt him!'

'Hurt him?' Snatcher chuckled softly. 'What gives you that impression, you foolish girl?'

'What are you going to do with him?' she asked fearfully.

243

'What do you want with all these children?' James was out of sight now, tucked away in the dusky folds beneath the tree with the accomplice.

'What we want is no business of yours,' Snatcher said softly, dangerously. 'And the fact that you can see us does not make it so. Be assured, the child will be well cared for. So I suggest you go back to your nice warm bed and forget you ever had a brother.'

'Never!'

The low chuckle came again. 'You are a fiery one, aren't you?' He lifted a handful of her hair. 'Fiery, just like your red hair.'

Tears ran down Rowan's face. Her one good arm was still in his grasp. Her other arm hung uselessly at her side in its plaster. Yet, even as she thought it, she wondered if it really was so useless . . .

'If you take him, I'll find you,' she said through her teeth. 'I won't rest until I get him back!'

Snatcher gave an amused whistle.

'You hear that?' he called into the shadows. 'She's just made me a promise.' He leaned closer, his breath rushing past her ear. 'The thing is, I don't like promises that can't be kept. They upset me.' He released his grip on her arm and she collapsed forward in relief.

'Now, go,' he threatened. 'Before you come to real harm.'

Rowan stayed where she was, allowing herself a couple of little sobs. Just enough time to make it seem convincing that she was beaten. Then in one fluid motion she was on her feet, twisting her body around with her plastered arm cutting through the air. It

244

slammed into Snatcher's jaw. A split second later he spat teeth and blood. Rowan ran for the trees.

She had only taken a few paces when from behind her she heard a growl and a swoop. Snatcher had sprung into the air. Once more she was taken down, and this time, as he kicked her over to face him, she knew she really was in trouble. His eyes glowed red, and as he leaned over her, drops of his warm blood fell in her face.

'That was a mistake.' He grabbed her by her hair and forced her to her knees. 'I was willing to go easy on you,' he said, through a crooked jaw. 'I like your spirit. But now I'm tired of being patient. And when people cross me, I like to leave them a little souvenir.'

'What do you mean, a souvenir?' Rowan gasped.

'Come on, Snatcher,' his companion called anxiously. 'She's just a child.'

'Something to remember me by,' Snatcher said, his words wet and bloody. His companion remained quiet. 'Just in case you ever think of trying to cross me again.' He laughed. 'What do you say?' he called to his hidden companion. 'Shall I give her some wings?'

'What do you mean? What are you doing?' Rowan struggled, swinging her plaster behind her once more, trying to catch his knees – but this time he was too quick for her, dancing out of her way. She felt her hair being yanked from her nape and twisted into Snatcher's meaty fist. As it grew tighter, pulling at the tender skin on her neck, she suddenly felt something cold and hard being pressed into her skin. An image of Snatcher's ring with its wing insignia flashed into her mind. Then a white-hot, excruciating pain seared into the centre of her back at the top of her shoulders. It felt like her back had been set on fire.

She screamed – then choked on grass as Snatcher pressed her face into the earth, cutting off her cries. Then the pressure relented and a new sound filled her ears – a cry of pain deeper and louder than her own. Lifting herself to her elbows, she spat dirt out of her mouth and rolled onto her back in an attempt to let the cool grass ease her seared flesh. It was then that she saw golden light flickering, illuminating the darkness – and the rest of what was happening.

A terrible smell wafted over her, along with howls of pain and fury. Snatcher's wings had burst into flame, and now he was batting at them with his hands and screaming incantations to try and put them out. But nothing seemed to work. In the time it took for his companion to reach him, the flames and Snatcher's wings were gone.

'My wings!' Snatcher was shrieking, as he was led away. 'My beautiful wings! What has she done to them? How did she do that? The little witch!'

Weakly, Rowan tried to stand but the pain on her back was too much to withstand. She lay there, drifting in and out of consciousness as Snatcher and his companion vanished into the night . . . taking her little brother with them.

20

HAT WAS THE LAST TIME I EVER saw my brother,' said Red, staring into her beesmead. She lifted her hand to the top of her back, tracing the burn.

It was late now, and quiet in the Pauper's Platter; most of the punters had either left or retired to their rooms. Only a few stragglers remained, the occasional drunken snore reaching them from where someone had fallen asleep on a table, or under it.

'My shouts finally woke some of the staff and the children that were left. I was hysterical at first, shouting about fairies, but of course no one listened. Eventually I calmed down. I had to think quickly, but I was in a lot of pain. I hid the burn and dealt with it alone. I couldn't think of a way to explain it. When the police arrived I told them that I'd seen someone take James, and ran after them. It was the truth, just not the complete truth. The area was searched, but of course they never found anything. The next day they moved me to London. By then, I'd thought it all through. I knew that if I went to live with my Aunt Rose there would be no chance of finding James ever again. So I waited until my plaster was taken off two weeks later, packed a few essentials, and ran away. It's easy to disappear in London. So many people, and no one even looks at you.' She stopped to stifle a yawn, and Stitch placed a hand on her arm.

'I think that's enough for tonight,' he said. 'We need to get some rest if we're to leave early.'

Gredin nodded, looking thoughtful.

'You're sure that neither of your parents . . . had the second sight?' he asked.

Red shook her head in surprise. 'I'm sure,' she said. 'Why do you ask?'

'No reason,' said Gredin, but his eyes did not meet hers.

They rose from the table and found their rooms. As the goblin had described, they were small, but as Red sank down into a feather-stuffed mattress and wrapped a fur around herself, it was the biggest luxury she'd had in a long time.

Raven found them the next morning as they were saddling up and preparing to leave.

'The housekeeper is safe. The gypsy woman found her in the woods near to Tinker's End.'

'*Tinker's* End?' Red interrupted. 'Do you mean *Tickey* End?'

Gredin shook his head.

'Tinker's End is the name of the area in the fairy realm,' he said. 'Sometimes, in your world, the names have merged to become something similar. Occasionally, you will even find that some place names are exactly the same. It's a result of the two worlds mixing over many years – things overlap.'

'That makes sense,' said Red.

They mounted the horses and set off. This time, Stitch took the colt and Gredin and Raven rode the stallion. A chilly breeze curled around them as they travelled; a stark reminder that summer was over. The dark months were beginning.

As Gredin had promised they rode hard, stopping only once on that second day. Red's body ached from riding. Each jolt from the horse rattled her bones and her teeth but she did not complain. Every minute that passed was a minute closer to the Unseelie rule. That night, they bedded down under the stars.

On the third day the sun rose in a red sky.

'Samhain,' said Gredin.

The word sent fear slithering down Red's back like an eel.

'We're a little further away than I'd hoped,' Gredin continued. 'But we can still make it in time.'

They journeyed relentlessly, over hills and past villages large and small. All the while the sun rose above them and then gradually fell in the sky.

'Are we nearly there?' Red asked time and again. 'How much further?'

At first Gredin would grunt a response, often lost in the wind. Then he appeared not to have heard, and so she stopped asking. When yellow lights dotted the horizon she had all but given up hope that they would make it in time, but then Gredin yelled for them to keep up, and she spurred her horse on with all the strength she had left.

Faint music reached their ears as they neared the lights and, as they approached, Red saw a town similar to the one they had stayed in on the first night.

'This is it,' Gredin called, slowing his horse. 'Our destination: Avalon.' He dismounted and beckoned them to follow as they passed into the town. The music was louder now, raucous and frenzied. They followed it along the narrow stone streets, which grew busier the closer the music got. Red peered out from beneath the fox-skin coat. She was careful not to fasten it, for she did not want to transform but simply conceal herself a little from those around her.

Soon the paths were clamouring with fairies; old and young, alone and in groups, ugly and beautiful. Red felt dazed as they milled past, yet she held a thought in her mind as she looked into each face. At least one of these fey people knew where her brother was – and there was every possibility that James himself might be amongst them. She found herself staring into the face of each child as she passed, trying to imagine what he would look like now.

The centre of the town was the rowdiest. A manic dance was taking place.

'That's them!' Stitch hissed suddenly, pointing to the centre of the crowd.

Red looked and saw three musicians: a faun, a goblin and a crooked old winged man leaping about to their own music.

'They're the ones who caught me in the fairy ring!'

Beyond the fey musicians was a maypole, with dozens of fey folk dancing in time to the beat while knotting the coloured fronds of red-gold leaves that spiralled out from the pole. Some of the faces were alight with joy. Others betrayed a sense of doom and impending obligation. It was these fey people who were afraid.

'The Samhain dance,' said Raven, in a low voice. 'It is danced every year in this place, and fairies travel from all over the realm to partake. In spring, there is another dance – the Beltane dance, which celebrates the Seelie rule.'

'Keep walking,' Gredin murmured. They passed the bulk of the crowd and moved on through the streets, where the throng of fairies lessened. Now they were less conspicuous, Red allowed herself to take in her surroundings a little more. All around them was a mixture of homes, shops and inns. Half of them bustled with life, decorated in autumnal colours. The other half were dark, their shutters closed. In one little shop, curiously named 'The Cat and the Cauldron', a hand-painted sign was propped in the window.

Closed for Samhain, it read. *Back in Spring.*

Red raised her eyebrows. 'So they really do just up and leave.'

'Yes, unfortunately,' Raven grumbled. 'I was hoping we'd catch them in time but obviously we've just missed them. They do some of the best remedies around.'

'What kind of remedies?' asked Red, peering into the darkened window.

'Oh, the usual,' Gredin replied. 'Ear tip salve, that kind of thing. And their wing repair service is second to none.'

'*Ear tip* salve?' Red wondered aloud.

'For pointed ears,' Gredin explained, gesturing to his own. 'If you've been using a glamour to entice them into a rounded, more human shape they can become a little tender after a while.' He turned to Raven expectantly. 'Was it the wing-rot treatment you were after?'

Raven nodded. 'Not for *me*, you understand,' she told Red and Stitch, hastily. 'For the Mizhog. It suffers the most horrendous breakouts. Drives us mad with the scratching—' She broke off as an indignant noise sounded from the folds of her dress where the Mizhog was nestling.

Stitch's eyebrows shot up. Evidently wing-rot was not a desirable subject for discussion.

'Let's leave the horses here,' said Gredin, as they came to the end of the street. They were on the edge of the town now, with fields and pathways ahead of them. As Red looked into the distance she saw flickering lights, seemingly in mid-air.

'What are those?'

'Torchlight,' Gredin answered. 'From the Tor.'

'Glastonbury Tor,' Stitch added. 'The home of the courts.'

'We have to climb that?' she asked. 'But look how high up they are!'

'It's not as bad as it appears,' said Raven.

They set off, following a barely visible footpath that took them away from the town. Gredin led the way, pointing out a narrow stony path that had been carved into the surface of the grassy mound.

'We must hurry,' he said grimly, and after that nobody else spoke, instead saving their breath for the ascent.

Red's thighs burned with the exertion of the climb. After three days of travelling and little sleep, she was weaker and wearier than she'd ever been in her life. But now she was close – closer than she had ever been before to James.

It took around twenty minutes to reach the top. Stitch was the last to arrive. Red handed him her flask as he made it to the summit, for his lips were dry and cracked. The wind was high at the top, whistling around them and carrying strange, echoing sounds of laughter and singing. The land surrounding the vast hill was lost to darkness; just a few tiny, lit windows from the faraway town were visible.

'Are you ready?' Gredin's voice caught her off guard.

She nodded, shivering.

Gredin and Raven walked to the centre of the hill. Red and Stitch joined them.

'So where is it?' she whispered, her eyes searching. She had been expecting a grand palace once they had reached the hilltop. But all that was there was a circle of torches on the empty hill.

Gredin nodded towards his feet.

'It's below us.'

'Then how do we get in?' Stitch asked, clearly baffled.

'Like this,' said Raven. She spread her arms, motioning for them to stand in a circle and join hands. Red's heart drummed as she stepped in and completed the circle. The moment her hands touched Stitch's and Raven's, the ground rippled beneath their feet. Red jumped back in surprise, beginning to unclasp her hands – but Gredin shook his head fiercely.

'Don't break the circle!'

Red understood then, and held on tight with her eyes fixed on the ground.

The grass rippled again, and then a tuft of it curled back into a thick roll that landed at Stitch's feet.

A chink of light burst from the ground along with a chorus of voices and music. The circle of light widened as the grass unfurled, peeling back like the skin of an orange until there was a hole in the ground before them.

What it revealed was astounding: an ornate staircase of twisted roots that curved down and then split into two separate sets of steps, spiralling around each other. Beyond it, snatches of a vast hall, full of light and movement. It was magnificent, beautiful, terrifying.

It was the fairy court.

21

ASKED FIGURES IN ELABORATE costumes lifted their heads to view the newcomers on the stairs. They descended in pairs on the staircase to the right; Raven and Stitch at the front and Gredin and Red following on.

Red did not know where to look. Her eyes were being drawn everywhere; to the grandness and splendour of the hall they were coming into, the intricacy of the staircase, and the way the inhabitants of the hall were divided into two, almost cleanly split down the middle. Their eyes were disturbing her; staring and unreadable behind the masks. Her own exposed face left her feeling like prey.

A feast was in progress. Two long tables were set on either side, both laid with exquisite food and drink: roasted birds and hog, ripe, glistening fruit, golden-brown nuts, and goblets of fiery, blood-red wine. The sights and scents of it all sent saliva rushing into Red's mouth.

Each table mirrored the other, but the seated guests paid attention only to their own. Those at the table on the left of the hall were loud and boisterous, eating and drinking with gusto. In contrast, the table on the right was subdued. Red quickly deduced that the former must be the Unseelie fey, preparing for their new term of power, while the latter was the Seelie, regretful to relinquish theirs.

Beyond the tables a masked dance was taking place on a dimly lit floor. From the hillside above, twisted roots tumbled down from the domed ceiling, the longer ones culminating in gnarled wooden pillars, and the shorter ones home to garlands of autumn leaves that cascaded down to decorate the entire hall.

Overseeing the dance and the feast on a raised altar, two figures sat side by side on carved thrones, neither speaking to, nor looking at each other. The figure on the left was male, dressed in dark brown fur. His face was hidden behind his mask: the head of a stag with enormous antlers. On the right sat a woman. Her dress and mask were of brilliant blue; the iridescent, shimmering feathers of a peacock splaying out defiantly.

As they twisted further down the staircase Red saw two guards standing at the foot of each set of steps, waiting to receive them. She saw Stitch's cheek twitching, and realised he was clenching and unclenching his jaw nervously. She wondered if he regretted accompanying her, but knew as he must, that now he was here, it was too late for him to turn back.

'State your business,' one of the guards barked at Gredin, blocking the final steps into the hall.

'We have given safe passage to these two travellers,' said Gredin, gesturing first to Raven and himself, then stepping back to motion to Red and Stitch. 'They seek an audience with the court.'

The guard scoffed, the sound stifled a little from behind his mask.

'Then they have had a wasted journey. No one comes for an audience on Samhain or Beltane. It is unheard of.'

'We know of no rule that forbids it,' Raven said, her voice insistent, but respectful.

The second guard leaned in, his eyes glittering through his tree bark mask.

'It is ill-advised. I urge you to return when one court is in power – not when it is neither and both, like tonight. In less than an hour the changeover will be complete.'

'No,' said Red, clenching her fists at her sides. 'It has to be *now*. You have to let us try.'

'As you wish.' The guard stepped aside, and though Red could not see his face, she thought she heard a smile in his voice. 'On your head be it.'

They moved forward into a susurrus of whispers. The entire court was now aware of their presence, and if Red had felt exposed before on the steps, it was nothing to how she felt now. All eyes were upon them, and their simple, tatty clothing and lack of a mask marked them out as different – and more importantly, uninvited. A quick glance back at the stairwell confirmed that the grassy entrance had folded back into place after them. They were now at the court's mercy.

When they reached the dance floor the dance had stopped. The guests stood still, frozen as they waited for them to pass. Grudgingly they parted, allowing a clear path to the altar. Too soon they were there, frighteningly close to the horned man and the peacock-feathered woman. Following the example of Gredin and Raven, Red and Stitch bowed their heads and knelt before the thrones.

The whispering around them escalated to a rabble of voices, and even the music had stopped playing. Red sensed a movement from the altar. A deathly silence stole over the hall. All she could hear was the rush of her own blood as it pulsed through her ears. Daring to raise her eyes she saw that the horned man had lifted his hand for silence.

'To what do we owe this interruption of our festivities?' he asked, in a slow, musical drawl.

Red could not decide whether he sounded annoyed or bemused.

Gredin stood up, bowing his head once more before he spoke.

'Forgive us, my lord. We bring two travellers – humans – who would like an audience with you.' He beckoned Red and Stitch forward, and stood aside with Raven.

'You ask for an audience tonight, of all nights? The night of the Unseelie?'

'Yes,' Red managed, finding her voice. Hastily, she added, 'My lord,' though it pained her.

'The night is not yet yours,' the peacock woman said coldly, staring straight ahead, though her words were clearly directed at the horned man. 'Until the witching hour, it belongs to us both. Remember that.' She turned her gaze upon Red and Stitch. 'Speak, and quickly. What is your business here?'

Red heard Stitch draw breath to speak, but she got there first.

'I've come to ask for my brother.' Her voice carried easily across the silent hall. 'He was stolen from me by one of your kind. I don't know why he was taken, but I want him back.'

Her eyes skittered wildly from one to the other. She still could not see their faces, but she knew she had their utmost attention now. After all, it couldn't have been often that the relatives of human changelings knew what had happened – let alone entered the fairy court and demanded their return.

'And how is it that you have gained entry to our world?' the horned man asked. 'Were either of you invited?'

'No,' Red said quietly. 'I willingly took the place of another – someone who was imprisoned here – in order to try and find my brother.'

'Then even if your brother were to be returned to you, you are still bound by the laws of that person's imprisonment,' said the woman. 'You cannot simply leave.'

'I understand,' said Red. 'And so I'd like to enter into a bargain with you. If you give me my brother – unharmed – and my freedom, then I'll give you something that you ask in return.' She glanced at Stitch and saw that beads of perspiration dotted his upper lip.

'And you?' the horned man asked him. 'How did you come to be here?'

'I was . . . brought here against my will,' Stitch answered. 'By a group of revellers.'

'Then there is nothing to keep you here,' said the horned man, dismissively. 'You may leave.'

'This girl keeps me here,' said Stitch. 'Whatever her task is, I want to help her.'

'Well, well,' said the horned man, rubbing his hands together in cruel delight. 'What to do with you?' He glanced from Red to Stitch, and then back again. 'What makes you think you have anything that would interest *me*? That you have anything I would like to bargain for?' he sneered.

'I . . .' she began feebly, but stopped short as the peacock woman slowly turned to face the horned man – the first time she had done so in their presence.

'Their fate does not rest in your hands!' she hissed. 'The changing of the courts is not yet complete. There is one last hour of Seelie rule here tonight!'

The horned man leaped to his feet, looking down on his female counterpart.

'This is *our* night, as you well know!' he snarled. 'The feast is in progress, and no judgement shall be made that disturbs it. Instead,' he chuckled, 'they may wait until midnight is past. *Then* they shall have an audience . . . with the Unseelie Court alone!'

At this there was a roar of applause from the Unseelie table. Fists flew into the air brandishing roasted drumsticks in approval, and goblets of wine were spilled. This clashed with angry protestations from the Seelie guests nearby.

Red's knees were quaking now. This was everything she had feared. She could not afford to enter a bargain with the Unseelie court. It would be doomed to failure before she had even begun.

The Seelie leader got to her feet also, meeting the horned man's glare.

'I will not allow it. This court is still under my rule, and the plea has been entered in the presence of us both.'

Red waited for the Unseelie leader to retort – but no objection came. Instead he stood, staring hatefully at his enemy, his shoulders heaving with angry breaths. He gestured to a leafy curtain behind the two thrones.

'Let us discuss this in the chamber,' he said coldly.

The peacock woman nodded her agreement, and the curtain parted to reveal a glimpse of another room beyond. Through it Red could see a smaller table, and beyond it, a glass case of shining silver. With a jolt she recognised the Thirteen Treasures as the curtain came down like the closing of a theatre show.

The whispering in the hall began again. Red turned to Gredin and Raven, her eyes wide with fear.

'What's going on? Why have they gone back there?'

'To try and reach a decision,' said Raven. 'One that will suit them both.'

Whatever decision had been reached, it happened swiftly. For before Raven had even finished speaking the curtain lifted once more and the two fairy leaders entered the great court again. They did not take up their thrones, but gestured towards the crowd.

'Bring forth the elders!' the horned man roared.

Red turned to Raven and Gredin. 'The elders?'

Gredin leaned over and whispered into her ear. 'Each court has an elder; a fairy who has served many years upon it and can give advice and wisdom in extreme situations.'

This sent another tingle of apprehension up her spine. Scanning the courtroom, she saw a wizened little figure arise from one table and hobble towards the altar. Another was being pushed across in a wheeled chair by a younger fairy. As the chair rolled closer, Red studied its ancient passenger. Painfully thin arms and legs were twisted and weak-looking, and two bent and useless wings trailed limply over the chair's sides. From behind a feathered brown mask fashioned to look like an owl's face, wispy tufts of fluffy white hair stood up at odd angles. The mask obscured only the top half of the face, revealing a droopy white moustache with bits of food caught in it.

The other fairy was female and looked to be in slightly better condition – although no more attractive for it than the first. She had but one long tooth which protruded from her wrinkled lips, and only one functioning eye, for the other had been sewn shut a long time ago. Her working eye peered out from a helmet-like mask decorated with snails' shells.

Physically they looked close to death, but the venomous

looks they exchanged as they were assisted up onto the altar suggested that their shared hatred was very much alive. They wheeled and hobbled respectively into the chamber beyond the curtain. It fell shut with a swish.

A ripple of excitement went through the courtroom and Red's heart filled with dread. She could not bring herself to look up at Stitch, for she was afraid of what his face might tell her. However much he had insisted on helping her she knew now that she should never have agreed to it. Time dragged by unbearably. She caught the rise and fall of an animated conversation from behind the curtain but the increasing volume from the rest of the hall meant that none of the words was fully audible.

Eventually the fairies emerged from the chamber, the horned man and peacock woman taking up their thrones once more, and the decrepit elders returning to their seats in the hall.

'The elders have spoken,' the Seelie leader announced. 'And we have decided on a way forward.' She paused to look distastefully at the Unseelie side of the hall. 'This situation has arisen only once before in the known history of the courts,' she continued. 'At Beltane, almost three hundred years ago. The course of action taken was this: both courts decided upon an outcome . . . as one great court.'

A collective gasp filled the hall. Red's body was taut with anxiety.

'And so now, we will look to the ways of our forefathers. Tonight, we have heard your plea as one court, and it is as one that we will decide how it will be resolved. Fetch the stones!'

A goblin woman with a set of keys on her belt hurried to kneel before the thrones. For the first time Red saw a padlocked casket positioned between them. From it the goblin withdrew a drawstring bag of velvet, with seven tiny emblems on one side and six on the other. Red could not see what they were, but she saw the silver thread they were embroidered in and remembered the two sides of the coin Gredin had shown her at the Pauper's Platter.

The goblin snapped the casket shut again and jostled the bag. Its contents clinked softly, like bone on bone.

'You will draw stones,' said the horned man. 'Whichever stones you pull will determine a task of some kind for you. If you accept, and complete it, what you have asked of us shall be given. But first you must roll a dice from each of us. This will decide how many stones you will draw, and thus how many components your task will have.' He smiled, flashing a gleam of white, predatory teeth.

Another thrill of anticipation hummed through the court. Red felt sick. It was just a game to them, she realised. Just entertainment. And she was under no illusion that the Seelie leader had insisted on involvement through any kind of pity. It was a power play, pure and simple.

In unison the leaders withdrew two small objects from their robes. The goblin collected both and bounded eagerly over to where Red and Stitch stood, offering them each a dice from two equally sweaty hands.

Grimacing, Red took her dice, her hand shaking.

'Now throw,' the goblin instructed, poised like a cat about to pounce on a bird.

'Let's do it together,' Stitch said. 'On the count of three. One, two . . . three!'

The dice clattered across the stone floor, halting just short of the two thrones.

'Read them,' the peacock woman commanded. The goblin scurried to obey.

'It's a one,' she called eagerly, 'and a . . . another one!'

Stitch shot Red a look of relief. This was a huge stroke of luck in their favour. The more stones they pulled from the bag, the more complicated their task would inevitably become.

'*Two?*' the horned man repeated, seething with this result.

'Yes, my lord,' the goblin said with a bow. She picked up the dice.

'Now this is where it gets interesting,' the Unseelie leader said. 'Draw from the bag!'

The goblin giggled, rattling the velvet bag like it was something living that she was trying to throttle.

'Who wants to go first?' she grinned, offering the open neck to them both.

'I will,' said Red, plunging her hand into the bag. Her fingers brushed against the cool, smooth surface of stone. She closed her fist around one and pulled it out, keeping her hand wrapped around it.

Stitch reached in after her, making his choice just as swiftly.

They handed their stones over and watched as the goblin skipped over to the two thrones. The horned man plucked the stones from the goblin's hand and held one up for the court to see.

'The first stone is the Quest!'

'Is that good or bad?' Stitch mouthed to Gredin and Raven, who had moved aside a little.

'It all depends on the second stone,' Gredin said quietly, drawing closer now that the selections had been made.

The Seelie woman held the second stone aloft.

'The girl has pulled the Heart!'

The word echoed in Red's head. Whatever the symbols stood for, their fate was now sealed.

'The stones have been chosen,' the horned man announced. 'Your quest will be something precious to you; something *close to your heart!*' He threw the two stones back into the velvet bag, and the goblin hopped off to return it to the casket. He held up a hand to a guard nearby.

'Search them!'

'What?' said Red, clutching her belongings fiercely.

Stitch stood his ground, but Red could see that he was as alarmed as she was. 'Just co-operate,' he murmured as the guard approached. In one hand he held a cruel-looking spear. Its base hit the ground with a resounding click as he stopped next to them.

'Empty your pockets and your bags,' the guard instructed. 'Your possessions are to be reviewed by the court.'

Bewildered, but mindful of the weapon in the guard's

hand, Red did as she was told. Kneeling, she undid her bag and rooted around for her precious book, placing it carefully on the floor, then upended the bag so the rest of her belongings came cascading out. Out tumbled her flask, the map, a toothbrush, and numerous other items. Grudgingly, she took the magical scissors from her pocket, and her knife from her belt, and added them to the pile before stepping back.

'That's everything of mine,' she said.

Stitch had fewer items than her in his bag, all of them – and the bag itself – taken from the Hedgewitch's cottage. From his pockets he threw some matches, a coil of string, a bunch of keys and a pencil stub. But as he reached into his top pocket he flinched as though he'd put his hand into a wasps' nest. It was then Red remembered the bracelet. It rattled like a dangerous snake as he pulled it from its pocket, the twelve charms knocking into one another. He placed it on the floor, adding the loose thirteenth charm – the Cauldron – afterwards. Then he backed away, looking as uncomfortable as Red felt.

One by one, their belongings were picked up and placed on a fat cushion, then presented by the goblin to the two throned figures. The horned man's fingers glided from one object to the next.

Not the book, Red thought silently. *Not my book.*

His fingers lingered over it for rather longer than the rest of the items, and she bristled with anger as he carelessly lifted the cover.

'Fairy Tales,' he said mockingly. 'Something I've never understood about humans. Why call them "*fairy* tales" when there are so few, if *any* fairies in them?' He let the book fall closed and gave a petulant sigh which suggested that so far the selection of items did not excite him at all. Then the peacock woman reached out and lifted the bracelet to the light. She held it there, examining each of the charms with a critical eye, and then she and the horned man exchanged a long look.

'Where is the thirteenth?' Red heard her say softly, and she knew that they had recognised what the bracelet replicated. The horned man scanned the cushion and plucked the Cauldron charm from it. Red glanced at Gredin and Raven and saw that they were looking uneasy.

'I think we've made our selection, haven't we?' the horned man murmured, and the peacock woman nodded her approval, almost amiably.

'An object has been chosen,' she announced, raising the bracelet. 'One that is more fitting than any of us could have predicted! A piece of human jewellery, modelled on the Thirteen Treasures of the great court!'

'Wait!' said Stitch. 'There's been a mistake. The bracelet doesn't belong to either of us – I picked it up to fix the broken charm for someone else!'

Already, Red knew that his plea was wasted. The fairies' excitement was too tangible. The bracelet's link to Avalon clearly excited them beyond words.

'The rules of the quest are these: the object,' the fairy

woman said, 'will be cast out into your own world. Your mission is to retrieve it.'

'Retrieve it from *where?*' Stitch burst out.

'That is part of the challenge,' the horned man cut in. 'The object will decide that. And as the nature of this object is so *delicate* . . .' he lifted the broken Cauldron charm to a sea of sniggering, '. . . there will be several components to the task.' He took the bracelet with its remaining charms and snapped another off easily. '*Thirteen* components, in fact!'

'No,' Stitch whispered – before the hall roared its applause and drowned him out. Red could not bring herself to look at him.

The horned man removed the charms – one by one – with increasing relish. When the bracelet was stripped bare he tossed it back at their feet. Then he threw the handful of charms high into the air. As they came down Red expected them to ping as they hit the floor – but on the moment of impact each one vanished from sight.

'You, girl,' he addressed Red. 'When you are ready to return, simply put the bracelet on. You will be brought back here and, if you have found all thirteen charms, we will remain true to our part of the bargain. If you fail you will become our prisoners. And you will never see your brother again.'

'What about me?' Stitch asked.

The Seelie woman's lips curved beneath the peacock mask.

'Your part in the task is to remain here,' she said.

'What? Why?' Stitch stammered.

'Let's just call it insurance,' said the horned man. 'We want to make sure the girl comes back.'

'Why wouldn't I come back?' Red asked. 'You think I'd leave my brother here?'

The fairy man shrugged.

'Just in case you . . . change your mind.'

'I won't,' Red said firmly. 'I'm coming back for him – and for you, Stitch.'

The horned man laughed.

'So be it. The task is set and no other will be given. If you do not accept, you fail. If you attempt to employ the help of any fairy, you fail. Do you accept?'

Red knelt and picked up the bracelet.

'I accept.'

The Unseelie man smiled.

'Now leave us.' He turned, and lifted a goblet to his side of the court. 'The time of the Unseelie is almost upon us! Let us feast!'

It was a swift dismissal that left them scrabbling to collect their belongings. Red had barely shoved the last item of hers in her bag and closed it when a guard's hand was clamped around her arm, pulling her roughly to the stairs and escorting her to the top in a relentless march. She twisted around in the guard's grip to see Stitch being led away by two more guards, his face a mask of disbelief.

'I'll come back for you!' she yelled. 'I'll do it! I'll find them all!'

270

Cool air rushed in as the grass above the hill rolled back to reveal the gateway, and then a hard push sent her sprawling to the damp ground outside. By the time she had got to her feet the entrance had hidden itself once more, leaving no sign of what was hidden beneath.

She stood there, breath clouding the air. It tasted different, Red realised: metallic and dirty. An ancient building loomed above: the ruin of a church that had not been there when they had climbed the tor earlier that night. She walked to the edge of the hill, joining Raven and Gredin who were standing there quietly. Together they stared down in silence at the well-lit towns surrounding it. In the distance, the headlights of tiny cars travelled along the streets, confirming to them all that they were no longer in the fairy realm.

They had come out on the other side; in her own.

22

THE HOUSE IN CHALICE ROAD *had been derelict for some time. It was a three-storey townhouse in a part of London where people kept their heads down and turned a blind eye to the comings and goings of the neighbourhood.*

Rowan wasn't the first to get in through one of the boarded-up windows. Other people stayed there at night as well as her, mainly teenagers but occasionally older homeless people, too. None of the twelve rooms was exclusive; nightly accommodation was generally on a first come, first served basis amongst the comers of a similar age. When the older, or meaner, ones came, however, all that went out of the window. If trouble looked likely, those younger or newer to street life soon learned to make themselves scarce or put up a good fight for their corner.

The best room was the only one with furniture: an old sofa bed with broken springs and a cracked mirror on the built-in cupboard door. Generally, Rowan didn't stay there long after waking up. Today she'd remained until there was enough light streaming through the missing board at the window to see clearly, for the electricity had been cut long ago. Standing in front of the mirror she tied her hair back and peered over her shoulder to look at her back.

Ten weeks had passed since the night James went missing. She had told no one of the burn between her shoulder blades during the time between James's abduction and running away, the same day her plaster cast was removed. At first, the choice was simply because she could not think of a way to explain the winged brand that was seared into her skin. As time went on she thought of another good reason for keeping it to herself – the mark was something that could easily identify her. And now Rowan had made up her mind to disappear, being identified was the last thing she wanted.

The burn had blistered and wept during the first couple of weeks following the attack. Now it had healed to a red outline detailing the winged pattern of Snatcher's ring. Rowan traced it with her fingers then rearranged her clothing to cover it. She was realistic enough to know that the scarring would never fade completely. She was marked for life.

Collecting her bag, she squeezed out of the window and left the house without a second glance. She wouldn't be going back. Places to stay were only good for a short while before word got out and too many people came. It was time to move on.

Breakfast was the usual: a couple of pieces of fruit swiped from a market vendor on her way to the library, washed down with water from a public fountain. She had become thinner at first, but now her thieving skills had improved the weight was gradually going back on.

In the library, she headed for the folklore section and pulled a few books off the shelf. Once settled in a corner, she flicked to the

273

pages she had marked out the day before and continued to read from where she had left off, absorbing the information off the pages. Over the past two months Rowan had crammed a vast amount of knowledge into her mind; things about the fairy courts, changelings and methods of protection. Never give them your name, *she read*. Not if you can avoid it, for they'll be sure never to give you theirs. Names are powerful.

Everything she filed in her mind had a bitter edge, for she knew it was too little, too late. The truth was, she had no idea how to get her brother back, or where to start looking.

She had the first inkling that she was being watched about an hour later. Looking up, she saw a scruffy boy of about the same age sitting across from her on another chair. He was reading a local paper, and one of his knees was bouncing up and down as he read, making the paper crackle. Every now and then he glanced her way, then went back to reading the paper.

On the third occasion their eyes met Rowan held his gaze. She had already guessed that, like her, he was a runaway, for the look of the streets was all about him. His fingernails were rotten and his hair greasy. Under his seat he had tucked a huge backpack and a rolled-up sleeping bag.

The boy nodded amiably at her, then to Rowan's annoyance, got up and came over to the table and pulled up a seat.

'What you reading?' he said, nodding to the stack of books in front of her. He had a northern accent and one of his front teeth was chipped.

'Mind your own business,' Rowan snapped, gathering the

books and preparing to leave. 'Just because I looked at you, it wasn't an invitation.'

The boy leaned back and held his hands up, his eyebrows disappearing into his shaggy hair.

'Steady. I didn't mean nothing, just thought I'd come and say hello. You don't have to go. I was just being friendly, like. Being as we're both tomorrow's fish and chip paper.'

Rowan planted herself back down on the chair, glaring.

'What are you talking about?'

The boy looked around before putting his newspaper on the table and turning to one of the pages in the end section. Twenty or so black and white faces stared out of the page, all under a heading of 'MISSING – CAN YOU HELP?'

'There's me,' the lad said, pointing to one of the photos in the middle section. Rowan stared at the picture, taking in the boy's distinctive chipped tooth. He covered his name with a cheeky smile before she had a chance to read it, and then pointed to the bottom of the page.

'And there's you, if I'm not mistaken.'

Rowan stared at her picture, blood rushing to her cheeks. Self-consciously, she ducked her head. The boy smiled and flipped the paper shut.

'You're pretty new to it then,' he said in a low voice. 'Being on the streets, I mean. Says you went missing back in March, and it's what . . . May, now.'

Rowan shrugged. 'I'm getting used to it,' she muttered. 'How about you?'

'Six months.' The boy scratched his scalp through his dirty

blond hair, and gestured to their surroundings. 'Good places, if you can get into them, libraries. Warm and quiet, and you can usually get away with staying for a few hours so long as you don't nod off or smell too bad.' He chuckled. 'Both a bit of a challenge.'

Rowan said nothing.

'So,' he persisted, craning his neck to look at her books once more. 'Fairies, is it?'

She scowled at him. 'So what if it is?'

'There you go again, all defensive, like,' he said. 'I'm just curious.'

'Well, don't be. It's nothing to do with you.'

The boy leaned back, a knowing look in his eyes. 'Maybe it is.'

Rowan had had enough.

'Just say what you came to say and go. I'm busy.'

'All right,' said the boy. 'I see them, too.'

Rowan stared at him. 'Is this some kind of a joke?'

'Do I look like I'm joking?'

'How should I know? I've known you for two minutes.'

'Fair point.' The boy leaned down and picked his bag up. 'Come with me. There's something I want to show you.'

'Forget it,' said Rowan. 'I'm not going anywhere with you.'

The boy dug into his pocket and pulled out a handful of loose change. He counted it.

'Come on, what's the harm? There's a cup of tea in it for you.'

'Last time I had an offer like that I had all my money stolen,' Rowan answered. 'So no thanks.'

276

'Look,' said the boy, exasperated. 'I just wanted to talk to you, not to frighten you or rob you.' He counted out some coins and put them on the table next to her. 'Think of this as good will,' he said. He pointed through the library window, past a park bench, on to the street corner. 'I'll be in that café just over there for about half an hour if you change your mind.' He paused. 'Well, I say half an hour but it depends on how long I can make a cuppa last before they sling me out.' He grinned his chipped grin again and got up, tucking his paper into his coat. 'Call me Sparrow, by the way.'

'Sparrow?' Rowan repeated.

'That's me. Common as muck and gets everywhere!'

She watched as Sparrow sauntered out of the library, then got up and went to the window. He was as good as his word, straight into the café and up at the counter.

She returned to the table and stared at the money the boy had left for five minutes. Eventually curiosity got the better of her. She slid the coins into her pocket and picked her bag up, returning the books to their shelves on the way out.

Sparrow looked up from across his mug of tea as she bought her own drink from the counter and pushed the meagre change towards him on the table as she sat down.

'Keep it,' he said.

She didn't need telling twice.

'What should I call you, then?' he asked.

Rowan rolled her eyes. 'You already know my name if you recognised my picture in the paper,' she said in a low voice.

'Don't matter.' Sparrow drew his cuff across his mouth.

'Never know who might be listening.' He flicked his eyes around the café. 'Best to stick to good practice, if you know what I mean.'

Rowan shrugged, wrapping her hands around her warm cup.

'I don't know. Call me whatever you like, except my real name.'

Sparrow studied her, his eyes appraising.

'Your hair stands out the most,' he said bluntly. 'So . . . Red. Not too fussy and to the point. I think it suits you.' He grinned again, and for the first time, Rowan saw a dimple in his cheek when he smiled.

'So what did you want to talk to me about?' she asked.

'Fairies,' Sparrow said simply. 'I wasn't having you on before. About seeing them, I mean. It's not something I go saying to just anyone.'

'So why me?' said Rowan, her heart hammering.

'The books, for one thing,' said Sparrow. 'And because I've seen you around a couple of times now.' He lowered his voice. 'I've watched you, watching them.'

Rowan studied the boy's face for any sign that he was pulling her leg, but his expression was deadly serious.

'Prove it,' she said hoarsely.

'That's why I got you over here,' said Sparrow. He lifted his bag onto the table and pushed it at her. 'Have a look in that side pocket. Discreet, like.'

Suspicious, Rowan pulled the bag closer and unzipped the side compartment. As she lifted the pocket flap a horrid smell drifted up. She glimpsed something small, crushed and bloody, hair matted around two broken wings. Shoving the bag away with a cry, she knocked Sparrow's tea over.

A flicker of irritation came over Sparrow's face – but it was nothing compared to the fury on Rowan's. She leaped up, grabbing her bag, and ran from the café amid tables of curious customers. She was over the road and going through the park when footsteps pounded the path behind her.

'What did you do that for?' Sparrow demanded. 'I told you to be discreet! Wasted two drinks, that did. Plus they'll probably kick me out next time I go in!'

'Discreet?' Rowan whipped round to face him, her eyes blazing. 'You're the one carrying a dead fairy around in your bag, you lunatic!'

'I was just trying to prove to you that—'

'That what?' Rowan hissed. 'That you're sick?'

'That I can see them!' he finished. 'Look, I'm sorry. Probably not the best way to get your attention, but not exactly buzzing with them around here, is it?' He motioned to the grey buildings around them. 'They're a bit harder to come by here, you know? Couldn't really afford to be picky.'

Rowan calmed slightly.

'Did you . . . kill it?' she asked, eyeing him distrustfully.

'Course I didn't! What do you take me for? No, don't answer that. It was in the gutter, near to where I been staying the last couple of nights. Must've been hit by a car.' He opened the compartment again and showed her. 'See? Empty. I don't make a habit of it. It was just to show you.'

'All right,' said Rowan, her anger subsiding. 'I believe you. So what do you want?' She started to walk through the park, keeping to the path.

Sparrow wiped his cuff across his nose and followed.

'I seen you reading those books in the library,' he said, somewhat apologetically. 'For a few days now. Saw you marking the pages, so I had a nose after you left yesterday. It's changelings, isn't it?'

Rowan felt the burn on her back twinge as her shoulders tensed. The skin there was still tender. Sparrow hurried on.

'I'm not prying, like—'

'Well, you are . . .'

'All right, I am, but—' He broke off and pulled his hand through his hair. 'Why are you reading that stuff? Did something . . . happen?'

Rowan stopped to face him, trying to assess what he might know.

'Yes.'

Sparrow nodded. 'Thought as much. Took someone, did they? A kid?'

'How do you know this? Did it happen to you?'

'No, not me. I've met other people though, who've known kids to be switched over.'

'You have?'

Sparrow nodded again, his hair bobbing. 'Met one of them in this park, in fact. We got talking one day when it was obvious we were both watching the same fairy in a birdbath. I thought he had the second sight at first, but it turned out that he was fey, in disguise, like. His niece was taken by them, a couple of years ago.'

Sparrow had Rowan's full attention now.

'When they took her he refused to give up looking. And eventually, he got her back.'

'How?' Red said urgently. 'How did he get her back?'

'Says he used the one that was left in her place – the impostor – as a bargaining chip. He's got contacts – fairies on the other side who never wanted the switches in the first place – half of them are done out of spite or mischief. So they're only too eager to get their own back, same as us.'

Rowan's head reeled.

'So you mean it's possible to switch the changeling back for the same child it was taken for?'

'Sometimes,' Sparrow conceded. 'But they don't always want to give a human child back if it was taken as a replacement – like if the fairy was sick, for example. But most of the time a trade can be arranged.'

'What if there's no replacement to trade with?' Rowan interjected, stricken. 'What if a child was taken and no replacement left? How would that work?'

Sparrow whistled through his teeth.

'Tricky. Don't think I've ever heard of it being done that way. I suppose you'd have to find one – a fairy that's been left in place of a human – and steal it somehow. So it'd be dangerous, because you can't just go round stealing babies, can you? Or you could, but you'd get into a lot of trouble. And even then, if the switch was made, it would more than likely be for the kid that particular fairy was switched for in the first place, if you follow me.'

281

'But it's not impossible?' Rowan persisted. 'And even if you got back a different child, not the one you wanted, but one that had been stolen anyway, it'd still be worth it, wouldn't it? It'd still mean another child got returned to its family.'

Sparrow shrugged. 'I suppose so.'

Suddenly Rowan found herself facing him, gripping the sleeves of his filthy coat in her fists.

'This fey man,' she said urgently. 'Who is he?'

Sparrow looked down at her hands on his coat.

'He's a traveller. Works with a circus.'

'I need you to take me to him. Right now.'

'Steady on,' said Sparrow, gently releasing himself from her grip. 'I can't just take you to him. It's not that simple.'

'Why not?'

He gestured to a park bench nearby. 'Let's sit down for a minute.'

'Why can't you take me to him?' Rowan demanded again, remaining on her feet as Sparrow sat.

'Because I don't know where he is.'

Rowan swore and kicked an empty drinks can on the path. It skidded across the concrete with a clatter.

'Why bother telling me about him, then?' she said angrily. 'You must have known I'd ask to meet him!'

'Course I did,' said Sparrow, looking bemused at her outburst. 'And if you calm down for long enough to let me talk, I'll explain.'

Rowan sat, breathing heavily.

'I don't know where he is now,' Sparrow continued. 'But I know where he'll be in a couple of weeks' time.' He nodded to a lamp post a few metres away. Rowan looked over and saw a brightly-coloured poster had been pasted to it.

'You mean . . .'

'He'll be coming here,' Sparrow finished. 'The show doesn't open until the start of June but they always arrive two weeks early to settle in and set up. Once they're here I'll take you to him, if you're planning on sticking around that long.'

'I'll be here,' said Rowan.

'In that case,' he said, 'keep an eye out for me. I'll come by the library and find you. Until then, if I don't see you before, stay out of trouble.'

Rowan didn't see Sparrow before, despite looking out for him everywhere she went. She visited the library daily, continuing to cram information from books, though her concentration lapsed every time the library doors opened. Sparrow's comment about staying out of trouble preyed on her mind. What if something happened to him? It would be too easy for him to disappear without anyone knowing – or caring.

Then, thirteen days after she had met him he reappeared, scruffier than ever and slightly out of breath as he hurried over to where she sat.

'They're here,' he said.

Her books were closed before he even finished speaking, and then she was on her feet, following him out into the bright afternoon.

As they approached the park Rowan saw a huge area over the back where a cluster of old-fashioned caravans had gathered. More were arriving.

'They're all pulled by horses,' Rowan said in surprise, noting the snarled-up traffic surrounding the park.

Sparrow nodded. 'It's traditional – one of the oldest circuses still going. Many say it's the best – their acts are second to none.'

'So what's this man's name, then?' Red cut in, as they neared some of the parked caravans.

'Calls himself "Tino",' said Sparrow, edging round some chestnut-coloured horses tethered to a knot of trees.

Rowan felt uncomfortable suddenly, seeing people milling between the vans and feeling their eyes upon her and Sparrow. They were strangers; uninvited.

Sparrow's friendly grin deflected a couple of hostile stares, but it wasn't long before a tall, thin man barred their way.

'Something I can help you with?' he asked coolly.

'We're looking for Tino,' Sparrow answered.

'Tino's busy,' was the flat response.

'Tell him it's Sparrow.'

The thin man assessed them a moment longer.

'Wait here.' The man turned and strode off, his face surly. Eventually he returned, giving only a jerk of his head to indicate that they should follow him. He led them through a maze of gypsy wagons, each more beautiful than the last. Finally they stopped outside a large van that was painted a deep midnight blue. The man knocked, then left without another word. Behind them a door snapped shut as the one before them opened.

A swarthy-looking man stood in front of them, one eyebrow raised. His dark blond hair was a similar colour to Sparrow's, but longer, skimming his shoulders. One of his eyes was hazel, Rowan noticed. The other was green. His expression softened as he took in Sparrow's untidy attire, then he turned his gaze to Rowan.

'Who's this, then?' he asked, his voice a lazy drawl.

As his head moved Rowan thought she saw the tip of a pointed ear protruding from his hair momentarily.

Sparrow nudged her forward.

'She wants to talk to you about the trade.'

The mismatched eyes narrowed, then Tino shifted in the doorway.

'You'd better come in.'

The interior of the caravan was sparser and less ornate than the outside, though it was adorned with rails of glittering costumes. Some even hung on the doorframes and curtain rails, and on a dressmaker's stand a gown of shimmering silver was half finished. Apart from a shaggy wolfhound sprawled on the kitchenette floor, the caravan was empty of any other living being. It seemed that apart from the dog, Tino lived alone.

From a pot on the stove Tino poured three glasses of a steaming mixture and handed them out, keeping one for himself. He motioned to the seating that ran around the edges of the van.

'Sit.'

Rowan and Sparrow sat. She sniffed her drink but did not taste it. It smelled of fresh mint, but despite her temptation she resisted. All the books she had read had advised never to drink or eat anything offered by a fairy.

'Who did they take?' Tino asked, sipping his own drink.

'My brother,' she mumbled.

Tino nodded slowly.

285

'So you want him back.'

'More than anything,' she said fiercely. 'Only, I don't know where to start . . . Sparrow said trades can be arranged – with the changelings that are left behind. But when my brother was taken, no replacement was left.'

Tino pressed his fingers together in an arch and took a long time replying.

'It can still be done,' he said eventually. 'A switch is a switch. Some of them are straightforward, some aren't. Wherever possible we try to match the child that was stolen to the one it was replaced with, but it doesn't always work that way. Sometimes we return fairy changelings and it's weeks, months even, before the human counterpart is found.' He finished his drink and poured another, declining to offer Sparrow or Rowan a refill as neither of them had touched a drop of their first glass.

'If you want us to search for your brother then I can take some details. Can't promise anything though.' He cocked his head suddenly, studying her. 'Can't really divulge much more information, either . . . unless . . .'

His eyes met Sparrow's. Rowan turned to the boy, who had been sitting quietly the entire time. A question of some kind hung between them.

'Unless what?' she asked.

Tino ran his forefinger around the rim of his glass.

'Well, it all depends on how involved you want to get.'

Rowan felt a tremor pass through her; fear and anticipation combined. Somehow, she sensed she was standing on the edge of a precipice; a turning point in her life which would change everything.

'I think,' she said hesitantly, 'that I'm already involved. I'll do whatever it takes to get my brother back.'

'"Think" is no good to me,' said Tino, his voice low, insistent. 'You have to be sure. Otherwise you're no use to us.'

'I'm sure,' she said, clenching her jaw to try and bring her nerves under control. 'I'm in. Tell me what you want me to do. I've got nothing to lose.'

Tino's lips stretched into a smile. He extended his hand and gripped Rowan's in a firm, business-like grip.

'All in good time. Now, first things first. I don't know your name.'

Her voice, when it emerged, sounded different. Harder. As though something had crossed over in her that could never go back.

'You can call me Red.'

23

HE DAY AFTER HALLOWEEN was dark and drizzling. Everyone at Elvesden Manor apart from Nell and Amos was gathered in the kitchen. The housekeeper had decided to barricade herself in her room and was refusing to speak to anyone.

Fabian took a butter knife from off the table and punctured the now soft pumpkin that he and Tanya had never got around to carving.

'I can't believe this,' he said hotly. 'I can't believe Warwick has decided that he'd rather go off with that baby-stealing vigilante than come back to his own home! What if he never comes back?'

Florence sighed. Since Warwick had been missing she had barely eaten and looked thin and ill.

'I'm taking Amos his meal,' she said. 'Then I'm going to check on Nell.' She got up and left Tanya and Fabian alone.

'Warwick's just trying to help Red,' Tanya said quietly. 'He's doing what he thinks is best.'

'How can that be for the best?' Fabian exploded. 'His place is here, with us – not with her!'

A light scratching at the back door interrupted them. Tanya opened it and stepped back, stunned to see a small red fox looking up at her in earnest. Then she held back a scream as a hand emerged from the fox's coat, followed by a head and a body, and then Red was standing before her, holding the coat at her side.

'Red!' Tanya managed. 'How did you . . . how did you *do* that?'

'It's a glamour,' Red said simply.

Fabian ran to the door and touched the coat, speechless for once.

'They've let you go,' Tanya said, her eyes shining. 'You're back. But where's your brother? And Warwick?'

Red came into the kitchen and sat, her face sombre.

'They're still there.'

'What's happened?' Tanya asked in confusion.

Red reached out to stroke Oberon who had come over to greet her. He remained with his head on her knee and wagged his tail a little before returning to his bowl to gobble down some biscuits.

'I'm in trouble,' she said. She raked a hand through her tangled hair. 'A lot of trouble.'

'What kind of trouble?' asked Tanya.

'The kind where we've been set a task by the fairies,' said Red. 'And if we don't complete it I'll never see James again – and we'll all be prisoners of the fairy realm: me, James, and Stitch.'

'Stitch?' Fabian asked.

'Your father. That's what I called him while we were there. It's dangerous to use real names in the fairy realm.'

'Why is Warwick still there though?' Tanya asked.

Red slumped forwards, her face in her hands.

'They've kept him to make sure I go back. And I don't know how I'm going to do it. How I'll ever find them all . . .'

'Find what?'

But Red was no longer listening.

'If only he hadn't picked up the bracelet. Anything else, anything at all would have been better than this. They were drawn to it immediately . . . the charms and what they represent . . .'

'Bracelet?' Tanya asked, as the truth began to dawn. 'You don't mean . . . surely not *that* bracelet?'

Red nodded, her face still hidden.

'Warwick took it? *Why?*' she exploded.

'He found the cauldron charm in the sink. He was going to fix it for you—'

'I never wanted to wear it again!' Tanya cried. 'I thought it was beautiful at first, but then the drain-dweller died because of it . . . and the fact that it belonged to Elizabeth Elvesden is just creepy!'

'Well, you'll probably never get to wear it again anyway,' said Red. 'But if you change your mind, it'll be much lighter.'

'What do you mean?'

Red reached into her pocket and threw the bracelet onto the table.

'Where are all the charms?' Fabian asked.

'I don't know,' Red said quietly. 'That's the point. That's the task. I have to find them . . . and I don't even know where to begin.'

'You mean they could be anywhere? Anywhere at all?' said Fabian. 'Anywhere in the *world*?'

'I know.' Her voice was muffled behind her hands. 'It's hopeless.'

'It can't be hopeless,' said Tanya, slowly. 'Why would the fairies set you a task that was impossible to complete? There *must* be a way to solve it.'

'Tanya's right.' Gredin and Raven materialised at the back door. 'No task can be set by the courts that cannot be completed, however difficult. It is a fairy law.'

'Can you help us?' Tanya asked. 'Surely you'll have an insight into where—'

Gredin cut her off.

'Even if we did, we would be forbidden from revealing the locations of the charms. It would be viewed as treachery and result in serious consequences for us both. What we *can* tell you is that in any fey task there will always be an element – a key, if you like – that once discovered, will unravel the entire thing.'

'So we need to find out what that key is,' said Fabian.

'We?' Red shook her head. 'This is my task. I only came back to tell you what had happened to Warwick.'

'He's my dad,' Fabian argued. 'And by the looks of it, you're going to need all the help you can get.'

'How long do you have to find the charms?' Tanya asked.

'I—' Red stopped short. 'They never said.'

'So time isn't an issue,' said Tanya. 'But we don't know how Warwick is being treated. The sooner we save him, the better. So where do we start?'

This time, nobody objected to the 'we'.

'Perhaps we should start with what the bracelet is based on,' said Red. 'What attracted the fairies to it in the first place . . . the Thirteen Treasures. We need to go over everything we know about them.'

Fabian obligingly removed a pencil and his brown leather-bound book from his top pocket.

'What are they? And what do they do? Remind me. Call them out.'

'The Platter that will never allow its owner to go hungry,' Tanya began. 'The Cauldron that will restore the dead to life. The Sword that'll allow only victory and not defeat . . .'

'The Heart of courage,' Red continued. 'The Key that will open the door to any world. The Goblet of eternal life; the Cup of divination. The Mantle – a staff of strength, the Light that never diminishes, the Book of knowledge, the Dagger that drips blood which will heal any wound . . .'

'Hang on,' said Fabian, catching up. 'All right, keep going.'

'The mask of Glamour,' said Red.

'And the Halter, a ring that will render its wearer invisible,' Tanya finished.

One by one Fabian scribbled them all down. Then they stared in silence at the list.

'The Platter,' Red said suddenly. She looked at Gredin. 'You told us a story about a family that was rewarded by the court with its power. Perhaps the Platter charm could be in the location of where that family lived. Perhaps all the charms could be in places where their powers were used. Do you know where that place was?'

'It was hundreds of years ago,' Gredin answered. 'The story will have changed over time, and so it would be hard to pinpoint where it happened. And there's a problem with that theory – not all of the Thirteen Treasures were used. Some of them never had the chance to be used before the dividing of the courts – and after that, they were never used again.'

'So that's not the connection, then,' said Fabian, glumly.

'What about the owners of the bracelet?' Tanya asked. 'I know it's old, but how many people have owned it? It must've been lots. Perhaps it could be linked to them!'

'It's a good idea,' said Fabian. 'Although if that *is* the link then it could involve both you and Florence – you've both owned it.'

Tanya went very still as she considered that prospect.

'In that case,' she said, 'the best place to start is with Elizabeth Elvesden – the first owner of the bracelet.'

'That means that at least one of the charms could be in the house,' said Fabian, jumping to his feet. 'We should start with her room, I bet there are loads of good hiding places in there . . . under that thick rug, maybe, or behind the portrait.'

'But that isn't the only place linked to Elizabeth Elvesden,' Tanya said. 'There's also the place she died – the asylum.'

'Maybe we should also think about where Elizabeth lived before she came here,' Fabian added. 'The bracelet was given to her by Lord Elvesden as a gift after she agreed to marry him.'

'Do you know where that was?' asked Red.

'No,' said Fabian. 'But I know how we can find out.'

'Of course,' said Tanya. 'We have some of Elizabeth's diaries! The ones she stashed around the house. Maybe we can find clues in them. Shall I ask my grandmother to let us see them?'

Fabian shook his head.

'I don't think we should tell Florence anything until we know what we're dealing with. She's got enough troubles looking after Amos and Nell, without finding out what's really happened to my father. And if things get dangerous she'll stop us searching for the charms. It's better if she doesn't know – at least for now.'

'But what about me?' said Red. 'If she sees me she'll want to know where Warwick is!'

'So we'll hide you,' Fabian said calmly. 'Tanya did it

before. We can do it again. Only, this time . . .' he nodded at her fox-skin coat, '. . . you've already got the perfect disguise.'

'Let's do it,' said Tanya. She turned to Gredin and Raven. 'You've heard our reasoning. I'm begging you not to tell my grandmother, at least not yet. We're Warwick's only chance, not to mention Red's brother.'

'As you wish,' said Gredin. 'There is little else we can do for you.'

With that, they left.

'Let's go upstairs,' said Fabian, urgently. 'Put that coat on – we'll have to smuggle you up, just in case anyone else sees.'

Obligingly, Red put the fox-skin coat on, feeling their eyes on her as the startling transformation took place.

Looking around the kitchen, Fabian grabbed a pile of clean bed linen that was ready to go upstairs and lifted it from the basket. 'Get in,' he said.

Red leaped into the basket and Tanya tucked the folded sheets around her until only her nose was visible.

'My grandmother will never go for this in a hundred years,' she muttered. 'If she sees us with this basket she'll know we're up to no good – we're never helpful.'

'Doesn't matter,' said Fabian. 'All she'll find is a fox. And we can say it's injured and we're trying to look after it. That's the beauty of it.'

They need not have worried. As they carried the basket upstairs they saw no one.

'It feels strange being here again,' said Red, as they passed the grandfather clock on the landing.

'Shh,' said Tanya. 'Foxes can't talk, remember?' She pushed her bedroom door open and went in, placing the basket on her bed. Red leaped out, leaving muddy prints and fox hair on the laundry. She threw the coat off once more.

Fabian sniffed and wrinkled his nose as it landed near him. Tanya caught the hint, and was subtler.

'If you want to go ahead and use the bathroom I'll sort out some fresh clothes for you. They might be a bit small but I'm sure I can find something. Meantime, Fabian – you go and see if you can make any progress with the diaries.'

'What about newspapers?' Red asked, as Fabian left. 'Has there been anything more about me, or the children I took?'

'Nothing in the papers,' Tanya answered. 'But I remember a radio bulletin about a changeling you took in Suffolk – Lauren Marsh?'

Red nodded.

'She's been returned,' Tanya said. 'Warwick and I both heard it together, but we guessed it couldn't have been you who brought her back if you were in the fairy realm.'

Red shook her head. 'No, it wasn't me. Remember I told you before, that I have contacts? Someone else must have brought her back, which can only be a good thing for me.'

'They're still looking for you, though,' said Tanya.

'Yes,' said Red. 'But now, all the children – or change-lings – I took have been replaced with the human children that were stolen, which means that the only missing child

296

connected with me now is James – and they know I'm not responsible for his disappearance. At least if I'm caught now they're likely to be more lenient than they would be if the children were still missing.'

Red went into the bathroom and locked the door behind her. Hunting through her bag, she pulled out her toothbrush eagerly, then helped herself to a generous dollop of toothpaste. The cool explosion of mint in her mouth after so long a time of only using water to brush her teeth was extraordinary – and wonderful. She brushed, spat and rinsed, then repeated the whole thing again out of sheer indulgence.

Afterwards, she wiped her tingling mouth with the small hand towel on the rail, and turned on the taps over the bathtub. Her scalp and skin itched with dirt, and she stared as the bath filled annoyingly slowly.

When she climbed out of the tub twenty minutes later the water that slid down the drain was tepid and grey. Scrubbed and clean, she dressed in a baggy T-shirt and some too-short jeans of Tanya's, then went into the bedroom.

Fabian was standing sheepishly in the fox-skin coat and Tanya was sitting on the bed with a plate of food raided from the kitchen. Fabian slipped the coat off and laid it meekly on the bed.

'It only works for me,' Red explained.

'Tell us everything that happened to you in the fairy realm,' said Tanya, pushing the plate of food towards her.

Red tore into a chunk of bread and swallowed without chewing properly, trying to figure out where to begin. When she eventually started, the story came out in a jumble. Tanya and Fabian listened in silence, their eyes growing wider with each incident related. Finally, as she came to an end, Tanya reached for a pile of shabby, battered journals from beneath her bed.

'Are those Elizabeth Elvesden's diaries?' Red asked.

Fabian nodded.

'We'll need to be careful, and as quick as we can. Because if Florence finds out we've got them it'll ruin everything.'

24

FOR THE NEXT TWO HOURS, THE shuffling of papers was the only sound that could be heard.

'Bookmark any pages of interest,' Tanya said before they started. 'Places, events, anything at all that could be important. We'll read for two hours, then discuss our findings.'

'We should just search the house,' Fabian grumbled. 'It's not as though we don't know what we're looking for.'

'It's all very well knowing what you're looking for if you know where to find it,' said Tanya. 'But this would be like searching for a needle in a haystack. We need to know where to look. The diaries are the best way forward. Once we've been through them we can take a closer look at the bracelet's other owners.'

There were six diaries in total, two for each of them to read. The final one had been split into parts; with pages secured together with twine.

When two hours had passed they set the diaries down.

'Who wants to go first?' said Red.

'Me,' said Fabian promptly. 'I've got the first part, which begins when she was sixteen and ends when she was eighteen. Her maiden name was Sawyer, Elizabeth Sawyer. She lived with an old woman called Miss Cromwell, who took her into her care when Elizabeth's parents died. Elizabeth describes her as a mean old spinster – she basically treated Elizabeth as a slave and paid her very little. She was also spiteful to her every chance she got. She never knew Elizabeth could read and write, and Elizabeth kept it a secret from her – saving her wages to buy paper and ink, and hiding the diary under her mattress. She only ever wrote in it when Miss Cromwell had gone to sleep. She writes about the fairies – how she'd always seen them, and how when her mother was dying and delirious with fever, she told her how she'd suspected that Elizabeth had been switched for one of the "little folk" when she was born.

'She met Lord Elvesden in the marketplace one day. She was there selling eggs from Miss Cromwell's hens and she caught his eye. Everyone in the town knew he was rich – but Elizabeth was wary. He started to hound her, bringing her gifts of jewellery and clothes. Still Elizabeth turned him away. But soon she realised that marrying Elvesden was her best chance of escaping Miss Cromwell. So the next time he asked, she said yes. The bracelet was his wedding gift to her; he'd commissioned it from a jeweller in Tickey End—'

'What was the name of the jeweller?' Red interrupted.

'Stickler and Fitch,' said Fabian. 'There's a card here with the address. And as we'd already guessed, Elizabeth had asked for those particular charms. She'd read about the Thirteen Treasures in a book, though she didn't tell Elvesden about the fairy connection. Apparently they're mentioned in stories of King Arthur, too – so Elvesden was happy with this explanation. The diary ends when she moved into this house, which Elvesden had just had built.'

'So we have the name of the shop where the bracelet was made,' said Red. 'We might be able to trace it. Same for the house where she lived with this Cromwell woman – does she give an address?'

Fabian nodded. 'In the front of the diary.'

'Good. What next?'

'That would be me,' said Tanya. 'Elizabeth found it hard to adjust to having money for the first time in her life, and also began to feel trapped very early on by the expectations that were now upon her. One of her pet hates was posing for the portrait that hangs in their room – it took months to complete and she detested having to sit still for hours on end.'

'No wonder she looks miserable in it,' said Fabian.

'When she'd been married a year, she was lonely, and bored, and spent most of her time outside, near the woods, making a friend of the local wise woman, Agnes Fogg.'

The name made Red's skin crawl. 'Who later became the Hedgewitch,' she said, continuing as Tanya shut her diary. 'She was given a little black kitten by Agnes Fogg, whose cat had just had a litter. Elizabeth adored it, so much so that she had one of the charms taken off her bracelet to adorn the cat's collar. Soon after, the witchcraft rumours began.'

A creaking sound from the door made everyone turn. With no time to put the fox-skin coat on, Red dropped to the floor and rolled under the bed.

Tanya went over to the door. Opening it, she craned her neck to see out into the hall, and sighed with relief as she saw the culprit.

'It's only Spitfire,' she said, watching as the fat ginger cat loped off. 'All the same, we'd better hurry up and finish the diaries. If my grandmother finds out they're missing . . .'

'If we haven't finished reading them by tomorrow I'll put them back for a while anyway,' said Fabian. 'Just in case she suspects. But we've got enough information to make a start.'

Red crawled out from under the bed.

'It makes sense to start with what's closest, and that's the house and the shop in Tickey End,' said Fabian.

'We can search the house later on,' Tanya said. 'We should try the shops first – they'll be closing in just over two hours. What's the address on the card you found, Fabian?'

Fabian checked his notes.

'Thirteen Wishbone Walk.'

'We can find it,' said Tanya. 'The likelihood is that the shop won't still be there – but the building might. It's worth a look.'

'I'm coming too,' said Red.

'But what if you're recognised?' said Fabian. 'Maybe you should stay here.'

Red shook her head stubbornly.

'I'm going. No one will recognise me – it's been too long. I doubt they're even looking for me in this area any more. Plus they've always known me to be alone, or with a young child. If I'm with you two no one will look twice.'

It turned out that she was right.

In her glamour disguise they sneaked Red out, and as they walked the lanes to the bus stop, she skirted their ankles, dipping in and out of the tall grass at the side of the road. By the time the bus came, the girl had replaced the fox, and three children boarded.

It was a quiet day in Tickey End. The cobblestone streets were almost deserted, inhabited only by a few last shoppers and withered leaves that chased each other across the ground. They hurried through the town square and into the narrow side streets.

Wishbone Walk seemed a little livelier, with music and voices coming from some of the inns. They passed the Spiral Staircase pub, from which a delicious smell of home-cooked food wafted, and moved further along.

Suddenly Red stopped dead.

'There it is.'

'The shop?' Fabian asked.

'No,' said Tanya, following Red's eyes to a derelict building with boarded-up windows. 'The children's home, where her brother was taken from.' She tugged at Red's sleeve. 'Come on. Don't stand here staring – it could draw attention to us.'

They set off again.

'Hardly any of the shops have numbers,' Red muttered. She was keeping her head down despite the empty streets, wearing an old cap of Fabian's to help hide her face.

'There,' said Tanya. 'Pandora's Box is number twenty-five, and Clifford's Accountants over there is twenty-one. Number thirteen will be on this side, further down.'

They ran the rest of the way, counting down the numbers as they went. But as they halted outside number thirteen, all three of them stared in dismay at the painted out windows and 'closed' sign hanging in the door. A lease board above the door confirmed the shop was empty.

'I don't believe it,' said Fabian, rattling the door. He cupped his hands around his face and peered through.

Tanya and Red squeezed into the doorway beside him. The shop was bare inside, save for a pile of unopened post clustering around the inside of the door. Fabian moved out of the doorway and stepped back into the street.

'It's not even a jeweller's any more,' he said, pointing at the name of the shop. '"The Baker's Dozen". I remember it now. Horrible pies, no wonder they closed down.'

'So that's it,' said Tanya, joining Fabian. 'A dead end.'

'Not necessarily,' said Red. She brushed past them and walked a little way on. To the side of the shop was a wooden gate. It opened as she lifted the latch. 'Through here, quickly.'

'What are you doing?' said Fabian, as Tanya slid through the gate after Red. 'We can't do this, it's trespassing!'

'Like she's worried about *that* when she's wanted for kidnapping!' Tanya said scornfully.

Fabian couldn't argue with that. He closed the gate behind them, with a quick glance either way to check they weren't being watched.

'It's all clear,' he said. 'I don't think anyone saw us.'

At the back of the bakery was a little kitchen, visible through a glass panel in the door.

'There's a key in the lock on the other side!' Fabian said. He rooted in his pocket and pulled out a piece of folded paper. 'I bet I can have that key out of there in five minutes.' He patted himself down. 'I usually carry a piece of wire to push the key through with . . .'

'Or we could just do it the fast way,' said Red, stooping to the ground. Her fingers curled round half a broken brick that had come loose from the wall, and then she stood up, brought her arm back and threw it at the window.

The glass shattered, and Fabian looked on in unabashed admiration. Scouting the yard, Red collected a handful of newspaper from by the dustbins and wrapped it around her hand to push out any jagged edges of glass left in the frame. When the pane was free of shards, she slipped her arm through and unlocked the door.

'Search every inch of this place,' said Red, closing the door quietly behind them. 'We need to be quick. I'll search the kitchen, and you two look in the front of the shop. Fabian, you comb the floor and Tanya, you check all the drawers and surfaces.'

They set to work, and it was fast work as the drawers in the counter were empty and the floor was swept clean. After only a few minutes Fabian gave a small cry and pounced on something.

'Here!'

'Show me!' Red demanded.

'Oh,' said Fabian, adjusting his glasses. 'It's nothing, just a silver button.'

They continued to search, but even after going over everything twice they had found nothing.

'Don't get too close to the front door,' Red warned Fabian. He was sorting the post on the floor and had stacked it neatly to the side of him, checking the floor where it had lain and prodding each envelope for a telltale bulge.

'There's nothing here,' Red said, disheartened.

'Don't these shops usually have basements?' said Tanya.

'Some of them do,' said Fabian. 'But there's no sign of a trapdoor or any other kind of door that might lead into one.' He stared at the floor, pushing a leaflet around with his toe.

'Let's go,' said Red, heading for the back door. 'We should get back – it's going dark now anyway.'

'Hang on,' said Fabian. He bent down and picked the leaflet up. 'This is advertising a sale in a local jeweller's.'

'So?' Red said impatiently. 'It's not much good if it's not the shop where the bracelet was made, which was *here*, remember?'

'But look at the name,' said Fabian, holding the leaflet up.

'Stickler and Sons,' Tanya read.

Fabian pulled his notes out of his pocket. 'The original

306

shop was called Stickler and Fitch,' he said. 'But what if they decided to part ways, and this Stickler person set up on his own – a family business?'

'It's possible,' Red said. She took the leaflet from him. 'But even if it was the same company, it's not the same place. It's moved.'

'Only to a few streets away,' said Fabian. 'Look, it's in Turn Again Lane – that's only round the corner!'

'It's worth a shot,' said Red. 'But why would they change locations just to move a street or so away?'

'Lots of reasons,' said Fabian. 'More space, or less – if they were having problems with the rent.' He looked at his watch. 'We'd better hurry – it's nearly closing time.'

They left the shop, slipping through the gate and into the street once more.

'This way,' said Fabian, beckoning them back in the direction of Pandora's Box. They passed it and went into the next street, then Fabian took a right into an alley.

'This is a short cut,' he said, calling over his shoulder as he jogged ahead. Soon the alley gave way to another little tumbledown road of shops and cottages. 'This is Turn Again Lane. Stickler and Sons is at number thirty-one.'

'Thirty-one,' Tanya repeated. 'That's thirteen, with the digits swapped around. Anyone else think that's just a coincidence?'

The shop, when they found it, was tiny. Seemingly, Fabian had been right about the move to smaller premises. The place was run-down, its windows adorned with birds' droppings, and its doorway littered with leaves that no one cared about enough to sweep.

'What a dump,' said Fabian.

'Some family business,' Tanya agreed, nodding to the shop's name, for either through vandalism or neglect, several of the raised letters on the sign had dropped away, leaving it to read: *TICKLE & SO.*

'Let's go in,' said Red, but as she reached to open the door a balding man ducked through it, fumbling with a bunch of keys.

'Sorry, I'm closing,' he said with a slight frown as he saw them waiting there.

'But it's not five o'clock yet,' said Fabian, pointing at the opening hours in the window, and then at his watch.

'It is in my book,' the man grumbled. 'I've not sold a thing all afternoon. Come back another time.'

'Oh, please,' said Tanya. 'Can't you spare just a few minutes? It's my grandmother's birthday tomorrow. I need a gift for her.'

'We know what we're looking for,' Red added.

The man hesitated.

'Please?' Tanya said again.

'Oh, all right,' he muttered. 'But just a couple of minutes, mind.'

He turned on the lights again and held the door open as they poured into the shop.

'What exactly are you looking for?' he asked, as they scanned the glass cabinets and counters.

Red pulled the bracelet from her pocket.

'Silver charms,' she said. 'To go on this. She collects a different one every year.'

'But it's bare,' the shopkeeper said, peering at the bracelet.

'It was stolen,' said Tanya, thinking quickly. 'The bracelet was recovered, but all the charms were gone. We're trying to find replacements.'

The man scratched the bald spot on his head.

'We don't do much of a trade in silver charms,' he said. 'Gold, yes. But silver, only a few, and most of those are second-hand. Shame really, as it's what we used to specialise in.'

'Can we see what you have?' Fabian asked politely.

The man nodded and bent down behind the counter. They heard a drawer open and close, and then he bobbed up with a velvet tray of six or seven silver charms.

There, in its centre, a silver heart was pinned to the velvet. It was duller than the rest and appeared much older. Engraved into its surface was a tiny pair of wings.

'Any of those take your fancy?' the shopkeeper said, clearly wanting to hurry things along.

Red exchanged glances with Tanya and Fabian. They were both wide-eyed. She pointed to it with a trembling finger.

'That one. The heart. How much is it?'

The man leaned forward, prodding at the charms.

'Don't remember that,' he said. 'Funny. It doesn't seem to have a price.'

Beside her Red heard Fabian gulp.

'Let me check my books.' The man vanished through a doorway into the back of the shop.

'We're such idiots!' Fabian hissed the moment they were alone. 'We don't have any money to buy the stupid thing! Unless either of you do?'

Red and Tanya shook their heads.

'That's settled then,' said Red. 'We'll just have to steal it.'

'Wait,' said Fabian. 'Look.' He pointed to a handwritten sign behind the counter. *We Buy To Sell*, it said.

In a flash, Fabian took off his watch and laid it on the counter, just as the shopkeeper came back through.

'I don't know where that came from,' he said, shaking his head. 'There's no record of it coming in. Looks like you've got yourselves a bargain, kids.'

'Will you take an exchange?' Fabian said, pushing his watch forward.

The man narrowed his eyes and stared at them suspiciously. For an awful moment, it looked as though he was going to refuse.

'I think we all know that the watch is worth more than the charm,' he said. 'Wouldn't you rather come back with the cash?'

'We don't have the cash,' said Fabian. 'And it's important.'

The man shrugged. 'All right. It's for a present, you say? I'll get you a box.' He scooped Fabian's watch up and took it with him into the back.

'Are you sure it's one of the charms?' Fabian whispered. 'I mean, it looks like it, but . . .'

'It is,' said Tanya. 'I'm certain of it.'

'Let's ask him to put it on the bracelet, then,' said Red. 'No point having a box.' She reached out to unpin the charm from the velvet tray with her thumb and forefinger, the bracelet tucked into her hand. As her fingers skimmed the charm a curious thing happened. There was a small, metallic clink, and the charm vanished from the tray. Red dropped the bracelet in surprise.

'Where did it go?'

'There,' said Tanya, pointing to the bracelet in amazement. 'It's attached itself to the chain.'

'It must have been drawn to it, almost like a magnet,' said Fabian, his wide blue eyes even huger behind his glasses.

'Then there's no doubt,' Red said in a low voice. 'This is it. We've found the first charm!'

'Let's get out of here,' said Fabian.

They called their thanks to the shopkeeper, who was still rummaging around in the back, and then left the shop.

'What about the box?' he said, coming back through to an empty shop. Through the grimy windows he saw the three children vanishing from view. He stood shaking his head for a moment, then put on his coat, ready to shut up shop for the second time that evening.

Outside, it had started to rain. Tanya, Red and Fabian ran to the bus stop, their spirits lifted with their find.

'I can't believe we figured it out,' said Fabian, whooping as they headed to the back of the bus and sank into the seats. 'We actually did it!'

'Yeah. We did it,' said Red, but she could feel her smile fading on her lips as the thrill of the find wore off. It had just hit her that this was only the beginning; the first charm.

Somewhere out there, twelve more charms were waiting.

25

ACK AT THE MANOR, RED, Tanya and Fabian worked into the night in Tanya's room.

'We must be on the right track,' said Fabian. 'The clues must lie with the owners of the bracelet – it makes sense if we found the first charm in the place the bracelet was made.'

Soon, there were more discoveries.

'Just after the Elvesdens were married, they were robbed while out in their coach one day,' Tanya read. 'Elizabeth's bracelet and some other valuables were taken. After Elvesden offered a reward, the bracelet and most of the other things were discovered hidden in the chimney of an inn a few villages away. The landlord was then exposed as a highwayman.' She tapped an open page of the phone book. 'The pub is still there, and to this day it's known as the Highwayman.'

'Good,' said Fabian. 'What else?'

'When the rumours of witchcraft started flying about, the townsfolk drove Agnes Fogg away,' said Red. 'They also accused Elizabeth of keeping a witch's familiar: the black cat that Agnes had given her. Soon after, it vanished, and she knew it had come to harm.'

She looked up from the page she was reading. 'She discovered her husband was reading her diaries. That's why she started hiding them. Then one of the maids heard the plans to put Elizabeth in the asylum, and told her in secret. So she tried to run away.

'She knew about the escape tunnels under the house. The evening before she was due to be taken away she acted as if she didn't know anything. In the night she went into one of the tunnels, the one leading to the church. She walked for two miles underground, until she came to the fake gravestone . . . but something had gone wrong. Elvesden had found out somehow . . . he was waiting for her at the other end.'

'And we know the rest,' Fabian said grimly. 'She died in the asylum.'

Tanya gathered the diaries together.

'I think that's enough for tonight,' she said. 'Now we've finished the diaries we should move on to the next stage – what happened to the bracelet after Elizabeth died.'

It was past midnight when they decided to turn in for the night. Tanya went to the kitchen for a glass of water before going to bed. It was only then she realised that she had forgotten to feed Oberon earlier that evening. But as she heard him gobbling his biscuits in the corner she knew that someone else must have fed him. He thumped his tail when she scratched his head, then she went wearily back out into the hallway, more than ready for bed.

Red awoke to the sound of a door closing. She lay for a few minutes, wrapped in her fox fur and some blankets beneath Tanya's bed, then, unable to get back to sleep, she got up and peeked through the curtains. It was early, and a thin mist crawled over the land outside the manor. A small movement attracted her attention. A figure was hurrying out of the back garden, away from the house. Though she could not see her clearly she could tell it was a plump, middle-aged woman.

Thinking quickly, she strode over to Tanya and shook her awake.

'Red?' Tanya whispered.

'I've just seen someone in the garden, running away from the house.'

Tanya got up sleepily and stumbled to the window.

'It's Nell,' she said. 'Our housekeeper. Looks like she's heading for the woods!'

Hurriedly, Tanya grabbed the previous day's clothes from the floor. She wriggled out of her pyjamas and pulled on rumpled jeans and a jumper, which she turned inside out. She finished by pulling on her trainers and stood up, remembering the compass just in time. She pulled it out from its hiding place and pocketed it.

'I'm going after her,' she said quietly. 'Coming?'

Red nodded. 'What about Fabian?'

'No time. And anyway, we'd have to go past my grandmother's room to wake him.'

They crept down the stairs and into the kitchen.

Oberon looked up from his food bowl and gave a soft belch.

'That's odd,' said Tanya, peering into his full bowl. 'Maybe Nell is the one who's been feeding him.'

'He needs to go on a diet,' said Red. 'I swear he's got fatter since I've been here.' She ignored Tanya's hurt look and unlatched the back door. 'Hurry up.'

They stepped out into a chilly autumn drizzle, leaving the house and the rest of its inhabitants shrouded in sleep. Once they were beyond the garden walls they scanned the land between the house and the forest.

'There she is.' Tanya pointed into the distance. Nell's stout little body was just visible approaching the stream. 'Come on, or we'll lose her!' She started to run, and Red followed.

They reached the edge of the stream a couple of minutes after Nell had vanished into the woods.

'We can still catch her up,' said Red. 'We're quicker than she is.'

'I can't believe she'd come back into the woods again,' said Tanya. 'Of all the stupid things to do!'

Red opened her mouth to reply, but at that moment, they both heard it. A shrill voice was calling out ahead of them.

'Carver? General Carver? Where are you?'

'She's looking for that bird of hers!' Tanya said furiously.

They followed Nell's calls deeper into the woods.

'Careful where you walk,' Red whispered. 'The forest floor's still rife with fairy rings.'

Tanya nodded. 'I think we're safe with our clothes inside out – it's Nell I'm worried about. If she's not careful she could end up getting carried away by fairies again.' She paused. 'There she is. She's right by Mad Morag's caravan!'

'Time for you to call her back,' said Red. 'I'll have to stay hidden – I can't let her see me in case she tells Florence . . .' But as she crept behind a tree to hide, she stumbled and tripped, falling with a cry and landing in view. Nell turned with a surprised squawk.

'Why are you following me?' she said guiltily. She peered at Red. 'And who are you?'

Red didn't reply. Instead she regarded Nell as familiarity swept over her.

'I followed to make sure nothing happens to you,' Tanya was saying pointedly. 'Like the last time. I can't believe you'd come out here and put yourself in danger again. When are you going to accept it, Nell? Fairies are *real*.'

Nell shifted uncomfortably.

'I know,' she said quietly. 'I mean, I believe what I saw.' She gestured to her clothes, and for the first time Red and Tanya saw they were inside out. 'Florence gave me a few tips, see?' she said. 'But all the same, I can't stay there. As soon as I find my bird I'm leaving. Florence can stick her bleedin' pay rise!'

'So that's it?' Tanya snapped. 'You're just going to leave?

You're running away after the mess you've created? Warwick's missing because of you and your stupid parrot!'

'Wait a minute,' said Red, edging towards Nell. 'I know you. You worked at the children's home in Tickey End!'

Tanya looked from Red to Nell in surprise. 'You know each other?'

Nell squinted at Red, taking in her appearance. 'I don't recall . . .'

Suddenly, her face drained of colour. 'I do remember you,' she whispered. 'Your hair was longer. Long and red. Your brother was one of the children that went missing. You said it was . . . that it was . . . fairies. No one believed you. And then you ran away.' She looked down, and to Red's surprise and Tanya's, her plump shoulders shook in a huge sob. 'It was true!' she whispered, sudden tears streaming down her face. 'It was all true, and nobody believed . . . and now I know . . . oh, now I know what I did!'

'Know *what?*' Red said sharply.

'It's my . . . my f-fault!'

Red's pupils narrowed to pinpoints.

'What do you mean, *your* fault?'

Nell sank to the ground, wringing her hands in her lap.

'I was on duty the night your brother disappeared. I was meant to be looking out, keeping everyone safe. And then the little boy went missing, and you were hysterical afterwards . . . all I remember you saying is that he should have been protected, because you'd put a red tea towel over him.'

'I did,' said Red, remembering. 'And when he was taken,

afterwards, the tea towel was gone. There was no sign of it in his cot.'

'It didn't make much sense to anyone,' Nell sobbed. 'We all thought it was just the shock of what had happened . . . but . . . but when Florence was telling me ways to protect myself from fairies in the house, she told me about the colour red being a deterrent. I remembered then, I thought of you when she told me!'

'Go on,' said Red. 'And stop snivelling.'

Nell wiped a podgy hand across her face, streaking it with dirt.

'It . . . was . . . me,' she whispered. 'Just before midnight, I looked in on you and James. You were both sleeping. I remember him looking so peaceful, like a little golden-haired angel.'

Red's eyes clouded with tears.

'Then I saw the tea towel,' Nell continued. 'And I wondered what on earth it was doing there, in his cot. It wasn't even clean. So . . . so I took it away with me. Put it in with the laundry.'

Red closed her eyes. A tear fell and landed on her cheek.

'I'm so sorry,' said Nell. 'I didn't know. And now I'll never forgive myself.' She buried her face in her hands and wept.

'That makes two of us,' said Red. 'Because I'll never forgive you, either!'

Nell looked up, her face puffy and bloated. At Red's words she gave an anguished howl and clambered clumsily to her feet. 'I'm sorry,' she repeated.

'Sorry isn't going to bring my brother back, is it?' Red yelled, pink in the face with rage. Her hands were balled into fists at her sides. 'All this is your fault! It's your fault he's gone, you interfering, meddling old busybody!'

Nell cowered at her words, sobbing uncontrollably.

'Red,' Tanya said softly. 'That's enough.'

Red turned away, her tirade over with. Her throat ached with unshed tears. She knew it wasn't really Nell's fault. She hadn't understood what she was doing.

The only sound in the clearing was Nell's muffled sobbing. Then an ear-splitting screech made them all turn.

'What was *that*?' said Red.

'*Skulduggery, that's what it is!*' said a familiar voice.

'It's the General!' Tanya exclaimed. 'It's coming from Morag's caravan – she must have found him!'

Nell looked up, sniffing. She shuffled to the caravan door and knocked; there was no answer. The General squawked again from inside.

'There's something else,' said Nell, pressing her ear against the door. 'Like a sort of . . . mumbling.' She knocked again, then tried the handle.

None of them expected it to open – but it did.

Tanya rushed forward.

'Hello?' she called, peering inside the darkened caravan.

'I can hear it too, now,' said Red. 'Someone's moaning in pain!'

'I'm going in,' said Tanya, stepping inside. As the light from the doorway streamed in it revealed a cage on the table. Inside, the General was perched halfway up, and had puffed his feathers out to twice his normal size. Outside the cage, Morag's smoke-grey cat was sitting still as a statue, staring in hungrily. Its yellow eyes glinted as they entered.

'How rude,' said General Carver.

'Oh, look . . .' Nell sniffed, calming a little at the sight of her bird. 'He's wearing his . . . suit of . . . armour!' She swatted the cat away. He hissed and fled for the open door.

'Tanya!' Red called. 'Over here, quickly!'

At the rear of the caravan, past a dresser of dozens of bottles of liquids and powders, was a dark velvet curtain. Red was standing before it, her hand outstretched. Tanya came up behind her. The moaning was coming from behind it.

With a quick flick, Red flung the curtain back to reveal the rear portion of the caravan.

In a single bed propped against the wall, Morag was huddled beneath the bedclothes. In an instant, it was clear something was terribly wrong. The old woman's eyes were rolling about in her head and her hair was slicked to her face with sweat. Even though she was radiating heat she still shivered and shook beneath the bedclothes and she murmured and moaned incoherently under her breath.

'What's wrong with her?' Tanya cried. 'She looks delirious!'

'And it looks as if she's been this way for a while,' Red said. 'Get her some water, quickly!'

Tanya ran back into the kitchen area.

'What's going on back there?' said Nell, her voice

quivering. She had circled her arms around the General's cage as though to protect him.

'I don't know,' Tanya muttered, fumbling with some tumblers on the draining board. She grabbed one and filled it with cold water and then ran back to the bedside. Red took it from her and tilted the glass to the old woman's dry lips.

'Drink,' she instructed.

Morag took a little and her eyes slowed for a fraction of a section before flickering again. In the moment they were still they rested on Tanya, and she flung her hand out, knocking the glass from Red's hand as she reached past her.

Tanya knelt down and took the old woman's hand.

'What's she saying?' she said, leaning closer to Morag's face.

Red shook her head. 'I don't know. I was trying to listen but couldn't make out the words – she's speaking too quickly – it's all distorted.'

Tanya leaned in closer. Morag's breath was sour from dehydration.

'*Won't stop . . . won't stop, can't make them stop,*' she whispered, the words tumbling over each other in a jumble. '*Won't go away . . . won't stop . . .*'

'What won't stop? Talk to me, Morag . . .'

Nell appeared in the doorway.

'Is there anything I can do?' she said, eyeing the old gypsy woman fearfully.

'Yes,' Red snapped. 'Just stay out there in case you cause another catastrophe.'

Nell shrank back, stung.

'This is no good,' said Red. 'We need a doctor—'

'Wait,' said Tanya. 'I think she's trying to tell us something.'

'*Can't make them stop . . . too many, all I can see . . . won't go away . . . visions won't stop . . . haunting me . . . everywhere . . .*'

'She said, "visions won't stop",' said Tanya. 'She's having visions! Something's wrong with her, I don't understand!'

'We need her to snap out of it,' said Red. 'Let's get her up.' She pulled back the cover. 'Poor old girl even got in bed fully clothed.'

Under the bedclothes, Morag was clutching a shawl around herself tightly. In the dim light, Tanya could see glittering beads that were sewn to it winking like tiny stars . . . except for one, duller and heavier than the rest, not a bead at all but instead an object that was very familiar.

'*Terrible things . . . make them stop . . . people dying, buildings falling . . . visions won't stop . . .*'

'Red,' Tanya whispered, pointing to Morag's shawl. 'Look!'

Red followed her gaze to the woollen fabric wrapped around the old woman's shoulders, where instead of a round, silvery bead, a squat silver goblet had been sewn in its place.

'It's from the bracelet – the Cup of divination,' said Tanya. She reached out to tug at it, but it was firmly secured in place. 'It's what's giving her these awful visions – we have

323

to make them stop!' She tugged at the shawl, trying to pull it away from Morag, but the old woman held it in her claw-like hands with an iron grip.

'She won't let go – we'll have to cut it off,' said Tanya. 'Give me your knife!'

Red pulled her knife out from her belt – then hesitated.

'Quickly,' said Tanya. 'What are you waiting for?'

'She might be able to tell us where the rest of the charms are,' said Red.

'You can't be serious? We've got to help her!'

'We will,' said Red. 'But think about it – we could solve this right now. If she's having visions maybe she could see where we need to look next.'

'No,' said Tanya. 'Look at her – we need to make it stop.'

'And I need to find my brother!' said Red. She slid the knife back in her belt and pulled the charm bracelet from her pocket. She held it up to Morag's face.

'Tell us where to find the missing charms,' she said urgently. 'Where should we look?'

Morag's eyes flickered and rolled back in her head. Her whole body went rigid.

'*Connected*,' she whispered. '*All connected . . .*'

'Connected how?' Red pressed.

'*To the past . . .*'

'Whose past? The bracelet's owners?'

'*Connected to the . . . bracelet itself . . . shadow moments . . . some events leave a trace. The past . . . is the key . . .*'

'So that's it,' Red breathed. 'The charms will be in places

significant in the history of the bracelet itself! We were on the right lines – but not close enough!'

'That's enough!' Tanya shouted, lunging for Red's knife. 'Make it stop – or I will!'

Red drew the blade out from her belt and severed the charm from the woollen thread. She held it in her palm before slowly bringing it to touch the bracelet. As soon as they made contact there was a small clink of metal on metal. The charm had attached itself to the bracelet once more.

Morag's eyes closed and she lay back, still in her bed, peaceful at last.

'Morag?' Tanya whispered, brushing a damp strand of grey hair back from the old woman's face.

Morag's eyes opened slowly.

'Some water . . . please?' she croaked.

Tanya rushed into the kitchen to refill the tumbler. When she went back into the gypsy woman's sleeping quarters, Red had helped her to sit up. After a few minutes she was well enough to be helped into the kitchen area.

'Are you sure you're all right?' Tanya asked.

'I will be,' said Morag. 'Once I've got rid of this raging headache.' She peered at Nell, sitting in an armchair with the General's cage balanced on her knees. 'I see you've been reunited, then?'

Nell gave a meek nod.

'I found him in a hawthorn bush,' said Morag. 'He must have had quite an adventure.' She handed a small key to

Tanya, then sank down into her chair by the window tiredly.

'What's this for?' Tanya asked.

'My cabinet,' said Morag, nodding to the various ingredients in pots, jars and bottles. 'You can mix me a remedy – I'll tell you what to do. And then I think it's about time you told me what's going on, don't you?'

26

ENERAL CARVER CHATTERED and clacked all the way back to the manor, seemingly none the worse for his little escapade. He was also the most talkative of the group. Since leaving Mad Morag's caravan, Nell had not uttered a word, and every attempt Red made at conversation with Tanya was cut short with an abrupt reply.

'What's wrong with you?' she asked finally, as they went through the garden gate. 'You've hardly said a word all the way back.'

Tanya pulled the compass off from over her head and pushed it into her pocket. Her dark eyes were fixed ahead as they marched through the weeds.

'I think the question should be, what's wrong with *you*,' she answered. 'You saw Morag was in a bad way, and still you pressed her for answers. How could you do that?'

'I did the same as what I always do,' Red retorted. 'What I *had* to.'

Tanya stopped and faced her.

'I know you've lost your brother, Red, but it's not just about him any more. Morag might have lost her mind if she'd been left in that state much longer. You can't just let things happen to people because it suits you and your search for James. Didn't you see what that charm was doing to her?'

'Of course I saw,' Red said angrily. 'And once we're safely inside I'll explain myself.' She turned to Nell. 'I need you to do something for me. I need you to keep me – and what's happening – a secret. You mustn't tell Tanya's grandmother about any of this. Forget everything you saw and heard in Mad Morag's caravan.'

Nell looked torn.

'I don't know,' she quavered. 'I've a responsibility . . . what if something happens to one of you?'

'It's just for now,' Tanya added. 'If things get worse, we'll tell my grandmother, I promise.'

'And you owe me,' said Red, her eyes narrowed. 'If you want to even attempt to make up for what you've done then you'll stay quiet.'

With that, they had her. She nodded miserably, and, satisfied, they all went in.

'We only saw the charm by accident,' said Red. 'It was sewn onto the gypsy woman's shawl – she didn't even know it was there.'

'As soon as we removed it the visions stopped,' said Tanya. 'I dread to think what would have happened if we hadn't found her when we did.'

328

They were gathered in Tanya's room, relating the morning's events to a sleepy-eyed Fabian.

'Morag confirmed what we thought after we told her about the task,' said Tanya. 'She knew it was no coincidence that the Cup of divination had come to her. Firstly, she already has visions – but she's able to control them, and she said they've never been relentless like these visions were. Secondly, she's a descendant of Agnes Fogg, the wise woman who was connected to Elizabeth Elvesden . . .'

'And the woman who became the Hedgewitch,' Red put in.

'. . . And that's the link between Morag and the charm.'

'So the charms' locations aren't just to do with the owners of the bracelet?' Fabian asked. 'Because Agnes Fogg never owned it – she just knew Elizabeth.'

'Tell him the rest,' Tanya said, with a cold glance at Red. 'Tell him how you refused to remove the charm straight away.'

Red stared back defensively.

'When we realised Morag was having the visions I questioned her about where the rest of the charms might be. I didn't think we'd get as lucky as specific locations, and I was right. But what she did tell us is that past events can leave a trace on things. The charms will be found in places significant to the history of the bracelet itself.'

'So that's the link,' said Fabian. His bushy hair was sticking up comically where he had slept on it. 'I don't understand why the charm would give Morag visions, though.'

'Neither did I – at first,' said Red. 'But then it hit me. What we discussed about the fairies not specifying how long we have to find the charms . . . well, I think I know why. The charm that was with Morag had some kind of power over her – and not just any power. The power of *divination*, which relates to the object itself. Except that its power was warped – swamping Morag with visions she couldn't control. If we hadn't taken the charm from her she would have been driven mad.'

'The charm was cursed,' said Fabian.

'Exactly,' said Red. 'And the Cup of divination is just one of the Thirteen Treasures . . . one that isn't as bad as some might be, if their power was corrupted.'

'But the Heart,' said Tanya. 'Nothing happened when we found that – it was just sitting with the other charms.'

'Sitting in a tray in a shop,' Red pointed out. 'Looking for an owner. Waiting for someone to buy it – and wear it.' She looked at Tanya. 'That's why I pushed Morag for answers – not just because of James, but because of the damage the rest of the charms could do if we don't get to them first. We need to find them as soon as we can. Because I think the Cup of divination is just the start of how dangerous they could be.'

'But the bracelet must have had dozens of owners,' Tanya said dismally.

'I was thinking the same thing myself,' said Fabian. 'Last night I couldn't sleep so I sneaked back into Florence's study and found some old papers, tracing the bracelet back through the family. And what I found was that it was buried with Elizabeth.'

'Then how was it passed down through the family?' said Red.

'It reappeared in the family after a hundred years. Which means that someone must have dug it up.'

'Someone dug the grave up?' Tanya said in disbelief. 'Just to get the bracelet out? Who would do such a horrible thing?'

'Someone who wanted to make money,' Fabian answered. 'Florence opened the house to visitors a few years ago to make some extra money, but she wasn't the first. When times were hard it was opened once before to the public. The Elvesdens' room was, of course, the most popular. And the more original objects and artefacts there were, the more people flocked to see them. Elizabeth's bracelet was displayed in a glass cabinet in the room, along with other things of hers.'

'So during that time, it never really belonged to anyone?' Tanya asked.

Fabian nodded. 'Which means that the bracelet has only ever had three real owners – Elizabeth, Florence and you.'

'That should make things easier,' said Red. 'It means that the bracelet has hardly ever been out of this house.' She glanced at Tanya. 'You didn't take it to your home, did you?'

Tanya shook her head. 'I only wore it here.'

'It may make finding the charms easier, but it doesn't make it any less dangerous,' said Fabian. 'We should all search together whenever possible.'

331

'It makes sense to search my room first,' Tanya said. 'The only place I ever kept it when I wasn't wearing it was here.' She knelt down and pulled back the carpet, lifting out the loose floorboard.

She took the shoebox out and removed the lid, then the contents one by one.

'No charms,' Fabian said grimly. 'Oh, well. We might as well search the rest of the room, but it's probably a waste of time. You haven't owned the bracelet long enough for anything significant to have happened to it.'

'Wait,' Tanya said suddenly. 'Something significant *did* happen. The drain-dweller died because of the bracelet. It became obsessed with it after I gave it one of the charms!'

'The Cauldron,' said Red.

Tanya got up and went into the little adjoining bathroom. 'Warwick pulled it out of the sink when he was going to fix it.' She leaned over the basin and peered into the plughole. 'I can't see anything, but it's dark in there. Do you think there's a chance . . .?'

'Only one way to find out,' said Fabian. 'Back in a minute.'

He ducked out of the room and returned a few minutes later armed with a spanner and an empty bucket.

'Do you know what you're doing?' Red asked doubtfully.

'Of course I do,' he answered. 'I've seen Warwick do it.' He bent down and began dismantling the pipe under the sink, holding the bucket beneath. As he pulled a section of the pipe away grey water dribbled into the bucket and a faintly eggy smell arose. 'That's odd,' he said, holding the section of pipe up to his eye. 'There seems to be something clogging it, some kind of sludge . . .' He gave the pipe a tap.

'What is it?' Tanya asked. 'Soap, or hair or something?'

'I can't really tell what it is,' he said. 'But it doesn't look pleasant.'

He gave the pipe a vigorous shake – and let out a yell of alarm as, with a gurgle, a wave of glistening, grey-green slime slithered from the tube. It splattered wetly against the base of the bucket, some droplets bouncing up and hitting Fabian's T-shirt and glasses. A revolting stench hit the air – the rotten egg smell of a few moments ago magnified by a hundred.

'Ugh!' Red exclaimed, backing away. 'What *is* that stuff?'

'I don't know,' Fabian said, taking off his glasses to clean them. Unlike Red, he was leaning forward in obvious fascination to peer at the slime. 'It reminds me of frog-spawn, but the cells are bigger. And definitely smellier. But they seem to be empty.' He tilted the bucket to show Tanya.

'Just get rid of it. Throw it down the toilet.'

'Don't you want to find out what it is?'

'No!'

Fabian put his glasses back on and swilled the contents of the bucket. Suddenly, Red heard his sharp intake of breath.

'You're not going to believe this.'

The tone of his voice sent her hurrying to the bucket. Holding her breath, she looked in.

As Fabian had described, the bucket contained a frog-spawn-like substance. Each cell was about the size of a grape, and at the centre of every one a grey-green tadpole was suspended in a clear jelly.

'I thought you said the cells were empty?' she said.

Fabian frowned. 'They are – except that one.' He pointed to one of the cells on the outer corner. 'That's why I called you over.'

The cell he was pointing to did not contain a tadpole. Instead, the jelly held a small, familiar object – the silver Cauldron charm.

'How the hell did it get in there?' Red said.

'I don't care,' said Tanya. 'At least we've found it. Now the question is, how do we get it out without getting covered in tadpoles and slime?'

'Tadpoles?' Fabian asked.

In the bucket, the tadpoles began to wriggle.

'They're moving,' said Tanya. 'And if you can't see them, that can only mean one thing – they're drain-dwellers!'

'But it's been dead for months!' Fabian protested. 'How can there suddenly be spawn in your sink?'

'The Cauldron,' said Tanya. 'Its power restores the dead to life, remember? This was the drain-dweller's home – and now it's been brought back by the power of the charm – with dozens more!'

One of the tadpoles burst free from its gooey cell and began flapping about in the bucket.

'Quick, water!' said Tanya. 'They're starting to break out.'

Fabian hoisted the bucket into the bath and filled it from the taps.

'We'll need to transfer them into pond water,' he said. 'Tap water's no good for them.'

'We'll take them down to the brook,' said Tanya. 'Can you imagine the destruction they'd cause once they're all hatched? The house would be overrun!'

As she spoke, more of the tadpoles were breaking free and wriggling in the water.

As Red looked on in horror, she spotted something.

'Oh, no . . .'

'What?'

'One of the first to hatch – it's got legs!'

'That's impossible – it takes weeks before that happens,' Fabian snorted.

'They're legs! They're changing fast – it must be the magic of the charm. We need to get them out of here now, and we need to get that charm out of their grasp otherwise we'll never see it again!' Steeling herself, she plunged her hand into the slimy contents of the bucket and tried to grab the Cauldron. The spawn was slippery and surprisingly difficult to handle. It slid out of her fingers and splashed back into the bucket, bursting more of the tadpoles' cells as it landed. By now, some of them had four legs. She shuddered as they half swam, half crawled over her hands.

'Let me try,' said Tanya, plunging her hand into the bucket. She wrestled with the spawn.

'Quickly,' said Red. 'They're changing fast!'

'I can't get it – and we need to get them out of the house before they hatch!'

'I'll take them,' said Fabian.

'No – you can't do it if you can't see them.' A glance in the bucket revealed that the creatures had grown and were starting to lose their tails. Suddenly one of them leaped free of the bucket. Already it had the huge, bulging eyes and greenish-brown amphibian skin. In a flash it had slid into the plughole and vanished.

'We need to cover the bucket!' Tanya gasped, looking around the room desperately. Her eyes settled on a book, but it was not wide enough to cover the brim. In the end she ran and snatched a cardigan from her wardrobe and arranged it over the opening, tying the arms together around the sides. Then she ran from the room, trying to keep the bucket and its contents steady.

Tanya hurried downstairs and through the kitchen. She was just about to go through the back door when she heard Oberon gobbling in his food bowl yet again. Placing the bucket down on the floor for a moment, she went to investigate and saw that, once more, his bowl was full.

'Who keeps feeding you?' she murmured, exasperated.

Oberon wagged his tail at her voice and hiccupped.

'I think you've had enough,' she said, lifting the bowl away from him and placing it on the worktop. 'Come on, let's go for a walk.'

She picked up the bucket and opened the back door. There was a lot of splashing inside it now, along with low, unintelligible muttering. Suddenly, a hole appeared at the centre of her cardigan and a slimy, grabbing hand came through. One of the drain-dwellers had bitten a hole in the fabric. Before Tanya could react its head was through, followed by its body, then it leaped from the bucket in a smooth arc, landing neatly in the drain outside the back door. It was swiftly followed by more.

Groaning, Tanya spied a saucepan lid on the draining board. Grabbing it, she launched herself off the doorstep and tore through the garden, out of the gate and towards the sparkling water near the forest. With one hand she held the bucket in front of her. With the other she clamped the saucepan lid over the bucket. The splashing in the bucket was frenzied now, and her cardigan was soaked with slimy water. Her arms ached with the weight of it. Oberon ran along beside her, jumping up at the bucket. He could clearly smell that there was something inside.

She reached the brook, breathless, and with legs as jelly-like as the contents of the bucket. Quickly, she threw the saucepan lid onto the grass and fumbled with the sleeves of the cardigan, unknotting them and pulling it away. Inside, the bucket was a writhing mass of drain-dwellers, clambering over one another and hopping in their bids for freedom.

Only as she sank to the ground did she hear the thud of an approach. Red was in her fox form, the charm bracelet clamped in her jaws. Oberon growled as she approached, and she stopped and stiffened warily. Then he caught her scent, calming and wagging his tail.

Holding the bracelet firmly between her teeth, Red dipped it into the slimy bucket. There was a popping noise as the cell burst open, and when she withdrew the bracelet, the Cauldron was attached. Tanya seized the bracelet, hooking it out of reach of the grabbing drain-dwellers, which were already clamouring for the shining object.

Oberon thrust his nose inside the bucket with interest, then took a step back and sneezed. Gripping the sides of the bucket, Tanya tipped it towards the flowing water. A tide of fully-fledged drain-dwellers spewed into the water with squeaks of pleasure. Then they vanished beneath its surface and, as Tanya and Red watched, were carried away downstream.

'Some escaped,' Tanya said. 'At least two went into the drains.'

'They'll end up in the house, no doubt,' said Red. 'But a few are manageable. A whole bucketful *isn't*.'

They walked back to the house. Before entering the kitchen Tanya checked the coast was clear for Red. Oberon immediately ran to his bowl, and Tanya stopped to watch.

'Who keeps feeding him?' she said in exasperation. 'Every time I look at him he's eating, and I just took his bowl away from him.'

'Perhaps it's Nell,' Red said in a low voice. She was sitting under the kitchen table with only her forepaws visible.

'Well, it's not me,' Tanya said bad-temperedly. 'But the bowl isn't filling itself now, is it?'

'Or maybe it is,' Red said, as a horrible thought occurred. 'Tip the biscuits out.'

'What?'

'Do it – anywhere, just tip them on the floor.'

Tanya upended the bowl. Brown dog biscuits showered the floor like hailstones. She placed it on the floor, empty – then before their eyes it refilled with biscuits once more, stopping at the brim.

'The Platter,' Red said. 'Whoever receives its power will never go hungry. I think we've found another charm.'

'You think *Oberon* has the charm?' said Tanya.

'Only one way to find out,' Red answered. 'Where is he?'

Tanya stuck her head out the back door. The dog had slipped off after she'd taken his bowl away.

'Oberon?' she called into the garden. He was nowhere to be seen. 'Where is he?' she muttered, stepping back inside. 'Oberon!'

A long brown nose came into view from around the side of the door. A moment later, the rest of Oberon appeared, skulking towards her guiltily. A length of potato peel was caught up around his ear. He scuttled past her with his tail between his legs and ran over to his bowl.

'Where's the charm?' said Tanya, worriedly. 'Do you think he's eaten it? How will we get it if he has?'

'He hasn't swallowed it,' said Red. From within the coat she reached out her arms, still half in her fox form, and stroked Oberon's large head with one hand, scratching him behind the ears to relax him.

'That looks bizarre,' said Tanya, eyeing the hands protruding apparently from the fox's neck.

With Red's other hand, she undid the buckle on Oberon's collar and slid it off, handing it to Tanya. 'There's your charm.'

A small silver disc was at the centre of Oberon's collar. The Platter.

'It looks just like his name tag,' said Tanya. 'Only it's not engraved. I'd never have noticed . . .'

'None of us would,' said Red. 'That's the idea. If you hadn't noticed how much Oberon was eating he just would have carried on and eaten himself . . . well . . .'

'To death,' Tanya whispered furiously. 'How did you guess, Red?'

'The diaries. Elizabeth Elvesden had a cat, remember? She had one of the charms attached to its collar. It's like the history of the bracelet is repeating itself in a really warped way.' Red removed the bracelet from her pocket and held it close to Oberon's collar. The charm attached itself once more.

'That's three lucky escapes now,' said Tanya. 'Mad Morag nearly driven out of her mind by the Cup of divination, the Cauldron spawning about a hundred drain-dwellers in place of the one that died, and now Oberon nearly gorging himself to death. The Thirteen Treasures have become the Thirteen Curses.'

27

ED FOUND IT DIFFICULT TO wake up the next morning. She had slept more deeply than usual, worn out from the searching of the previous day. Fragments of dreams clung to her, in which the silver charms were guarded by changeling children. She lay there awhile, warm in her fox fur. The house was silent, and for a moment she thought it must be too early for anyone else to be awake. Then she heard the sound of the front door closing, and a minute later Florence's battered old Volvo roared into life. Tanya's grandmother had gone out. She crawled out from beneath Tanya's bed and stuck her nose in her hand.

'Stop it, Oberon,' Tanya murmured.

'It's not Oberon, it's me,' said Red.

Tanya's eyes opened.

'I just can't get used to a talking fox,' she murmured, sitting up and rubbing her eyes.

'Your grandmother has gone out. Any idea how long she'll be?'

Tanya got up and dressed.

'She's probably gone to Tickey End for some groceries. Let's go downstairs and get some breakfast for you while she's not here. Stay in the coat – if she comes back unexpectedly, that way we're covered.'

In the kitchen, in the prime spot in front of a newly-lit fire, Spitfire was giving himself a half-hearted wash. His ears flattened against his head and he hissed when he scented Red. Oberon looked on warily, sensibly keeping his distance. The General was also watching Spitfire, and was uncharacteristically quiet. Red inched closer and growled softly. Spitfire gave a defeated yowl and fled the kitchen, his matted ginger tail vanishing through the door.

'Pop!' said the General, suddenly looking much happier. 'Pop goes the weasel! Pop!'

'What's the plan for today, then?' Red asked.

'The Elvesdens' room,' Tanya answered. 'We'll get you in there, Fabian and I, but you might have to search alone if my grandmother comes back.'

'Sounds like a good idea,' said Fabian, as he entered the kitchen. He headed straight for the cupboard where the cereals were kept and, grabbing a box, shook it, then proceeded to pour its contents into his mouth. 'The only problem is that we need a skeleton key to access the different parts of the house. Last time I checked, the Elvesdens' room was locked. Without my father's key that only leaves Florence's, and we don't know when she's likely to be back or how easy it'll be for me to steal her key.'

'So how do we get in there?' said Tanya.

Fabian's and Red's faces were equally blank. Then someone shuffled out of the pantry and into the kitchen. From Nell's expression she had heard everything that had been said.

Red growled. 'You decided to stay, then? Haven't run away yet?'

Nell stared past her spindly legs at her flip-flopped feet.

'No,' she mumbled. 'You were right. I caused a mess, so it's only fair that I try and help put it right.'

'You'd be more of a hindrance than a help,' Red said rudely.

Nell bit her lip and collected the dustpan and brush from under the sink.

'You might find what you need in the pantry,' she said quietly, then went out into the hallway.

'What does she mean?' Tanya frowned.

Fabian set down the cereal box and wiped his hands on his pyjamas. Tanya and Red followed as he stuck his head round the door of Florence's pantry. At first they saw nothing other than rows of tins and jars. Then Red saw it, resting on a sack of potatoes: an old key.

'I don't believe it,' said Fabian. 'Nell's left us her skeleton key!'

Red was silent as Tanya picked the key up. Shame washed over her at the memory of her unkind words to Nell. She strode to the hallway to look for the housekeeper – but Nell had gone.

*

To reach the Elvesdens' room, Tanya and Fabian took Red up to the second floor of the house and into the alcove where a squat chair guarded a dirty tapestry like a bulldog. Behind the tapestry was a door that led to the servants' staircase; the only entrance that didn't involve going into another room. As before, it was unlocked, and a stale blanket of air oozed around them as they slid through into the darkness. When the door closed behind them, Fabian lit the way with a pocket torch and then they counted the doors along to the Elvesdens' room.

It was by far the grandest in the house. Red took in the ornate wooden furniture as Fabian threw off the dust sheets; the four-poster bed and its elaborate brocade coverings, the fur rug before the fireplace and the portrait of the Elvesdens that hung above it. She took off the fox-skin coat and stood in front of the painted couple, glad to feel properly human once more.

'So you're Elizabeth,' she said to the young woman.

Elizabeth stared back at her, locked in the painting. Her slender hands were folded in her lap. The bracelet gleamed on her wrist; painted faithfully by the artist.

'Let's talk about what we've found so far,' said Tanya, sitting down on the rug.

Red and Fabian sat next to her, and Fabian pulled out the notes that he had made from Elizabeth's diaries.

'So we've found the Heart, the Cup, the Cauldron and the Platter,' he said. 'All of them have been connected to the bracelet's past, and all of them apart from the Heart have had some kind of horrible power.' He checked the first sheet of paper. 'Perhaps if we look at the remaining ones we can figure out the rest of the puzzle. We've still to find the mask of Glamour, the Goblet of eternal life, the Book of knowledge, the Sword of victory, the Dagger that drips healing blood, the Light that never diminishes, the Key that'll open any door, the Mantle of strength, and the Halter – the ring of invisibility.'

'If the charms are taking powers related to the object, that leaves us with at least one problem,' Tanya said uneasily. 'If the Halter's power is invisibility, what if the object itself is invisible? How would we ever find it?'

'There has to be a way,' said Fabian, though he looked unconvinced.

'Fabian's right,' said Red. 'And don't forget that Gredin said that any task set has to be possible. "Invisible" could just mean it's concealed – after all, none of the other charms have been hidden when we've looked in the right place.'

'And you could say the same for glamour,' Tanya added. 'The charm could be disguised to look like something else, and we have no way of knowing what.'

Fabian let his notebook slide to the floor.

'It's hopeless,' he muttered. 'We're not going to do it, are we? We're never going to get my father back!' He stared at Red resentfully.

'Don't you look at me like that,' she said angrily. 'I never asked your father to help me, he took it upon himself. And in case you've forgotten, he was the one who picked up the bracelet in the first place!'

'Shut up, both of you,' Tanya snapped. 'Fighting isn't going to help. We won't get anywhere by analysing the charms. We need to focus on the bracelet's history – that's what will lead us to the answers. That's how we found the first one in the shop, remember?'

Fabian snatched the notebook back up, fuming quietly.

'All right,' he said. 'We know where the bracelet was made – that led us to the first charm. We know the bracelet was given to Elizabeth when she lived with Miss Cromwell, so we'll need to check whether the address still exists. And we know that the bracelet was displayed in this room after Elizabeth's death—'

He broke off at the sound of a car rumbling over the gravel outside.

'Florence is back,' he said urgently, snapping the notebook shut. 'We'll have to talk about this later.'

'So where should I start?' Red asked.

'This room,' said Tanya. 'I feel certain the bracelet has a connection to it.'

'And afterwards?'

'Just wait here until we come back for you,' said Fabian. 'It might be a while until we can get away – Florence is really jittery at the moment, she doesn't seem to want us out of her sight for long.'

Tanya and Fabian left quietly through the servants' door, then Red was alone. She felt intrusive, being in this room with its history and secrets. Elizabeth Elvesden stared at her plaintively from her portrait. After unsuccessfully trying to ignore the painting, Red hit upon an idea. If the bracelet was immortalised in the painting with the Elvesdens, then perhaps one of the charms could be concealed behind it.

She dragged a chair over to the fireplace and stepped up onto it, trying not to think of how much it might be worth. Then, carefully, she lifted the painting off the wall. It was difficult to do alone. The painting and its frame were exceedingly heavy, and only after she had lain it across the bed did she realise that it would be impossible to put it back on the wall by herself – she would need Tanya's or Fabian's help. She flipped the painting over to inspect the back. There was nothing, no charm, and the way in which it was framed showed that there was nowhere for anything to be concealed. The canvas was stretched and pinned tightly around a wooden frame.

She checked the wall to which the painting had been fixed, looking for some kind of secretive opening or safe, but there was none. Her hunch had been wrong.

Another couple of hours passed as she combed the room, searching the carpet, the fireplace, the bedding, and even the fur rug. There was nothing, and no sign of Tanya or Fabian. Fear began to gnaw at her again. What if their previous discoveries had been nothing but good luck, a fluke? It would only take for one charm to not be found, and the whole task would never be complete – no matter if they got as far as finding twelve of the charms.

She threw the fox-skin coat around herself once more before stepping out into the dark servants' staircase. Until Tanya and Fabian returned for her there was little point in staying put. Other rooms could hold clues.

In her fox form, the mouldy scent of the staircase was magnified tenfold, and her acute hearing picked up on tiny scuffles and rustles beneath the wooden stairs. Then, from the top of the house, she heard a thump. She padded up the stairs, her claws clicking on wood, until she reached the very top of the house. There was a door, slightly open, which she nosed through.

Her first thought as she surveyed the vast attic was that it would take weeks to search. There was years' worth of old belongings: trunks, mirrors, toys, furniture, books; some of it broken, some of it outdated. Everything was swathed in dust, and cobwebs hung thick from the ceiling like broken chandeliers.

Her second thought was the realisation that she was not alone. At the far end of the attic there was a faint flickering that could only be candlelight. Red stepped closer, her fox ears twitching. She could hear a voice now, not quite a whisper but still low. She felt her hackles rise as she recognised the voice to be a child's.

She edged closer, trying to make out what the voice was saying. Soon she could make out the tone, though not the words. It was a playful, sing-song voice, like that which a child would use to talk to its toys. What was a child doing in the attic?

She followed the voice, around broken chairs, boxed-up board games and jigsaw puzzles. Then a ghostly sight sent her skittering backwards. A female figure in Georgian dress loomed above her, its arms outstretched from the lacy folds of the dress. For a heartbeat she was terrified – before realising that the figure was in fact a dummy, simply employed to keep the dress in shape. Too late, she had knocked over a jar of marbles and sent them rolling noisily across the wooden floor. The voice shut off immediately as Red cowered behind the dummy.

'Who's there?' the child asked in a frightened voice.

Red hesitated, then crawled out of her hiding place. As she rounded a tall dresser, the owner of the voice came into view. Before a beautifully crafted doll's house sat a little girl of about seven years old, clutching a doll to her chest, her eyes wide. She relaxed as Red came into view, and her expression changed from one of fear to one of wonder.

'A fox!' she whispered. 'How did you get in here? Daddy doesn't like foxes.'

Red stayed still, wondering whether to speak or not. If she did, there was no telling what the child might do. But she had to find out who this child was ... and what she was doing in the house in the first place. Tanya had never mentioned any younger relatives at the manor, and Florence didn't look the type to keep small girls in the attic.

'I won't hurt you,' the little girl breathed. She was sitting very still, as though scared that a movement might frighten Red away. Her clothes were a little old-fashioned, Red saw –

a blue pinafore dress and white stockings – and her brown hair was curled and tied in ribbons. A strange little warning was starting to tap in the back of Red's mind. Something wasn't right here. She decided to take a chance.

'What's your name?' she asked.

The child's eyes widened again, but she did not look as surprised as Red had anticipated. She gave a little laugh.

'You can *talk*! Are you a magic fox?'

Red went a little closer.

'Sort of. There's a spell on me – I'm really a girl . . . just like you.'

'A spell? What happened?'

'A witch made this coat of fox fur,' said Red. 'It's enchanted, and it's turned me into a fox.'

The child tugged at one of her curls.

'I know someone who can change into a bird,' she said.

'Really?' said Red. 'Who?'

'I'm not supposed to talk about it,' said the child. 'She'll be cross.'

Red stayed silent. An odd thought had just occurred to her.

'A bird, you say?' she asked eventually.

The girl nodded.

'Is it a big, black bird?'

Another nod.

'A bird called . . . Raven?'

'You know her?' the little girl asked in surprise.

'Yes,' said Red, her blood chilling as her suspicion was

confirmed. 'So that must mean that you're . . . Florence.'
She took in the girl's old-fashioned attire once more, trying
to make sense of it all. Fabian had just seen Florence come
back to the house – so how could this apparition of her in
her childhood be in the attic?

'How long have you been here?' Red asked.

The child Florence shrugged.

'A long while. It feels like forever.' She reached into the
doll's house and placed her doll carefully into a seat at a
dressing table. And there, on the dressing table, an object
caught Red's attention. It was a miniature silver goblet.
Immediately Red knew that this was not just any goblet, for
there was a tiny hole in its base, a hole where a link should
be. It was one of the bracelet's charms: the Goblet of eternal life.

'What's your dolly doing with that funny old goblet?' Red
asked, trying to sound casual – but her heart felt as though
it was beating as fast as a humming bird's wings.

'She has to hide it,' said Florence. 'It's priceless treasure
from a smugglers' cave – but the smugglers know she stole
it and they're after her.'

'Where's the rest of the treasure?' Red asked.

'It's in the garden,' Florence said in a confidential whisper. 'Buried where "X" marks the spot at two.' Snapping out
of the fantasy suddenly, she turned back to Red. 'Can I
stroke you? I've never touched a fox before.'

Red moved closer. All the while, she kept her eye on the
charm, and allowed Florence to pat her head. It was a

351

strange feeling, she thought as Florence scratched behind her ears, to be fussed over by a child.

'You're not soft, like our dog,' Florence was saying. 'You feel rough and scratchy.' She giggled, and with her distraction Red took the opportunity to lunge into the doll's house and snap the Goblet charm in her jaws. Then she twisted out of the little girl's reach, scampering through the attic to the staircase.

'What are you doing?' Florence called after her in alarm. 'You can't take the charm . . . I'll get told off if I lose it! Wait, come back!'

Red did not stop until she reached the bottom of the staircase. The metallic tang of the charm was strong in her mouth. In the darkness she fumbled with the catches on the coat and threw it to the floor. Once back in her human form she reached into her pocket and pulled out the bracelet, then spat the charm into her other hand. With fumbling fingers she held the Goblet to the chain. It reattached itself at once, and from the attic, the little girl's voice stopped.

Cautiously, Red crept back up the stairs and went through the dusty attic. This time, there was no candlelight, and when she reached the doll's house its front was closed and blanketed with grey dust. Nearby, a charred candle stump was draped in cobwebs. There was no sign of Florence, or the game she had played with her dolls as a child. It was just a dusty old attic full of things that were once loved, but now forgotten.

Red went back down to the Elvesdens' room.

She had not been there long when a creaking noise came from the staircase. Someone was outside the room. With no time to put the fox-skin back on, she grabbed it and rolled under the bed, the door just visible from under the bed-clothes. A pair of trainers came into view. She relaxed and crawled out from her hiding place. It was Tanya.

'Any luck?' she asked.

Red held the bracelet up.

'I found the Goblet.'

'Where was it?'

'In the attic . . . with an apparition of your grandmother as a child.'

Tanya stared at her in confusion.

'Florence took the charm off the bracelet and pretended it was stolen treasure as a child. She played with it in her doll's house.'

'But what do you mean there's an apparition of her in the attic? An apparition is a ghost, isn't it? How can that be true if she's downstairs right now?'

'Think about it,' said Red. 'The Goblet's power is eternal life. It's as though the twisted power of the charm opened that small window in Florence's childhood and let it play out. As soon as I attached the charm to the bracelet she vanished.'

'But if you hadn't found her she might have been left up there forever,' said Tanya, biting her lip. 'Each time we find one of the charms it seems to get more dangerous. It's like they're gaining power all the time.' She paused and looked about the room. 'I can't believe you didn't find anything here. I really thought there would be some kind of link.'

'So did I,' said Red. 'But one thing your grandmother said – I mean, the child version of your grandmother – was that the rest of the "treasure" had been buried in the garden as part of her game. I think that might be another hiding place. And if I have my coat on, it means I can search the garden undetected.'

Tanya nodded – but she seemed distracted, and was still looking around the room. 'You searched the painting, then,' she said, eyeing the portrait which was on the mantelpiece, leaning against the chimney.

'It was a dead end,' said Red. 'I thought a charm could be hidden behind it, perhaps.'

Tanya hesitated.

'What if . . . oh, never mind. It's a stupid idea. Come on, let's go.'

'No, wait,' said Red. 'No idea is stupid. What were you going to say?'

'One of the treasures is the Halter . . . the ring that makes the wearer invisible,' said Tanya slowly. 'Maybe we *can* see it . . . but we're not meant to realise it's there. Can I have the bracelet?'

Red handed it over, watching as Tanya went over to the fireplace and stood before the portrait, her eyes fixed on the painted bracelet. Lifting the real bracelet up to the flat canvas, she brushed it so that it touched the area where the ring was painted.

They both heard the distinctive linking noise. When Tanya brought the bracelet back down, a sixth charm had attached itself to the chain.

'You were right,' said Red, quietly. 'The ring was invisible . . . yet visible all at once.' She put the bracelet back into her pocket. 'Come on. Help me get this thing back on the wall, and then let's get out of here.'

28

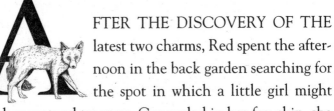

AFTER THE DISCOVERY OF THE latest two charms, Red spent the afternoon in the back garden searching for the spot in which a little girl might hide her pretend treasure. Concealed in her fox-skin, she was able to scour the overgrown garden without the worry of being seen. A couple of times she even saw the goblin, Brunswick, come in and out of his little abode beneath a holly bush, and both times he was singing a little song to himself.

Try as she might, however, she saw no sign of a place marked with an 'X'. She searched high and low, scouring tree trunks in case they had been engraved, and large stones, and even the ground itself. There was nothing. If Florence had left a mark as a child, more than half a century before, it now appeared to be long gone and she felt foolish to have hoped that it would have remained.

It was an overcast day, with occasional bursts of sunlight breaking through thick cloud. Every so often, Red saw Florence at the kitchen window, staring out towards the woods as if in search of answers. She was looking older by the day, and was noticeably distracted by Warwick's absence.

Red had agreed to wait for Tanya and Fabian to come out in the afternoon when they took Oberon for his walk by the brook. This would provide them with a chance to discuss their next steps, without being seen or overheard.

When they finally appeared, Red was waiting underneath a bush near to the garden gate, and they quickly exited the garden and headed away from the house. When they reached the brook they sat down, tossing sticks for Oberon to fetch until he was exhausted, throwing himself down and panting next to them, grass stuck to his long, pink tongue. Red cast her fox-skin coat off, relieved to be out of it once more, and Oberon gave a little yap and proceeded to sniff at the coat with interest.

Tanya and Fabian had been busy. Fabian took their notes out from under his coat, and weighted them with stones on the grass in front of them. His glasses were smeary and speckled, and his hair more bush-like than ever. Clearly, his missing father was troubling him deeply.

'The more charms we've found, the more clues they've given us to the whereabouts of the others,' he said. 'We've got several leads from the diaries as to possible locations, but we need to think logically about how realistic some of them are.'

'And how we'd be able to get to them,' said Red. 'The asylum Elizabeth died in is going to be a problem – if it's even there, still. How on earth would we get into a place like that?'

'We don't need to,' said Fabian. 'That's my point. The asylum seems an obvious place, but in reality I don't think the bracelet was ever there. They don't tend to allow personal belongings like that in those sorts of hospitals. It would have stayed here, at the manor.'

'So we can probably strike that off our list,' said Tanya. 'If our options run out we can go back to it.'

'The other thing is that the diaries that are still missing seem to be from Elizabeth's time there,' Fabian added. 'Florence once said that Elizabeth had the diaries brought back secretly by the maid she trusted, but they were intercepted by Lord Elvesden and destroyed. Even so, if we work to the theory that the bracelet was never at the asylum then we don't need to worry about the missing diaries.'

'What else?' Red asked.

'I've traced the location of Elizabeth Elvesden's first home,' said Fabian. 'The cottage she lived in with Miss Cromwell when Lord Elvesden first gave her the bracelet. The cottage is still there in a village about twenty miles from Tickey End. We could take a bus but it would take a whole afternoon to get there and back – and of course we'd need a plan for getting into the house.'

'We'll think of something,' said Tanya.

Fabian nodded.

'If the clues are anything to go by, I think one of the

358

charms might be in the underground tunnels that Elizabeth used when she tried to escape from the manor. The bracelet broke and fell off when she was down there in the darkness.'

'It'll be dangerous,' said Red. 'Maybe even impossible to reach – I've been down there, remember? Some of the tunnels have collapsed.'

'It gets worse,' said Fabian. 'Because think about what happened next, after she ran away.'

'Well, she died shortly afterwards, didn't she?' Red asked.

Fabian nodded. 'And it was buried with her – the last significant thing to happen to it in Elizabeth's lifetime.'

Red felt her stomach turn.

'You think one could be in the grave, don't you? We're going to have to dig her up.'

'It's not like she's going to mind,' said Fabian, although he looked as uncomfortable with this prospect as she felt. 'She's been dead for two hundred years. And if it helps bring my father back home then I'm prepared to do whatever it takes.'

'I'll do it,' Red said grimly. 'Neither of you needs to get involved. Just tell me where the grave is.'

Fabian looked over towards the church.

'You can't go now, it's broad daylight. You'll be seen.'

'Obviously,' said Red, her voice scornful. 'I'll have to go at night.'

Fabian ignored the comment.

'The grave is one of the grandest in the churchyard,' he said. 'A huge stone slab in the centre of the cemetery, next to an identical one where Elvesden was buried. You can't miss it.'

'You've got that wrong,' Tanya objected. 'I went to her grave in the summer with my grandmother and there was no slab. It was a headstone, and it wasn't in the centre of the graveyard at all – it was right at the edge, over that way.'

'What are you on about?' Fabian snorted. 'I *know* where it is.'

'Clearly, you don't,' said Tanya, also getting annoyed. 'I just told you – I was there. I saw her name. We left flowers.'

'Come on, then.' Fabian jumped up. 'Let's settle it.'

On the way over to the churchyard, Red told them about her search of the garden.

'There's no "X",' she said. 'I've hunted high and low and there's nothing. I don't see a way of finding out where Florence kept her imaginary treasures.'

'Unless we question her,' said Fabian. 'But in a way that she won't realise what we're doing.'

When they reached the church, Fabian led them through the maze of graves to two stone slabs, just as he'd described, in the centre of the graveyard. They were overgrown, but he knelt and brushed aside the trailing ivy to reveal the two names side by side: Edward and Elizabeth Elvesden.

'See?' he said smugly. 'I was right.'

Tanya stared at the name in front of her in disbelief.

'That's not right,' she said. 'It can't be. I remember. Let me show you!' She headed off determinedly, despite Fabian's protestations, to the edge of the graveyard.

Red stayed rooted to the spot, staring at the grave. She recognised the grave; she was sure of it. Scanning the surroundings and the nearby church, she did a quick lap of the graveyard as Tanya and Fabian moved further away, then she arrived back at the spot she had started. It was the one, as she had suspected. Looking up, she saw that Tanya was waving at her, and so she jogged over to meet them.

'It doesn't make sense,' Fabian was saying. 'There must be two people with the same name!'

Tanya pointed to the worn name on the stone. *Elizabeth Elvesden.*

'*This* is the one my grandmother showed me to. Not the other one.'

'Then what is that one?' said Fabian. 'How can someone have two graves? *Why* would someone have two graves?'

'Because only one is real,' said Red. She nodded to the one in the centre of the graveyard. 'And it's not that one.'

'How do you know?' Fabian demanded.

'You remember what I told you in the summer?' said Red, looking at Tanya.

'How I got into the house when I was hiding out?'

'A grave,' said Tanya. 'You said you got into the tunnels by a fake grave.'

'Right. And guess which one it was?'

All three of them stared back into the churchyard.

'*That's* the fake grave?' Fabian said.

Red nodded. 'I didn't remember the name, just the

location of it and some of the decorations. It's quite lavish, not like this one.'

'This one is a lot simpler,' said Tanya.

'And it looks newer,' said Fabian. He was quiet for a few moments, scuffing the earth with the toe of his shoe. He looked at the grave, then back at the churchyard, then to the grave again.

'Notice how it's a little way out from the others?' he said eventually. 'There are only a few this far out from the church. And there, look.' He gestured to a small area of a crumbling stone foundation at ground level that divided the land into two. 'See it?'

'What is it?' said Tanya.

'It looks like the remains of a wall,' said Red. 'But then that would mean that a few of the graves were outside of the churchyard.'

'Weird,' Tanya added. 'The graveyard couldn't have been full, because Edward Elvesden died *after* Elizabeth, and in any case it looks like their graves were plotted many years before their deaths. Some people still do that, don't they?'

'I'll tell you why she was outside the churchyard,' said Fabian thoughtfully. 'And why the gravestone is new. It's what they used to do to people thought of as sinners in the olden days. They were buried in unmarked graves on unconsecrated ground. Elizabeth Elvesden was thought to have dabbled in witchcraft, and she committed suicide. Those are the reasons why. And it means that it was only more recently that anyone thought to mark her resting place with a stone. The grave within the churchyard is just to save face. At the time, no one would have known that she was really buried here, all along.'

'So she was just thrown in the ground, with nothing to say who she was?' said Tanya indignantly.

'But which grave would the bracelet have been buried in?' Red asked. 'We'd be lucky to get away with looking into one, let alone both!'

'That's something we need to think about,' Fabian said. 'Let's go back.'

Grudgingly, Red put the fox-skin on again and they went back across to the manor. Once inside, they checked the coast was clear before hurrying upstairs to Fabian's room.

For once it was reasonably clean, though there was still a considerable amount of clutter lying about. With a sweep of his arm he cleared a space on the bed for Tanya and Red to sit down, and a shower of clothes and other bits and pieces went flying to the floor. Fabian did not sit, however. He remained on his feet and proceeded to pace the room.

'What are you doing?' Tanya asked, after a few minutes. 'Apart from wearing the carpet out?'

'Quiet,' said Fabian. 'I'm thinking.' He continued to pace, then went to stand by the window, staring out. 'I can't think of a way we'd find out which was the right grave to search in. But I think that the fake grave would be the best place to start, because we can get to it from the tunnels, where we're going to search anyway. That way we can kill two birds with one stone.'

'That makes sense,' said Red. 'We can get into the tunnels from the house and find our way to the grave. It's the route I used when I hid in the house before, and I left string in the tunnels marking out the way. It should still be there.'

'Plus if we go through the tunnels to the graveyard we won't be seen,' said Tanya.

'I say we do it tonight,' said Fabian. 'There's no time to waste.'

Outside the window, the sun came out once more, throwing gold light onto Fabian's face.

'All right,' said Red, impatiently. 'But we need to keep looking. What shall we do in the meantime?'

A slow smile spread across Fabian's lips as, suddenly, his gaze shifted and refocused. Instead of staring into space his vision was now fixed on something in the garden.

'I think I've got the answer to that, too.' He beckoned, and Red and Tanya joined him at the window, Red standing with her hind legs on the bed and her forepaws on the windowsill.

'What are we meant to be looking at?' Red asked.

'There, in front of the rockery,' said Fabian. 'See it?'

They both saw it at the same moment. It was a shadow, cast by the sun coming over the house, a faint and misshapen 'X'. For two or three seconds they stared before the sun went behind a cloud, taking the shadow with it.

Fabian held up his alarm clock and shoved it under Tanya's nose, not taking his eyes from the spot.

'"X" marks the spot at two. What time is it now?'

'It's half past two,' said Tanya.

'That means that the place we saw it will be slightly off the mark,' said Fabian. 'Tanya, go outside and I'll direct you until you're standing in the right place. Then leave something to mark it – a stone or something – and we'll come down. We don't want to go out there and forget the spot we've been looking at.'

'But what is it that's casting the shadow?' Tanya asked.

'You'll see when you're out there,' said Fabian.

Tanya took the hint and left. A few minutes later she appeared in the garden accompanied by Oberon and walked over to the rockery, standing a few paces from where the "X" had been. She stooped and picked something up from the ground, then looked up at the window. With his eyes still glued in place, Fabian lifted the window and leaned out, gesturing for Tanya to move further back, and to the left, until she was finally standing in the correct spot. When he gave her a thumbs-up, she crouched down and marked the spot with whatever she had picked up from the ground, and then Fabian and Red went cautiously back through the house to join her. Red skulked along behind him, ready to hide or run if Florence should appear, but she didn't, and as they passed by the sitting room they heard her scolding the General, who had just called her a whippersnapper.

Tanya was waiting patiently for them in the garden. She pointed to a distinctive flat pebble that she had laid on the spot, and looked up at the house.

'It's the weathervane,' she said, pointing. 'That's what's throwing the shadow.'

Red looked up and saw the dark shape outlined against the sky. Its intersecting arrows pointed to the four corners of the earth, forming the 'X' the young Florence had described. Sitting on top like a witch riding a broomstick was a mermaid that mirrored the one on the fountain in the front courtyard.

'Let's dig,' said Red.

'Didn't you hear what I said?' said Fabian. 'It's not the exact spot because the timing was off.'

'How do we pinpoint the spot then?' she demanded.

'We have to wait and hope the sun comes out again,' said Fabian. 'If we can plot the path the sun's taking we can use it to work backwards.'

'You're confusing me,' said Tanya. 'And it doesn't look like there's much chance of the sun coming out again anyway – look at the cloud.'

Fabian squinted up at the sky.

'There's a break over there, and the cloud seems to be travelling in that direction. If we wait it could work, otherwise we'll have to do it again another day, when it's next sunny.'

Red didn't like the idea of that at all, and neither did Tanya.

'I'm only here for a few more days,' she reminded him. 'Half-term is nearly over, but I can't go back until this is solved!'

Privately, Red thought that Tanya didn't have much choice in the matter. But as luck would have it, ten minutes later the sun came out when the patchy cloud broke and allowed it a quick escape. It was only a few seconds but enough, judging by Fabian's gleeful whoop, to plot out the path of the sun. They marked the spot – this time a short distance away from the first – with another stone, and watched as Fabian scratched his head while he backtracked.

'It doesn't just go in a straight line, see,' he said. 'It curves slightly as it moves, which means we could really do with one more marked place to get the idea of the curve. But I don't think our luck's going to hold out.'

He was right. Now the break in the cloud had passed, the rest was coming over thicker and darker. Soon, droplets of rain were spitting.

'Just make a guess, then,' Red snapped.

Fabian's eyes darted from one point to another, and then he collected a third pebble and dropped it a little way from the first.

'That's my guess,' he said, with an apologetic shrug. 'It shouldn't be too far off – I'd say the right place should be within a metre of that area. The good thing is that as Florence was only little when she buried it, it probably wouldn't have been buried very deep.'

'You two go in,' said Red. 'I'll get to work here. If Florence sees a fox digging up her garden the most she'll do is chase me off, whereas if it's one of you it'll raise questions.'

They left her and went back in. The rain started to come

367

down more heavily, in fat droplets that ran off her wiry red fur. Using her paws, she began to scrape at the ground, turfing up the grass until her claws met soil beneath. The rain helped soften it a little, though the deeper she went the harder it became; baked solid from the hot summer. Soon she had dug several holes, but after fifteen minutes she had found nothing. Then a strong scent caught her fox senses; the distinctive smell of a rusty tin. She dived in its direction, digging faster, mud caking her claws. As she went deeper the smell strengthened, until finally, only a few inches into the ground, her claws scraped metal. Moments later she had cleared the earth away from a small tin. There was old-fashioned writing on it, just legible through a layer of rust: *Beazley's Treacle Toffee.*

This was it. She had found Florence's box of treasures. In her excitement, as she pawed the tin out of the hole, she noticed the approaching footsteps too late – and then a loud clapping made her jump almost out of her fox-skin.

'Shoo!' said an indignant voice.

Red turned and froze, pinned to the ground in fright like a butterfly pinned to a board. Florence was marching towards her, her thin mouth twisted in annoyance as she clapped her hands to ward Red off.

'Off you go,' she said crossly. 'There are lots of places for you to dig – but not in my garden! Go on, hop it!'

Red finally found her feet and fled, off through the garden and around the side of the house. There she stopped and peered back out, correctly guessing that Florence wouldn't follow – and wouldn't expect her to stick around. She saw the woman tutting at the mess, and using the toe of her shoe to nudge some of the little heaps of dirt back into their crevices. But then Florence stopped what she was doing and slowly bent down.

'Oh, no,' Red whispered to herself, as she realised what was happening. 'Oh, no, no, no . . .'

Already she knew it was too late. With a small cry of surprise, Florence had scooped up the long-lost box and was carrying it back to the house. The look of joy and astonishment on her face was one that made it difficult to believe that the rusty tin contained not real, priceless treasure but the mementos of a small child with no value other than sentimental.

She became aware that someone was behind her and turned quickly, ready to run again – but it was Tanya. She had come down the side of the house from the front.

'What happened? We were watching from Fabian's window when my grandmother came out – did you find anything?'

'I found a box,' said Red. 'But I didn't get a chance to look inside. She came out and shooed me away, and now she's taken it inside with her!'

'We have to get it back,' said Tanya, pushing her dark hair away from her face. 'If she finds the charm it could put her in danger and ruin everything.'

'What shall I do?' Red asked. She felt helpless and angry with herself for failing to get away with the box.

'There's nothing you can do,' said Tanya. 'You'll have to leave it to Fabian and me. Come with me, we'll go back in the front way.'

They went back round the side of the house to the front, pushing through the brambles and wild rose bushes, and then crunching on the gravel path to the front door. Once inside, Red crept upstairs to Tanya's room alone and crawled under the bed; wet and cold and miserable. There was nothing to do but wait.

When Tanya went into the kitchen, Fabian was already there with her grandmother.

'It's extraordinary,' Florence was saying. 'I only went outside to shoo the fox away – I never dreamed it had dug something up. How peculiar! And to think that it's my old tin of treasures. Why, I'd forgotten all about it! I can't even remember what's inside! Now, if I could just get the blasted thing open . . .'

'Let me try,' said Fabian, doing his very best to look innocent and helpful.

Florence handed the box to him, along with a knife she had been using to scrape away more of the caked-on mud. Fabian wrestled with the lid.

'It's stuck tight. Seems to be rusted on,' he said. He ran the knife under the rim of the lid, pulling out another curl of mud. Something gave and the lid shifted a little. With a flourish he finally got it off, and Florence swooped on it like a magpie.

Tanya leaned further over the table, peering into the tin as her grandmother turned over the contents. There were small collectable cards, a tiny doll, some glass beads rattling about with a broken costume brooch, and a couple of toffees, still in their faded gold wrappers. Underneath, not immediately noticeable, was a glimpse of tarnished silver . . .

Tanya caught Fabian's eye and gave the slightest nod of her head to show she had seen it. It was long and thin, and mentally she recalled the charms that were still missing. It had to be either the Mantle or the Sword.

'This was my mother's,' said Florence, lifting the broken brooch out of the box. 'I always loved to see her wear it. Then one day it fell to the floor and chipped, and she let me have it.' She gave a wry smile. 'It's funny, the little things you treasure as a child. Once I even buried the old charm bracelet – the one that you've got now, Tanya. I did get a telling-off for it, too, when my mother realised what I'd done.' She lifted out one of the toffees. 'These were my favourite. They don't make them any more.'

By now Tanya was itching to grab the charm, but her grandmother's attention was fully on the box. She shot a desperate glance at Fabian, wondering if there was a way they could distract Florence somehow.

'Did you hear that?' she said suddenly. 'It sounds like the General – do you think he's all right?'

'I didn't hear anything,' said her grandmother. 'But I'm sure he's fine. He's safely in his cage in the other room.'

'What's that?' Fabian asked, pretending to be interested in something. He lunged clumsily for the box, knocking it straight off the table. The contents, apart from the brooch in Florence's hand, mostly went clattering and rolling across the kitchen floor. But Fabian had misjudged, and some of the objects fell into Florence's lap.

'Oh, Fabian, do be careful,' said Florence, but as she said it, an odd thing happened. Her voice changed from scolding to wistful. She lifted her hand to her forehead, making no attempt to pick up any of the dropped objects. Instead she stared into the empty tin as Fabian scrambled around on all fours retrieving the things from the floor.

'Perhaps some things should remain in the past,' she said in a queer voice. 'It doesn't do to dwell on it.'

'Are you all right, Gran?' Tanya asked, concerned. From down on the floor behind Florence, Fabian caught her eye.

'I can't find it!' he mouthed.

'Yes,' said Florence. 'I'm all right. I just feel tired, all of a sudden. Tired, and awfully old. What with Warwick gone . . . I just don't know how to cope with it all.'

Tanya was worried now – she had never heard her grandmother express herself in this way before. She had always been so sprightly and energetic. Even as she watched, Florence's shoulders drooped and the colour drained from her face, leaving her grey and haggard.

Behind Florence, Fabian went rigid. Tanya followed his gaze, and then when he saw her looking he frantically gestured to her grandmother's side. Only then did Tanya realise what had happened. Fabian was trying to tell her that he could see the charm – and it was in a fold of her grandmother's skirt.

'I think I'll go and have a lie-down,' said Florence. 'I'm not feeling well.' She rose from the table, her eyes staring blankly ahead. As she stood, the objects in her lap fell to the floor with various pings and clatters, but Florence did not give pause for any of them. She left the kitchen, leaving Tanya and Fabian to collect the fallen objects.

'There it is,' Fabian said, pouncing. He lifted up a tiny silver item. Tanya saw that this time it was the Sword.

'Be careful,' she told him fearfully. 'Did you see what it did to my grandmother?'

'Yes,' he said. 'She went all funny, like she'd given up on everything. What's the power of the Sword?'

'It's for victory,' said Tanya, remembering. 'And from what we just saw it's like the power was the exact opposite. The look on her face and the things she was saying – it was like she was completely defeated. It did something to her mind.'

'But she wasn't even wearing it,' said Fabian. Even so, he put the charm on the table, looking at it as though he was afraid it might bite him.

'Neither was the young Florence that Red saw in the attic with the Goblet,' Tanya pointed out. 'Don't you see? They don't have to be worn to take some kind of horrible effect. The more time that passes, the more powerful they're becoming!'

29

HEY TOOK THE SWORD CHARM up to Tanya's bedroom in a cup of salt. It was Tanya who hit upon the idea after remembering that salt could be used to dispel magic. There, Red took off the fox-skin coat and attached the seventh charm to the bracelet. As Tanya and Fabian told her what had happened to Florence, her pointed face paled.

'Perhaps you'd better check on her,' she said.

Tanya nodded and left, leaving Red and Fabian alone to stare awkwardly at each other and the cursed piece of jewellery.

'We're only halfway,' said Fabian. 'We still have another six charms to find. What if our luck runs out and we can't find them all?'

'Luck?' Red scoffed, but she could hear the fear in her own voice. She knew Fabian could hear it too. 'You think it's luck that's led us this far? Think again. If they'd really wanted to, the fairies could have hidden the charms any-where – anywhere at all. Instead they've put them in places they knew we'd track down.'

'What are you saying?'

'It's all a game,' said Red. 'If they hadn't wanted us to find the charms they'd have made sure it was impossible. So we haven't been lucky. We've been led exactly where they want us to go – with a few added scares along the way. They *want* us to find the charms, I've no doubt about it.'

'But why?' said Fabian. 'Surely they don't want us to win?'

'Of course they don't. So that must mean there's something else, something bigger to all this. I just haven't figured out what it is yet.'

'Do you think they'll really release my father?' he asked, his voice troubled.

It was a question Red had been dreading, and so she was grateful for the sudden distraction of voices from outside the room.

'You're sure you're all right now?' Tanya was asking.

Florence's reply was brisk. 'Yes, yes, fine. I don't know what came over me.'

The stairs creaked as Florence went down them, and then Tanya came back into the room, closing the door behind her.

'She's fine,' she said, her voice weak with relief. 'Whatever power the charm held over her is gone.'

Rain pattered at the windowpanes. The afternoon sky had darkened, and now dirty grey clouds swirled across it like a witch's brew.

'When Florence goes to bed we'll sneak out to the grave,' said Fabian. 'We've got all evening to prepare.

I'll gather as many torches and candles as I can get away with.'

'What about protection?' Tanya asked. 'If the fairies think we're getting too close they could attack.'

'Red thinks they want us to find the charms,' said Fabian, and went on to relate their earlier conversation.

'We should still be prepared,' said Red. 'Just in case.'

The evening crawled, interrupted only by Florence's call for dinner – none of which could be successfully smuggled up to Red. It was ten o'clock before they managed to bring her a meagre plate of cold leftovers, and by which time Fabian, who had been going over and over the information they had from Elizabeth's diaries, had pinpointed another possible location.

'The church!' he said, banging his fist on the bed and making Tanya and Red jump.

Tanya glared at him. 'Quiet, idiot!'

'Sorry,' said Fabian, pushing his glasses back up his nose. 'But it stands to reason that one might be there. It's where the Elvesdens were married.'

'It's worth a try if we can get in,' said Tanya.

'And if we've enough time – we've no idea how long it'll take to search the tunnel and the grave,' Red added, stuffing a whole potato into her mouth.

It was past eleven o'clock when Florence creaked up the stairs for the final time that evening. They heard her take Amos his bedtime drink, then come back down to her own room. Waiting a further twenty minutes to allow her to drop off to sleep, they slipped downstairs one by one and, after collecting Oberon from the kitchen upon Tanya's insistence, went into the library.

Red's fingers found the indents in the circular wooden panel at the edge of the bookshelf. She turned her wrist clockwise once, twice, and the mechanism clicked into place. She sensed Fabian trembling with anticipation behind her. It was the first time he had ever been into the secret opening in the library. As the partition swung open, revealing the small, black gap, she felt Oberon push past her legs, eager to explore. The musty air that met them sent him recoiling, and he hid behind Tanya's legs.

'Coward,' Fabian muttered, but he didn't sound much braver.

Red stepped into the passageway, flicking on a torch.

'Careful,' she whispered, as she stepped down onto the stone staircase. 'These steps are steep. If one of us loses our footing we'll all go down.'

Fabian was the next into the tunnel, holding a slim silver torch in his teeth. His hands were pinned either side of him on the damp walls to steady himself.

'Come on, Oberon,' Tanya hissed, as she followed them into the tight space.

Red looked back, past Fabian, to see Oberon's long brown nose peering around the edge of the bookshelf. He looked petrified, shifting from one large paw to another.

'Make your mind up!' Tanya said crossly. 'We haven't got all night!'

'Just leave him!' Red said in a fierce whisper. 'We haven't got time for this!'

A low scraping noise alerted them that the partition was closing, and Red remembered that this entrance only stayed open for a short time before the mechanism sprung back. With seconds to spare, Oberon squeezed through the gap and joined them; the thought of being left behind evidently worse than the gloomy tunnel.

With a final click the doorway was sealed. There was nowhere to go except down. They followed the staircase, their footsteps tentative. The flickering of the torches was disorienting and the dank smell of mildew invaded their lungs.

'Keep your eyes open for a charm,' said Red, flashing her torch in every direction.

'I don't think I'll ever get this taste out of my mouth,' said Fabian disgustedly, shining his torch at the dripping green walls as they came to the bottom of the steps. His voice echoed off stone. They had arrived in a small cavern, with four tunnels ahead of them.

Red searched the ground with her light. Soon she picked out a large pebble, wound and knotted with string leading off into one of the tunnels.

'Follow me,' she said.

No one spoke as they went into the tunnel. They sensed as well as saw the space become tighter above their heads. The air grew thicker and icier, like a freezing, rotting soup. Oberon whined, his tail tucked firmly between his legs.

When the air turned even cooler – but cleaner – Red knew the cavern was ahead. Only Fabian paused to look at the old-fashioned bed, table and chair that stood abandoned there. They moved quickly on past to where the underground room closed off into a tunnel once more, following the limp string on the ground.

'It's not far to the grave now,' said Red. 'If we don't find any charm in the tunnel we can search on the way back, too.'

Following Tanya's example, Red now carried the bracelet in a drawstring pouch of salt in her pocket. Though none of the charms had shown signs of enchantment after being reattached to the bracelet, she was taking no chances. Several times she drew breath in a false alarm as her torch-light caught some damp glimmer in the darkness, but always it turned out to be a water droplet, or a shard of glass broken long ago.

It was Fabian who spotted it.

'There it is!'

It was not tucked in some underground crevice, or wedged behind some loose rock. It was on the ground perhaps three metres away, directly in their path, brazenly waiting to be discovered. They stopped, their torches aimed at it, bouncing off the smooth silver.

'Which one is it?' Tanya asked, through chattering teeth. Oberon pressed himself into her legs.

'I think . . . it's the Light,' said Red, stepping uncertainly towards it. As she did, her torchlight flickered. She shook it until it righted itself, then shone it further along. 'The exit is just up ahead. About twenty metres away.'

Tanya's torch wavered and then went out, leaving their light reduced by a third. In the darkness of the tunnel it made a lot of difference.

'Did you put fresh batteries in these, Fabian?' she said, shaking the offending torch and flicking the switch a few times.

'Brand new, all of them,' Fabian said in a small voice. He reached into his backpack and pulled out a candle and some matches. Lighting one, he passed it to Tanya.

Red took another step towards the charm. Her torch dimmed for a moment, then came back to full strength. Her breathing quickened.

'This isn't coincidence,' she whispered.

'You mean the way the lights keep flickering?' Tanya asked. Her hand shook, and she winced as hot candle wax dripped onto her skin.

Red nodded.

'Keep hold of the torch,' she said. 'I want you to carry on through the tunnel and get out through the grave. Once you're out, try the torch again. If it works you'll have to use it to guide us out.'

'What do you want me to do?' said Fabian, no longer attempting to mask his fear.

'Stay where you are, and shine your torch ahead to guide Tanya.'

Tanya moved past them, giving the charm a wide berth.

As she and Oberon drew level with it her candle dimmed, then finally died, leaving the tunnel ahead pitch dark.

'Keep going,' Red told her, and as Fabian lifted his torch she willed it to reach the furthest recesses of the tunnel. Instead, the shadows seemed to stretch even further and Tanya was swallowed by the darkness.

Finally they heard her call out.

'I'm here, but I can't lift the slab!'

Red cursed under her breath. She had forgotten about the heavy stone. It was difficult to shift, but not impossible. However, Red was bigger and stronger than Tanya – and lifting it from below was twice as hard as doing it from above.

'Go and help her,' she told Fabian.

'What about you?'

'You can come back once the slab's shifted if I need you,' she said. 'Go.'

She lifted her own torch as Fabian ran headlong into the darkness, for as she had expected, his torch went out as he passed the cursed charm. She heard his voice and Tanya's, but not their words, and then the scrape and shifting of stone on stone. Seconds later, gusts of cold, fresh air blew into the tunnel, and she sucked them in gratefully. Up ahead, she heard a shout of encouragement, and then torchlight shone in from above. Tanya and Fabian had made it out, away from the darkness. She was alone.

Gathering her courage, she took another step towards the charm. It looked so innocent, lying there. It could be a dropped trinket, nothing more. But it was more than her imagination that sent shadows scudding across the walls of the tunnel. The shadows were lengthening, thickening. Another step, and Red's torch was rendered useless. With a feeble sputter, the light went out for good. Trying to keep her nerve and a cool head, she stuck the torch in her pocket and continued. The charm was now only five paces away, and all she had was the thin light that came from Tanya and Fabian's torches, twenty metres further on, that barely stretched to her.

'Have you got it?' Fabian called.

'Not yet,' she shouted back, her voice echoing off the walls. She took another step. At first she thought the lights ahead had dimmed, but as a wisp of black swirled in front of her face she knew that the shadows were growing. They were stretching along the walls of the tunnel as far as she could see, going both away from her and coming towards her. Time and again she thought she saw shapes within the shadows . . . a face, or perhaps a hand. But trying to distinguish anything real was like trying to make sense of the shapes in a cloud formation. She was afraid now, unsure of what was happening. Slowly, slowly, she knelt down to the bone-chilling ground and began to crawl towards the candelabra.

And that was when everything went black.

Tanya and Fabian were gulping in the fresh autumn air with relief after being stuck in the clammy tunnel. The moon hung overhead, highlighting the gravestones all around; it was an improvement to the tunnel, but a small one. Only Oberon appeared completely at ease with his surroundings.

Tanya leaned through the opening in the grave, stretching as far as she was able, and held her torch up for Red's benefit. She too had seen the darkness thicken as Red had got nearer to the charm.

'It's getting darker down there,' she murmured. 'Our torches aren't doing anything.'

'I'm going back down,' said Fabian. 'Here, hold my torch.'

He began to scramble into the tunnel, squeezing himself through the narrow square onto the steps. In front of him, they watched as Red lowered herself onto her hands and knees and started crawling towards the charm. The torchlight picked out her movements, and the tiny silver object in front of her. Suddenly she froze, and reached her hands out blindly in front of herself.

'I can't see!' she shouted. 'Are you still there?'

'We're here!' Fabian yelled. 'I'm coming back to you!'

'No! Stay where you are – something's happening! It's all gone dark! Are the torches on?'

'The torches are shining right on you!' Tanya called in alarm. 'Do you mean you can't see them?'

'I can't see anything!' Red had stood up and turned now, facing back into the tunnel, back the way they had come. Her voice was high-pitched, nothing like the calm, cool Red Tanya knew.

'She's panicking,' Fabian said. 'We've got to get her out!'

'It's the charm,' said Tanya. 'Its power is working against her – it's taking all the light and leaving her completely in darkness.'

As they watched, shadowy figure formations swirled all around Red. They were blurred and fragmented but as one reached out with its shadow hands, holding them over Red's eyes, both Tanya and Fabian saw it. The sight of it sent Fabian recoiling but he managed to stand his ground.

'Get out of there, Fabian,' Tanya said in a low voice. 'If either of us go down there the shadows will get us too, and then we'll be no good to her. We need her to keep her head so we can direct her out.'

Fabian didn't need telling twice.

Red held her hand in front of her face and couldn't see it. There was nothing but darkness, as though an inkwell had been upset and the contents had gone into her eyes. She found the wall of the tunnel and clung to it for support, her thoughts of the charm pushed from her mind.

Eternal darkness . . . was this to be her curse? Never to see light, never to see anything again? Something forced its way up her throat, a sob mingled with a scream. It erupted as a strangled sound that sounded alien to her.

'Red!' Tanya called. 'Try not to panic! We can do this – once you get the charm it'll be all right. Trust me! We're going to get you out.'

'How?' she cried. 'I can't even see an inch in front of my face!'

'Just stay calm,' Fabian shouted. 'The darkness has confused you – you're facing the wrong way. Turn back around,
listen to our voices to guide you.'

Red turned, still keeping one hand on the wall to steady
herself, and started back the other way.

'Good,' said Fabian. 'Now you need to come out into the
centre of the tunnel. Take three small steps to your right.'
He paused while she did as instructed. 'Now get back down
on your hands and knees and start moving slowly in this
direction. The charm is directly in front of you.'

Red crawled forward, grit digging painfully into her knees
and the heels of her hands. The darkness was all-consuming,
and Fabian's voice was her only beacon. She tried to block
out everything else and just concentrate on what he told her
to do.

'Now stop,' he instructed. 'The charm is right in front of
you! Reach out slowly until you find it.'

Red patted the ground in front of her, careful not to brush
the charm away. Her hand found it, cold and hard. She
curled her fingers around it and felt in her pocket with her
other hand.

'What are you doing?'

'I'm getting the bracelet out. If I can get the charm back
on it—'

'No!' Tanya shouted. 'You could drop it. Just get the
charm and get out of there.'

Reluctantly, Red pushed the bracelet deep into her
pocket, though every instinct was fighting to do whatever it

took to try and see again. Attaching the charm to the bracelet was the only thing that would stop the curse . . .

She stood up uncertainly and began to move on. No sooner had she stepped past the point where the charm had lain than the air changed again, growing heavier, swirling around her in fierce gusts. And suddenly she realised it was not just air . . . it was the shadows, fighting angrily against letting her go . . .

'Red, keep moving!' Tanya yelled. 'The shadows are all around you – just keep coming towards us, you're nearly there!' Her arm was aching with the pressure of keeping the torch trained on Red. Fabian had taken his torch back and also had it pointed at the girl staggering blindly towards them, her arms outstretched. All around her the shadows loomed, engulfing her, growing more turbulent by the second.

'The steps are in front of you!' Fabian called.

Red stumbled, landing heavily on the cold stone. She cried out as her wrist took the brunt of her fall, but somehow managed to keep her fist clamped around the charm. Close to tears, she crawled up the steps, feeling the welcome air of the outside on her cheeks. Then hands were on her, hauling her out of the cavity and onto her back where she lay on the spongy wet grass in the blackest night she had ever seen.

Tanya grabbed Red's clenched fist, prising it open to reveal the charm in her palm and taking care not to touch it. She looked into the girl's eyes, and saw them dark and blank and unseeing. It was a terrifying sight, and she prayed that whatever curse the charm had put on her would be dispelled once it was back on the bracelet.

Fabian had drawn the drawstring pouch from Red's pocket, and was now carefully lifting the bracelet from the mound of salt inside. He brushed it over the candelabra. The moment the charm reattached, Red gasped and her eyes cleared.

Simultaneously, a vast, hissing wall of shadow burst forth from the tunnel entrance like lava from a volcano, whooshing past them and sending Tanya's hair flying skyward. It curled up into the sky and then filtered back down, settling into the darkened cracks and crevices of the churchyard. The shadows were now as they should be.

Red lay on her back, half laughing, half crying, with Oberon licking her face enthusiastically and Tanya and Fabian looking on in relief. The navy-coloured sky was full of cloud, allowing only the brightest stars to shine through where it parted.

It was hardly perfect, but to Red it was beautiful. She allowed herself a minute to take it in. Then she got up, pushing any thoughts of defeat or vulnerability from her mind, and faced Tanya and Fabian.

'Are you ready to look for the next charm?'

30

ENEATH THE FAKE GRAVE-
stone the entrance to the tunnel was sur-
rounded by a low stone frame which held
the slab a little way from the ground. There
were three sections to the slab, the centre-piece being the
one that concealed the tunnel. Had the three sections been
one, it would have been impossible to lift. Under the end
sections there was just earth. There was a dip in the frame
in which they sifted through dirt, dead leaves, dead insects
and mice, with bated breath, for the next charm.

'Remind me of the ones we still have to find,' said Fabian,
poking a twig into another crevice. 'We might be able to try
and prepare . . . you know, what to expect.'

'In the way of curses, you mean?' Red asked.

Fabian nodded.

'There's the Mantle, which is a staff to give strength; the
Dagger, which drips blood that can heal any wound; the
mask of disguise: Glamour; the Key which will open any
door – even to other worlds – and the Book of knowledge.'

Tanya sifted through a handful of soil.

'I don't fancy finding any of those in a graveyard.'

'Well, one thing's certain,' Red said grimly. 'There's nothing here.' She shook dirt from her lap and stood looking over to the edge of the graveyard.

'Shall we shift the slab back in place?' Tanya asked.

Red shook her head. 'Leave it open in case we have to make a quick escape.' She started walking, away from the centre of the graveyard and over to where the real grave was. She sensed Tanya and Fabian dragging behind reluctantly, and pointed them over to the caretaker's keep where two heavy shovels sat.

'Why don't you see if you can find a way into the church?' she said to Tanya, once Fabian had brought the shovels over.

Tanya did not relish the idea, but it was preferable to sticking around while Elizabeth Elvesden's grave was dug up. She vanished round the side of the church, leaving Red and Fabian staring at the ground.

'Let me dig up the grass,' Fabian said at last. 'I can do it in sections, so we can replace it afterwards.'

'You mean like turf?' Red asked. 'All right.'

Fabian set to it, removing small, square sections of grass piece by piece. The dampness of the ground made it easy work, and thankfully the grass was holding together. Once enough had been removed, Red picked up the other shovel and they began to dig.

'I can't believe we're doing this,' Fabian muttered. 'We could go to prison, you know.'

'We'd have to get caught first,' said Red, throwing another shovel of soil to the side.

Soon they were three feet down into the grave. The deeper they got, the less they spoke, nerves overtaking everything. Soon Tanya returned from the church.

'I think I've found a way in,' she said, purposely avoiding looking into the grave. 'Round the back – there's one of those narrow windows that doesn't have any glass. It's got mesh over it instead, but it's coming away. We could probably pull the rest of it off. There are bottles of turps and things on the window ledge, so I think it must be a storeroom. It's too narrow for an adult to get through, but I might be able to manage.'

'We'll try the church last,' said Red.

Tanya turned from them and went to sit a little way away, near to one of the other unconsecrated graves.

'I don't know how you can bear it,' she said. 'I won't be able to look when you open the coffin.'

'There won't be much left,' said Fabian. 'Only dust and bones. The decomposition process would have happened much quicker back in those days when—'

'Thanks, Fabian,' Tanya interrupted. 'I didn't want a science lesson.'

Fabian shut up and carried on digging. As he struck the shovel deep into the earth a loud rumble came from nearby. Red stopped what she was doing.

'Whose tummy was that?'

Fabian paused and looked at Oberon, who was sitting at the edge of the grave, looking in.

'Not mine. It must have been greedy guts over there.'

'He's not greedy,' Tanya began crossly. 'He can't help having a big appetite—'

The rumbling came again, louder this time and more of a shaking, rattling sound.

'What *is* that?' Fabian said.

There was another sound now, a creaking, groaning noise over where Tanya was sitting. She leaped to her feet at once with a shout.

'It's coming from . . . from *underneath* us!'

All around the graveyard, the ground scratched and creaked and shifted. Roots shot up through the earth, and as Red looked down at the disturbed ground she saw writhing masses of underground creatures oozing out of their habitats: worms, beetles, centipedes and slugs. She shook a worm off her foot and stepped back, placing her hand against the side of the grave, then jumping and flinging away something slimy that it landed in.

'What's going on?' Fabian whispered. 'It's as though something's driving everything out of the earth!'

They got their answer that very second when Tanya screamed; a shrill, piercing sound that rang through the graveyard. Something long and pale had burst from the earth and wrapped around Tanya's ankle, holding her in place. Red grabbed her torch from the side of the grave and jerked it sharply in Tanya's direction. It took a moment to get a proper glimpse, for Tanya was struggling against it. When Red finally saw what it was the torch slipped from her hand and fell to the ground.

'Tell me that's not a hand?' Fabian yelled. 'Or to be more precise – a *skeleton's* hand!'

But that was exactly what it was. With a shout and a kick, Tanya had freed herself of the hideous thing that gripped her and started to run – as a second skeletal hand broke free from its grave and clawed at the air in front of her. She dodged it, only to be faced with another.

Red opened her mouth to shout to her, but was silenced as the dirt beneath her and Fabian trembled.

'Get out, now!' he yelled, pulling himself out of the grave. He reached for Red's hand but she ignored it and remained where she was.

'We must be near a charm!' she said. 'It's the only explanation – there has to be one in the grave! We can't leave now!'

'You're nuts!' Fabian shouted. 'We can't stay here, look what's happening – look around you!'

'Exactly – we're close!'

Oberon yelped as bony fingers pushed through the dirt and brushed his tail. He fled to Tanya's side, whimpering.

There was scratching beneath Red now, the scrabbling and tapping of bone on weak, rotten wood. Red heard it give, splintering as the thing inside that should be dead pushed against it, forcing it to yield. Then from the dirt a hand of ivory bone pushed its way into the night air for the first time in two centuries. Tattered fabric flapped at its wrist like an injured bird; the lacy remains of some once grand burial dress that was now barely more than a cobweb. The hand reached around wildly, seeking something to grab that would help launch it from its grave. Red stood well back, rooted half in fear and half in determination. Another scratch, more splintering wood. A second hand, balled into a fist, escaped the depths of the earth. And within the gaps in the bones, something tiny and silver.

'The Key,' Red whispered, the short hair on her nape rising like a cat's. 'Now it makes sense.'

'What makes sense?' Fabian yelled, hopping from one foot to another, dodging the rapidly increasing number of hands appearing all over the graveyard. From the fresher, more recent ones was nothing but thuds and dull moans. These were the fresh graves, where wood was still good and strong, keeping the contents in. And suddenly Red thought of her own parents, dead in the ground.

'The Key can open other worlds,' Red said softly. Her fear ebbed away with understanding. 'It's opened the world of the dead, bringing us to them, or perhaps even them to us. We don't have to be afraid of them.'

Tanya had jumped on top of a large, square plaque that was high off the ground, and was surveying the graveyard like she was on a stony island surrounded by sharks.

'How can we not be afraid when they're grabbing at us . . . from the dead?' Fabian squeaked as he narrowly missed being caught once more.

'Because that's all they are,' Red said simply. 'They're dead. Look around you, look at their names. Look at how they died.' She turned and read from the grave nearest to them, inside the walls of the yard. "'Thomas Goodfellow, died 1907 aged thirty-six. He gave his life to save another." These aren't demons, or ghouls out to get us. They were just people, like us. We don't need to be afraid of them – even though that's what the fairies want. They wanted us to be scared and to run away – but I won't.' She bent down and, bracing herself, reached out and gently touched the clenched bone hand with hers. It was cold and smooth, and at her touch it opened like a flower to reveal the charm. Her jaw clenched as she saw that the link was connected to a fine bone, and for a moment she wondered how she was going to get it off. Then she remembered how the bracelet worked. Pulling it out, she brushed it against the dead hand of Elizabeth Elvesden, and as she pulled it away the charm came with it, back in its rightful place on the bracelet once more.

With its reconnection the life went out of the dead. Skeletal hands and feet – and in one case a skull with raggedy tufts of hair still attached – sank back into their graves, sighing to be at peace once more. Soon, only one remained: the one holding on to Red's own hand.

'Rest in peace, Elizabeth,' she said softly, releasing the hand. It remained momentarily, then retreated back into the ground like a snail drawing back into its shell.

'You're brave, Red,' Tanya murmured, climbing down from where she had perched.

'They were just people,' Red repeated, looking down at the bracelet. 'That's all.'

'I still think you're nuts,' said Fabian, but his voice held a grudging admiration. He scuffed a clod of earth back into its rightful place, then paused to scan the rest of the grave-yard. 'A lot of the ground is disturbed. We should try and put it all right again.'

'Yes,' Red agreed, clambering out of the hollow grave where she still stood. She folded the bracelet into the leather pouch and picked up her shovel again, heaping the soil back in. Tanya and Fabian skirted around the yard fill-ing in clumps of overturned dirt and turf. Finally, when all the soil was replaced in Elizabeth's grave they covered it with the grass turf they had taken off to start with.

Afterwards, Red's clothes clung to her skin, damp with sweat. She was exhausted. Tanya and Fabian didn't look much better off; Fabian had smeared dirt above his upper lip, giving himself an extraordinary moustache, and Tanya was shivering with cold and looking longingly back in the direction of the manor.

'Go back if you want,' said Red, but not unkindly. 'Both of you. But I'm staying. While I'm here I'm going to try and search the church.'

Tanya shook her head, her hair dancing around her face in windblown tangles.

'We're in this together.'

Red felt a rush of warmth for them both. A dull ache began in her throat, and she swallowed it away before it crept into her voice.

'Let's go, then,' she said gruffly.

Tanya led them to the side of the church, past a stone well with a battered bucket. Tucked away into the church wall, as she had described, was a tiny window roughly an arm's length higher than Red was tall.

'You think you'll be able to squeeze through that?' she asked Tanya doubtfully.

'I might,' said Tanya. 'It's worth trying.'

'We need to get rid of that mesh first,' said Fabian.

'Hmm,' Red agreed. She lifted her shovel, using the handle end to batter at the mesh. It was tough, but the tears had weakened it and eventually it gave. Bottles and jars balanced on the windowsill crashed and smashed to the floor on the other side.

'We could probably go to prison for that, too,' said Fabian resignedly.

Tanya took her jacket off and handed it to Fabian, turning to Red. 'I need you to give me a leg-up.'

Obligingly, Red moved closer to the wall and linked her fingers together. Tanya stepped into the foothold she had created and launched herself towards the window, grabbing the sill. She pitched herself onto it, balancing precariously on the narrow, sloping ledge and gripping the sides until she was secure. Already, Red could see that Tanya's slim frame would fit through easily.

'Pass me a torch,' Tanya said.

Fabian handed her one, and she shone it through the narrow slit.

'It's a storeroom,' she said. 'There's lots of bottles and a mop and bucket. And there's a door – it's closed but maybe it's unlocked. I'm going in.'

'Wait,' said Red, grabbing her ankle. 'Make sure there's something for you to stand on to get out first, in case you can't go through that door.'

Tanya leaned further through the window, lifting the torch.

'There's nothing . . . oh, wait – there's a chair. It should be high enough to get back up.'

'All right.' Red released her ankle. 'Be careful. If you notice anything odd, anything at all, come straight back out.'

Tanya slithered through the window, twisting to get her legs through, followed by her shoulders. Then she vanished into the dark window altogether and they heard her drop nimbly to the floor. Through the window they saw flickering light from Tanya's torch, and then came the sound of a door creaking open. After that the torchlight vanished and there was silence. Oberon sat very still, his head cocked to one side and his eyes trained on the dark spot which Tanya had vanished into.

Red and Fabian waited, increasingly anxious with every moment that Tanya was gone.

'What if she's found something?' said Fabian. 'What if she's found another charm . . . and there's now some horrible curse on her? How will we get in to help her?'

'She won't go near it if she sees it,' said Red, but inwardly she was worried. Tanya was impetuous – and from what had happened earlier she knew that none of them would need to get too near to a charm for it to take effect. Worse still, Tanya was alone, and there was no way for Red or Fabian to get in and help her.

She called Tanya's name a couple of times and listened for a reply. When none came, Fabian started to chew his fingernails and Red began to pace back and forth.

'That's it,' she said finally. 'Fabian, come here. I'm going in after her.'

'You won't fit,' Fabian snorted. 'It's way too small for you – too small for me, even.'

'I've got to try,' she said. 'Give me a lift up.'

With difficulty, Fabian linked his fingers together, mimicking the way Red had for Tanya, and hoisted her into the air. It was a clumsy attempt. Fabian wasn't strong enough to hold her and she failed to get a grip on the window ledge. She slid back down the wall, skinning her palms and bumping her knees, while Fabian ended up with his hands full of mud from her boots.

'What are you doing?' a bemused voice asked.

'Coming to look for you!' Fabian retorted as they spun around to see Tanya watching them.

'There's a side door,' she said, beckoning. 'It's got one of those old-fashioned latches and a bolt – it was jammed at first.'

They followed her round the other side of the church to where a studded wooden door was ajar in a narrow stone archway. The door was very small, testament to how old the place was. Tanya was the only one of the three who did not need to duck as she went through it.

Inside the church was no warmer than outside. Red was anxious. If they were caught in the church they were likely to get into a lot of trouble. Their only advantage was that the church really was quite alone, a good half-mile from its closest neighbour in any direction. But the thought of being caught, this close to finding James, made her exceedingly twitchy.

'I've found the lights,' said Tanya. 'Shall I put them on?'

'No,' Red answered. 'Just stick to the torches, and keep them low.'

It was a simple church, laid out in a 'T' shape, with plain wooden pews and an equally plain altar adorned only with a lectern and a low, wide table. There was little that looked to be of value; even the candlesticks on the table were brass. The one thing of beauty was a vast stained-glass window high up on the wall, overlooking the entire church. Once or twice their wayward torch beams caught it, lighting up the vibrantly-coloured glass. Against the wall below it was an area of scaffolding where some kind of work was in progress.

'Is it even safe to be in here?' said Tanya. 'What are they doing to that wall?'

'Looks like it's being restored,' said Fabian, nodding to a pile of new bricks in a crate nearby. 'The stonework is all crumbling and weathered – the wall must be breaking down gradually.'

'I don't even know where to begin,' said Tanya, turning away from the scaffolding.

'If there's a charm here we'll find it,' said Red. 'I'm certain of it.'

They shone the torches under the pews and over the hard floor, even conducting a fingertip search on hands and knees until their knees bruised and their hands were numb with cold. The air grew even cooler as the time ticked by. The night was ebbing away from them.

'I think we should give up,' said Fabian. 'There's nothing here.'

They neared the far wall with the scaffolding once more, sweeping their torches around one last time. On their way towards the door Oberon jumped up at the scaffolding suddenly, nosing past two sticky workmen's mugs and into a half-eaten packet of biscuits. He wolfed down one or two before Tanya got to him and pushed him down. It took both hands for her to wrestle the greedy dog away, and in doing so, she placed her torch on the scaffolding. Only when she went to pick it up again did Red notice what the torch's beam had picked out.

'Stop,' she said, her eyes fixed on the wall.

Tanya followed her gaze and Fabian, who had been almost out of the side door by then, hurried back over.

Lodged between the crumbling stonework, something small and silver was directly in the light from the torch.

'It's the Mantle,' Red said, peering closer. Her voice was steady though her insides were not. 'The staff of strength.'

She clambered onto the scaffold and edged over to the wall. 'It's wedged between the stones.'

'Can you pull it out?' Tanya asked.

'That's the whole point,' said Red. She touched it very gently. Only a small section the length of her thumbnail was visible, along with the link. The rest was buried beneath the stone. She felt her forehead prickle with a sudden sweat. 'If we pull it out we don't know what damage it could do. The wall's obviously unstable or it wouldn't need repairing. If we remove one of the stones to get to it the whole thing could collapse.'

'The staff of strength in a weak wall,' Fabian said grimly. He pulled himself up next to her and leaned in to touch it.

'Careful,' Red snapped. 'We need to think about this.' She pulled out her knife and ran the point of its blade around the edges of the stone. Even with the light pressure the mortar holding the stone in place crumbled a little, a fine dust falling to the wooden scaffold.

'It's brittle,' said Fabian. 'We could scrape it away and have the stone loose in no time.'

'Getting it out is easy,' said Red. 'All we have to do is touch the bracelet and it'll reconnect. Doing it with enough time to get away if the wall comes crashing down is the problem. If it came in on us we could get killed.'

'Not if we're fast enough,' said Tanya, absent-mindedly giving Oberon another biscuit without really meaning to. 'The scaffold would act as some kind of support and buy some time – enough to grab it and run.'

'It's risky,' said Red.

'But there's no other way,' Tanya argued. 'Listen, I can run fast. Let me do it. As long as my path is clear to the door I can make it in a few seconds.'

All three of them stared at the distance from the scaffold to the door. It wasn't far. Tanya's plan sounded very possible.

'Be quick,' said Red, handing the pouch with the bracelet to Tanya. Then she and Fabian made their way to the door with Oberon, kicking the path to the door clear from obstructions; workmen's tools and a couple of unused scaffold poles.

Tanya climbed onto the lower level of the scaffold, nearing the charm. With a last glance at the door, she took the bracelet out and held it to the protruding silver Mantle. As it attached itself she drew her hand back furtively, allowing the length of the charm to slide out of the crevice. A fine, powdery dust came with it as a section of the crumbling brick shifted.

'I've got it!' she called, tucking the bracelet tightly into her hand and rolling off the scaffold. As her feet met the ground, a heavy thud confirmed that a brick had fallen free from the wall onto the wooden scaffold. Before the second brick could fall Tanya was already halfway across the church.

Fabian, seeing her near the door, held it open wide for her to make a clean exit. No sooner had she cleared it to join them safely outside than Oberon, unable to bear the thought of uneaten biscuits, shot through the door in a flash, bounding towards the scaffold. Behind it, several bricks slipped from the wall, hit the wooden platform and then crashed to the floor.

'Oberon, NO!' Tanya cried. Before Red or Fabian could react she was hurtling back into the church.

'Tanya, get out of there!' Fabian yelled. 'You'll get yourself killed!'

Grabbing the wretched biscuits from the scaffold, Tanya flung them with all her might, ducking as more chunks of flying stone came her way. The packet soared through the door and landed clear outside, joined a moment later by Oberon who proceeded to gobble them down without a second thought.

Tanya was neither as fast nor as lucky. She made it partway to the door when a section of brickwork came toppling inwards, skidding across the scaffold, and crashed to the floor in front of her, forcing her to stop. Its destruction left a gaping hole in the top part of the wall. More sections disintegrated. Within seconds the wall came down, falling like a shoulder drooping in defeat. Its collapse heralded the end for the stained-glass window too, for with nothing to support it, it came soaring into the church and shattered. Almost at the door now, Tanya cried out. A terrible, ominous creaking sounded from above. Helpless, Red and Fabian could only encourage Tanya to keep moving, but now the girl had frozen and was looking skyward.

'Get away!' she gasped. 'Away from the door! The roof—'

If she finished her sentence, Red and Fabian never heard it, for with a sound to rival a clap of thunder, a section of the church roof plummeted towards them, blocking off all access to the door – trapping Tanya inside.

'TANYA!' Fabian cried, rushing forward. Red caught him and held him back.

'The window!' she hissed.

They ran round the back of the church, past the half-demolished wall, and to the window where Tanya had first got in. Fabian cupped his hands together and shouted, calling her name. Red joined him, and Oberon, who had suddenly realised his mistress was missing, began to bark in distress.

After a minute of shouting there was still no reply. Red heaved Fabian up to the window, straining under his weight as he looked through. Oberon barked relentlessly. For once, Red did not mind – it was a sound that was likely to comfort Tanya . . . if she could still hear it. Fumbling with the torch, Fabian shone it through the window.

'There's so much dust,' he croaked, coughing suddenly. 'Tanya!'

'I can't hold you for much longer,' Red grunted. 'Plus we don't know how stable *this* wall is now!'

'I can see her!' Fabian said suddenly. 'She's by the store-room door, on the floor!' He choked back a noise like a sob. 'She's . . . she's not moving. She must have run for it when the roof came down. Tanya, wake up . . . *please*!'

Red's strength gave out, forcing her to let Fabian go. He

continued to call while she shook out her aching arms. Still there was no answer. Another crash came from inside the church. More of it was collapsing.

'We're running out of time,' said Fabian. 'We can't even go for help – the whole building could come down.'

'She's probably just unconscious,' said Red. 'If only we had some water to throw on her face – it might bring her out of it.'

'Water . . .' Fabian repeated. 'The well!' He ran back in the direction of the graveyard, vanishing beyond the front of the church. Minutes went by, during which Oberon's barks became whines, and more thuds sounded from within the church as its walls creaked and shifted. Finally Fabian reappeared, carrying a pail of well water.

Garnering the last of her strength, Red lifted Fabian up to the window again. This time it was even harder with the added weight of the full pail, plus by the time Fabian had steadied himself a good pint or so had slopped all over Red and was dripping icily down her face and neck. Giving it his best aim, Fabian launched the water through the window, the bucket bouncing on the other side of the wall as he dropped it.

'She's moving!' he cried. 'Tanya! Tanya! Get up!'

A groggy voice answered him.

'Fabian? My head hurts . . .'

'No, don't lie back down, you've got to get up, *now*!'

There was a shuffling sound, followed by a fit of coughing.

'I feel dizzy.' Tanya's voice was weak.

'Of course you're dizzy,' said Fabian, panicking. 'You've got an enormous gash on your forehead and— *Ouch!*'

Red, desperate to shut him up and with no hands free to pinch, had nipped his leg with her teeth. 'Don't tell her that, you idiot!'

'Well, it's not that bad, really,' Fabian gabbled. 'Just a scratch. Now, climb onto the chair and take my hand.'

The chair scraped across the floor and clattered. Red groaned as Fabian's weight shifted.

'Steady,' he said. 'Try again. Just take it slowly.'

'Not *too* slowly,' said Red, through gritted teeth. Her hair was in her eyes and worse, Fabian's bottom was in her face. A groaning, creaking noise had started in the roof. 'Hurry up!'

'That's it,' said Fabian. 'Now grab hold of me. Good!'

Twisting her head, Red saw that Tanya's head and torso were through the little window, her arms draped around Fabian's neck. She looked dreadful – and as Fabian had described, there was a horrible cut on her head. Her face was smeared with blood.

'I feel sick,' she moaned. 'It hurts.'

'Just throw up if you need to,' Fabian said, trying to sound cheerful. 'But only if you really, really need to.'

Her arms burning, Red could hold on no longer.

'I'm letting go, hold on to her!'

Fabian slipped out of her grasp, bringing Tanya tumbling down on top of him. As she slid through the window the rough stone tore her top and scratched her skin, causing her to cry out again. Fabian was on his feet at once, and together he and Red half lifted and half dragged Tanya away from the wall, away from the church and through the graveyard, Oberon bounding along beside them.

They paused only to seal the entrance to the secret tunnel – for none of them wanted to go back through it. While Red and Fabian shifted the slab back into place, Tanya staggered out of the graveyard and heaved the contents of her stomach into the grass. Though the front of the church was intact there was a final, obstinate crash from the back as the wall collapsed altogether.

Dirty, dishevelled and stunned, they left the graveyard and headed for the manor. Above them, the edges of the sky blushed pink as daylight dawned along with the realisation that they had been out all night.

31

N THE BATHROOM THAT ADJOINED
Tanya's room, Red tended to Tanya's wounds.
Fabian hovered in the doorway, refusing to go
to bed. Watery sunshine filtered through the
window. Were it not for their dirty, bloody and drawn
faces the night would have seemed nothing more than a bad
dream.

'How are you feeling?' Red asked.

'Better,' said Tanya. She lifted her hand to touch the
makeshift bandage that Red had made by ripping up one of
Florence's clean white towels.

'You look better,' said Red. 'But it's a nasty cut. You'll
need to get it looked at.'

'But that means I'll have to tell my grandmother,' Tanya
said.

Red hesitated.

'I know. And I think . . . I think it's time she knew. About
everything. Because this is getting way too dangerous.'

'But she'll stop us from searching for the charms,' Fabian
protested. 'And we've still got three more to find.'

'She can stop you two,' Red answered evenly. 'But she can't stop me, because I'll be gone.'

Tanya looked up and Fabian opened his mouth to interrupt, but Red carried on.

'I don't think the last three charms are in the house. I think they're in the places we discussed – Elizabeth's old cottage and the Highwayman inn. I'm going to them today. Alone.'

'But that's only two,' said Tanya. 'What about the third?'

'I think I know,' said Red, grimly. 'But you don't need to worry about that.'

'Red?' Tanya asked in a small voice. 'When you find James, what will you do? I mean, where will you go? You've been on the run for so long . . . what's going to happen to you when you've got James to think of? You can't carry on living like this. What if you're both put back into care?'

'I'm not going back,' Red said sharply. 'And neither is James. I'll find a way, some way for us to disappear. Maybe we can join some travellers, find work . . . keep moving around. I don't know, I'll think of something. But I'm not going back, not ever.'

She ignored the worried glances Tanya and Fabian gave each other and got up, walking back into the bedroom. She pulled her bag out from under Tanya's bed, and began methodically checking its contents.

Fabian followed her out of the bathroom.

'You're leaving now?'

She nodded, draping the fox-skin coat over the bag and checking the bracelet once more.

'I'll take the first bus.'

'I suppose you'll be wanting the directions then,' Fabian said quietly. He crept out of the room, leaving Tanya and Red alone.

'So this is goodbye,' said Tanya.

Red rubbed her nose awkwardly. 'For a time, maybe.' She tried to smile. 'Perhaps not forever. Who knows? When we're older, and people have forgotten about me, maybe one day it'll be safe for us to meet again.'

Fabian returned, offering Red a scrap of paper with his spidery writing all over it, and a rolled up ten-pound note from his money box.

'Here. You'll need the money for your bus fare. The cottage is the furthest. You'd be best going there first and working your way back to the Highwayman.'

Red squinted at the paper, trying to decipher Fabian's scrawl.

'I know this village,' she said slowly. 'Knook . . . My aunt lives there – I can't remember where exactly, it's been too long. Or at least, she *did* live there. I don't know if she still does.'

'Your aunt?' Tanya said in surprise. 'I didn't realise you had family. In the summer you said you had nowhere you could go.'

Red shrugged.

'It's true. She's the only one. My mother's younger

sister, Primrose – or Rose, as she insists on being called. She's the oddball of the family. I never had much to do with her when my parents were alive, even though I liked her. But my parents didn't like me visiting her for some reason. When they died, I hoped that she'd take me and James in. By the time the care home contacted her it was too late.'

'Maybe you could still try,' Tanya said. 'If you went to see her . . . perhaps she could help.'

Red looked unsure. 'Perhaps.' She threw the last of her things into her bag, and refilled her flask with water from the bathroom. She looked in the mirror over the basin. Her eyes were raging red from lack of sleep, her face thin and drawn. Her hair stuck up in short, elfin tufts. Finally, she fastened her bag and lifted it onto her shoulder. It was time to go.

Tanya and Fabian watched from the porch as Red slipped through the gates of Elvesden Manor onto the dirt track. Soon she was out of sight.

'Are you thinking what I'm thinking?' Tanya asked Fabian softly.

'If what you're thinking is that we carry on looking for the charms, then yes,' said Fabian, fiercely. 'I can't just do nothing when my father is being held prisoner – we have to keep searching.'

'Then we need to leave the house before my grandmother and Nell are awake,' said Tanya. She gestured to her head. 'Once they see this, the game is up.'

'I think the game might already be up,' said Fabian. 'I didn't say in front of Red but when I went back into my room to get the directions to Elizabeth's old cottage, the notes we made about the charms – and their locations – had been disturbed. Someone's been through my things.'

'Let's go now, before anyone has a chance to stop us,' said Tanya.

Fabian nodded. 'If we head straight for the Highwayman we should have located the charm by the time Red doubles back. That way we can wait for her and we'll know whether she was successful at the cottage.'

'And whether she's safe,' Tanya finished. 'And then, we'll get her to tell us where she thinks the final charm is so we can all search for it – together.'

The first bus to Knook left just after eight o'clock. With time to spare, Red walked the lanes from Elvesden Manor to Tickey End in order to save money, and was on the bus for five minutes as it sat in the station, ready to leave. In moments she was dozing, for the next hour drifting in and out of sleep. When it finally crawled into Knook, she hurried off the bus with a mumbled thanks to the driver, and strode off in what she hoped was the right direction.

The village had little to attract outsiders. Parts of it were even older than Tickey End, though here the tumbledown buildings were mainly cottages, and there was a distinct lack of the shops and inns that kept Tickey End thriving. At a public drinking fountain, Red consulted a small freestanding map of the village, and after working out which way to go, headed off.

After a wrong turn and a lengthy backtrack she eventually found the street she was looking for – Magpie Lane – and began making her way along it. The cottage she was seeking had a name rather than a number, and though Fabian had warned that it was likely to have changed over the years, he had helpfully noted that, on the old maps at least, it had been the only cottage to be completely detached. The others on the street were married in pairs or huddled together in little terraced rows.

'Honeysuckle Cottage,' she murmured to herself. 'Where are you?'

She was less than halfway down the street when things began looking familiar. She stopped, taking in a small pond adorned with ugly little gnomes in one garden, and a weathered swing seat in another. She stared at it, noting the flaky remnants of paint that had been bright, fresh blue the last time she'd seen it. She knew this street. She had been here before. A figure moved in the window behind the swing seat, and the net curtain twitched. Red moved on, keeping her head down. Memories stirred in her head: herself, five, maybe six years old, swinging her legs in the back of her parents' car as it drove down this very road.

'*An hour, and then we're leaving,*' her father had said. '*And if she asks for Rowan to stay over, just tell her we've got plans.*'

'*But you know she'll just keep asking,*' Rowan's mother had answered, with a fretful glance back at her daughter. 'She always does.'

'Then we'll just keep telling her 'no',' her father said. 'She's got to understand.'

'Why can't I stay at Auntie Primrose's?' Rowan asked absently. She had just seen two children on a swinging garden seat. It looked fun, and Rowan longed to have a go, but soon the car had driven past and she forgot it, her child's mind looking for the next distraction.

'It's Rose, darling,' her mother corrected. 'She doesn't like being called Primrose, remember?'

'Oh, yes,' said Rowan. 'I like Auntie Rose. She's got red hair, like me.'

'Of course you can stay at Auntie Rose's,' her mother replied. 'Just not tonight. Another night, perhaps.'

'That's what you always say,' Rowan whined. 'I like her house. I like all the animals. Why can't we have a pet?'

Her father muttered something that she did not hear.

The memory ended there, and Red stopped a little way in front of the only cottage that stood completely alone; a cottage that looked no different from the last time she had seen it, many years before. A wooden gate, painted crimson, opened onto a stone path leading up to a door of the same colour. The walls were white, though in the shade of the heavy thickets and trees that surrounded it, it appeared almost blue. A sign on the door, painted with familiar red berries to match those in the garden, read *Rowanwood Cottage*. It was Aunt Rose's house.

The realisation filled her with a heavy dread. Her aunt had lived here ever since Red could remember, yet all the while it had been the cottage that Elizabeth Elvesden had lived in. The coincidence was extraordinary, yet Red was aware that it had to be more than that. The bracelet had led her to this point, to this place, for a reason.

The curtains were all open, yet Red did not dare to knock at the door. Somehow she had to get into the house without being seen, but she did not know whether her aunt was even in or not. Taking a chance, she slipped through the gate and headed around the side of the house, where there was a second, larger gate of wrought iron that led to the back garden. Fixed to it was another sign, and this one said: *Beware of the dogs, goat and geese!*

Rowan cursed aloud. It was not the dogs she was worried about, but rather the geese her aunt kept. They were vicious creatures that delivered bruising pecks at every opportunity, and she had feared them a great deal when she was little. Now, as she peered into the overgrown garden, she could see two geese at the far end, one a great white thing called Boris, and another grey one that she remembered as Tybalt, which was ferociously chasing a little brown duck across the garden.

Nearer to the house, next to the shed, was an old grey goat with only one horn. Thankfully it was tethered on a long piece of rope and was preoccupied with chewing something.

There was no sign of the dogs, and as she lifted the latch

she realised that they were not in the garden or the house, for had they been they would have barked. Immediately she guessed that Rose must have taken them out for their morning walk, and that this was a perfect opportunity to get into the house. She sneaked into the garden, closing the gate quietly behind her. The garden was so sheltered from the house and from the nearest neighbours that she did not need to worry about being seen. Ducking under the washing line, she made her way to the back door. It was, of course, locked, but this did not deter her. She scouted round the garden, lifting plant pots, looking under the mat and for any place her aunt would have stashed a spare key, but she found none.

A hissing noise sounded from behind her, and she turned to see the fat white goose waddling towards her.

'Buzz off, Boris,' she muttered, skirting around him, but the creature would not be deterred. He lunged for her shin, delivering a painful peck, then backed off, honking as if with laughter.

'Oh, you think that's funny, do you?' Red began, rubbing her shin vigorously – but then a marvellous idea struck her. 'Let's see how funny you think this is!'

Pulling her bag off her shoulder, she opened it and removed the fox-skin coat. Tucking her bag safely beneath a nearby bush, she put the coat on and buttoned it up, letting the glamour take effect. The result was very pleasing indeed, and she couldn't help but give a few little warning yaps, just to make up for all the pecks of the past.

At the sight of the fox Boris honked again, but this time it was with fear as he retreated hastily to the other end of the garden. Tybalt, who had finished terrorising the duck and had been considering launching his own attack on Red, rapidly changed his mind. Only the goat looked nonchalant, munching on the white thing which looked suspiciously like a pair of knickers. Red sat in the centre of the lawn feeling pleased with herself, but the feeling faded as she remembered why she was there. She had to get into the house.

The answer hit her as she heard the side gate opening. Her disguise was the perfect solution, for Rose would never know the difference. All she had to do was to play on her aunt's sympathy.

As her aunt's dogs came round the side of the house, panting heavily and worn out from their walk, their hackles went up at the sight of her and they started to bark.

Red froze with fear until she realised they were still on their leads, and however much they stretched and strained, her aunt was holding them back. She came into sight a moment after the dogs, her pale, pointed face in a frown as she sought to find what the commotion was about.

'Whatever is the matter with you lot—' she began, then stopped as she saw Red cowering on her lawn. 'Quiet, boys,' she said, tethering the dogs' leads to a drainpipe.

Red turned away and limped in what she hoped was a convincing way.

'Oh, *dear*,' she heard Rose say in distress, and her shoes scuffed the patio as she came nearer.

Red took a few more steps and then collapsed on the grass, closing her eyes. She smelled her aunt's perfume, something lavendery mingled with the scent of dog, as Rose knelt by her side. Something soft and fluffy was being tucked around her: her aunt had taken a towel from the washing line.

Red gave a little whine.

'Hush, now, I'm not going to hurt you,' Rose murmured, lifting her expertly into her arms.

Red felt herself being shifted gently into one arm as Rose felt in her pocket with one hand. Then there was the jangle of keys and the sound of the back door being unlocked. She was in.

Rose threw her keys on to the kitchen worktop. Red opened her eyes a crack and saw that they had landed next to a plump cat scavenging on the work surface. The familiar smell of the house washed over her; the ever doggy odour mixed with the smell of fishy cat food. The entire house was dominated by its animal occupants, yet the smell was strangely comforting. It brought back further memories: Red's first taste of ice cream soda one hot summer (complete with cat hair garnish), splashing in the washing-up bowl in the back garden as a toddler (along with her aunt's excitable puppy), and being read to in Rose's living room (animal stories, of course). There was not one bad memory among them and, not for the first time, Red wondered what her parents' aversion to Rose had stemmed from.

Her musings stopped when Rose brought her into the

living room and set her down on the rug in front of the wood burner. Unwrapping the towel, she ran her hands lightly over Red's fox coat, applying light pressure here and there as she checked for injuries. Rose's long red hair tickled Red's nose as she leaned over her.

'I can't see any injuries,' she muttered. 'How odd . . . unless it's poison. Good grief, that might just be it.' She tucked the towel around Red again, then got up and went back out into the hall, returning a moment later with her keys. 'I won't be long,' she said worriedly. 'I'm going to get the vet. He'll make you well again, I'm sure of it.' She left the room, closing the door behind her, and a moment later Red heard the front door open and close. She was alone in the house.

In a flash she was up, throwing the fox-skin coat off. Her plan had worked better than she could have hoped. Now she just had to find the charm, and hoped that her aunt wouldn't return at the wrong moment and be endangered.

Despite the generous amount of land that came with it, the cottage had no upstairs, existing only on one level. Red knew her way around perfectly, and with the exception of the wallpaper and some furniture, little had changed. There were only three rooms: the kitchen, the sitting room and one bedroom, plus a tiny bathroom that had been added on in recent years, for in Elizabeth's time there would have been no bathroom, just an outhouse. For this reason she dismissed searching the bathroom and decided to concentrate on the rest of the house.

The kitchen was not dissimilar to that of Elvesden Manor, though on a smaller scale. The ceiling and doorways were low and dark beams ran the length of the room. She rummaged in the cupboards and drawers, finding countless tins of pet food and animal care manuals, charity stickers and vet bills. The walls were adorned with framed pictures of the numerous pets, and several of Red herself, before James had been born. After that she had not seen much of her aunt at all. Red frowned as she studied the pictures, for all of them were crooked on the wall, at angles.

The cat on the worktop eyed her lazily before stretching and turning its back on her. In the moments that it got up, she saw that it was lying on a stash of unopened letters, and suddenly she remembered how her aunt disliked opening letters; in fact disliked any real contact with the world outside her little cocoon of animals. She did not even have a telephone. No wonder the care home had struggled to contact her, she thought in disgust.

She ducked out of the kitchen, beneath an iron horseshoe hanging above the doorway. There was one above the door of every room, and she recalled Rose telling her that it was for luck.

She went into her aunt's bedroom. A single bed was heaped with cushions and two more snoozing cats. Above the bed was another crooked picture. Halfway down the chimneybreast was a thin mantlepiece with trinkets and knick-knacks, all of which she peered into. In the centre was another picture of Red, taken when she was about six years old, in a frame that she had made herself from lollipop sticks as a gift to Rose. She picked it up, and as she did, another photograph slid out from behind it and fluttered away from her, landing in the empty grate.

Except the grate was not quite empty. Though it had been swept out, there was a small pile of ashes that the brush had not managed to reach. And in those ashes was a tiny, blackened mask. Unthinkingly she picked it out of the ash and rubbed it between her fingers. The soot came away, revealing silver beneath. The mask of Glamour. Delving into her pocket she shakily removed the bracelet, connected the charm, then shoved it back into the drawstring pouch. She had what she had come for, and it had been the easiest one of all, yet the knowledge only made her more *uneasy*. She picked the photo out of the grate and reached for the frame it had fallen from. For the first time she registered what the picture was of, and it shocked her.

A much younger Rose had been snapped in a hospital bed, looking tired and wan. Her auburn hair billowed around her head in a wild cloud, and in her arms was a tiny baby. Far from looking happy, however, Rose looked troubled and vulnerable.

Red slowly slid the picture back behind the image of herself, not knowing what to think. She knew that she had stumbled on some secret in her aunt's past, but she could not begin to imagine what might have happened. She had never heard her mother saying anything about Rose having a child; yet it was clear from the photo that that was indeed the case, and Rose had always seemed to like children. Had something happened to the baby?

She turned to leave, but hesitated. A nagging feeling would not let her go until she had at least tried to resolve what had happened in Rose's past, and a horrid little thought pushed its way into her mind. She edged closer to her aunt's built-in cupboard next to the fireplace. Opening it, she breathed in the ever-present scent of dog hair on the clothes hanging on the rail, but ignoring them she looked above to where there was a shelf of clutter including a box and a pile of well-thumbed books. Taking the box down, she opened it to find a small pile of baby clothes. She snapped the lid back on and pushed it on to the shelf, her heart thudding. There was something eerie about those clothes in isolation. Just clothes, and no baby . . .

As she withdrew her hand she caught it on one of the books, and the two nearest the top came sliding down towards her. She caught them, and stared as she took in their titles, first: *Protection from the Little Folk*, and the second: *Ward: The Power of Protection Against Magic*.

'It can't be,' she whispered to herself, thumbing through the books in disbelief. 'It just can't . . .'

She paused to read a page that had been folded over at the corner.

Faeries can be discouraged from coming into your home by keeping iron objects, using herbs and flowers (see page 122) and with careful use of salt. Smaller deterrents include keeping pictures and mirrors at angles to prevent faeries from settling on them.

'Crooked pictures,' Red said, turning to the other book, where a page had been marked with an envelope.

Natural Protection Against All Things Fey, read the heading. *To ward off unwelcome attention from the little folk, there are numerous easily obtainable plants that are known to discourage fey activity.*

'Ash,' she read aloud. 'Bay, blackberry, clove, garlic, linden, rowan, sandalwood, witch hazel . . .' Her eyes lingered over the word 'rowan', then ran down the page where there was a second heading. 'Plants to Avoid . . . bluebell, elder, foxglove, hawthorn, primrose . . .'

'Rowan? Is that . . . is that *you?*'

Red spun round, dropping the book. Aunt Rose stood in the doorway, staring at her like she was an apparition. She still had her coat on, and her keys were in her hand.

'I don't understand . . . what . . . what are you doing here?'

'I—' Red faltered, searching for some kind of explanation, or possible escape – but there was none. She was well and truly cornered, and, stupidly, had left the fox-skin coat in the living room. The irony was not lost on her – that she had found the mask of Glamour, yet it was the very thing she was prevented from using.

'I . . . left an injured fox in the living room,' Rose whispered. 'The vet was out on an emergency call . . .' She shook herself. 'And now there's just a fur coat . . . and you're in here. It was you, wasn't it? It's some kind of glamour. Why?'

Red shook her head, nauseous. It was too much to take in – her aunt's carefully hidden knowledge of fairies and glamour. Hidden for so long, and now revealed.

'I was . . . looking for something,' she said.

'What?' Rose implored, still frozen in the doorway. 'I don't understand. What were you looking for?'

'A charm,' said Red. 'Just a tiny little charm . . .'

A shadow crossed Rose's face.

'You mean that mask, don't you?' Her eyes searched and found Red's sooty fingertips. 'It just appeared one day, out of nowhere. I knew it must be something to do with . . . *them*, so I tried to get rid of it. Threw it into the bin at first. It came back. So I threw it into the stream . . . It still found its way back. I was hoping that the fire would get rid of it for good . . . but obviously not. Why do you want it? Where is it?'

'In a safe place,' Red whispered. She could not take her eyes off her aunt, this woman she thought she had known. 'And you don't need to know why. It's better that way.'

'People are looking for you, Rowan,' Rose said sadly. 'Is it true you took those children? Why would you do that?'

Red gave no answer.

'My little Rowanberry. What's happened to you?'

'Can't you guess?' Red said bitterly. She gestured to the fairy books. 'Is it really that difficult? Why didn't you tell me you could see fairies? You must have known I could see them too! Why didn't you share some of this with me, some of this protective knowledge? Instead you kept it all to yourself, along with your other secrets. Oh, don't look so surprised.' Her anger was reaching boiling point now. 'I found the photograph, and the baby clothes. I know your big secret. You had a baby, didn't you? And I think I can guess what happened to it – the same thing that happened to my brother while we were in care! It was taken, wasn't it? Taken by the fairies!'

Rose clutched her hand to her throat as if she'd been stung by some poisonous insect.

'James . . . you mean, *they* took him?'

'Yes,' Red spat. 'And I've been trying to get him back ever since. But maybe, just maybe if you'd shared your knowledge with me, or even cared enough to come and get us sooner after my parents died, none of this would have happened! Instead you left us there for weeks!'

'I didn't mean to,' Rose said weakly. 'I didn't know what had happened until four weeks after the accident. I'd been abroad, working in an animal sanctuary. Came back to the awful news. I wanted to come sooner, but I'd contracted malaria – I was bedridden for weeks.' She came into the bedroom and slumped on the bed, no longer blocking the door. Red's route was now open to escape, but her aunt's words had pierced her and she was unable to move.

'But I did come for you, both of you,' she continued, her head in her hands. 'By then it was too late. James had already gone missing . . . and so had you.'

'Why didn't you tell me about the fairies?' Red repeated obstinately. 'Why didn't you tell me you could see them?'

425

Rose looked up, her eyes shining with tears.

'Because I can't.'

'You expect me to believe that?'

'It's the truth. I know they exist, but I don't see them, at least . . . not in the way you do. I don't have the second sight.'

Red held her gaze.

'Then what is all this? Why do you live all alone in this little cottage, surrounding yourself with rowan and iron horseshoes? What are you so afraid of? And what happened to your baby?'

Rose stared back into her lap, and took a deep, shuddering breath.

'If you really want to know, then sit down, and I'll tell you. It's time you knew the truth, about everything.'

Red hesitated, then slowly walked over to the bed and perched at the end, away from her aunt. She looked mad, sitting there with her frizzy red hair cascading down her back, and her hands twisted in her skirt like a scolded child.

'Everyone knows how I like to be called Rose,' Rose began. 'And not Primrose, which is my real name. But no one, *no one*, knows the reason why except me. I vowed I'd take it to the grave, because even if I'd told anyone they wouldn't have believed me.

'I'd always liked my name,' she continued. 'Until one day, in the summer when I was seventeen. It was the day of the carnival. There was one every year at midsummer, and I'd been chosen as a carnival queen. The theme that year was

426

girls who were named after flowers. Naturally, there were a number of girls who took part: a Jasmine, a Lily, two Roses and two Ivys. But I was the only Primrose. Of course, we dressed to reflect our names. I wore a pretty yellow dress, with green ribbon threaded through it, and a headdress that I made from real, fresh primroses.

'As the carnival rode through the streets and by the woods near to where we lived, I noticed a young man, smiling up at me from the crowd. He had the blackest hair, and eyes to match. He followed with the crowd all the way until the carnival procession finished, and there was dancing in the street.

'I danced with him all night, until my feet were blistered and sore. Even then he didn't want to stop. He had eyes only for me, despite the other girls watching and waiting, hoping for a dance. The night passed in a dream, I felt giddy, dizzy.

'I asked him why he'd chosen me, out of all the other girls. He just laughed, and said he liked my name. He liked it *very* much, he said, and he told me how, if used correctly, primroses could be used in a magic to see fairies.

'I thought he was messing about, or was perhaps a traveller that believed in that kind of thing. By that time, of course, I'd realised that I didn't know *his* name. But when I asked him, he simply laughed, and said it was better that I didn't know.

'When I could dance no more, he took one of the primroses from my hair. "To remember you by," he said. Foolishly,

I asked what he would leave *me* to remember *him* by, to which his only reply was a strange little smile as he went on his way.' Rose fiddled with her hands in her lap. 'I never saw him again after that night. No one did, and no one knew who he was. But whoever he was, he did leave me something to remember him by.' Subconsciously she held a hand to her stomach. 'Nine months later I had a child, a tiny, flame-haired baby.'

'A fairy child?' Red whispered. 'You had a fairy child?'

Rose nodded bitterly.

'Of course, I knew what was happening to me a long time before the baby was born, even though none of it made sense. At first I denied it could be possible, but it was futile. My body was changing, and there was nothing I could do to stop it. I remembered the strange little smile, his talk of fairies. How he'd been so fascinated by my name – and refused to give his.' She gave a wry smile. 'After a little research it all made sense. He was a fairy, and he'd left me with a child. I was terrified, to have this thing growing inside me, this thing I'd neither wanted, nor asked for. I had my life mapped out – I was going to be a vet. There was no room for a child.

'I told only my sister, your mother,' she whispered. 'I couldn't tell her the father was a fairy. Didn't need to. She'd seen me dancing with the young man at the carnival and drawn her own conclusions.

'I was desperate. Young, and foolish, barely more than a child myself. And Anna, who had been married to your father for four years already, was yearning for a child. It was she who suggested it. A perfect solution. I would go and live with them, hiding myself away until the baby was born, and meanwhile Anna would fake her own pregnancy and take the child when it was born. It went like clockwork. Except when the baby was born, I knew I'd made a mistake. I didn't want to give it up. I loved it as soon as I saw it . . . but by then, it was too late. I'd agreed to hand the baby over. I knew it would break Anna's heart if I went back on my word. And so I didn't – but it broke my heart instead.'

'My parents had another child? Before me?' Red repeated.

Rose shook her head, bringing her eyes to meet Red's own, green eyes, so very alike . . .

'No, Rowan,' she said softly. 'There was no other child. The baby I'm talking about . . . it was you.'

Red recoiled.

'It's not true,' she whispered. 'Tell me it's not . . .'

'I'm sorry,' Rose croaked. 'I'm so sorry. You were never meant to find out, not like this. Not at all . . .'

'You gave me up?' Red whispered, horrified. 'You gave me away? How could you do that?'

'Because I thought it was for the best.' Rose reached towards her pleadingly, but Red sprang away.

'And James?' she asked, her lip quivering.

'He was their son. Not your brother, but your cousin . . .'

'NO!' Red shouted.

'I made them promise, before you were born, that I could choose your name . . .'

'Oh, big deal!' Red snarled. 'You pass me off to someone else and then expect me to thank you for choosing my name? Does that make you a better mother, somehow?' Her mouth twisted at the word. 'You're not my mother. No! I don't believe it – I won't!'

But the look on Rose's face – the face that was so like her own, now that she knew the truth – convinced her otherwise.

'I chose the name Rowan before you were born,' Rose continued. 'I knew it would work whether you were a boy or a girl. Protecting you was all that mattered, and your name was the only way I could think to do it. Because it was my name, you see, that got me into trouble in the first place . . . the thing that brought him to me, like a moth to a flame. And so now, I'm Rose. Just plain, ordinary Rose—'

'*No!* It doesn't make any sense – if that was true it makes me half fairy! I can't be one . . . I'm not! I can see them, I'd *know* . . .'

Rose shook her head. 'The name created a barrier, protecting you from everything – even from knowing what you were – and it stopped others with the second sight from seeing what you were—'

Red had heard enough. With a choking sob she jumped up and ran through the cottage. Then she was outside, grabbing her bag from beneath the bush. As she ran back through the garden, out of the side gate and past the dogs, she heard Rose's voice calling after her desperately.

'Rowan, come back! Please, come back!'

She vaulted the front gate and ran, too late remembering the fox-skin coat. She'd left it behind, her source of glamour. Unmasked, exposed, a useless disguise. A pretence that was no longer valid . . . just like her real mother.

Her whole life had been a lie, just one big mask of deceit. The fairies had known it, and let her enter into a bargain she could never win. For how could they give James back now? How could they give her brother back, if she'd never had one to begin with?

32

ED WENT BACK TO ELVESDEN Manor. She didn't know where else to go.

She forgot about the Highwayman, forgot about the last two charms. None of it mattered, because James wasn't her brother and there was no way she could win the task. She had been defeated before she had ever begun, and the fairies had known it all along.

She made no effort to try and get in secretively. She had neither the will nor the motivation, for by now she guessed that Tanya and Fabian would have told Florence the truth about what had really happened to Warwick. For the first time, she walked up to the grand front door – but as she reached out to knock she stopped abruptly. Something wet and red was smeared on it.

A chill ran through her. She hammered at the door.

It was Fabian who answered.

'Red!' he said, his mouth dropping open. 'You came back – you've got to come quickly!'

He pulled her inside, not giving her the chance to speak.

The urgency of his tone alerted her that something had happened, and as he kicked the door shut she followed, feeling dazed and numb.

'It's Nell,' he said breathlessly, hurrying her towards the sitting room. 'She's in a bad way – we're waiting for the doctor.'

They went in. Nell was lying on the couch with her eyes closed, and she was taking deep, trembling breaths. Tanya and Florence were standing over her. Florence was holding Nell's arm in the air and pressing a cloth to her skin which was rapidly soaking crimson.

'Red? Quickly – the bracelet!' Tanya's words came out in a rush. 'Nell found the Dagger – but now she won't stop bleeding!'

Red jolted out of her haze as she took in the scene before her. She pulled the leather pouch out of her pocket.

'I don't understand,' she began. 'How did Nell get involved . . .? Where is it?'

Fabian pointed to a table next to the armchair. 'It's on there. It won't stop . . . *dripping.*' He shuddered.

The Dagger lay in a wet red pool that had spread to the edge of table. As Red watched, it dripped onto the floor, soaking into the carpet like wine.

Nell opened her eyes and tried to sit up.

'Found it . . . for you,' she said weakly, and coughed. 'Took some doing but I managed it. But somehow, an old scar on my arm opened up . . . so much blood . . . just kept getting worse—'

433

'Sit back, now,' said Florence, easing Nell back into the chair.

Red hurried over to the little table. Taking the bracelet out of the pouch, she dangled it over the widening pool, brushing it in the blood. They all heard it connect, and Red tucked it back into the pouch, still dripping and red.

Florence kept the pressure on Nell's arm for a little longer, but it was clear to see that the colour was starting to flood back into her cheeks.

'Fabian, go and make some hot, sweet tea,' said Florence. 'I think we all need a cup.' She looked Red up and down. 'And you, girl, need a good meal inside you.' She shook her head then turned back to Nell, cautiously lifting the towel. Beneath, Red saw an angry purple welt on Nell's skin. Around it were layers of dried red-brown blood, but as Florence wiped away the sticky residue she gave a relieved sigh.

'It's stopped. The wound has healed up again.'

She lowered Nell's arm and rested it across her chest.

'Just stay there for a few minutes,' she said kindly. 'You've had a bad shock.'

She motioned Tanya and Red out of the room, her finger to her lips.

'She needs to rest,' she said, once they were out in the hall. She led them to the kitchen, where Tanya explained what had happened.

'Nell found our notes about the charms in Fabian's room,' she said. 'She went to the Highwayman on her own to search,' she said. 'She wanted to do something to make up for her part in what happened to your brother. She rented the room the robber used to hide his stolen goods in and found the charm straight away – it was hidden in the chimney where the robber used to keep his stash. But as soon as she'd touched it, it began dripping blood . . . and not the healing blood of the treasure. With every drip from the Dagger, her old scar dripped too.'

'So how did she get back here?' Red asked, dazed.

Tanya flushed. 'After you left, Fabian and I continued to search. We didn't want to let you carry on alone, so the plan was to find it and meet with you when you got there. But instead we found Nell. That's when I sent for my grandmother to come and get us—'

'And finally told me what was going on,' Florence interjected sternly.

Fabian set a pot of tea on the table and poured from it. Red stared at her cup for a minute before mechanically lifting it to sip. It tasted of nothing.

'What about you?' Tanya asked. 'Did you find Elizabeth's old cottage?'

She nodded. 'I found it, and the charm, and a lot more besides.'

'Like what?' Tanya asked. 'Why do you look so unhappy? There's only one charm left to find!'

'It doesn't matter,' Red said quietly. 'It was all for nothing.'

'What are you talking about?' said Fabian.

'It was just a game,' said Red. 'A game I could never win, because James is not my brother. He's my cousin. My whole life is a lie and the fairies knew it. They never intended giving him back.'

'You're not making sense,' Tanya said gently. 'How do you know James isn't your brother?'

In fits and starts, the story came out. Once Red had finished, Tanya, Fabian and Florence sat in silence.

'So, you see?' she finished with a bitter laugh. 'I'm not Rowan Fox and I don't have a brother. I don't know who I am any more.'

'But you *are* Rowan,' Tanya said passionately. 'And James is still your cousin. He grew up with you and he loved you – does it matter that he's your cousin and not your brother? If you say he belongs with you then he does. And no one can change that.'

'And you can't give up now,' Fabian pleaded. 'What about my father? He's still there, and you're his only hope!'

'Exactly,' said Tanya. 'We can't leave Warwick there. You have to try, for his sake as well as James's. We just need to find the last charm . . . the Book of knowledge.'

'I know where it is,' Red said softly. 'The only place left that it can be.'

'Where?' said Tanya and Fabian at once.

'The last place the bracelet went to,' she said. 'It's in the great court in the fairy realm. The place where the bargain was made.'

'Of course!' Fabian hit the table, upsetting his cup.

Red stared at the pouch in front of her. Then, for the last time she opened it and took the bracelet out.

'I'll do it,' she said. 'I'll go back. There's nothing more they can take from me now, anyway.' And before she could change her mind, she slipped the bracelet over her wrist.

Before her eyes, Tanya's and Fabian's faces and the kitchen of Elvesden Manor swam before her, as though she was viewing them from underwater. Colours and features merged into one great swirling pool, and she thought she heard Tanya call out to her, as if from a long distance away. New faces appeared, slowly coming into focus.

She found herself kneeling, looking down at a marbled floor. Laughter echoed in her ears, and she followed it to two familiar thrones ahead of her. The fairy court had gathered once more, divided in its entirety, waiting expectantly. This time there were no masks, no festivities. Just her and the court, split evenly down the middle, and only one throne was occupied. The other remained empty, its only occupant a crown of withered brown summer flowers.

As everything focused and sharpened, the figure in the winter throne stood; and she looked up to meet the eyes of the young man who had worn the horned mask on the night the bargain was made. Now he wore a crown of berries and leaves, but still the horns, antlers in fact, were present. For the first time Red saw that they were not part of any mask, but part of him. He smiled down at her, and it was the smile of a predator; a wolf, or perhaps a fox. It was a triumphant smile, a victorious smile.

'Welcome back,' he said in a voice as smooth as cream.

Red got up, wrenching the bracelet off her wrist and throwing it to the floor.

'There,' she said viciously. 'There are your charms, your precious Thirteen Treasures. I've fulfilled my part of the bargain. I've come for my brother – and for my friend.'

The fox-like smile widened, more a baring of teeth than a real smile. The winter king clicked his fingers, and a goblin minion hurried to collect the bracelet from where Red had hurled it. Placing it on a fat velvet cushion, it waddled over to the young man and bowed in a grovelling gesture that made Red sick to her stomach.

In a deft, theatrical motion, the bracelet was swept up into the horned man's fingers, where he made a show of counting for the benefit of his audience.

'Only twelve?' he said mockingly. 'That is not what was agreed.'

'That's because the thirteenth is here,' Red answered, holding his gaze. 'With you, where the pact was made. It never left the court.'

'Clever,' said the horned man. 'I'm impressed.' With a speed that stunned her he pitched the bracelet back at her.

Somehow, with pure reflex, she caught it before it hit her in the face. Turning it over in her hand, she counted thirteen charms. The Book of knowledge was now connected. The bracelet was complete. Yet she knew that the task was not. There was still one, final curse to be delivered.

'What happened to my brother?' she asked. 'Where did he go when he was taken?'

Anger welled up inside her as the horned man cupped his hand behind his ear.

'I said, "*Where's my brother?*"' she yelled. Her voice filled the courtroom, extending to every last dark corner. Things like rats and mice scurried out of the corners, disturbed from their sleep by her cry.

The horned man relaxed in his throne, looking content.

'But you already know the answer to that,' he said, his eyes like dark pools. 'You don't have a brother. You never did.'

He laughed, and the court joined him. It was an ugly sound that rippled through the air. But she stood her ground.

'I want to know what happened to him,' Red repeated. 'I entered your agreement believing that child was my brother. So I don't care what you say. It still stands. He belongs with me, and I love him. That makes him my brother, even if not by blood.'

She trembled visibly, waiting for some terrible wrath to be unleashed. Curiously, there was none. The horned king put his head on one side and studied her.

'You *really* want to know what happened to the child?'

'Yes,' she croaked, aware that she was still holding the Book. *The Book of knowledge, that would answer any question . . .*

'Bring forth the child!' the horned king roared.

439

At the rear of the court a commotion broke out. Red turned to see two huge wooden doors that lay beyond the twisting staircase opening, and then three fairy guards stepped through, hauling a fey family with them. Red held her breath as they approached, herded like cattle to the front of the courtroom. The fairy woman was sobbing bitterly, and in her arms was a small, golden-haired child who was clinging to her in terror, his face buried in the woman's neck.

The man had his arm around her shoulders in an attempt to give some comfort – but Red could see his own eyes were brimming with tears as well. As they drew closer, stopping a short way from her before the throne, they were close enough for Red to see that the child did not share the characteristic pointed ears of the fairy couple. They were rounded, human . . . but as the woman reluctantly put the child down, Red's heart sank as he turned.

'James?' she whispered.

The child regarded her – but with curiosity, nothing more. No recognition or love lit up his face. And Red saw that this child was far older than her brother's years, closer to six rather than the three James would be now. A mixture of emotions raged inside her: disappointment, anger and resentment, that the fairies thought they could fob her off with an impostor. But then she saw something that sent those feelings crashing down in ruins. On the child's cheek, a birthmark the colour of a tea stain and the shape of a fish . . . proof beyond proof that this was James.

'Take him,' the horned king said, smiling widely. 'He's yours.'

'No!' the fairy woman sobbed, dropping to her knees and pulling the child to her. She turned her face to Red's, her anguish raw. 'Please, don't take him away from us, I beg you!'

'We love him,' the fairy father said hoarsely. 'He's our son . . . our second son – our first son died! Please, he's our only happiness . . .'

Red swallowed the lump that had risen in her throat. So James had not been taken for mischief, or pain, she realised. But taken to replace a child that was loved and lost.

'I'm sorry,' she said, and she meant it. 'But he was my happiness before he was yours.' She averted her eyes from the fairy couple and knelt before James.

Turning to the throne she met with the triumphant gaze once more.

'He's older,' she said. 'Make him the way he was.'

The horned king spread out his hands in a gesture of innocence.

'Time passes, and differently here. I cannot undo what is impossible. I cannot unmake the time that has passed.'

'You can do *something*,' said Red fiercely. 'You can make a glamour that makes him look younger – I can't take him back like this! That's not the way it works in my world!'

'As you wish.' The horned king bowed. 'When you leave the realm, it shall be done.' He nodded to the back of the court, and once again, the doors at the rear opened. This time, a lone prisoner was brought forward in chains, shoved

441

spitefully to his knees once he was level with Red. Warwick looked up at her – and in that one glance Red knew that he had never expected to see her again.

Grunting, the guard removed the chains and retreated, leaving Warwick on the floor. He looked thinner but otherwise unharmed.

'You're free to go,' the horned man told them pleasantly.

The fairy woman continued to sob into her husband's shoulder.

Red leaned towards the child. Gently, she reached out and brushed her fingers over the birthmark. Then, reaching down, she took his hand in hers.

'Come on, James. It's time to go home.'

The child snatched his hand back at once, shaking his head and burying himself against the woman he believed to be his mother. His blond curls bobbed around his head with the movement, and the fairy mother cried harder.

'James, come on,' Red pleaded. 'Don't make this any harder for me . . .' She put her arm round the child and tried to pull him away.

'NO!' he screamed, kicking out at her. 'I don't want to go with you!'

'Well, you're coming,' said Red. She lifted the child up, despite his struggles. Her eyes were blurring with tears at his words. 'You don't belong here, James!'

'I'm not James!' The child sobbed, collapsing against her in exhaustion. 'That's not my name! I don't want to go with you, I don't know you! I want my mother!'

Red was crying too now, openly. For finally she knew that, despite everything, it really was too late. James did not remember her. If she took him now all he would remember was being torn from a family he loved, by a stranger he didn't know and didn't want. It was the crueller choice. The selfish choice. And she knew she couldn't go through with it.

She sank to her knees, releasing the child, who ran to his mother and was swept up in her arms. The fairy mother stared at her through tears of grief and confusion.

'I can't,' Red said, beaten. 'I can't do it.'

'Why not?' the horned king demanded, jumping to his feet. 'This is what you wanted, so take him!'

Red looked into his cruel, arrogant face and saw the truth: this was not what he'd wanted. He wanted the chaos, and the upset.

'I won't take him,' she said. And suddenly, an image of Rose came to mind, and the way she had spoken of doing what she thought best. Now Red understood. It was called sacrifice. 'I can't, because I love him too much.' She braced herself for jeers from the court, but only silence met her ears.

'Then how about a compromise?' the horned king suggested slyly.

'What kind of compromise?'

'The kind where you stay here, with us . . . as one of us. After all, you know what you really are now, don't you?'

'You're talking about my real father. Aren't you?' she said. 'That he was fey.'

Another flash of those sharp little teeth.

'Indeed.'

She saw Warwick look up at her in bewilderment, and nodded very slightly to inform him that what had been said was true.

'You can even visit the child,' the smooth voice continued. 'There. He'll have the best of both worlds, and you will finally have somewhere to belong.'

His words stung her to the core, reaching the part of her she'd fought to keep hidden. She had been about to tell him how absurd the idea of her staying in the fairy realm was, until he had spoken those last words. For they were true. She had always felt like an outsider, but now she really did belong nowhere and with no one.

'What is there to go back to?' the horned king coaxed. 'Except more trouble?'

'Don't listen to him, Red.' Warwick stood up, his jaw squared. 'Don't listen to a word they say. It's all a game, just words.'

'But it's true,' Red said, her voice as broken as her spirit. 'What is there for me to go back to? Nothing. Nothing but trouble. And if I'm half fey then maybe I should stay . . . maybe I *could* belong.'

Warwick grabbed her and shook her.

'Listen to me! That's what they want you to think! They want you to give up, and think like them, and *be* like them! And maybe you are half fey, but you're half human too. And that half has a heart, and a place back in our world, not in this twisted one. There *is* somewhere you belong – with *us*. At Elvesden Manor! We want you there.' He released her shoulders suddenly, aware that perhaps he had said too much. 'Only you can choose, Red. You must decide what you want.'

'But what will I say, if I do go back?' Tears streamed down Red's face. 'I've done things, things that can't easily be put right.'

'Running away isn't going to make them right,' said Warwick, sadly. 'And some things aren't easily repaired, but it doesn't make them impossible.'

'But they are!' Red cried. 'I don't see a way to fix things!'

'There's always a way,' Warwick answered.

Red stared back at him, looking from his kind eyes to the horned king's dark, emotionless ones. She thought of Tanya, and Fabian – and even Nell – and how they had gone out of their way to help her. And she thought of Rose again – so alone, and desperate to make it up to the daughter she had lost. There were still choices to be made and things to put right. But none of them were here. She felt it in her heart.

'I choose to leave,' she said.

'I don't think you mean that,' the horned king said, settling back into his relaxed place on the throne.

'Yes, I do. I do mean it.'

At the forefront of the crowd, two figures emerged and watched from afar: Raven and Gredin. They nodded, encouraging her to go on.

'I don't think you do,' the horned king repeated. 'You

don't know your own mind, or yourself. You don't even know who you are.'

The fire of Red's anger started to go out, clinging only now to the tiniest embers of hope. The horned king glowed, feeding off her sapped hope and strength, drawing power from her weakness. She replayed the words in her mind, over and over until only one thing remained, the one thing that was true.

'I know enough,' she said. 'Because I know that my name is Rowan.'

A collective gasp went up around her, including Warwick. The horned king's smug expression fell.

'Red, what are you doing?' Warwick hissed. 'You can't give them your . . .' He trailed off as he saw the triumphant light in her eyes.

'It was the name given to me by my mother,' she continued, her strength flooding back. It all made sense . . . what Rose had been trying to tell her. The Hedgewitch and Snatcher . . . everything finally fell into place.

'The name I've been called all my life, except since my brother has been missing I denied it, kept it secret and hidden. But even then, it protected me – protected me from harm. I defeated your Hedgewitch, even if I didn't understand how at the time – but now I do. I defeated her because she tried to harm me, but she couldn't because of my name and what it means. And she paid the price because of it. I'm Rowan . . . and you have no power over me!' She shouted the last words at the horned king, who sat glowering on his throne. He could do nothing – for he knew as well as she did that she spoke the truth.

'You can't touch me,' said Rowan. 'All you could do was crumble what was around me – my lie of a life. But now I know the truth, and I accept it. I'm going back, and I'll face up to the things I've done, no matter what happens. Because I'd rather be there than here with you!'

She turned to James and his fairy parents, taking one long, last look at the little golden-haired boy.

'Take good care of him,' she told them. 'I know you will.' She reached out and tousled the boy's hair. 'Goodbye,' she whispered, under her breath. 'Goodbye, James.'

Fresh tears leaked from the fey woman's eyes as she hugged her son to her.

'Some day,' the woman said, 'we'll repay you for your kindness, in a time of need—'

Rowan shook her head. 'You don't owe me anything. Just . . . look after him.' She began to walk away, with Warwick at her side. Then suddenly, she turned back. 'Wait,' she called to the fairy parents, who were hugging and sobbing.

They looked up, their expressions fearful, and she knew they thought she had changed her mind. Hurriedly she took off her bag and searched inside until she found what she was looking for. Pulling it out, she offered it to them.

'There is something you can do,' she said, holding the book of fairy tales. 'This was our mother's.' She ran her fingers over the rough fabric of the cover, touched the

447

smooth gilt edges of the pages for the final time. 'Perhaps . . . perhaps you could read it to him, from time to time.'

The fairy mother accepted it, smiling through her tears, and then Rowan and Warwick vanished into the crowd of fairies, that was now bubbling with excitement and anger. The horned king remained on his throne, his face shrouded in fury at his defeat, but powerless to stop them.

As they ascended the stairs, the guards parted warily to let them past.

Halfway up, Rowan reached out and took Warwick's hand.

'Stitch?' she whispered, not daring to say his real name aloud. 'I'm scared. What's going to happen to me when we get back? How do I make things right? What do I say?'

Warwick squeezed her hand as they continued to climb. The entrance to the hilltop was almost upon them.

'You just tell the truth,' he said, staring straight ahead. 'That's all. You tell them that you missed your brother, and that you wanted him back, but no matter what you did, no matter which children you took, nothing could replace him. Because that is the truth, isn't it?'

Cool air washed over their faces as the hillside rolled back to allow them to pass. They ran the final few steps, leaping free of the staircase and jumping onto the boggy grass, saturated with rain. Fat drops fell from the sky, soaking them in seconds, and as the hillside closed behind them, a terrible roar of anger erupted from the horned king. It was cut off as the entrance sealed itself once more, breaking the connection between the two worlds.

Or perhaps, not quite.

A low rumble began in the distance, rolling over the hills and vales surrounding the tor. As they started on the stone path on the way down, Warwick turned to her and grinned.

'I think there's a storm coming,' he said.

Epilogue

There was thick snow on the ground when the Land Rover pulled up outside Elvesden Manor.

Two people got out of it: a man with long, grey-streaked dark hair and a tall, thin teenager. From the back of the vehicle, the man pulled out a battered brown suitcase, and then, together, they walked up the gravel path to the front of the house, hunched up against the biting cold.

The hallway smelled a little musty as they went in, the way most old places do, and it was quiet and still except for a matted ginger tail slinking beneath the telephone table, keen to keep out of sight.

Further back through the house, voices and the smell of roasting food wafted out from the kitchen like an invisible invitation. As the kitchen door was pushed open and the new arrivals went in, the voices inside quieted, then erupted into a chorus of shouts and cheers. Chairs scraped as their inhabitants jumped out of them, and the teenage girl who had entered with the man was enveloped into hug after hug, a large brown dog jumping up at her and a parrot cackling in excitement all the while.

Only one person remained seated at the old oak table: a woman with a pointed and pale face, and long red hair worn loose. She looked up at the girl, her eyes searching.

'Your hair has grown,' she said. 'It suits you.'

Rowan lifted a hand to her head, where her hair, an identical auburn to that of the woman who had spoken, now skimmed her jaw line in a neat bob. She gave a shy smile. 'Thanks.'

Rose stood up, and for a moment they regarded each other awkwardly before embracing.

When they released each other, Tanya stepped forward and tugged at Rowan's sleeve. 'I'll show you your room,' she said, her eyes shining. 'It's next to mine, so we share a bathroom—'

'And a drain-dweller!' Fabian crowed. 'It's already had a necklace of Nell's—'

'And a thimble from my sewing kit,' Florence put in, with a smile. 'It's a particularly troublesome breed.'

'I don't mind,' said Rowan, laughing as Tanya and Fabian dragged her from the kitchen. She followed them as they ran up the stairs, past the grandfather clock and stopped outside a door on the first-floor landing.

Hanging from an iron nail in its centre was a wreath of green leaves and masses of dried red berries.

Rowan took a deep breath, closed her eyes . . . and went in.

THANKS TO:

My family and friends – special thanks to Darren for making me thousands of cups of tea while I was away with the faeries, and to Carolyn and Janice for helping me to research children's homes.

Julia Churchill, and Becky, Maddie and all at the Darley Anderson Agency.

Last but definitely not least, thank you to Venetia, Jane, and everyone in the children's team at S&S.

Michelle Harrison was born in 1979 and is an editorial assistant in children's publishing. She is a former bookseller at Ottakars/Waterstones in Stafford. Originally from Grays in Essex, she is an illustrator as well as a writer and now lives in Oxfordshire with her partner. Her first novel *The Thirteen Treasures*, won the Waterstone's Children's Book Prize and has been sold in fourteen other countries as well as the UK. *The Thirteen Curses* is her second novel for children. To find out more about Michelle, visit her website at: www.michelleharrisonbooks.com

**If you enjoyed *The 13 Curses* why not
find out how it all began in *The 13 Treasures*.**

While visiting her grandmother's house, Tanya discovers
an unsolved mystery. Fifty years ago, a girl vanished in
the woods nearby – a girl that nobody will speak of.
Fabian, the caretaker's son, is still tormented by the girl's
disappearance as his grandfather, the last person to see
the girl alive, has lived under suspicion ever since.

Together, Tanya and Fabian decide to find the truth.
But Tanya has her own secret: the ability to see fairies.
Will it help unravel the mystery? Or is the manor's sinister
history about to repeat itself . . .